HOME FIRES

HOME
FIRES

Luanne Rice

BANTAM BOOKS

NEW YORK • TORONTO • LONDON • SYDNEY • AUCKLAND

HOME FIRES

A Bantam Book / August 1995

Library of Congress Cataloging-in-Publication Data
Rice, Luanne.
    Home fires / Luanne Rice.
        p.   cm.
    ISBN 0-553-09728-8
    I. Title.
PS3568.I289H66   1995
813'.54—dc20   94-23911
                                                    CIP

Published simultaneously in the United States and Canada

Bantam Books are published by Bantam Books, a division of Bantam
Doubleday Dell Publishing Group, Inc. Its trademark, consisting of the
words "Bantam Books" and the portrayal of a rooster, is Registered in
U.S. Patent and Trademark Office and in other countries. Marca
Registrada. Bantam Books, 1540 Broadway, New York, New York 10036.

PRINTED IN THE UNITED STATES OF AMERICA
BVG   0   9   8   7   6   5   4   3   2   1

Chapter 1

The fire started in the tangled old wires behind the bathroom heater. At first there was no flame, only a core of intense heat. The wires' frayed insulation, gray weave with the texture of a man's jacket, began to smolder. One spark popped, then another. The orange line crackled to the panel board, causing a momentary blink of the house's microwave, stereo, television, and alarm clocks.

In that instant the portable phone beside Anne Davis's bed clicked, resetting itself. Usually the sound would awaken her, but tonight it barely penetrated her deep sleep. She had been traveling all day; it had been months since she had slept well. She half turned toward the bedside table, but she was engulfed in a sweet dream that would not release her.

Tendrils of blue smoke wisped through the wallboards three rooms away. They dissipated like ghosts into the thin winter air. Flames licked the wall from behind, trying to follow the smoke. They raced in all directions, searching for cracks. One line of fire spawned another, and another, all crazy to escape. They filled the space like agitated spectators in an arena crammed beyond its capacity. They sped down the wires, and that was all it took. When the electrical system exploded, the flames burst through the wall in one thunderous blast. The house was on fire.

Iᴛ was another Karen dream that enveloped Anne as she slept. A dream of hazy images, clear bliss. Karen in her arms. At the beach, with Matt nearby. The sun's heat sensual and intense. Anne's nose pressed against Karen's skin, the spot where her neck and shoulder met, smelling of summer. Baby sweat, Coppertone SPF 40, salt water, chocolate from a Good Humor bar. Karen's weight on Anne's lap, and the sound of waves lapping the shore.

A clack. Sounds from the outside world.

Anne shifted, her face burrowing into the pillow, anything to preserve the dream. The family on summer vacation. Matt, Karen, and Anne together on a beach blanket. The hot summer day: she had it back, that feeling of joy and closeness. It was perfect, and so very real. She could touch Matt's leg, lick salt grains from the nape of Karen's neck. All her senses were awake; contentment throbbed through her body like lifeblood.

Then the house exploded.

Anne jumped out of bed. For a second she didn't know where she was. She started for Karen's bedroom, just yards away, then realized she wasn't in their New York apartment. She had come to the island, to her family home, the place where she'd grown up.

Smoke drifted in from the hall, under the closed bedroom door. Shivering in the dark, Anne touched the door with her hand. It felt scorching hot. Grabbing a bureau scarf, she wrapped it around the brass knob and pushed. Fire roared inward, burning her hand as she slammed the door.

She ran to the window and saw the snow glistening orange a long drop below. Her room was on the second floor, and the land sloped steeply away. In the distance, coming from town, she heard a siren. She returned to the door and touched the knob, as if to check that it hadn't somehow, incredibly, cooled down. Then, with no other choice, she turned back to the window.

"Karen," she said, choking with smoke and panic. There was no time to tie bedsheets together, no time to wait for the Island Volunteer Fire Department. She opened the window and looked down. Height, even this twenty-foot height, terrified her. She gulped air, but the smoke was catching up with her. She could jump out the window, she thought, then reenter the house by the porch door.

Climbing over the sill in her white nightgown, she let herself hang against the side of the house. It took forever to summon the power it took to let go. Don't think about it, she told herself. You have to do this. Jump. Jump. Finally her fingers obeyed. With bare feet she kicked off. Her eyes were closed. She tried to forget she was falling. A snowcapped yew bush broke her landing, and she rolled a few yards down the hill before she could stop herself.

Flames had broken through the bathroom roof, and the west upstairs windows glowed. Sirens screamed down Salt Whistle Road. Before Anne reached the porch, she heard men shouting, spools creaking as the hoses were unwound. Suddenly her mind was clear, and a superhuman burst of will propelled her across the yard, across the porch floor.

"Stop! Don't go in there," someone called. Anne glanced over her shoulder at the fire truck and saw a big man running toward her. He towered over everyone: a giant in black rubber coat, *Star Wars* mask, and yellow fireman's hat.

Anne rattled the door. Locked. She let out a cry of panic and frustration. From a nest of dry brown leaves she grabbed a smooth rock painted with the dark spars of a sailing ship by Anne herself, at age seven, and used by the family ever since as a doorstop. Smashing it through a pane of glass, she reached inside to find the dead bolt.

"Please, no!" the man shouted, running closer. Anne's hand shaking, she glanced back again. He had flipped the mask up, and

Anne was shocked to see that his left cheek was melted, like wax on a candlestick. His eyes had battle in them—urgency and alarm.

If he wanted to stop her, he was Anne's enemy. Moaning with panic, she groped for the dead bolt. Finding it, she gave it a turn. And then she was inside.

THOMAS X. Devlin of the Island Volunteer Fire Department stood outside the old house on Salt Whistle Road, watching black smoke seep through the attic vents. Flames lit the west windows on the second floor. He felt a shiver go down his spine, the way it always did at a fire ground. His skin grafts felt stiff, and he flexed his hands a few times, getting ready to work.

Car and truckloads of volunteers were streaming around the marsh, sounding a cacophony of air horns and sirens, a parade of pulsating blue strobe lights. Martin Cole lined up the cherry picker and Thomas Devlin was reaching for the roof saw when he spied the woman.

With her black hair and white nightgown, she was nearly invisible against the snow and night sky. She staggered up the hill, seeming to sway for an instant before charging onto the porch with the force of a locomotive and the grace of an apparition. Thomas Devlin shouted to her.

She glanced over her shoulder, and he bounded off the truck. She was trying the door, searching the porch for something. She was on a rescue mission; he saw it in her eyes. He crossed the yard in four strides, his arms out to catch her before she entered the burning house.

He called again, but a patch of ice tripped him up. He stumbled, just missed falling, heard the glass break. When he looked up, she had disappeared into the smoke.

Where was she heading? Upstairs? To a bedroom for a sleeping husband? Child? He'd seen the mad look in her eyes during the split second she'd glanced back. The woman had appeared small, desperate, and breathless. She wouldn't have much time before the smoke got to her. Thomas Devlin felt for his regulator, pulled down his face mask, and entered the house. No newcomer to fire, he had been a paid firefighter in Boston before coming to the island ten years ago. But every fire was new, every fire could mean death.

Blue-and-red strobe lights bounced through the smoke until he was three feet inside, and then everything was black. He crawled into the room, his breath through the air mask sounding artificial, like an iron lung. He envisioned the house's floor plan; he had been in plenty like it. It was the design of choice for working-class island families during the thirties, a tinderbox built to withstand hurricanes.

He fixed on the stairs, where he figured she was heading. Moving toward the fire, he heard something drop to the floor off to his left. He changed direction. Feeling his way along the wall, he touched her body before he saw her. He swooped her off the floor and cradled her in his arms. Through his thick rubber coat, he felt her chest rise and fall.

Outside, he held her close, to protect her from the bitter cold. Away from the smoke, he could see she was clutching a diaper bag. By the way she lay limp in his arms, he knew she was unconscious. Firefighters and police-band groupies milled around; Sarah Tisdale came running with blankets and a tank of O_2.

"Anyone else inside?" Brian Grisky shouted.

"She went back after something," Thomas Devlin said.

He laid her on one blanket and covered her with another while Sarah placed the oxygen mask over her face. Gently, he pried the bag from her hands, intending to look for clues. At the sight of the stuffed toy, the tiny dresses and sweater, his heart began to race. Almost instantly, she came to. She struggled to rise, then fell back. Her hand reached for the bag.

"There's a child inside the house?" he asked, shaking the woman's shoulder. "Where? Tell me where!"

The woman blinked, trying to swallow. She pushed the oxygen mask away. "The house is empty," she croaked.

"It's empty," Brian called out. "All clear!"

Soot coated the woman's pale face, making it nearly as dark as her hair. The smoke had swollen her eyes nearly shut. But even though she was half-frozen, half-asphyxiated, Thomas Devlin could see that she was lovely. She had a small body, but only a heart of steel could have made her enter that burning house.

"Where's the child?" he asked, watching her fumble through the soiled diaper bag. She suddenly regained the air of panic he had seen about her when he had thought she was on a mission of rescue. Her eyes darted back and forth, from one side of the bag to the other. She bit her lower lip.

And then she had it: the moment of relief. She threw her head back, then raised it again to look. Her hand closed around something, withdrawing it from the bag. A crumpled sheet of manila paper, one side covered with crayon marks. Tears squeezed out of the corners of her eyes.

"The child?" he asked again, more softly.

"There is no child," the woman answered, and she turned her head away.

Chapter 2

"I mean, my God," Gabrielle said, bracing herself against the kitchen counter. She had made Anne a plate of sliced apples and cheese, but she couldn't seem to deliver it to the table. Every time she thought of the fire, the danger Anne had put herself in, she'd feel the most dizzying combination of relief and fury.

"Everything is fine," Anne said.

"Everything is not fine!" Gabrielle said, serving the plate with a forceful clatter. "What were you thinking, running back into a burning house?"

"I had to get something."

"Something. You nearly died going in after a thing. A thing!"

Anne just sat there, staring. Gabrielle felt so helpless, completely unable to connect with her younger sister. Growing up, they had kept no secrets from each other. Adulthood and the dramatically different turns their lives had taken had changed that somewhat, but Gabrielle would have said they were still close.

Until Karen's death. Because now, no matter how much Gabrielle wanted to help, no matter how badly she wanted to ease her pain and protect her, she couldn't imagine exactly how it must have felt for Anne to see her four-year-old daughter die.

"I wish you had let us know you were coming to the island," Gabrielle said, instead of what she really wanted to say.

"I didn't know myself until yesterday morning."

"A spur-of-the-moment thing?" Gabrielle asked, hating the small talk.

"Yes."

"Most people want to get off the island in February, not come to it. But then again, you're not most people."

"No," Anne said blankly. "I'm not."

Great, Gabrielle thought. She'd been trying to pry a smile out of Anne, alluding to what she teasingly called Anne's "jet-set life." But all conversational gambits led back to Karen. In the seven months since Karen died, Gabrielle had lost the ability to talk to her own sister. It was like talking to a shell. Like one of the channeled whelk shells Gabrielle collected on her daily walks on the beach: empty, cold, self-contained, and silent. Talk into one, and your words would echo right back to you.

"I'd been thinking for some time about coming out," Anne said slowly. "To stay for a while."

"How long is 'a while'?"

"Until . . . I don't know. I just know I can't stay in New York anymore."

Gabrielle wasn't sure whether Anne intended this as an opening, but she dropped the towel she had been folding and took the chair beside Anne's.

"It must be so hard for you," she said, holding Anne's hand.

Anne squeezed back, hard enough to startle Gabrielle. Tears were running down her cheeks, but even now she wouldn't speak.

"I don't know how you've stayed this long," Gabrielle said, completing the sentence in her mind: *in the apartment where Karen died.*

"I can't stand being in the same city as Matt," Anne said.

"I was thinking more of . . ." Gabrielle began.

But Anne wouldn't allow her close to the subject of Karen. "I still love him, you know. It's ridiculous, but I do."

"I'd like to get my hands on him," Gabrielle said. Matt had left immediately after the funeral. He had been planning to move out anyway, apparently; Karen's death was just his excuse.

"Gabrielle?" Anne said, giving the name an inflection at once stern and plaintive.

"Anne," Gabrielle said, finally exploding. "Is there anything I can talk to you about? We can't talk about Matt, you won't let me near Karen. I loved her, too, you know."

"Everything's lost," Anne said, her voice barely a whisper, her eyes focused on the untouched plate of fruit and cheeses.

"Not everything," Gabrielle said emphatically. "You can't think like that."

Anne didn't reply.

Frustration, the desire for closeness, had pushed Gabrielle over the edge, and now Anne had retreated even more. Gabrielle needed to be in control of her relationships, and when she wasn't, it drove her crazy. Her mind would start to sizzle; her body must have produced some sort of chemical, because she could actually taste frustration in the back of her throat.

Absently, Gabrielle plucked some lint off the sleeve of Anne's beige sweater. Cashmere, she thought, hating herself for noticing. Despising the fact that envy was creeping in.

Gabrielle, who had adored Anne since the moment their parents had brought her home from the hospital, couldn't stand the way she felt. But here she was, married to her perpetually debt-ridden high-school sweetheart and living on the same godforsaken island she had grown up praying would sink into the sea, while Anne was living the good life.

Anne and Matt, so gorgeous and in love, so rich! Every year his business just got better, necessitating more and more exotic business trips, always with Anne along, of course. Every postcard of the Taj Mahal, the northern beaches of Thailand, the Baie des Anges, another trigger for Gabrielle's envy.

And who would have thought that Anne's silly childhood hobby would bring her fame and an income all her own? That Anne could have become well-known for the delicate little collages she fashioned of images cut from postage stamps? Her quirky collages hung in galleries in New York and Tokyo, and the unique pieces had recently been used on the covers of a line of classical-music CDs.

The great irony being that as a child, Gabrielle had been the better artist, had won prizes for her work all through childhood and college—even in contests against Anne.

Now, gazing down at her sister who had "lost everything," Gabrielle felt poisoned with resentment and the guilt it brought. But life on the island was hard. Especially in winter, when the construction business would stop dead.

She would see Steve drinking beer and watching TV, and instead of screaming at him to get his feet off the goddamn table and his butt out of the easy chair and help her do the dishes, she would stand at the sink wishing Anne's galleries would dump her. Gabrielle would imagine her own teenage daughter, Maggie, making high honors and getting into Harvard while secretly hoping that Karen, who'd been enrolled at some fancy New York kindergarten, would grow up into a troublemaker and a dropout.

Thinking of the bad luck she had imagined for Karen, Gabrielle had to turn her face away from Anne. Karen had died a month before she would have entered kindergarten.

"Can you smell the smoke?" Anne asked, raising her wrist to her nose. "One night in the hospital and two showers, and I can still smell it and taste it. The poor house. I burned down our childhood home."

"Steve says the damage isn't too bad, considering. Three rooms upstairs are ruined, and the roof. And the wiring was a disaster waiting to happen. He'll fix it."

"It's nice to have a builder in the family," Anne said, smiling for the first time since coming to Gabrielle's house.

"Yes, well . . . the insurance check will be a welcome, welcome sight."

"Your business must be slow this time of year."

"That's putting it mildly. Although we'll get a boost at Valentine's Day." The Seduction Table, her catering business. Gabrielle was aiming for the love market, and although it went over big with the summertime yachties, the year-round islanders were too practical and unromantic to buy it.

The telephone rang. Gabrielle saw Anne close her eyes wearily, probably hoping that the call would bring a reprieve from Gabrielle's ministrations.

"Hello," Gabrielle said, all business, planning to cut short whoever was calling and get back to Anne.

"Gabrielle, hi. It's Thomas Devlin. May I speak with your sister, please?"

"Just a second," Gabrielle said, covering the mouthpiece with her hand and jostling Anne. "It's for you."

"Who?" Anne asked, hope shimmering behind the frown in her eyes. She probably thought it was Matt.

"Thomas Devlin. The fireman who went in after you."

Anne's frown deepened, and she waved the call away. "Tell him I'm asleep."

Gabrielle hesitated, wishing Anne would make the simple gesture of thanking the man for saving her life. Wouldn't that be the healthy, life-affirming, getting-back-to-normal thing to do?

"Please," Anne said, sensing that Gabrielle was about to push. "I don't feel like talking. I'll send him a note later."

"I'm sorry, Thomas," Gabrielle said directly into the receiver, turning her back on Anne. "She seems to be asleep. But I'll tell her you called."

"How is she doing?" he asked.

"She's going to be just fine," Gabrielle said, without a trace of conviction in her voice.

THOMAS Devlin hung up the phone in his workshop and tried to put Anne Davis out of his mind and get back to work. Cuckoo clocks, grandfather clocks, gold watches, Swiss chimes, inner works without faces covered every inch of wall space and every available tabletop. He had inherited his father's tools and some of his knowledge, but he considered clockmaking a hobby, not a trade.

Every time he entered a burning building, he'd prove it to himself over again: he was a firefighter through and through. The fact amazed him. After the bad fire in Boston so many years ago, the one that had burned off half his face and all of his joy, a betting man would have said that Thomas Devlin was finished as a fireman.

Thomas had believed in himself.

He'd taken refuge on the island, set himself up as a clockmaker, and one day astounded himself by joining the volunteer fire department. Most of the calls they got were routine: grease fires at the Fish House, kids playing with matches behind the school, barbecues run amok. Then there were calls like the one they'd had this week, the house on Salt Whistle Road.

He kept seeing the woman.

His first sight of her, when she was standing in the snow, was vivid in his mind: the fierce beauty in her dark eyes, her clenched fists and the tension in her shoulders, her nightgown molded to her body by the wind.

He remembered how his heart had pounded when he saw her enter the house, even more when he followed her in and realized how hard it would be to find her in the smoke. She had been moving with hurricane force, full of some life-or-death purpose, so it had seemed doubly shocking to find her crumpled on the

floor. She had seemed somehow invincible, a woman of superhuman strength. He had lifted her with so little effort: she was light
as a feather. Her body had been supple in his arms, and cold, from
her standing barefoot in the snow.

Now, working on Emma Harwood's mantel clock, Thomas
Devlin pushed the glasses up his nose. The left earpiece rubbed on
his scars, making them itch. The wind howled outside, but all he
could hear was the clock. Strange that someone who had chosen
to work on clocks half the day couldn't stand the sound of ticking.
It made him feel trapped. Six-foot-four and using doll-sized tools.
Hot and uneasy, he pushed back his chair, knocking over a cigar
box full of springs.

"Damn it," he said, watching the minuscule springs roll under
the desk, into floor cracks, behind the bookcase. He just stood
there scratching his scar. His concentration was useless.

Time for a ride. Anything for some open air, maybe take a drive
out to the dunes and watch the waves build. The wind had shifted
east, and some good breakers should be rolling in. Stop thinking
about the mystery woman who had come to the island. She had
upset his balance in a way he couldn't quite define, and that made
him feel nervous and ornery.

He threw on his parka and grabbed the truck keys. Just as he
stepped outside, damned if Peggy Lawson wasn't pulling down the
driveway. She climbed out of her red Neon holding Mac's gold
watch at him like a hypnotist on the stage in a New Bedford dive.

"Loses ten minutes every other day," Peggy said, her voice
raspy from cigarettes.

"I'll give it a look," Thomas said.

"Sure you have time? I hear you're pretty busy being a hero
these days."

"Oh, the Salt Whistle fire?" he asked casually, recalling that
Hugh Lawson, Peggy and Mac's nephew, had been at the scene.

"I hear you saved the lady of the house," Peggy said in a way
that made it clear she had a story to tell.

"Anne Davis. Do you know her?"

"Of course. She's an island girl, born and bred, just like me. Though she certainly tried to put it behind her. Know what I mean?"

Thomas Devlin knew that nothing but sorrow could come from listening to rumors, so he started to edge toward his truck. But Peggy's car was blocking him.

"I went to school with her sister, Gabrielle. You know Gaby Vincent, don't you? Steve's wife?"

"Sure," Thomas said, amazed all over again. He couldn't quite picture it, the woman he had rescued being related to Gabrielle. Gabrielle had big bones, big red hair, a big Ford van, and a laugh he swore echoed from here to Nantucket. Nothing seemed to faze her. Anne was small. Entering the house, she had moved like a linebacker. But later, when Thomas had laid her down and she opened her eyes, Thomas could see that something inside had broken. That whatever had hurt her was worse than the fire.

"She was a wild one, Anne was. And trouble has certainly followed her. Money can't always buy happiness."

"No, well . . ."

"She married it, and a lot of good it did her."

"She's married?"

"Separated. Divorced, something like that. He walked out."

Thomas didn't want to hear any more. The wind stung his ears, and he could practically see the waves, mountains of green water trailing foamy crests behind. He would park by the clay cliffs and walk to the lighthouse. Clear his head. Tonight he'd eat leftover beef stew and write a letter to his son, Ned, away at boarding school. Have a quiet night and try to shake this case of nerves.

"I'll see what I can do about Mac's watch," Thomas said. "Thanks for bringing it by."

"Well, who else would I take it to? And I did want to tell you we think you're quite a hero. Anne Davis is lucky to be alive. She has you to thank. She might have gone the way of her child."

The hair on the back of Thomas Devlin's neck stood on end, and it wasn't the wind.

"Her child?"

"Oh, you haven't heard? It happened last summer. A darling little girl. She used to play with Hugh's daughter, Sadie."

Thomas Devlin had the impulse to walk away, to deprive Peggy of the satisfaction she was getting from this. But he had to know.

"What happened?" he asked, his pulse drowning out the sound of the wind.

"The little girl died. Fell four stories. Anne was right there, poor thing. Although the police were very suspicious. For a while we thought there'd be charges."

Somehow he had known. She had said there was no child, but he hadn't believed her. He thought back to the fire, to the way she had run back to the burning house. Everyone at the scene had been disgusted, that the woman would risk her own life and everyone else's for what had appeared to be a diaper bag.

Everyone but Thomas Devlin. He had seen the clothes and toys of a little girl, had recognized the look of loss in the woman's eyes. He had recognized himself. Anne Davis had witnessed the death of someone she loved.

His scars were throbbing, as they often did when the weather changed. Snow was coming. He could feel it in the air. He made a little more small talk with Peggy, gave her some excuse about having to be somewhere. By the time he got into his truck, the pain was shooting up and down the left side of his face. He scowled, knowing his only salvation was to empty his mind. Images of fire were flashing behind his eyes, and he fought to put them down. Passing a girl who might have been Maggie Vincent, Anne's niece, he was blind to the landscape. He thought only of driving toward the east wind.

MAGGIE Vincent had dropped off her schoolbooks, changed into tighter jeans, and headed out to meet Kurt, Eugene, and Vanessa, all without running into her evil mother. Or Anne. She knew Anne was in the kitchen with her mother.

Maggie wore a white angora sweater she'd liberated from the Living Doll Shop, Kurt's leather jacket, six gold hoop earrings (not counting the one she'd recently inserted in her nipple), zero makeup (eat your heart out, Vanessa), and motorcycle boots she'd found at the South End Sally Ann last time she and Vanessa had hitched to Boston. So they were a little too big—like three sizes— but she'd stuffed the toes with Kleenex and everything was cool.

She was walking down Teatime Lane. God, she couldn't wait to move someplace where every road didn't have some cutey-pie historical, tourist-pleasing name. Like New York City: Fifth Avenue. Forty-second Street. No bullshit there. Out of nowhere, a kick-ass Chevy Blazer came screaming along, and everyone was in it, Kurt at the wheel.

"Tell me I'm not seeing this!" Maggie said, tonguing his ear as she climbed onto his lap.

Even with his mouth on Maggie's, Kurt managed to execute an Indy-worthy burnout, his eyes never leaving the road.

"Do I want to know where you got this?" she asked when Kurt stopped kissing her.

"Marcy whatever-her-name-is, the bank chick," Vanessa said, handing Maggie the pint of Southern Comfort, "left it at the ferry, and we found the spare key in her little magnetic key box."

"How'd you know there was one?" Maggie asked.

" 'Cause with a chick like that, there's always a spare key in a little magnetic key box," Kurt said.

"Little Miss Perfect type," Vanessa said, squealing at whatever Eugene was doing to her.

"So, where are we going?" Maggie asked. "I guess we can't use the old house."

"Yeah, real sweet," Kurt said. "Your dipshit aunt's there less than a day, and she burns the place down."

"Sorry to inconvenience you," Maggie said, stung. She climbed off his lap and sat as far as possible away from him in the passenger seat.

"She the one who killed her kid?" Eugene asked.

Maggie shrugged. Kurt didn't realize how badly he could hurt her with his words, the tone of his voice, the way he'd act all displeased and angry with her.

"Maybe she burned the place down on purpose," Vanessa said, giggling. "Maybe she's a pyromaniac *and* a killer."

"You gotta admit, she's got one hell of a touch," Kurt said. Although Maggie was staring out the window, she caught a glimpse of him reflected in the glass. He'd glanced her way. That made her feel a little better. She turned her head toward him slightly. The bottle came around again, and Maggie took a swallow.

"My dad said she acted real strange at the fire," Eugene said. "She ran back inside, and everyone thought she was going after a kid or a dog or something, but they carry her out and she's holding a paper bag or something. Guys could have gotten killed, and for what? A paper bag? Probably had her jewelry in it or something."

"Rich bitch," Vanessa said.

"The freaky giant, Mr. What's-his-face Devlin, ended up going in after her," Kurt said.

"The jolly green scarface," Vanessa said.

"I mean, who gives a flying fuck if she wants to kill herself?" Eugene asked. He took a long slug, then burped. "Serves her right, after what she did. But those guys are out there risking their lives for a kid killer and her jewelry?"

"Can we please talk about something else?" Maggie asked quietly.

"Hey, your aunt ruined our party spot," Vanessa said, jabbing the back of Maggie's shoulder. "The least you can do is give us the gory details. Tell us what she did to her kid."

"It was an accident," Maggie said.

"That's not what the papers said," Vanessa said. "Or the TV news."

Sometimes Maggie hated Vanessa so much she couldn't stand it. Didn't the idiot ever listen to herself? Like anyone would consider the TV news an authority on anything.

"I distinctly remember hearing that it was way more than an accident," Vanessa said. "Like murder. What are you defending her for? I thought you hated your family. Just admit she killed your cousin, and get over it."

Karen. Maggie thought back to last August, when Anne, Matt, and Karen had come out to the island for their usual summer vacation. Everyone knew you couldn't drag Maggie to a family thing, but it was different when the Davises were around.

Especially Karen. Maggie hadn't known a little kid could be so smart and funny. Better company than anyone she knew. She had found herself hanging out with them all the time, baby-sitting for Karen at night when their parents would head into town. Maggie and Karen were like sisters, really. At least, that's how Maggie felt and it's what Karen had said.

Just thinking about it, Maggie used the knuckle of her right index finger to wipe away tears.

"All choked up?"

"Shut up, Vanessa," Maggie said.

"Just tell us. Where does the news get off calling your aunt a murderer if she's not one?"

"There was an investigation. That's all. There's always an investigation when someone dies."

"Your aunt was the only one there, though. And everyone saw her looking out, even before the kid hit the ground. That's sick. She must have seen the whole thing."

"I didn't know about that part," Kurt said, looking over at Maggie. "Gross."

Maggie couldn't stand thinking of Anne seeing Karen die. She closed her eyes, as if she could block the image from her mind. But that only made it more vivid. Her eyelids flew open, and she looked wildly around at the landscape flying by. Red barn, snowfield, power lines, lighthouse way off in the distance. She watched the light flash red, white, red, white, red, white for a few seconds, until she felt calm again. She reached back for the bottle.

"Not till you tell," Vanessa said, hugging the nearly empty bottle to her chest.

"She fell out the window," Maggie said. "That's all, she just fell. She hit the sidewalk and died. Now give me the bottle."

ANNE Davis lay under a blanket on the sofa, pretending to sleep. They had given her a sedative at the hospital, but she had fought it, as she had learned to fight sedatives last August, and she felt tired but wired. Gabrielle was putting the finishing touches on a dinner she had made for two people celebrating a fifteenth wedding anniversary. Between canapés and sauce moutarde she kept slipping in from the kitchen, to make sure Anne hadn't moved. Anne couldn't wait to be alone in the house. Faking sleep, she thought of her daughter.

Even at four, Karen had liked to read after bedtime. Anne had totally approved. As if they were unaware, Anne and Matt would kiss Karen good night and turn out the light. They would put a CD on the stereo and try to forget that Karen was waiting for the coast to be clear.

How could they forget that their four-year-old, who had nursery school at eight-thirty the next morning, would read until midnight if they let her? Karen would wait until they left her room, then turn on her flashlight. She would open a book— *Desmo the Incredible Kitten* or *The Little Mermaid* (she especially liked stories with lots of animals in them)—and read until someone stopped her.

Karen had an amazing imagination. You could hear her talking out loud, conjuring up characters. While she was reading *101 Dalmations* she would pretend to be Lucky, the littlest puppy who hadn't yet gotten her spots, and she would hide under the covers with her imaginary parents, Pongo and Perdita, from Cruella DeVille. Anne would stand in the hall, listening to her incredible child.

She would always make noise before going in to check on her, to give Karen enough time to fake sleeping. She would shuffle her feet, or clear her throat before opening the door. Then she would tiptoe over to the maple bed. There Karen would be, her lashes resting angelically on her pink cheek, the covers drawn to her chin, her arm convincingly tucked, pillowlike, under her head.

Perhaps unwittingly, Anne imitated her now. She lay on the sofa, her arm crooked under her head, the sound of her wrist-watch ticking in her ears as she tried to fool Gabrielle into think-ing that she was fine, resting comfortably. She was Lucky playing dead, to escape detection by Cruella. The effort made Anne feel easy, closer to her daughter.

Lying there, Anne's mind darted to Maggie, then away again. Maggie hadn't once spoken to her since she had come to the island. Since Karen had died, for that matter. Anne vaguely re-membered seeing Maggie at the funeral. Anne had lunged, to kiss her, and suddenly Maggie wasn't there. Deep down, Anne won-dered whether Maggie believed the rumors, but she didn't won-der too hard. If Maggie did believe them, Anne didn't really want to know.

The kitchen door opened, closed, then opened and closed again. Anne heard Gabrielle approach, sigh audibly, and shuffle her feet. Anne breathed steadily through her mouth, her elbow tucked under her head. Gabrielle stood still, watching. With her eyes closed, Anne could feel Gabrielle's gaze; just as surely, she knew that Gabrielle realized that Anne was faking sleep.

The sisters let it be; Gabrielle packed up her van, and she left.

This was the first time Anne had been alone in the house since she'd been released from the hospital. She rose from the sofa and went into the family room. A gallery of family photos covered one wall. Stuffy portraits of grandparents, wedding photos, Maggie's school pictures, shots of the Vincents and Davises on holidays and summer vacations.

Anne stood before the wall, as if challenging it. Her eyes went directly to a picture taken on the beach last summer. It showed Anne, Matt, and Karen building a sandcastle by the water's edge. Maggie stood in the background. She had been helping with the castle, Anne remembered, but had stepped away when Gabrielle said she wanted to take a shot of the Davises alone.

There was Karen, placing a piece of pale green sea glass over the princess's window. She was smiling for the camera, but her eyes had a sidelong glance, as if she didn't want to be torn away from working on the castle. She had already adorned it with garlands of periwinkle and mussel shells. Using her little hand, she had scooped out and molded balconies of sand for the princess, king, and queen.

Her brown hair curled damply; the day had been scorching hot, and Karen and Anne had just taken their third swim of the morning. Her skin was brown, and she wore the pink bikini Maggie had given her the first day of vacation.

Anne stared at the photo for a long time with no change in expression. It was a happy moment frozen forever on film. That was how she viewed it. It didn't particularly move her one way or another.

The photograph didn't show that Anne and Matt had had a bitter fight before breakfast that morning, or that before sunset he would be on a plane to La Guardia. It didn't show that ten minutes after Gabrielle snapped the shot, she served a picnic lunch, and Karen and Anne had shared a tunafish sandwich and a glass of lemonade. It didn't show Karen and Anne waiting for low tide, to go crabbing in the tidal pools. It didn't show Karen falling out the window eight days later.

The photograph didn't make Karen seem real or present or faraway to Anne.

For those sensations, Anne dug into the canvas bag she'd rescued from the fire.

Karen's drawing. Sitting on the floor, Anne spread it across her knees. She loved to touch it. The paper was yellow manila, coarsegrained, the variety favored by kindergartners everywhere. Karen had used fourteen different crayons to color the picture for Anne.

Anne brought the paper to her face. It smelled like smoke now, but if she concentrated she could bring back the scent of crayon wax. Touching the surface, she could trace the smooth, slick tracks of Karen's crayons. It was so real, something she could hold in her hands, a drawing Karen might have finished just five minutes ago. It felt the same, smelled almost the same, looked exactly the same, as it had the moment Karen had presented it to her.

It was a picture of things Karen loved, all blended together in the epic vision of a preschooler.

It showed her room—everything pink, her favorite color—at home; Mommy, Daddy, and Karen playing in Gramercy Park; Karen and Maggie building a castle at the beach. Between Karen in the park and Karen at the beach were two puzzling whitespeckled boxes.

For a four-year-old, Karen could draw beautifully. She gave her people smiles and eyebrows, five fingers on each hand, clothes that she had seen them wear. Her beach had rocks and shells; her ocean had a shark (sharks scared her more than anything. For weeks after seeing *The Little Mermaid,* she'd had nightmares about the shark), a sea horse, and minnows. Gramercy Park had squirrels, a low wrought-iron fence protecting red tulips, and a multistoried white birdhouse. Karen on the beach had red fingernails, like Maggie; in the park with her parents, her nails were unpainted.

"It's my best and favorite thing," Karen had said proudly, giving the picture to Anne.

Anne had accepted it, delighted. She and Karen had examined it together, not speaking. Except for the white boxes, she recognized every image and knew where it fit in Karen's conception of her world.

"What's this?" Anne asked, pointing at one spotted box.

"Don't you know?" Karen asked, her brow creasing. Suddenly she looked troubled, as if her mother had failed to understand something basic and vital.

Anne shook her head.

"It's paradise," Karen said.

"Oh, I love you," Anne said, pulling Karen into her arms. A picture of the people and places Karen loved the most: paradise. The boxes didn't matter. Nothing mattered compared with that.

Now, sitting on the floor of Gabrielle's family room, Anne stared at Karen's picture of paradise. Karen had colored it the morning of her fall. When Anne was alone with the picture, when she blocked everything else out, she could believe that Karen had done it five minutes ago, not seven months. She could believe that Karen was right beside her.

It was a real piece of paper, colored with real Crayola crayons from the big box with all the colors, by Anne's real little girl. Photographs were just frozen moments, but paradise was forever.

The telephone rang. It startled her. She started to stand, but then her gaze was drawn back to Karen's picture. Every time she put the picture away, she had the sense of leaving Karen. She wasn't ready to do that yet today. Not right now. She closed her eyes and smelled the crayon again. She felt full and as close to peaceful as was possible for her. The hollowness would return soon enough.

Sitting on the floor with paradise, Anne blocked out the ringing phone and let the answering machine do its work.

Chapter 3

M att Davis had an affair, and it ruined his life. Until it happened to him, until he'd been swept away by another
woman, he would have said that he believed unfailingly in marriage. He believed in the love, nourishment, and challenges that it
brought two people; he believed in Anne. She had given him so
much. Together they'd had a child, the most precious thing in
their lives. But by last summer, when Matt and Anne celebrated
their tenth wedding anniversary, he was in the midst of a love
affair that had been going on for eight months.

Flying home from Paris, he tried to concentrate on paperwork.
He was the president of the American branch of a French perfume
company; his job was to sell design houses and celebrities on the
idea of launching their own fragrance line. He traveled all the
time. Although work could be tiresome, it was the only thing that
kept his sorrow at bay. He wondered about Anne, alone all the
time. Not working. Sometimes when he thought of Karen, it was
all he could do to keep from smashing windows, from howling at
the moon.

His life was full of glamour. He lived in New York, but kept a permanent bungalow at the Beverly Hills Hotel and a suite in Paris's Plaza Athénée. He flew the Concorde twice a week, often with a movie-star client. He made frequent excursions to Grasse, in Provence, where the flowers were the most beautiful, their scents the most refined.

He and Anne had planned to buy a farm near Grasse.

Anne had come into his life eleven years ago. They were both twenty-five; he was a perfume executive and she was temping in his New York office. He noticed her immediately. She had big, dark eyes that would have been sultry if they weren't so wide-open and innocent, as if she was taking everything in. She seemed very different from the girls he was dating, and he liked looking at her. He had the feeling she hadn't been in New York for very long.

Even after they married, after ten years on Gramercy Park, Anne hadn't really seemed comfortable in New York. She needed sea air and sand in her shoes. She was always happiest on the island. So, although it made sense to Matt that she would return there now, it scared him because it put her just that much farther out of his reach.

Sometimes he wondered whether Anne would eventually have forgiven him if Karen hadn't died. But his betrayal and Karen's fall were so closely linked in time and event that Matt believed he'd created some evil confluence. If Anne hadn't seen him and Tisa together, if she hadn't had that on her mind, she might have been paying more attention to Karen, and it might never have happened.

The strange thing was, he'd been planning to leave Anne for Tisa. He had fallen in love with another woman. He felt terrible; he didn't understand why it had happened, but it had. For months, he and Tisa had been planning their life together. He knew he would have to tell Anne, and together they would have to tell Karen, but he kept putting it off.

He had planned to tell Anne before they went to the island. Then she and Karen would go away alone; by the time they returned to New York, he would have moved out. But when the moment came, he couldn't do it. Karen had spent winter Saturdays learning to swim at the Y, and he didn't want to miss her first summer in the waves.

He'd made the mistake of giving Tisa the island house's phone number. She was furious, and she called constantly. When Anne or Karen answered, she would hang up. Matt took to diving for the phone. Suddenly all those months of excuses seemed to add up for Anne. She didn't say anything, but Matt could see that she knew. It was mysterious, her sad anger, and he couldn't bear to confront it.

Instead, he picked a fight with her one morning before breakfast and was on a plane to New York by sunset.

Stupid bastard, he thought, staring at the airfone on the seat back ahead of him. Anne caught him two days later, when she herself returned home early. She'd left Karen with Gabrielle and Steve, flown to New York to try to patch things up with Matt.

Or maybe she'd had an inkling and wanted to catch him in the act.

Which she did. In their own bedroom at the rear of the building, with late-afternoon light streaming in, the light Anne had always loved most because it would turn their white sheets peachy rose and make their glistening bodies appear even more flushed. In her own bed, in her favorite light, Anne discovered her own husband fucking his girlfriend.

She kicked him out instantly. Tisa lost a diamond earring in the process. Matt left without his underwear. Standing on Gramercy Park West, dazed and ashamed, he hailed a cab. He held the cab door for Tisa; before following her, he looked up and saw Anne standing at the window of their fourth-floor apartment. She was staring down at him. From that angle he couldn't see for sure, but he thought she was crying. In that split second, before he climbed into the cab, he realized that his marriage was over. That he would never hold Anne again.

He was wrong. Eight days later he held her in his arms in the emergency room at Bellevue, where they had brought Karen's body. And two days after that he held her again, at Karen's funeral. That was the last time.

Now, thinking of Anne, he reached for the airfone. He zipped his credit card down the magnetic slot and dialed the island house. He got the same damned recording he'd gotten last night: "The number you have reached is not in service at this time. . . ."

He pulled out his green lizard Hermés agenda, looked up Gabrielle's number, and dialed it.

"Hello?" came Maggie's voice crackling through the air.

"Maggie? It's your uncle Matt. Do you know where Anne is?"

A long silence so venomous, Matt could taste it on the back of his tongue. "Just a minute," she said.

"Hello." Anne's voice didn't sound familiar. It was flat, with no welcome in it.

"I was worried about you," Matt said. "I've been trying the big house, and something's wrong with the line."

"There was a fire."

"A fire? Are you okay?" Matt sat bolt upright in his seat, picturing flames engulfing Anne's beloved home.

"I'm fine. I'm staying here for a few days, until I find a place to rent."

"Anne," Matt said, overcome with grief and frustration. "What the hell are you doing out there in the middle of winter? You have the apartment. You know I want you to have it."

"I don't want it," Anne said.

"Anne . . . it's your home. Please."

"I don't want it," Anne repeated, with all the animation of a hypnotized drunk.

"I just think you're in no shape to be making crazy decisions right now. After everything . . ." Matt's throat closed over. His eyes stung, and he blinked away tears.

"I have to go now," Anne said. But she didn't hang up.

"Don't do this," Matt said. "Don't you need me?"

"I can't have you," Anne said, her voice so full of anger and grief that Matt thought his heart would break.

"Forgive me, Anne," he whispered. "Please."

"You live with her, don't you?"

He didn't reply. After a moment the line went dead.

Matt stared blankly at the airfone for a minute. He remembered the first time he and Anne had gone out. He had planned to stop for roses on his way to pick her up, but he was late leaving the office. So he'd plucked one peach-colored rose from an arrangement on a table in the reception area. Standing in the tiny, dirty vestibule of her building, waiting for the elevator, he had felt so nervous.

When she opened the door, she looked so beautiful in black velvet, so sexy and pink-cheeked, that he tripped going in. She was thrilled by the rose; she found a glass vase, way too big for one flower, and filled it with tap water. But there was something about her, something so straightforward and guileless, that made Matt confess where he'd gotten it. He told her that he had wanted to bring her a dozen. But Anne had smiled, saying that a single rose was even better.

The next day, when he got to his office, he found eleven roses, of a similar peachy shade, in a vase on his desk. With a card blank except for the letter "A."

He sighed, still holding the airfone. He thought about calling Tisa, just to hear a familiar voice. She'd be waiting for him at home, in the apartment he'd taken across from the Metropolitan Museum of Art. She loved Matt. She would hold him through the night, to protect him from the dreams he had about losing Karen. That's what he needed now: love and protection. He wanted to give as well as take it. But he'd lost the privilege. Anne couldn't stand him, and he couldn't blame her.

W<small>HEN</small> Anne hung up the telephone, Maggie could see that her face was pure white. Maggie had the refrigerator door open, trying to decide what she wanted for a snack. But she was watching Anne surreptitiously. Anne didn't look very good. Maggie was sure her mother would have made Anne sit down. Maggie was tempted to push her into a chair, but that would mean talking to her. And she didn't know what to say.

Anne looked over, and their eyes met. Maggie tried to smile.

"Sounds like he was calling from a plane," Anne said.

"Yeah," Maggie said, but she had no idea of how a call from a plane would sound, or that such a thing was even possible. Except for the Island Commuter, a six-seat puddle jumper, Maggie had never flown.

"Mmm," Anne said, frowning. Lost in her own thoughts.

"So, you two split up?" Maggie asked.

"Yes." Anne gave Maggie a funny eyebrow sort of look. "Are you surprised?"

"Huh? I don't know. Not really. Well, sort of." God, Maggie felt so stupid. She had been one hundred percent totally amazed and flabbergasted when she heard the news, about a week after Karen's funeral. She had a million questions she wanted to ask Anne, but right now she felt dizzy and disoriented. There were so many things she wanted to say about Karen, it seemed strange that her first conversation with Anne would be about Matt.

"I never thought Matt and I . . ." Anne said. "I never would have believed. . . ." She looked at Maggie, as if she were seeing her for the first time. "Maybe I did see it coming."

"Oh."

"I mean, it has nothing to do with what happened. To Karen. I've been afraid you might be thinking that."

"No, I wasn't," Maggie said, even though she was.

Anne leaned against a kitchen counter and folded her arms. She wore an enormous gray Champion sweatshirt, faded jeans with frayed holes in the knees, and dirty white sneakers. Her hair could stand a shampoo. Maggie took all this in without actually looking at Anne. She could feel herself being watched.

"You haven't been around much, since I came to stay," Anne said.

"I've been pretty busy," Maggie said.

"What are you, a junior?"

"Yes."

"Oh. Junior year." Anne just stood there. Maggie could practically feel Anne's mind working, trying to find something to say. She was making conversation, just like every other adult. It had never been like this between them before. Anne had always given Maggie the feeling she could tell Anne anything, and Maggie had sometimes taken her up on it.

Last summer she had been bombed on peppermint schnappes, and Anne covered for her. She'd held Maggie's head while Maggie threw up into the toilet, and she'd let Maggie spend the night, telling her mother that Maggie and Karen were telling ghost stories to each other. Naturally, the next day, Anne gave Maggie the obligatory lecture on how everyone tries things like drinking, it's natural, but never ever get into a car with someone who's had more than one beer.

It depressed Maggie to have Anne suddenly talking to her just like any other adult.

"Junior year," Anne repeated. "Getting ready to look at colleges?"

"Yes," Maggie said, wanting to scream.

"That's good." Anne brightened, as if she'd discovered the perfect conversational groove. "Still painting your nails, I see. Nice color."

"It's called Very Cherry," Maggie said. She'd borrowed the

polish from Vanessa, and they'd both had a good chuckle, seeing as neither of them had been very cherry for quite some time.

"Pretty. Goes well with—"

"So, why did you and Matt break up?" Maggie asked in a rush. She thought her head would explode if Anne didn't quit being so polite.

"I caught him with someone else."

"You're kidding. Another woman?"

"Yeah."

"Uncle Matt?" Maggie was blown away. She had to steady herself, leaning against the refrigerator.

"Uncle Matt. Remember last summer, when he flew home to New York on business and I went back after him?"

"Right, and you left Karen with—" The words were out, and Maggie couldn't get them back. A gush of heat spread through her face.

"With you. Thank you, by the way. In case I never actually thanked you before. You were such a big help," Anne said, as if she were just thanking Maggie for any old baby-sitting job, as if there would be a thousand more to come.

"Oh God. You're welcome."

"I guess I was a little preoccupied, when I came back to the island," Anne continued. "See, Matt hadn't gone to New York on business. He had a girlfriend. Tisa. It's really pathetic, but I found them in bed."

"Oh my God." Maggie's eyes glittered with the delectability of having this conversation with Anne. She had once caught Kurt making out with Shelly Marshall, and she remembered that ice-cold shock, that heart-stopping moment when you realized that you were seeing exactly what you thought you were seeing.

"I haven't told your mother. I haven't told anyone," Anne said. "You, Matt, Tisa, and I are the only ones who know."

"Everyone thinks . . ." Maggie began, but she couldn't say the words: that Matt left because you let Karen fall out the window.

"Your mother doesn't. She knows there were other problems. There always are in marriages. You just hope . . . anyway, it's too embarrassing to give her the details. She's my older sister, after all," Anne said, and for once her smile was real enough to touch every part of her face.

"Yeah, she might not handle it too well," Maggie said.

"There's something about your mother, Maggie, that makes me want to be my best," Anne said. "It's always been that way. My own mother was way less strict than her."

"And your parents drowned fishing in a rowboat only twenty yards from shore and Mom had to take on the responsibility of the bakery and raising you and she had to give up all her dreams of going to college or ever getting off this island but looking back it's the best thing that ever happened because now she knows the value of a dollar and the island is the only place she'd ever want to live including Paris." Maggie knew the story by heart, even better than she knew her prayers.

Anne was laughing out loud, and that made Maggie smile. She twirled the silver snake ring Kurt had given her, pleased with herself.

"Do you think Matt is the one who keeps calling and hanging up when he gets the machine?" Maggie asked. It had been bothering her. She knew Kurt hated leaving messages, and it drove her crazy, playing back the tape and hearing all those hang-ups.

"No, I don't think so," Anne said. "It's not his style."

Suddenly Maggie heard her dad's truck pull into the driveway. That wiped the smile right off her face. He'd bully his way into the conversation, turning it into some big thing about a Democrat in the Governor's Mansion and how they were ruining the economy, when all he'd want was the excuse to drink beer and listen to his own voice. Her mother ran her ass off all year long, twelve months without a break, but her dad had the romantic notion that he only had to work when the sun was shining and the roses were in bloom.

"Excuse me," Maggie said to Anne. "I'd better get to my homework."

But it was too late. Big Belly Beardface lumbered through the kitchen door, not even bothering to wipe the snow off his boots, and practically pushed her away from the refrigerator. He pretended the maneuver was a hug, but it was just an offensive play to get to the Bud.

"A lot of water damage," he said to the air in general. "Smoke damage, water damage, the whole nine yards. We're looking at a healthy thirty grand."

"How long will it take?" Anne asked.

He narrowed his eyes, gazing at the ceiling. He shuffled his boots and looked at the floor. Then, as if only a beer would make sharp his powers of estimation, he reached for a long neck.

"Anne?" he asked, holding a bottle in the air.

"No thanks."

"We're probably talking April, beginning of May."

"You're going to work in the winter?" Maggie asked.

"Sure, Princess. Why not? If there's work we'll do it no matter what. And there's work to be done down at Grandma and Grandpa Fitzgibbon's, that's for sure."

It's weird, him calling the big house Grandma and Grandpa Fitzgibbon's, Maggie thought. They've been dead for twenty years. They died before they even had grandchildren. Her father was full of shit. She'd believe him working in the winter when she saw it with her own two eyes.

"April. That's not too bad," Anne said. "Guess I'll look for an apartment till then."

"That couch lumping up your back?" he asked, trading his empty for a fresh bottle.

"No, the couch is fine," Anne said. "Thanks for letting me stay. I know it's a pain, having someone take up residence smack in the middle of the living room."

"Hey, no bother."

No kidding, Maggie thought. Like he even knew Anne was there. She'd pull out the couch after he went to bed, and she'd make it up hours before he'd rouse his rotund hide.

"Princess, how about doing up a frozen pizza? Mom's got some in the freezer. Smelled her cooking 'em last week. Pesto, something yummy like that."

"They're for Valentine's Day," Maggie said. "She said everything in the freezer is on order for dinners and stuff."

Her father grinned, his red lips plumping through his thick brown beard. "Damn kids. Show no respect. Never mind."

He threw his parka on the kitchen chair, for someone else to hang up, and he headed down the cellar stairs to get his own stupid pizza. Anne was watching Maggie, waiting for her to say something, but all of a sudden Maggie had to get out of there. She felt so furious, she had the urge to break something. So it really confused her, the fact that her eyes were stinging, the way they did when she was about to cry.

She left the kitchen without another word to Anne. Damn it, she thought. Shitfuck. Upstairs, she slammed her bedroom door shut. She grabbed her pillow and yanked both ends, wanting to rip it apart. Maggie was boiling mad, and tears were burning her cheeks.

In the midst of her tantrum, she realized it wasn't her father she wanted to pull apart, but Anne. Anne, who had seemed to have the best life, a family so wonderful that Maggie had dreamed of being a part of it. She *had* been a part of it: when the Davises came to the island, anyway. Anne, with a rich, handsome husband and the greatest kid in the world, had thrown it all away.

Maggie beat on her poor pillow for a little while longer. She wiped off her old mascara and eyeliner and applied some fresh.

Then she picked up the telephone to call Kurt. After they had talked for a while, they would conference-call over to Vanessa's, and maybe they'd get a party going for later.

ON February 12, five days after the fire at the old Fitzgibbon house, the following note appeared on the bulletin board in the fire station's lounge area:

10 Salt Whistle Road
New Shoreham, CT

Captain Richard Wade
Island Volunteer Fire Co.
New Shoreham, CT

Dear Captain Wade,

I would like to thank all the firefighters and emergency personnel who came to my house the night of February 7. Everyone was very brave, and they worked very fast. My brother-in-law says the fire could have been much, much worse, considering how bad the wiring was.

I would especially like to thank Thomas Devlin. He came into the burning house to rescue me, and I'll never forget it. I'm sorry my actions put him in such danger.

You all did a great job.

Sincerely yours,
Anne Fitzgibbon Davis

One by one the firefighters, who were assembling for drills, read the note. Most read in silence, but some of them snickered.

"Sorry her actions put you in danger, Dev," Marty Cole said. "But at least she can sleep nights, knowing her jewelry ain't ashes."

"It wasn't jewelry, " Thomas Devlin said.

All week the guys had been ribbing him about rescuing Anne

and her silver and gold. It would have been much simpler to tell them what he'd seen in the bag, but somehow he felt that doing so would be a violation of her privacy.

"Yeah, whatever," Marty said, heading toward the coffee pot.

Thomas Devlin stood in a corner, waiting for the drill to start. His size always made it impossible to hide out, but he did his best. Ever since the fire, a dark mood had overtaken him. He felt stirred up, and the east wind had only made things worse. At night he'd lie awake, rigid as steel; when sleep finally did come, it brought dreams of the past, of a woman's body warm and silky suddenly transformed—mangled—by fire.

Exhaling, he turned back to the bulletin board and reread her note. She had looping, dramatic handwriting, messy in places, that didn't seem to fit his image of her. She had used a blue fine-line felt pen on a folded-over notecard. He removed the thumbtack to see the picture on the other side of the card.

He found himself looking at the damnedest, most exquisite thing he'd ever seen: a miniature collage, hardly bigger than a postage stamp, depicting Anne Davis's house on Salt Whistle Road. Surrounded by snow. In flames. With a dark hulking figure too abstract to make out as human but in which Thomas Devlin somehow recognized himself.

The collage was composed of tiny scraps of paper. Shards no larger than wood splinters, wisps of featherdown, watch gears. Purple shadows textured the snowfield, the house windows glistened black, and the flames were the brilliant orange of sunset. Bits of paper glued together to form something so perfect it brought back, exactly, Thomas's feelings of that night. The work was signed with a single letter, no bigger than the smallest dot of paper: "a."

Holding the note, he made his way to the station telephone. The guys talking made a cheerful buzz, and no one noticed him.

He didn't know why, but the number came to him right away. When a woman's voice answered, he hesitated. She said hello three times. Thomas hung up without saying anything, pretty sure the voice had belonged to Anne.

Dick Wade clomped into the station, kicking snow off his boots.

"It's a mother out there," he said. "Six inches on the ground and still coming. We should see a few fender benders tonight."

"Warm up the Jaws-of-Life," Bill Viera said.

"Did everyone see our nice commendation from the lady out Salt Whistle way?"

"Least she knows what's important, running back in after her jewels," Hugh Lawson said, and a flurry of laughter followed.

"Hey, hey," Dick Wade boomed. "None of that, now. Be nice, Hughie. And the rest of you. I don't know anything about the lady's personal life, but five nights ago she nearly lost her house. Maybe you think you're old hands at fire, but wait till it happens to you. Then it's a different story. You don't always act, let's say, predictable."

Dick Wade didn't have to look at Thomas Devlin for Thomas to know the speech was for him. Dick was the reason Thomas had come to the island in the first place. Thomas had served under Dick in Boston, until Dick retired to his wife's family place out here. After Thomas had recuperated from his burns, after he left the force, he came out to visit Dick, and he'd decided not to leave.

"Sorry, Captain," Hugh Lawson said.

"Never mind. Anyway, men, let me second Mrs. Davis in saying 'good job.' Now let's go to work. Search-and-rescue procedures."

Thomas Devlin nodded at his old friend the captain. He tacked the note back up on the board, glad he hadn't spoken when she'd answered the phone. There wasn't much to say. He just wanted to make sure she was doing okay after the fire. Her note actually made that clear enough. And he didn't need any complications in his simple island life.

Following the men out the door, Thomas Devlin made up his mind to concentrate on search and rescue, the task at hand. Even though he had the sickening, unholy feeling that he was rehearsing for a moment that had long since passed.

Chapter 4

Downtown New Shoreham consisted of eight restaurants, a market and a pharmacy, a bakery, a liquor store, one general store (open all winter), two seasonal art galleries, twelve seasonal boutiques, a carousel (boarded up until late May), two gas stations, three boatyards, and three old-fashioned hotels with rocking chairs on the front porches in summer. The main thoroughfare was called Transit Street because Venus, in her transit through the heavens, paralleled the street exactly.

Anne took the first apartment she looked at. It stood at the foot of Transit Street, occupying the second floor of a renovated stone warehouse and overlooking the ferry slip and parking lot. As soon as she walked in, she went straight to the front windows. A ferry was just docking. Mesmerized, as if she hadn't seen ferries dock a thousand times, she stood there watching.

When she turned away from the window, she knew she had found the place she wanted to live. She signed a lease and paid the deposit on the spot.

The rooms were spare, with high ceilings and tall windows. The landlord supplied a single bed, dresser, sofa, two shabby armchairs, and a small table and two straight-backed chairs. The floors were scuffed wood; long ago, the walls had been whitewashed. A web of fine cracks showed in the plaster.

In its austerity, the apartment reminded her a little of a monk's cell. But no monk ever had a view like this, she thought, watching the harbor.

Anne had always loved places with a view. When she and Matt had first found the penthouse on Gramercy Park, she had been so happy. Nursing Karen, she would sit by the window watching joggers circling the gravel path, the gardener planting bulbs or setting sprinklers, mothers playing with their children, people walking their dogs around the periphery, the neighborhood swearer who would interrupt his normally polite conversation with barking and obscenities, the cadets in blue on their way to the police academy, the old man who wore a scarf and beret even on the hottest days.

That view and the happiness it had brought her seemed very far away.

Anne bundled into her coat and headed for the pay phone by the ferry terminal. She had phone numbers for the local utility companies and a pocket full of quarters. A salty wind whipped off the harbor, forcing her to keep her head down. Crossing the street, she had to wait for a yellow school bus to pass and found that she had to look away.

At the phone, after making three calls and spending twenty freezing minutes on hold, she had switched the gas and electricity into her name and arranged to have a telephone installed the following Tuesday, sometime between eight A.M. and six P.M., with apologies of the order-taker for not being able to be more specific about the time.

Anne didn't mind. Setting up an apartment, even as a temporary place to live, would define her days, give her something to plan. Walking along Transit Street, she began making a mental list of things to buy: a bedspread, towels, a rug, a teakettle.

Passing Ruby's Slippers, a local coffee shop and island hangout, she noticed its cozy glow. The plate-glass window was all steamed up, and the scent of coffee and cinnamon buns drifted into the street. She stood on the icy sidewalk, looking in. There, sitting alone in a booth, was Thomas Devlin.

He was stirring a cup of coffee, reading a newspaper. His plaid flannel shirt strained across his broad shoulders, and his knees touched the bottom of the table, making Anne think of a big kid sitting at a first-grade desk. She stared at his face. The left side had been grotesquely burned. Covered with red and white patches, it was warped, crimped, as if someone had pinched it back together. The back of his hand was the same. Although his burns were horrible to look at, Anne couldn't take her eyes away. She had the sense of invading his privacy: spying on him.

Abruptly, she took a few steps toward her new building. If he hadn't been in Ruby's, she would have gone into the café. Her feet and hands were frozen. Her gas wasn't turned on yet, and she really wanted a cup of tea.

She wondered whether her note had arrived at the station, whether he had seen the collage. She had made it with him in mind. Standing still, she didn't know why the idea of facing him made her feel so nervous. Writing the note had been so much easier than returning his call. But very slowly, she found herself retracing her steps.

Once inside Ruby's, she stomped the snow off her feet. He looked up. At first he didn't seem to recognize her, but then Anne took off her hat and shook out her long dark hair. He rose to his feet.

"Mrs. Davis," he said.

"Hi," she said. She stood still, just inside the door. Then a group of men from the town crew came in behind her, and she realized she was blocking the way. At the counter she ordered a tea to go, then she stepped closer to Thomas Devlin.

"How have you been?" he asked. "Since the fire."

"Oh, fine. Thank you. I mean, thank you for what you did. Saving me." She blushed at the understatement.

He nodded. He smiled, and Anne felt her heart skitter. The right side of his face lit up. He had deep dimples, and his eye was full of warmth and happiness. His mouth was full, and his lips had a handsome way of curving up and then tightening at the outside corner. But the left side of his face, the burned side, was dead. The expression in his left eye was the same as the right—warm and excitedly pleasant. But the skin didn't lift. As if whatever had burned the surface had ruined his nerves and muscles, all the inner workings that made a person able to show a smile.

"Will you join me?" he asked, gesturing at the booth.

"No, thank you," Anne said. "You've got your paper. I don't want to bother you."

He watched her for a moment. He nodded, and slowly his smile went away. He seemed to make up his mind to let her go without insisting that it was no bother, that he'd already read the sections he was interested in, the things people say in restaurants when someone they know even slightly walks in alone.

Anne had turned her back, was halfway toward the door with her tea, when she heard him call her name again. Only this time he said "Anne" instead of Mrs. Davis.

"Yes?" she said.

"That note you sent," he said. "Your collage was beautiful."

"Thank you," she said, pleased that he'd noticed.

"How do you do it? Such little bits of paper."

"Postage stamps," she said, cutting the air with the fingers of her right hand. "And very small, sharp sewing scissors."

He was gazing at her with such intensity, as if he was listening to her explain the secrets of the universe, that she felt herself blush again. The look in his eyes had gone deep and searching, if possible even warmer than before.

"I'm glad you liked it," she said, waving good-bye.

She'd had the feeling that he'd been about to ask her to join him again, and it made her nervous to think that she almost certainly would have accepted.

It took six days and as many restless nights after Ruby's door closed behind Anne Davis for Thomas Devlin to figure out what he was so afraid of. He was back in Ruby's, having the blue-plate special before heading down to the firehouse for the weekly drill. He was enjoying his hot turkey sandwich, thinking about his son, Ned, when she happened to catch his eye.

She was hurrying along the street, glancing over her shoulder as she crossed just ahead of a delivery truck. She wore heavy winter clothes, but her grace was unmistakable. Thomas thought back to that first night, when he'd seen her bounding up the steps of her burning house. Something in her movements now reminded him.

When she saw him through the plate-glass window, she stopped dead. Their eyes met, and they gazed at each other without smiling. Then Anne raised a gloved hand to wave, and Thomas waved back. She moved along, more slowly now.

That's when it came to him: the reason he'd been feeling so jittery and crazed the last weeks. Something about the woman, about the things she had been through and felt and seen, made him know that he had found a kindred soul. Just looking into her eyes was like living a lifetime.

The realization was so powerful, he paid his bill on the spot and hurried into the fresh air. A knife wind slashed off the harbor, so he kept close to the buildings. His breath came hard. What he felt wasn't romance. It wasn't simple attraction, although he couldn't deny that Anne Davis was lovely.

What he felt was relief and terror, because he had met someone like him. He had made a home and wonderful friends on the island. They invited him to their parties, to their weddings, to the christenings of their children. They led beautiful normal lives that felt safe and secure and far from harm's way, and only Thomas Devlin knew that he was a pretender in their midst.

He had seen the worst, and he knew that no one could be made safe. Truly safe. You could install alarms, build fortresses, keep your kid on a leash like a puppy. You could put in a sprinkler system, place bars at the window, teach your children never to talk to strangers.

You could do your best, but you couldn't expect fate to respect that effort.

Thomas Devlin roamed the town, his hands stuffed deep in his jacket pockets, his eyes scanning the street for Anne Davis. Perhaps she was still nearby. If he found her he would approach her and say nothing. He would stare into her eyes and he would see if he was right.

He didn't see her again that evening.

After tossing all night, he awakened with the dawn. The sun rose, pale and watery through more snow clouds, then disappeared into a February gale. He brewed a pot of strong coffee and knew that he had to talk to her. That night he would leave the island for a long visit with Ned, and it seemed important that he see her before then.

At the earliest acceptable hour, when he knew Gabrielle would be getting Maggie breakfast before school, he called the Vincents' number.

"Hello," came Gabrielle's cheerful voice.

"Hi, Gabrielle. It's Thomas Devlin."

"Why, you old early riser," she said.

His mission had seemed so urgent, but now he felt embarrassed. What would he be wanting with Anne at six-thirty in the morning?

"I'll bet this isn't a call for my catering services," Gabrielle said dryly. "So you must be wanting a donation for the fire department. God knows we owe you."

"Actually, I was hoping to speak to your sister."

"Anne? She's not here."

He felt his heart quicken. Of course not; she'd probably left the island. Gone back to New York, to her husband, to her real life.

"She has a place in town," Gabrielle continued. "I'll give you the number."

Thomas sensed the curiosity behind Gabrielle's voice as she told him Anne's number and address: a building just across the street from Ruby's. He thanked her and hung up, but he didn't call Anne right away. She'd been born an islander, but she hadn't lived as one for many years. Habits change. Maybe she slept till noon now.

Besides, now that he knew exactly how to contact her, some perverse reluctance was overtaking him. Contacting Anne Davis could be a big mistake. Maybe he was asking for trouble, stirring up more than she could handle. Or more than he could.

THE worktable in her new apartment looked as if she'd been using it forever. A gooseneck lamp shone down on thousands of stamps from around the world. Many were canceled, sent to her by friends who knew what she needed them for. Others she had collected on trips with Matt, sending them on postcards addressed to herself. She had stamps depicting kings and queens, endangered species, tropical flowers, dead sports heroes, birds in flight, men on the moon, suicide poets, historic monuments. Reds of every shade from mute coral to brilliant scarlet. More colors than Crayola had names.

Three inches by three inches, Anne's collage-in-progress was a picture of an alpine lake. The original would be reproduced by Muniche Recordings for a CD of Chopin's nocturnes, then go on exhibit at her gallery on East Fifty-seventh Street in New York.

She had been at it since four or five in the morning, when she had given up trying to sleep. Chopin was playing in the background as she cut up stamps, trying to put together her collage, as seamless as possible for this purpose. Her swans' feathers came from stamps honoring the White House, the sunstruck side of a mountain, and the silvery surface of a rocket. She used tweezers and a magnifying glass, rubber cement, and tiny scissors that left her with a mountainous callus on the middle finger of her right hand.

She jumped at the sound of the telephone, cutting clear through a stamp she had been working for forty minutes.

"Damn," she said, glaring at the phone.

Finally, remembering she hadn't yet bought an answering machine, she picked up. She recognized his voice as soon as she heard it.

"Thomas Devlin," she said.

"It's nearly lunchtime," he said. "I was wondering if you'd like to grab a bite."

The invitation made her feel on guard. She felt grateful to him, but she hadn't come to the island to make new friends.

"Thanks anyway," she said. "But I'm working."

"You work at home?"

"Yes. I do collages. Like the one I put on your note." She expected him to laugh, if only because he felt nervous. People, especially islanders, often found it ridiculous that she could get paid for snipping postage stamps and turning them into pictures not much larger.

"Well, you do beautiful work. I can imagine buying one."

"Thank you," she said, surprised and even more wary. The man hadn't seemed like someone on the make, but he was sounding like it now. She felt a trickle of panic. Talking to the man who had pulled her out of the fire reminded her of what she had gone inside to retrieve, and that brought on an explosion of Karen. Her eyes felt hot and dry.

"It must seem strange, me calling you out of the blue and asking you out for lunch," he said carefully.

"Not really, but I do have work to do. Thank you, though," Anne said, needing to hang up the phone.

"Wait, please," he said.

She could hear his breath over the line, coming as hard as she felt her own.

"It's important," he said.

"I can't," she said, her voice falling. "I can't explain it to you, but I need to be alone right now. It's nothing personal. It's—"

"It's Karen," Thomas Devlin said.

Their silence ticked over the line. Anne should have hung up the phone. If she did, she would simply turn off the desk lamp, lay a cloth over her work to keep if from blowing around, and walk into the bedroom to lie down and take a long, long nap.

"I have to go now," she said, giving in to the exhaustion.

"I'll be at Ruby's," he said. "Never mind lunch. I'll be there at six tonight. If you change your mind."

"I don't talk about Karen."

"You don't have to. But I hope you'll come."

T HE day took forever. Still, she didn't take a nap and she finished the collage. All day she refused to admit it to herself, but she found herself reluctantly looking forward to going to Ruby's. She had heard something in Thomas Devlin's voice that she couldn't walk away from.

Six o'clock.

She bundled herself up and headed into the winter night. There he was, in the same booth he'd been sitting in the other day. She wondered how old he was. Forty-five? Fifty? She couldn't tell. The windows were steamy, the restaurant lit with a cozy glow. Anne walked inside.

He stood without speaking, giving her that same sweet, brilliant smile, tugging at his burned cheeks.

"Hi. Here I am," she said.

"Please—sit down."

She ordered tea with lemon and honey from a waitress who looked like Charlene Bowen, a girl she'd gone all through Island Consolidated School with. But the woman was icily indifferent. Anne had the feeling the woman had heard the tabloid stories, so Anne didn't say anything. Still, it made her chest hurt; she touched her throat.

"Is your breathing back to normal?" Thomas Devlin asked. "Smoke is wicked on the lungs, and the cold weather makes it worse."

"I think so," Anne said, not telling him that it had hurt to breathe since Karen had died, that having the smoke inhalation to blame for the pain had made her feel better.

"I'm glad you came."

"I'm not sure why I did," Anne said, aware that he was staring at her.

"Um, I could ask you something nice and general. Like, do you like the island in winter?"

The question was so benign, Anne started to laugh. "Yes. I always have. My sister used to curse it, dream of moving to Tahiti or someplace, but I loved it. We grew up here."

He nodded, and Anne was again aware that he knew things about her. She flushed, trying not to stare at his face, his hands. Now she saw that both his hands were scarred; she found herself wondering how many other burns were covered by his clothes. But she felt herself relax, a little. Something about the man made her feel comfortable.

"How about you?" she asked. "How do you like being here in the winter?"

"I'm from Boston. Except for the peace and quiet, it's not that much different."

"Peace and quiet," Anne said, laughing. "That's a nice way to put it."

"Okay," he said, laughing also. "Lonesome. It does get lonesome at times."

Lonesome. Anne gazed over is shoulder at the big corner booth where she, Matt, and Karen had eaten sundaes one afternoon last summer. Karen had loved the slogan emblazoned in red across the menu:

RUBY'S SLIPPERS . . . THERE'S NO PLACE LIKE HOME
HOME-STYLE COOKING AT A PRETTY PRICE

Karen had recently seen *The Wizard of Oz* for the first time, and when she and Anne were alone they would sometimes pretend that Karen was Dorothy and Anne was Glinda. That day, eating their sundaes, Karen had told Matt that he could be the Tin Man, which she pronounced "teen-man."

Anne and Matt had smiled, trying not to laugh, thrilled by their daughter.

Lonesome.

Anne looked back at Thomas Devlin.

"Are you called 'Tom'?" she asked.

"Thomas, usually. Much to my dismay, my parents didn't believe in nicknames. So 'Thomas' stuck. At least they didn't name me Aloysius or Ignatius."

"Yeah, my parents looked to the saints when they had kids, too. My sister and I always considered ourselves lucky to be Gabrielle and Anne, not Anastasia and Eustacia."

"Irish Catholic." A statement, not a question.

"Lapsed now, but yes. Born that way. Anne Magdalene Fitzgibbon."

"Thomas Xavier Devlin. They'd turn in their graves if they knew my colleagues at the firehouse call me 'Devil.' 'Dev' for short."

A shiver went down her spine. For some reason it upset her terribly, hearing that. She no longer went to church, but after Karen died, she'd discovered within herself a childish and pure belief in heaven. With it came a belief in hell.

"Why do they call you that?"

He lifted his elbows off the table, studied the backs of his hands. He frowned at them for a long instant, then hid them under the table. When he met Anne's eyes, she saw that he had neither eyebrows nor lashes.

"Because I was in a bad fire."

Anne didn't say anything. She looked away, but something about his face pulled her back. His burns were unspeakably ugly. Pocked and raised, like some primeval terrain, they made Anne think of screams and horror. But in some mysterious way, they were beautiful. They also made her think of Karen.

"They say only the devil could have come out from a fire like that alive," he said.

"How did you?" Anne asked, and she realized her voice was barely a whisper. "Come out alive?"

"Because I was with someone I loved. I had to get her out of the fire."

Time stood still. A song played on the jukebox, but Anne didn't register it. Her tea sat on the table in front of her, getting cold. Anne knew that this was the reason she had come to Ruby's. She heard her own voice before she realized that she was speaking.

"Did you save her?"

His hands were back on the table. Now they were palms up, and he was staring at them with the intensity of a fortune-teller.

"No," he said, looking into Anne's eyes.

"I'm sorry," she said. "Was it your wife?"

He nodded.

Anne thought of Karen, of how she had tried to catch Karen. So futile. One second Karen had been in her life, and the next second she was gone forever. Anne pictured the sun streaming through the window, backlighting her little girl. She saw the pigeon land. She herself had handed Karen the slice of bread. As if she was watching a movie, she saw Karen break the bread into pieces. She saw the pigeon take the crumbs from Karen's hand. And she saw Karen fly away.

Now, looking at Thomas Devlin, she wished she had scars. They would remind her of Karen. They would make tangible her longing, the passion she felt for her only child. With tears running down her face, she reached across the table and took his hands. She examined his burns, caressing them gently with her thumbs.

"I'm sorry," she said again.

"I know you are," he said.

She looked at him, perhaps quizzically.

"Karen," he said.

She stared. "I still can't talk about her."

"In your note? The one you sent to the station? You said that you were sorry that you put me in danger. You didn't say that you were sorry you went back inside the house, after the bag. I just want you to know that I understand the difference."

He was getting too close. She tried to pull her hands back, but he held them.

"Whatever made you run into the fire, it was all you had. All you had of her. I saw the toys, the dresses. I would have done the same."

"It was a picture," Anne said. "Her last picture."

"Did you get it? Is it okay?"

"Yes."

He nodded, and his expression was fierce. "Good," he said.

"It's not enough," she whispered. Tears ran freely down her cheeks.

The Charlene Bowen look-alike came by with a refill for Thomas's coffee. Anne could feel the woman's gaze, and her judgment. Thomas waved her away. Gently he withdrew his right hand from Anne's left. Digging into his pocket, he placed a five-dollar bill on the table.

"Let's go outside," he said.

She felt his hand on her elbow as they walked out the door into the bitter cold. Without speaking, they headed toward the ferry dock. The sun had set and splashes of burnished gold traced the black western sky. In the distance, they saw a ferry lit like a small city, steaming toward the island from across the sound. Six times, every summer of her life and two Christmases, Karen had ridden that ferry from the mainland. Anne felt the wind on her face, turning her tears to ice.

She slipped on the snow. She reached for Thomas Devlin, steadying herself. His arms encircled her, for just one moment. Self-conscious, she stepped back and continued walking on her own.

"I'm okay," she said. She was referring not to the slip, but to the flood of emotion she had experienced in Ruby's.

"Are you sure?" he asked.

"Yes."

"You don't have to be okay yet," he said.

She didn't reply, but watched the ferry draw closer to the terminal. Its horn sounded. People congregated on the upper decks, waiting to go to their cars. Anne heard the hydraulics operating the onshore ramp.

"One good thing about winter," he said. "You can get a ferry reservation at the last minute."

The statement seemed so incongruous, so normal, that Anne stopped in her tracks. She stared at him.

"Well, you can," he said.

"True," she agreed. You had to reserve months in advance or know Joe Dunbar, the head of the steamship authority, to drive a car onto the ferry in high season.

"I'm going off-island tomorrow," he said. "For a week."

"Oh," she said. This information, for some reason, brought her back to earth.

"To visit my son."

Anne stared at his eyes, but she couldn't see them in the dark.

He had a son. He had lost his wife, but he had his child. Drained, she turned away. She watched the big ferry graze the pilings, then bump the dock.

"Anne?"

She shook her head. She wanted to be left alone, but she knew it would be rude to say.

His arms came around her, and she pressed her face against his chest. She was clinging to another human being, and his name was Thomas.

"I'm glad you have a son," she said.

"So am I."

"I have to go home now." She had only the vaguest sense of what she meant by "home."

"I'll be back in a week," he said.

Gently, she pushed herself away. She couldn't see his face, but she smiled in its general direction. It was a crazy smile. A smile that didn't correspond to her feelings, a smile that hid as much from Anne herself as from the person at whom she had directed it. But it was a smile nonetheless, and her voice respected it.

"Have a good visit," she said. "With your son."

Chapter 5

Ned Devlin went straight to his dorm after hockey practice, expecting to find his father waiting. Winter afternoons at Deerfield felt like nighttime. The sun would dip behind the Berkshires, and a luminous, violet shadow would cloak the valley.

Ned ran past the red-brick dorms, his brown hair wet and freezing from the shower. He imagined he was on the ice, leading the Bruins to victory at the Boston Garden. He held an invisible stick, guiding the puck toward the goal.

It's a mind puck, he thought, cracking himself up so he laughed out loud. He passed a bunch of freshmen who looked at him as if he were crazy.

At seventeen he was six-four, gaining on his father's height, but more compact. He hoped he wouldn't grow much more. His father had had a collegiate growth spurt that had rendered him gawky, effectively ruining his prospects as a hockey player at Boston College, and souring his scholarship in the process.

Seeing his father's truck parked in front of his dorm, he slowed down. He was just old enough to affect a certain reserve in his father's presence. He didn't want to show his father, or his dorm mates, for that matter, how excited he felt. Tomorrow at dawn, he and his father would be taking off for a college tour.

Dartmouth was his first choice, but that was a long shot. The Ivies didn't give athletic scholarships. For Ned to attend Dartmouth, he'd have to rely on grants, a scholastic scholarship, loans, and a damned high-paying summer job. He and his father would also be visiting Middlebury, the University of Vermont, Bowdoin, and Boston College.

In spite of himself, he couldn't hold back. He ran up the granite steps, all in one stride. No one in the hallway, no one in the living room. He poked his head into the butt room, where Keith Harney and David Jorgensen were smoking French cigarettes and generally being too cool for words. They both had long, stringy hair, and they never wore anything but black. They should have been strumming guitars, to complete the picture.

"You seen my father?" Ned asked.

Keith shook his head, blowing smoke rings. David just stared moodily at nothing. Ned ran up to his room.

"Losers," he said under his breath, taking the stairs three at a time. Probably sitting there discussing metaphysics or suicide. They were sensitive show-offs; they wanted everyone to know they'd been injured by the cruel world.

Ned had them pegged for the types who would see his father and make fun of his face. If his father was anorexic like them, or wore nothing but black turtlenecks, they could accept his deformity. But guys like Keith and David would see his father as a jock, a fireman—to them, a municipal worker, just like a cop, or a garbageman, or a highway worker—who'd had his face burned off.

He burst into his room. Mark Mallory, his roommate, sat at his desk studying trig.

"Hey," Mark said, over his shoulder. "Your dad's here."

"Yeah, I saw his truck. Where'd he go?"

"I don't know," Mark said. "He's in a weird mood."

"What do you mean?" When it came to his father, Ned was always alert. Mark was a good guy who knew pretty much the whole story about Ned's parents; he'd spent a few vacations out on the island, and he liked Ned's father a lot.

"He had a big, goofy smile on."

"Interesting," Ned said.

He left the room and headed down the stairs, but more slowly than he had ascended them. His father was just about the most straightforward person Ned knew, but he certainly had his mysteries. As the years went by he was turning more and more into a hermit. Ned hoped this college tour would be good for him: get him off the island, away from his clocks. Maybe his father was looking forward to it, too. That could explain his mood.

Ned stepped outside. Lights had gone on in most of the dorm rooms as students headed home from practice or the library. The low, black mountains ringed the valley, their crests awash in the silver light of a sliver moon. Ned headed behind his dorm, to a path that led toward the playing fields.

Without the dorm lights, it was much darker back here. The stars seemed close enough to touch. Ned saw his father standing in the path, as tall as a tree, his head thrown back to look at the sky.

"Dad!" Ned said, before he got too close.

His father didn't hear him at first. He just stood there, staring at the stars, lost in his own world. Maybe something had happened. Ever since he'd lost his mother, Ned had a built-in anxiety when it came to his father. If his father didn't call when he was supposed to, if he was fifteen minutes late picking Ned up, if he didn't answer his telephone, Ned would worry. His pulse would quicken, the way it did now. Mark teased him, calling it his "old-lady heart."

"Dad, are you okay?" Ned asked.

His father turned then, and even in the dark, Ned could see that his face was radiant. You didn't see his father smile like this too often; he understood why Mark had called it goofy.

"Hello, son," his father said, and if anything, his smile got bigger. "Are you ready to find yourself a college?"

"Yeah," Ned said, puzzled. His father always told him how proud he was of him, for getting high honors and being all-American, and all that. But how big a deal was it, just looking at colleges? It wasn't as if Ned had been accepted anywhere yet. Or been offered financial aid. Still, it was the only thing he could come up with to explain his father's mood.

His father held out his arm, slapped it around Ned's shoulders. Ned, who towered over everyone at Deerfield, felt small for just that instant. He went back in time. His mother might have been waiting or them at home, ready to give them supper. Standing there with his gigantic father, looking at a skyful of stars, Ned remembered how it felt to be a little boy. And he didn't mind.

INSTEAD of going to school, realizing that their act would get them in trouble and not even caring, Maggie and her friends took the ferry off-island and hitchhiked to Boston. There were four of them, too many to hitch a ride in the same car unless it was a big empty one. If they got split up, they agreed to meet at Morning Glory, their favorite head shop in the Combat Zone.

They smoked a little pot on the ferry's upper deck, and Vanessa sipped from a bottle of Bailey's Irish Cream.

"Quit hogging it," Eugene said.

Eventually, she passed it around. Maggie hoped that getting all liquored up would make her warm. Even with her heavy sweater, leather jacket, and insulated mittens, she was freezing cold. This trip felt like a mistake. Vanessa had suggested it because they had a fourth-period history test that none of them had studied for, and if they were going to get in trouble anyway, they might at least have some fun.

But already it felt boring to Maggie. The same old thing: get high, get drunk, freeze your ass off waiting for a ride, then wind up in the grossest part of Boston. Every time she'd done this lately, she'd ended up having a different part of her body pierced.

Kurt was after her to put a ring in her pussy. Maggie knew how much it would hurt, and she didn't want to do it. Just the thought made her feel shaky. But she hated saying no to Kurt; the idea of losing him was scarier than facing any needle. Knowing her, she'd drink herself brave, and by the time she got back to the island, she'd have another hole in her body.

Standing at the rail, Maggie kept her eyes peeled for whales or seals. At this time of year you saw them all the time. Seals were her favorite. Their sleek round heads and enormous eyes, whiskering out of the water to watch the ferry slide by. Last summer she had promised Karen they'd ride the ferry alone together over Christmas, looking for seals. She'd even seen a seal toy at the general store, a fuzzy white baby that she had planned to give Karen for her birthday.

There. Maggie saw a real seal. He bobbed in the icy water, and she had the feeling he knew she was watching. She had the crazy desire to wave to him. But she didn't; her friends would think she was stupid.

"How much money do you have?" Kurt asked, coming to stand beside her. She leaned into his body and felt the thrill of love run through her limbs.

"About nine dollars."

"Shit," he said.

He had asked her to go through her mother's purse while her mother was in the shower, and to check the laundry for money her father might have left in his pants pockets. Maggie had said she would, but what Kurt didn't understand was that her family counted every penny. Besides, ripping off stores was one thing, but Maggie couldn't steal from her family. Instead, she had gone without school lunch the last few days in order to have a stash of cash for an occasion just such as this. When he would ask her how much she had.

"How about you?" she asked. "How much do we have alto-gether?"

He gave her a sarcastic look, to let her know there was no "altogether." She wasn't stupid. She knew that in Kurt's mind her money was theirs and his money was his. If he even had any. A little voice deep inside sometimes told Maggie that she could do better than Kurt. That there were boys who were nice, who knew the meaning of love, or at least respect, who were as good-looking as Kurt.

But they didn't live on the island. Kurt was the best boy in her class. Twenty years old! No one else had a boyfriend in his twen-ties. He was tall and handsome, with golden skin and flowing blond hair. His face reminded her of a beautiful cat, with exotic wide green eyes. He could easily be a male model.

Feeling guilty for even thinking about someone other than Kurt, Maggie pressed his hand to her breast and gave him a long, open-mouthed kiss.

"We need some more money," he said, pulling back.

"It's enough," Maggie said. "The ride'll be free, the ferry's free. . . ." The crew guys never charged island kids during the winter.

"I want to buy weed," Kurt said.

Boring, Maggie thought. But she didn't say anything. She re-sumed scanning the sea for seals.

"I'll figure something out," he said, heading toward Vanessa and her bottle.

They hitched a ride off the ferry with a refrigeration repairman who let them sit in the open back of his pickup as far as Wickland. Perched on the bare metal floor for all those miles made Maggie so cold she honestly thought she might die. She wondered whether her bottom was actually frostbitten.

She tried to convince the others to stop at a Friendly's for hot chocolate, but no one wanted to spend the money. They stationed themselves on the side of the highway. Maggie hugged herself. She very badly wished she hadn't done this. Her mother was going to kill her.

Besides, she knew that she could have passed the history test. She wasn't talking an A, or even a B, but she wouldn't have failed. She had just told her friends she hadn't studied because she didn't want them to think she was getting uppity.

After they'd gone thirty minutes with no luck, taking turns holding the cardboard with BOSTON in big letters printed on it and no one stopping, Maggie said maybe they should head back home.

"Party pooper!" Vanessa said.

"We're going to Boston," Kurt said.

Smirking, Vanessa sank to her knees. She folded her hands, like a little kid saying her prayers, and she looked at the sky.

"If only someone stops to give us a ride, so that we don't freeze to death, I swear I'll believe in God," she said, then started laughing hysterically.

Maggie went to church with her family every Sunday. Since Karen died she didn't know exactly what she believed. She didn't know how God could let such a thing happen to such a wonderful little girl. To an entire family! But it made her sick, Vanessa being so crude. She tugged Vanessa's collar, trying to get her to stand. But Vanessa flailed at her, pushing her away.

"I mean it," Vanessa said, and by now Kurt and Eugene were on their knees, too. All three of them were laughing so hard, they couldn't talk.

"Send us a ride, and we'll all believe in God," Kurt said before he collapsed again, whooping with laughter.

And at that moment a truck stopped. Not some dinky pickup, but a super-huge Peterbilt eighteen-wheeler. The driver opened his window.

"Boston?" he asked.

"Yeah," Kurt said.

"Hop in." He unlatched the passenger door. Kurt, Eugene, and Vanessa were still giggling.

"Aaaah, he would have stopped anyway," Kurt said.

"Yeah," Vanessa said. "We take the belief shit back."

Maggie felt so disgusted, she almost didn't climb in after them. But she was so cold. . . . Kurt reached down from the cab and pulled her in. He sat in the passenger seat, and the truck driver told the others they could ride in his little cabin.

Located right behind the cab was a tiny windowless room with a bed, some cupboards, and a bookshelf with a board across it, to prevent the books from flying around. Heat blasted out of a vent; Maggie huddled in front of it.

"It's adorable!" Vanessa squealed as Eugene pulled her onto the bed.

"It's home twenty-five days out of the month," the driver said. Maggie tried to size him up. With Kurt and Eugene there, she felt pretty safe, but you never knew. He was neatly shaven, with short blond hair. He wore a turquoise turtleneck under a colorful ski-style sweater. About thirty years old, very clean-cut. Maggie let herself relax.

"So, where are you all from?" the driver asked.

Kurt started telling him about the island. Maggie overheard part of it, but the Bailey's was having a delayed effect, and she started to feel drowsy. Next thing she knew, she smelled pot. Kurt and the driver were passing a joint back and forth.

"My name's Fritz, by the way," he said. "How about you?"

Kurt told him.

"Y'all got pretty girlfriends, Kurt and Eugene," he said. The more he talked, the more pronounced his southern accent became.

"Thanks." Maggie actually heard Kurt say the word.

"You bored back there?" he asked, checking his rearview mirror. He met Maggie's eyes dead on. Blushing, she looked away.

"No," she said.

" 'Cause if you were, I could offer you some interesting reading material. There in the bookshelf."

Maggie ignored him, but Vanessa reached right past her. She pulled down a battered paperback. Maggie didn't want to give her the satisfaction of looking, but Vanessa gently tapped her elbow. Maggie glanced over.

The cover showed a naked woman lying in a field. Purple bruises covered her body; a cord cut deeply into her neck. Her tongue, black and bloated, protruded from her mouth. It was a real photograph of a dead woman. The book's title was *Bitch*.

Maggie and Vanessa looked at each other. Eugene was stoned, his eyes closed. Quietly, Maggie slid the book back onto the shelf.

"What'd y'all find?" Fritz asked, half turning in his seat.

"Nothing," Maggie said steadily.

"C'mon—I saw you looking at one of my books. Don't keep it to yourself."

Kurt swung around to give Maggie a dirty look.

"He's nice enough to give us a ride," Kurt said. "Don't be a jerk."

Maggie stared at him calmly, trying to communicate to him that there was a reason why she wasn't eager to look through the books with Fritz. At the same time she kept glancing at Fritz, to make sure he had both hands on the wheel.

"Like I said, you boys have yourselves two sweet ladies."

That seemed to make Kurt feel okay. He relaxed, facing forward again. Vanessa reached for Maggie's hand, and she squeezed it.

"Matter of fact, I would be very happy to pay a hundred bucks to fuck either one of them. If that doesn't offend you, that is."

Maggie felt her throat close around a sharp cry. Vanessa's mouth had dropped open; she was shaking Eugene to wake him up.

Now Fritz and Kurt were conferring, their heads close together. Good, Maggie thought. Kurt's playing it cool. Instead of blowing up, causing a big scene and setting off God knows what kind of reaction a creep like Fritz might have, he's reasoning with him. Maggie tried to send Kurt a silent message. She gave him permission to tell Fritz anything he wanted: that she and Vanessa had STDs, AIDS, anything.

Fritz nodded. He seemed to understand Kurt's explanation.

Now Kurt was climbing into the little cabin, to hold Maggie in his arms. How could she have doubted him before? Shaking with fear, she let him protectively stroke her hair and kiss her face.

"It's okay," he whispered in her ear.

"Let's get out of here," she whispered back.

"I know. I know."

"Right now, okay?"

Reaching for the book, she laid it on her knee, so Kurt would understand that they were dealing with a sick one.

"The thing is," Kurt whispered, "he'll pay one hundred bucks *cash,* right now. All you have to do is let him . . . you know. It's no different than if he were some guy at school. I'm not your first guy anyway, and if it doesn't bother you, it doesn't bother me. He'll wear a condom. . . ."

Maggie couldn't believe her ears. She leaned back, to look Kurt right in the eyes. Had Fritz slipped him some bizarre personality-altering drug?

"Kurt . . ." she said. "Please?"

"Oh my God," Vanessa whispered.

They were slowing down. Maggie craned her neck, to see out the window, and saw that Fritz was pulling into a rest stop.

"One hundred bucks," Kurt said urgently. He held Maggie's upper arms with such force that they throbbed. She pushed him away.

"Get us out of this," she said.

His eyes narrowed, and she could feel his disgust.

"Hey, Fritz," Kurt said. "Never mind. We've really gotta get to Boston."

"My father's waiting for us," Vanessa said, her voice practically a trill.

"You got no daddy waiting in Boston," Fritz said pleasantly. Maggie could see that he'd taken one hand off the wheel. Between downshifts, he had unzipped his fly and was stroking himself.

"Fritz, man," Kurt said. "We've gotta book."

"We'll have us a little party," Fritz said. "Teach you boys a thing or two."

Kurt was stammering away, trying to change Fritz's mind, while Maggie looked around the cabin. She felt under the pillow, slid her hand along the bottom of the mattress in search of a weapon. Then she saw it: the bookshelf.

While Fritz parked the truck Maggie slipped behind Kurt. Very carefully, without drawing any attention to herself, she slid free the slat that kept the books from flying around. Flat and narrow, about twelve inches long, the wooden bar felt solid in her hand.

"Why'd we stop?" Eugene asked, coming to.

"No, please, no," Vanessa said to the back of Fritz's head. She started to cry.

From where Maggie sat, she saw Fritz reach into the door pocket. His hand closed around an object; she caught the glint of metal. Later, she would realize that she'd seen a gun. But in that split second, she merely reacted to her own sickening fear. She swung back and hit Fritz across the face with the bar.

He reeled back, blood spurting from his nose. He dropped whatever he'd been holding to cover his face with both his hands.

"Little bitch!" he screamed, blood burbling through his fingers.

Maggie and her friends scrambled out of the cab. Except for one other truck, the parking lot was empty. They ran into the woods, a shallow stand of scrub pines interspersed with trash cans and picnic tables. Two gunshots rang out; they kept running until they cleared the woods and came to a busy strip of gas stations, fast-food restaurants, and a Quality Inn.

Maggie paused, struggling to catch her breath. The others continued ahead, but stopped when they realized she had fallen behind.

"Come on," Kurt said.

She stared at him with a steady gaze, taking in his handsome face, his strong body, the shame in his wide, green eyes. Then she turned away. Shivering, and not from the cold, she walked in the opposite direction.

"Maggie!" Vanessa called. "Come on, we have to stick together."

Maggie just kept walking. She really expected Vanessa or Kurt to run after her, try to convince her to turn around, but they didn't. Actually, she was relieved.

She walked into the Quality Inn. The lobby was warm, and one of her favorite songs by James Taylor was playing on the loudspeaker. The desk clerk was a pretty black girl, not much older than Maggie herself.

"May I help you?" the girl asked.

"Do you have a pay phone?"

"Right over there." The girl pointed to a bank of telephones along the wall. Maggie thanked her.

She would call Anne. She'd make up some excuse and ask Anne to cover for her with her mother. She didn't ask herself why, but she knew she needed to hear a motherly voice. She'd hitchhike back to the ferry, slip onto the island, and everything would be fine again. Dialing Anne's number, she had to try three times before her fingers got it right.

"Hello?"

Maggie clutched the receiver, unable to speak.

"Hello?" Anne said again.

"Anne?" Maggie said. And then it all poured out. No excuses, no lies, nothing but the truth about Fritz and Kurt and Boston and having her nipple pierced and the Bailey's Irish Cream and seeing the seal and how she had never gotten to take Karen alone on the ferry at Christmas. She was crying very hard, and her face was wet from tears and spit.

"Where are you, honey?" Anne asked, her voice very calm.

"I don't know," Maggie sobbed.

"Can you find out? Just leave the phone where it is, and ask someone the name of the town and the route number."

Maggie pressed the receiver to her breast and tried to stop crying. The sobs subsided, but she couldn't stop the tears yet. Very carefully, like a beginning gymnast crossing the balance beam for the first time, she walked to the reception desk.

"Excuse me," she said to the girl. "Can you tell me the address? Of where we are right now?"

"Sure. It's Thirteen-oh-four Memorial Highway."

"Um, what town?"

"It's Wakefield. Massachusetts," the girl said with a soft, kind smile.

"Thank you," Maggie said.

She told Anne.

"Stay there," Anne said. "There's a ferry pulling in right now. I'll be there in two hours."

"Okay." Maggie didn't even try to argue.

"Will you be safe?" Anne asked. "Is it a nice place? Do you feel secure?"

"Yes," Maggie said, looking at the girl behind the desk.

"Two hours," Anne said. "Keep warm."

After Maggie hung up, she took a seat at one end of the plush sofa at the lobby's far end. A selection of magazines and sight-seeing brochures were fanned out on a long, low table. Maggie just stared at them. She tried to make herself very small so no one would notice her. So no one would ask her to leave.

She closed her eyes. After a few minutes she heard someone walking toward her.

Frightened, she started. But it was the desk clerk, smiling at Maggie, setting a mug on the table in front of her.

"Hot chocolate," the girl said. "You look like you could use something to warm you up."

"Thank you," Maggie said. Reaching for the steaming mug, she tried to smile. She couldn't quite, not just yet. But it was obvious the girl knew what she meant. The girl pushed the mug closer. Then she picked a discarded gum wrapper off the floor, as if she was cleaning up just for Maggie, and she went back to her desk.

For months Anne's life had been without shape. Without Matt or Karen. She had navigated her days like a sleepwalker, moving through time with neither hope nor purpose. She never answered the phone, avoiding the calls of even Matt or her closest friends. No one understood what had happened to her. They could sympathize, they could try to imagine her hell, but they couldn't know. Her silence made everyone doubt her. After a while her phone hardly rang at all.

Now, in the middle of the coldest winter she could remember, Anne felt something inside beginning to stir. She didn't awaken hating herself every day. She no longer spent those cloudy blue hours between midnight and three wishing that she would die.

In the week he was off-island, Anne often found herself thinking of Thomas Devlin. His loneliness, like her own, had driven him to seek even greater isolation on the island. He knew how it felt to lose someone he loved. Trying to save his wife, he had seen her life slip away. Hearing that had given Anne a bizarre kind of peace. She wasn't the only one.

She knew she was getting better because she had started reading the classifieds.

The *New Shoreham Star* had exactly one-half column of employment listings, and most of them were peculiar to island life. L.P. James's Shipyard needed a boat varnisher; Spera Seafood was seeking experienced lobster handlers. The Island Convalescent Home needed third-shift nurses, nurses' aides, and kitchen help.

Some mysterious "Wanda" with an island exchange was advertising for "open-minded women who like to talk on the phone." The ferry company was looking for office help, and the fire company needed a dispatcher.

Anne hadn't worked since Karen was born. She had wanted to stay home with the baby, and Matt's salary and her collage income had made it possible. But now she had the urge to be around people. She could still do her collages, but maybe she could find a friendly office to work in. She decided to call Stanley Gray at the ferry office.

MAGGIE slept the whole way from Wakefield to the ferry and through the crossing itself. It was the small ferry, with the open car deck, and they stayed in the car for the ride. Anne kept the engine running for heat, the windows cracked so they couldn't asphyxiate. Maggie smelled of smoke, sour milk, and liquor. Anne kept glancing at her, huddled in a ball on the seat. The ferry docked with a lurching thump, and Maggie woke with a start.

She sat up with "Where am I?" written all over her face.

"We're here already?" she asked.

"Home again," Anne said.

"Oh God," Maggie said. She smacked the crown of her head with her right hand and held it there. "Do I have to go home? Did you tell my mother?"

"Not yet."

"Not yet," Maggie said, her voice echoing with doom.

The ferrymen took their places, making fast the hemp docking lines that were bigger in diameter than Anne's upper arm. Ice glazed the dark brown pilings. Anne watched the men knock dagger-sharp icicles from the stocky bronze bollards, working fast but clumsily in their heavy gloves.

"I'm not going to tell her," Anne said. "But you are."

Vehement, Maggie shook her head. "I can't."

One of the men signaled Anne, and she shifted into first. The man looked familiar; she had the feeling he had been one of the volunteers she'd seen at the fire. Driving off the boat, she waved to him, but he seemed not to see.

"Asshole," Maggie said, staring at him over her shoulder. Anne drove up Transit Street, touched by her niece's reaction to the snub. Pulling into her usual parking spot, she patted Maggie's hand.

"Come on upstairs. I want you to see my new apartment."

Anne led Maggie up the narrow wooden stairs and unlocked the door. She hadn't done much in terms of decorating, but she had scrubbed the place clean, and her worktable looked busy. Stepping inside, she glanced out her window and noted with pleasure that the harbor lights were coming on.

Maggie didn't say anything. She stood in the doorway, just looking around.

"What do you think?" Anne asked.

"This is where you live?"

"Yes," Anne said. She motioned for Maggie to sit on the sofa, and she sat beside her.

"It's so empty," Maggie said. "I always loved your place in New York because it was so *you*. Your collages, all the stuff you and Uncle Matt brought back from everywhere, all the rugs and colors. . . ."

Anne nodded, picturing the apartment. She'd covered the hardwood floors with Oriental rugs, the furniture with bright silk and cashmere throws. Red was everywhere. She had covered one entire wall with picture frames: scrolled, carved, gilded, museum-quality picture frames that she'd picked up at tag sales on the island and elsewhere. Other walls contained her own collages, Matt's collection of small French paintings, and family photos. They had a three-foot-high bronze replica of the Eiffel Tower, at once monstrous and beautiful. Just looking at it made Anne smile. They had a *Webster's Second Dictionary* on a nineteenth-century lectern she'd found in Newport, Rhode Island. Karen's toys and books were everywhere, spilling from briar baskets. The rooms were full of life and passion: they were full of the Davises.

"This is so different," Maggie said, frowning. "I can't picture you happy here."

"It's been hard to be happy anywhere," Anne said in a quiet voice.

"What's this?" Maggie asked. Leaning forward, she reached for Karen's drawing of paradise. Anne had left it on the coffee table, within easy reach; she had been holding it hours before, when Maggie's call had interrupted her.

"Karen did that," Anne said, moving closer to Maggie.

"She loved to color," Maggie said. She traced some of the crayon markings with one finger.

Anne could see that Maggie was engulfed with feelings and memories of Karen. Here was a girl who had known and loved Karen as well as anyone but Anne and Matt. Maggie had baby-sat for her many times; she had played with Karen for hours and hours. Locked within Maggie were impressions of Karen that even Anne didn't have, and for Anne it was like sitting with a treasure chest.

"Tell me one thing," Anne said. "One thing you remember about her."

"Okay," Maggie said. "Remember one night last summer, when you and Uncle Matt went to Atwood's with my parents?"

"Our anniversary dinner."

"Yeah. Well, Karen was sleeping over at our house, and she wanted to try on my clothes. She loved to dress up."

"I know."

"She was looking through my closet, and she saw my prom dress. It was black satin, with lace—"

"Your mother sent me pictures of your prom. You were beautiful."

"Thank you. Well, Karen told me she would have liked the

dress better if it was pink. But she couldn't resist—it's a real party dress. She wanted to put it on. So I helped her into it and gave her the gloves I wore—very Madonna things, all black net. I mean, you probably hate me, right? Letting a four-year-old get dressed up like a high-school kid. Should I be telling you this?"

"You can tell me anything about Karen," Anne said.

"She was so cool. I could really picture her as a big girl. She wanted me to put makeup on her eyes, and polish on her nails, and she wanted me to call her 'Julia.' "

"She loved Julia Roberts," Anne said. It was a simple story, but for Anne it was cliff-edge suspense. She lived for every detail, every nuance. She knew she should be talking to Maggie about what was happening in her life, but Karen stories had the potency of a drug.

"She was Julia, and I was Lubie, her younger sister. Lubie! I mean, what a funny name."

"Lubie and Shella were her favorite make-believe names."

"I asked her why 'Lubie,' and she said it sounded pretty, just right for a younger sister. The whole time she was this little kid in black with raccoon eyes, and she was pretending to be a glamorous movie star, and I kept thinking she had the greatest imagination in the whole world."

"She did," Anne said, and her mind clicked off. She felt it happen, and she even knew why: she believed that Karen's imagination had killed her.

"I miss her," Maggie said.

Anne nodded.

They sat there in silence, both staring at Karen's drawing. After a few minutes Anne turned to face Maggie.

"Thank you for talking about her," Anne said.

"Don't thank me—" Maggie frowned, not understanding.

"Right after it happened, no one was talking about her. Matt had moved out, and my friends, even your mother, were afraid they would upset me if they mentioned her, which they would have. I hardly ever heard her name. I couldn't take it. I'd have to go into her room just to convince myself she had really existed."

"Honestly?" Maggie was staring at her, unsure of whether Anne was serious or not.

"Yes."

"That's so sad," Maggie said.

"Mmm."

"Well, anytime you want to talk about Karen, or if you need to check in with someone who knows she existed like crazy, you can call me. I mean it," Maggie said, flinging herself at Anne with what Karen would have called a train-wreck hug.

"Thanks, Maggie," Anne said, holding on to her niece for a long time, trying to remember how it had felt to hold her daughter. After a long while she gently pushed herself back so she could look Maggie in the eyes.

"What are we going to do about you?" Anne asked.

"I know," Maggie said, hanging her head. "I've been really stupid."

"Are you just saying that? So I'll think you're fine, that this was just another teenage adventure, and forget about it?"

"It was bad," Maggie said. "It wasn't an adventure."

"I think your mother needs to know."

"She'll hate me," Maggie said. "She's not like you. Mom does the right thing, all the time, and she can't handle people who don't."

"I'll help her handle it."

Maggie picked up Karen's picture and examined it more closely. She rested it on her knees, and Anne could see her drawing comfort from it, just as she often did herself.

"You don't understand," Maggie said, brushing hair out of her eyes. "Mom doesn't want to know. She looks the other way all the time. I know she loves me, and she wants me to be okay. But in order for her to respect me, she has to ignore things. She's caught me drunk before. But I tell her I have a cold and I took too much NyQuil, and she lets it go."

Anne stared at Maggie, weighing the options. She could tell Gabrielle, and Maggie would never confide in her again. Or she could keep the secret, taking Maggie's word that she wanted to change, and the next time Maggie could die in a drunken car crash. She thought of Karen, and she realized that no matter what Karen did, Anne would always want to know. On the other hand, she realized that she and Gabrielle were not the same person.

"I think you should tell the police about that guy, Fritz," Anne said, realizing that she had made her decision.

"I know. I wish I'd gotten his license-plate number. It was scary, that book with a picture of a real dead person on it. And the gun . . ."

"If you hadn't hit him," Anne said, hugging Maggie again, "I hate to think of what he might have done. Your friends are really lucky you thought so fast."

"I hope they're okay," Maggie said. "I just hope he didn't drive around looking for them."

"They're bad news," Anne said. "It's hard, growing up on the island. There's nothing to do, it's easy to get into trouble. Hanging around with the wrong kids. You need to stop; it's making you too unhappy."

"I'm going to try," Maggie said. "I want to make things better. Thanks for not telling Mom."

"I didn't say—"

"But I know you won't. I can tell you care about me, and I know you believe me about Mom not wanting to know. If it happens again . . ."

"Deal," Anne said, hoping she was doing the right thing. "It'll stay between us for now, if there isn't a next time."

Smiling now, Maggie pulled away. Once again she took a close look at Karen's picture. She looked from the paper to Anne and back again.

"This is amazing," Maggie said.

"Karen said it was of things she loved. That's you." Anne pointed to the drawing of Maggie.

"And that's you and Uncle Matt. The beach. Gramercy Park . . . what are those?" Maggie pointed to the white cubes.

"I don't know," Anne said.

Maggie narrowed her eyes, lost in thought.

"They look like rusty old stoves," Maggie said.

"I don't know. Karen told me the picture was of paradise," Anne said, gently taking the paper out of Maggie's hand.

"Paradise," Maggie said thoughtfully. She repeated it: "Paradise."

But when Anne turned to look at her, Maggie was frowning. It shook Anne deeply, seeing the expression on her face. As if Maggie had just thought of something terrible. Her heart in her throat, Anne was just about to ask what it was, but suddenly Maggie flashed a smile.

"Could I have a glass of water?" Maggie asked.

"Sure," Anne said. Knowing Maggie wanted to change the subject, she went into the kitchen. She took Karen's picture with her. When she returned, Maggie was leafing through a magazine. Anne's mind blocked out the question she had been about to ask. It was gone. Her mind was blank.

Just as well. Right now she had to focus on Maggie, on driving her home and making sure she would be okay. That's what mattered right now.

Chapter 6

It was a whirlwind tour of libraries and hockey rinks, deans and coaches, dorm rooms and student centers, and snow-covered college greens. Thomas and Ned Devlin took turns driving, and whoever drove got to pick the radio station. Behind the wheel now, Thomas Devlin tuned in to Country 96.6 and listened to some singer's sweet, lonely lament.

"Dad," Ned said. "You're listening to more of that tear-jerk stuff, and there's that lunatic smile back again. Are you going crazy or something? Should I be worried?"

"Far from it," Thomas said. "I'm happy, that's all."

"If you say so," Ned said, sounding profoundly unconvinced.

Thomas nodded, turning the radio up a notch.

"It's just that I keep expecting you to make some kind of bizarre announcement. Like you're moving to Florida or converting to some weird religion. Or like you have a girlfriend."

Glancing over, Thomas Devlin saw the blush spread up Ned's neck, behind his ears, and into his sideburns. Thomas felt the bad side of his face tugging upward in an even broader smile.

"Would any of those things bother you in particular?"

"Maybe the weird religion."

"You can relax, there. When you've spent as much time in parochial school as I did, you realize you're Catholic for life."

"You just seem different," Ned said, even as he seemed to relax perceptibly. He slouched in the truck seat, trying to get his big frame into a comfortable position. He had never really liked long car rides. Finally he settled in, one knee resting against the dashboard.

"Different?" Thomas Devlin asked, when Ned stopped fidgeting.

"Like something's going on."

"Hell, Ned. Plenty's going on! How often do I get to tour the best colleges in America and hear what a great kid I have?"

Ned shot him a glance full of boyish pleasure. Without leaning forward, he turned down the radio, the better to hear his father's praise.

"Yeah?" Ned said.

"All the coaches want you, the admission folks want you. Who wouldn't? You're an academic all-American," Thomas said. Even the players, who Thomas knew could start off feeling wary and competitive toward a potential teammate, had taken to him. Ned was as trusting and friendly as a big golden-retriever puppy, and people liked him right away.

"I liked Dartmouth best," Ned said. "I knew I would."

"It's a great school."

"I'm not sure I'll get in. I'd have to get a lot of scholarship help to go. And loans."

"I have the feeling you'll get in. I was glad to see you sent your poems. The admissions guy, Mister . . . ?"

"Mr. McCabe."

"Yes. He liked them very much. So do I, Ned. They're really something."

"Thanks," Ned said, embarrassed.

When Ned was fifteen, he had written four hauntingly beautiful poems about his mother. His freshman English teacher submitted them, with Ned's permission, to a colleague at the *Massachusetts Review*. They were published the following spring. The first Thomas knew of the poems was when he picked up his mail at the post office and found a package from Ned with a note to *please see pages 20–22*. It was the *Review*. That night Thomas Devlin didn't go to bed. He stayed up all night reading the poems over and over. They shimmered with love for Sarah, and an almost unbelievable knowledge of her, and they made Thomas Devlin see her through the eyes of her son.

Now, driving along, he felt a rush of sad, sweet pride. He wished that somehow Sarah could know that they'd made a boy like Ned. The miracle of it, to Thomas, was that she had died when Ned was six, and he'd still turned out so fine: in spite of being raised, not counting the year after the fire, solely by his father.

"Do you miss Mom?" Ned asked.

"Sure I do," Thomas replied, but the question took him by surprise. She had been gone for so long. Thinking of her as little as possible had been essential to his survival in the early days. He had trained himself to forget.

Right after the fire, when thoughts of Sarah had been most unbearable, Thomas Devlin had prayed that he would die. Nurses in the burn unit would pump him full of morphine, and it would zip through his veins straight into the air. You need skin to hold drugs inside a body, and Thomas Devlin had no skin. He had existed as pure pain. To him, his entire existence, his agony, was Sarah.

Later, when he could keep the drugs inside, he used them to forget. They dulled his memories and his love. They dulled Sarah.

"Do you think about your mother?" he asked.

"Yeah. A lot."

"Sometimes I wonder what you remember. You were pretty young."

"I have a long memory," Ned said. He stopped, as if he'd decided to keep the recollections private. But then, perhaps fearing that his father would think him rude, he continued. "I remember how pretty she was. How she smelled like soap and powder. Violets, or something."

"Piccadilly Violets, that's right. I'd forgotten." Thomas smiled at the lost memory. Every Christmas Sarah wanted a bath set you could only get at Filene's. It came with bath powder, guest soaps, and cologne, and the package showed a little girl selling violets in Piccadilly Circus.

"She'd sure be proud of you," he said.

"Thanks, Dad."

Thomas Devlin turned the radio back up. He wasn't certain why, but he didn't think they should talk anymore just then. Ned must have agreed, because they rode along in comfortable silence for the next twenty or so miles.

"We're here," Ned said as they passed the Deerfield Inn. The statement came out with a thud, as if he'd been reluctant to deliver it. Perhaps Ned, like his father, wasn't quite ready for the trip to end.

"This whole tour has been a thrill," Thomas Devlin said, driving slower than necessary.

"You know that stuff I said earlier, about being afraid your smiling meant you were about to drop a bombshell?"

"The stuff about Florida, religion, and a girlfriend?"

"Yeah."

"What about it?"

"I'd definitely mind you converting to a weird religion," Ned said. "But I'd mind if you decided to move to Florida, too. It's too far away."

"We'd miss the island."

"Yeah. Summers on the island definitely beat summers in Miami," Ned said.

"Yeah," Thomas said. He was waiting for Ned to make mention of the third thing, the girlfriend. But it never came. Ned's silence filled the car. It had the power and weight of a blessing, and it left both men's cheeks beet red.

"Take care of yourself, Dad," Ned said, when they pulled up in front of his dorm.

"You, too," Thomas Devlin said, beaming as wide as his face would allow: with love for his sweet son and with the anticipated pleasure of the woman he would see when he returned to the island.

EVER since the fire, Gabrielle had expected Anne to say that she had made a mistake by coming to the island in the middle of winter, that she was returning to New York. Instead, she'd taken an apartment in town and commenced looking for a job. It boggled Gabrielle's mind. Why would anyone with Anne's creature comforts abandon the finer things in a New York life for the hardships of an island winter?

The two sisters stood in Gabrielle's kitchen peeling root vegetables. Gabrielle had thought a chicken pot pie would be just the thing to warm everyone right down to their toes.

"Parsnips," Anne said. "Whoever would have thought we'd be able to get parsnips out here in February?"

"Excuse me, but are you saying islanders are food rubes?" Gabrielle asked, only half-kidding. "Granted, it might not be Balducci's, but for a market its size . . . Besides, what's so sophisticated about parsnips?"

Anne chuckled. She trimmed the parsnip, threw it into the crock, and reached for a turnip.

"I didn't say sophisticated. I was thinking of variety," Anne said. "When we were little, weren't carrots about the only fresh vegetables we could get out here? And maybe iceberg lettuce?"

"I like to think the Seduction Table has upped the culinary standards around here."

"I'm sure that's true."

Gabrielle dropped her peeler in the sink and fiddled with the portable-TV antenna. Oprah, her hero, was on, and a storm of static was drowning her out. At the best of times Gabrielle could get only two stations with any clarity, and high winds last week had blown the big antenna off the roof. Gabrielle turned the knobs, trying to clear the screen snow and let Oprah shine through, but it was a losing battle.

"I would trade my husband for cable," Gabrielle said.

Anne chuckled again. Gabrielle glanced over, on her guard. She had been half-serious, but she didn't like Anne agreeing with her.

"You're in a good mood," she said, clicking off the set.

"You make me laugh. I like it," Anne said.

Gabrielle wondered what Anne would say if she knew that Matt had called that afternoon, as he had called two other afternoons since Anne had come to the island. "Just checking in," he said, wanting to know how Anne was doing. Gabrielle had sensed something hangdog in his manner, a whipped-guy attitude that didn't suit him one bit.

He said he missed the family. Anne and Karen especially, but the Vincents also. Gabrielle acted stern and disappointed with him, but the truth was, she enjoyed his calls. They broke up the day. She harbored a dream that Anne and Matt would get back together, take whatever steps possible to patch up their marriage.

"Do you ever think about going home?" Gabrielle asked.

"To New York?"

"Yes."

Well, that wiped the smile off Anne's face. Gabrielle fought the impulse to give her a hug, get her feeling comfortable again. But this was a case of tough love: she wanted Anne to face some painful truths that might eventually make her life better.

"No, I don't," Anne said. "Not right now, anyway."

"It's just that . . . oh, I might as well spit it out. You shouldn't be out here, hon. You're past struggling."

Anne put down her peeler and faced Gabrielle head-on. Gabrielle had to admit, Anne had some color back in her cheeks. Something about island life was agreeing with her.

"What do you mean, 'past struggling'?"

Gabrielle realized she'd put her foot in it.

"I mean, don't go taking it wrong, now. Everyone knows you've experienced the worst thing that can happen to a mother. I know, Anne."

Anne nodded.

Gabrielle waited for Anne to say something, to express some of the terrible loss she must be feeling for Karen. But this wasn't the time. Anne said nothing, so Gabrielle continued.

"It's miserable out here. I go crazy in winter. The antenna blows away, you need four-wheel drive just to get your mail. You were smart enough to get yourself off the island, and it doesn't make sense to me, you coming back."

"I don't see it that way. I love it here."

That's because you have a choice, Gabrielle thought. In a minute she might boil over, say something she would regret. She stirred the cream sauce, tasted it, added a dash of pepper. Gabrielle had cushioned Anne's progress through life, and then Matt had taken over. Say what you want: Anne understood heartache, not struggle.

"I do," Anne persisted. "I love it here."

"Taste this," Gabrielle said. She coated a red plastic spoon with the silkily thickened sauce and held it to Anne's lips.

Instead of tasting, however, Anne lowered her head to Gabrielle's shoulder. She left it there for a long moment.

"Anne," Gabrielle said, overcome by a surge of love. Just because Anne didn't discuss her sadness didn't mean it wasn't there.

Sometimes Gabrielle wished she had a specific nickname for Anne, something dear for her alone instead of the generic "honey" or "sweetheart." The name "Anne" was so elegant, so refined and austere; in many ways the name was so like Anne herself. Still, Gabrielle did sometimes wish for a sweeter, cozier name that would fit Anne's soft side. "Annie" simply wouldn't cut it. It was too homespun, too quaint. Too Little Orphan Annie.

"Why did Mother and Daddy give you such a Queen of England name?" Gabrielle asked, stroking Anne's silky black hair.

" 'Cause I'm a royal pain?"

Gabrielle smiled. "No. It's just such a formal name. Have I ever told you that? That I wish I had something little-sisterish to call you?"

"Well, I've made it to my thirties without it," Anne said. A pause. "Gaby."

"Oh, I hate that," Gabrielle said, giving Anne another squeeze. "Makes me sound like a parakeet."

Anne eased herself out of Gabrielle's embrace and chose a potato to peel. Gabrielle wondered whether she had noticed that it was an Aroostock golden potato, one that had a buttery color without the addition of any butter whatsoever, instead of the usual pasty-white Maine variety. Until Gabrielle had started her business, the market hadn't known the difference.

The telephone rang. Gabrielle jumped for it. Steve was working on the big house, and many nights lately he had worked late. But it was Kurt.

"I'm sorry, Maggie is doing her homework," Gabrielle said icily.

"Tell her I called," Kurt said, and hung up, the mannerless loser that he was.

"I'll say one thing," Gabrielle said to Anne, replacing the receiver, "Maggie seems to be coming to her senses. She refuses to talk to Kurt Vibbert or Vanessa. You know Vanessa, don't you? Lynn Adamson's daughter?"

"I remember Lynn," Anne said. "So, Maggie's doing well?"

"Thriving. I'm telling you. Does her homework without being

reminded, no talking on the phone. Listens to the radio way too much, but she's at that age."

"Good," Anne said, smiling. "That's excellent."

"I know she enjoys having you around. The sense of family, you know? She always loved having you all at the big house."

"I'm not sure I'll go back there," Anne said. "I like my apartment in town."

"Really?"

"Yes. I need a job, and I think it's more likely I'll find something in town than cross-island."

Gabrielle tasted the sauce again. As if Anne needed the money! Matt had always been so generous, he wasn't about to get tight-fisted now. But she held her tongue. Instead, she decided to mention something she'd been mulling over for a long while.

"The taxes on the big house are outrageous. I realize that you and Matt have been carrying the load for a few years. Steve and I appreciate that."

"We wanted to."

"It's getting so islanders can't even own property anymore. The houses turn over so often now . . . every time the prices go up. And the taxes."

"Are you thinking we should sell?"

Gabrielle put her hand to her heart. God, even the idea made her sick. No, she wouldn't join the parade of old friends, selling their family places to rich out-of-staters, sailing into the sunset with their pockets full of gold.

"No way," Gabrielle said. "I was thinking more in terms of starting a bed-and-breakfast."

"Wow," Anne said, frowning. She was probably picturing the same thing that had kept Gabrielle awake nights when the idea had first occurred to her: strangers in their house. Strangers rocking on the front porch, strangers dozing in the hammock, strangers expecting breakfast in the morning.

"Paying strangers," Gabrielle said.

"Who'd run it?"

"Me? You? I don't know," Gabrielle said, although she had entertained a fantasy or two of herself greeting guests, serving breakfasts that would land her in the pages of guidebooks and *Gourmet* magazine.

"Well, it's an interesting idea."

"It's a way to keep the house in the family. Taxes are due to go up again in May," Gabrielle said, watching for Anne's reaction. But Anne didn't say anything. She was standing there, peeling too many potatoes, with an oddly dreamy look in her eyes.

"Penny for your thoughts," Gabrielle said, puzzled by the shifts in Anne's mood. From happy to sad to distant to moony. She reminded Gabrielle of a thirty-two-year-old version of Maggie.

"Oh, I was just thinking about a friend," Anne said.

Gabrielle waited for her to continue, but Anne didn't seem so inclined. She just reached for another potato. She would have peeled it too, if Gabrielle hadn't gently leaned over to hand her a carrot instead.

Chapter 7

When she had finished her commission for the Chopin CD, Anne began a series of collages she thought of as *Heaven*. She tried to keep her mind free, unencumbered by too much religion or sentimentality. In spite of this, her first effort showed cherubs playing on pillows of cloud. One cherub had Karen's dark features, her solemn gaze.

Thinking of Karen that way, in "heaven" with other angel children, depressed Anne so deeply that for two days she put the project away. But at the end of the second day, she added a gray dove, the pigeon Karen had been trying to catch when she fell. She changed Karen's somber red mouth to a smile. Anne felt a little crazy, but less depressed.

Her next collage in the series was a tunnel of deepening shades of red, meant to evoke a beating heart or maybe, she realized as she progressed, a baby in the womb. It was at once the most human and the most abstract collage she had ever done, but bending over it, she felt content. She found stamps containing the blue reds of blood, without a trace of orange, and she slivered over a hundred shards in the precise size and shape of a baby's fingernail paring.

Making these collages made her think of life and death and Karen, and they brought her peace.

Whenever she stopped, to eat or take a walk or sleep, she burned to get back to work. Away from her worktable she would sometimes think of Thomas Devlin. He stuck in her mind like a splinter, something that didn't belong there. For so long Anne had thought of herself, Matt, and Karen as a family. That dream had fallen apart, just as Thomas Devlin's had.

She couldn't stand the thought of letting someone new be important to her. Wouldn't it be disloyal? To Karen? The best part of Anne's life had been marriage and her child. That was over. Anne couldn't imagine anything good like that again. Evoking Karen, their family, was the closest Anne would come to happiness. She could do it through collage.

Thomas Devlin had swooped out of the smoke, a giant guardian angel who'd saved her life, and now he was gone.

Done with.

These collages, the *Heaven* series, would never be sold. Anne would work on them from now until August, one a month, getting herself past the anniversary of Karen's death. No one needed to know. Other people would consider it morbid; Gabrielle would be appalled. But working on the series would help Anne get through: she knew it was right.

She would need money.

Rent, gas, telephone, dinner, postage stamps.

Since Thomas Devlin's departure from the island she had stopped thinking of "meeting people," "friendly offices." She wanted only to sequester herself with memories and work, but she required an income.

That is why, late Thursday afternoon, she went to the ferry office, to apply for a job.

·   ·   ·

S TANLEY Gray, manager of the island terminal and childhood friend of Anne and Gabrielle, had gone to Salsbury, Maryland, on steamship business; Anne was about to leave, but Peggy Lawson stopped her.

"First, let me tell you how sorry I am," Peggy said. "About your daughter. I sent a mass card."

"I know. Thank you," Anne said. So many friends had written and sent flowers. Somewhere she had a list; she had intended to write back and acknowledge everyone, but somehow she kept putting off the task.

"It must be . . . awful for you," Peggy said, her eyes glittering. Anne didn't necessarily assume that her intentions were malicious. The best-meaning people couldn't help being avid for the details. But Peggy had been a mean gossip as a young girl, and Anne doubted that had changed. She just nodded.

"So," Peggy said, her lips tightening. Anne could see that she felt rebuked. "You're looking for work?"

"Yes. I saw the ad."

"Ah." Peggy was a secretary in the office. Suddenly Anne wondered whether this was such a great idea.

"Maybe I should come back when Stan—"

"I'm in charge of hiring," Peggy said. "We've commissioned a new ferry, and Stan spends most of his time at the shipyard."

"Well, I've worked in offices," Anne began. She paused, waiting for Peggy to start the interview. Her overwhelming impression was that of a smirk on Peggy's face. Outside, the air horn blasted, announcing the arrival of the four-thirty ferry.

"Anne," Peggy said with exaggerated patience. "I simply can't see it. This is a meat-and-potatoes job. The pressure in high season . . . well, you know. You've stood in line waiting for tickets, watching us go crazy behind the desk."

"I can handle it," Anne said, watching Peggy light an exceedingly long cigarette.

Peggy rolled her eyes, enjoying this moment.

"I know Word Perfect, Lotus 1-2-3—"

"We use Lotus for bookkeeping."

"I want the job," Anne said.

"It's high-pressure—"

"I know. Like you said, I've been on the other side of the desk. So have you."

"Hey, I *live* on this island," Peggy said. "Middle of July, I'm in the standby line at midnight for a six A.M. boat. You think I like getting out of bed before the sun comes up? Try explaining that's what it takes to some of the idiots who rent for two weeks and think they own this place."

"I know," Anne said, remembering with no slight embarrassment how Matt had once, three summers ago, successfully bribed Peggy to let him on a sold-out boat so he and Anne could go home four hours early on Labor Day.

"People won't take to this," Peggy said.

"To what?"

"To the idea of you working the reservations desk."

"Why not?"

Peggy took a long drag on her cigarette and blew a meaningful stream of smoke into the air. "Don't get me wrong," she said. "I'm not saying I agree."

"But what?" Anne felt sick to her stomach. Maybe she wanted to hear the rumors, what people were saying about her. She had sensed bad feelings everywhere, from the volunteer firefighters to the waitress at Ruby's.

"Nothing," Peggy said. "You'd better wait for Stan."

"Peggy," Anne said, her voice unsteady. "You have to tell me."

"Anne, don't do this," Peggy said, avoiding Anne's gaze. "I'm awfully busy right now. If you need a reason, it's just that people see you as the Fifth Avenue type. Above it all."

But Anne knew that Peggy was lying about the reason. She sensed a holier-than-thou attitude in Peggy, the superiority of one mother judging another mother. Karen had died because Anne was bad, or careless, or all of the above. Such a thing could never happen in Peggy's family. Imagining Peggy following the story on the news, night after night, Anne felt something harden in her chest.

"I'm not above anyone," she said.

"Well . . ."

"Okay," Anne said, barely able to catch her breath. "I'd better wait to talk to Stan."

"Mmmm," Peggy said, feigning indifference. She turned her attention to some paperwork, busily smoking in the process.

Anne left the office.

The ferry had docked. The sun had just gone down behind the buildings at the head of Transit Street. The harbor was bathed in golden-amber light, but the parking lot was a dark pocket. The off-loading cars had their lights on.

Anne stuck her hands in the pockets of her parka and headed up the hill. Her body quivered with intense anger and frustration. She felt rattled, trying to figure out the veiled sanctimony or derision or whatever it was in Peggy's voice. Peggy mentioning the mass card she had sent for Karen, and it made Anne want to scream. Peggy hadn't even known Karen!

Anne's good friends, the ones who cared for Anne, Matt, and Karen, had sent cards or brought casseroles, acts of kindness and sorrow that Anne couldn't even remember and knew it didn't matter. But Peggy, sending a sympathy card to a woman she obviously held in contempt, was too hypocritical for Anne to stand. She started to cross the street.

A horn sounded, and Anne jumped.

God, she felt like ripping the throat out of someone. She headed for the driver's window with sharp words racing through her head. She had the fleeting impression of a red truck or Jeep, a cab up off the ground. Her palm smacked the driver's window.

"Anne," came the voice.

It was Thomas. He had rolled down the window. Now he was reaching for her hand.

Anne stood there, in the middle of Transit Street, holding Thomas Devlin's hand through the window of his truck. His eyes had the same understanding as before. Staring into them, she felt her fury melt.

"Can I get in?" she asked, the words barely audible.

He nodded. People behind him beeped their horns, but he didn't seem to care. He got out of the truck. He put his arm around Anne's waist and helped her into the cab. She slid across the bench seat, her thigh grazing the gear shift, in a dream state.

He drove straight up Transit Street, past her building. She hardly noticed. He didn't know where she lived; the question of where they were going shimmered through her mind and disappeared. She just leaned back and felt warm air gusting out of the truck's heater.

The evening star hung just above the horizon in an amber sky. It would last as long as the sun took to set, and then it would dip behind the earth's curve. When they were children, Gabrielle had told Anne that the Indians who had once inhabited the island believed that the spirits of their beloved ones became stars, traveling through the sky until eternity, watching over their families on earth.

Staring at the evening star, Anne thought of Karen. She wanted to throw her arms around the star, pull it down to earth. The desire was electric, and it sizzled through every nerve in her body. She wanted Karen right now. She wanted to hold her daughter on her lap, surrounded by the truck's heat. A primal howl ripped out of her throat.

Blinded by hot tears, Anne hardly saw the truck pull to the side of the road. She felt Thomas slide across the seat, wrap her in his arms. The sound of her own sobs rang in her ears, muffled by the wool fabric of his jacket. She felt him petting her hair, the back of her neck. He didn't say anything; he just let her wail.

The agony of not having Karen. Of Karen not existing. There was a hole in the world, everything draining out. Karen's body in the cold ground. Under the snow, marked by the stone that would live forever. Images too horrible to believe flashed through Anne's mind: Karen at the window, Karen feeding the pigeons. There. Gone. Karen's tiny coffin. Karen's bones. Her *Heaven* collage couldn't change any of it.

"Oh, my God," Anne cried. She was suffocating. She would cut them into pieces, those stupid collages she had thought could "help her through." Gasping, she felt Thomas Devlin lean across her body and roll down the window. Instantly, cold air flowed into the truck.

"Breathe," he said.

Minutes passed; she opened her eyes. She wiped away the tears and looked west. No evening star; the sky just above the horizon was barren. Anne shuddered. Her eyes felt unbearably heavy. At that moment she felt she could go to sleep and sleep forever. The star had set.

Thomas Devlin pulled her across the bench seat. Numb, she let him drive with his arm around her shoulders. He drove like a one-armed man. With his right hand holding Anne, he drove with his left, now and then taking it off the wheel to make lightning-fast shifts. Small sobs hiccuped from her chest.

They headed cross-island, toward the big house. Anne wondered why he was taking her there, then realized that he probably thought she had returned after the fire.

"My family's house is empty," she said. "That number you called was at an apartment in town."

"I live out here," he said, and she felt his breath, warm in her hair. "You need to have dinner. I want to make it for you."

Anne didn't reply. She stared at the spot in the west where the evening star had been. It would be back tomorrow night, if the sky was clear. If only I could see Karen once a day, she thought, closing her eyes. I would trade anything to see Karen once a day.

She must have fallen asleep. It couldn't have been more than fifteen minutes, but she had a thousand dreams of Karen. Dreams as clear and beautiful as blue sea glass, filled with colors and laughter and the smells of a sleeping baby. Everywhere: deep blue sky. Images of Anne and Karen riding the funicular to a snow-covered alpine village; of rich island potato fields, the early-morning smell of dark earth encompassing Anne and Karen as they raised their faces to the sun; of castle building on their favorite island beach, with heartbreakingly beautiful blue water everywhere, Anne somehow knowing it was the last castle she and Karen would ever build together.

When Thomas's truck bumped down his dirt drive, Anne wakened with her cheeks wet.

"Here we are," he said, holding open the truck door. They walked to the door side by side, and Anne was aware of feeling slightly uncomfortable. She wondered whether she had made a mistake in letting him bring her here. He had seen raw emotion the likes of which she'd never showed anyone—not Matt, not Gabrielle—and she felt embarrassed.

"Thomas, I think I'd better go home," she said, stopping halfway down the walk.

"I think maybe you need company," he said gently.

"No, I'm okay. I just . . . sometimes I think of her, and it . . . it's too much. That's all."

"I used to say that," he said. "I wanted to be alone all the time because if I was with someone they might want to talk about the fire, they meant well and everything, but they didn't know."

"Thomas—" she wanted to put her hands over her ears.

"It will get better," he said, bending so his mouth was very close to her ear. "I promise you."

"You can't know," Anne said. Standing in the frozen mud, she held tight to her vision of Karen. She wanted to go home and work on her collage. She would do a sandcastle. The best sandcastle in the world.

"I want to help you," he said.

Anne shook her head. Her eyes were dry. Rubbing them with her fists, she said, "I have work to do."

"Stay," he said. "We don't have to talk about anything you don't want to."

"I have work . . ."

He stood close by, and she could feel him looking at her. This part of the island was very dark. There were no street lamps, and he hadn't left any lights on in his house. She couldn't see his face.

"You can't work on an empty stomach, can you?" he asked after a moment. "I have some groceries in the car. I thought I'd make you some soup."

"Oh," she said, thinking that soup sounded good. A canopy of stars, the winter constellations, filled the sky and silhouetted his massive shoulders.

"Mushroom-barley soup," he said. "With the best French bread you've ever had. I bought it on my way home from a bakery in Massachusetts."

"Okay," Anne said. In that instant she felt the tension in her back knot up, then begin very slowly to spin itself out. But she was still thinking of her stamps, of what she could use to make a beautiful sandcastle, one Karen would be proud of.

"Good," he said, and she heard the smile in his voice. He unlocked the front door.

Inside, he turned up the thermostat first and switched on a light second.

"Be right back," he said, running out to the truck.

Anne stood in the middle of the living room, looking around. There was a braided rug, made from colorful scraps of tartans, checked wools, and what appeared to be old tights. Ansel Adams posters hung on the walls, photographs of soaring mountains and craggy canyons. The sofa and chairs looked comfortable, well sat in. But the room's most striking feature was its abundance of clocks.

Anne counted twelve clocks. With so many timepieces, some obviously antiques, you'd expect some to be off by at least a few minutes. Amazingly, these clocks all showed the same time.

Thomas Devlin stomped his feet on the mat and entered the room. He swung a blue canvas duffel bag off his shoulder, laying it by the stairs. His arms were full of grocery bags. Anne hadn't seen him in the light yet; looking at his face, she steeled herself against the shock she always felt upon seeing his burns. But the warmth in his eyes made her smile without even realizing it.

"Are you just getting home?" Anne asked. "From your visit with your son?"

"Yes," he said, nodding at the paper bags. "I did my food shopping on the mainland. It costs about half what it does out here. Plus, wait till you taste the bread. Can I get you a beer? Or a glass of wine?"

"Whatever you're having."

"Say it's wine—do you like red or white?"

"Both."

"Say it's red, and you were forced to choose between a nice Burgundy and a nice Bordeaux—what would it be?"

The question reminded her of something Matt would ask; coming from Thomas Devlin, it seemed incongruous and made her smile. "Depends," she said.

"Leave it to me," he said, nodding reassuringly.

She watched him disappear, in the direction of what she assumed to be the kitchen. Feeling slightly awkward, she leaned down, to see what books he had on his bookshelf. A lot of Hemingway, Rex Stout, Simenon, Rendell, and Follett. A stack of *Sports Illustrated* and a few copies of *Road and Track*. *The Ultimate Motorcycle Book*. *The Joy of Cooking*. Yearbooks from the Boston Latin School, Deerfield Academy, Boston College, and the Massachusetts General Hospital School of Nursing. Six leather-bound photo albums.

A moment later she heard Thomas standing behind her.

"I was just thinking," he said. "It's nice and warm in the kitchen."

"I wasn't sure whether you mind having an audience when you cook," she said.

"I thrive on it," he said, giving her that radiant half grin.

"Okay, then," she said, following him down a dim, narrow hallway.

The kitchen was tiny, but he moved around with ease. He had placed wine glasses on the blue tile counter, and Anne glimpsed the Burgundy he had chosen: a 1982 Corton. Opening the bottle, his movements were deft and graceful. She saw him glance at the cork upon removing it, nothing more. He was following a ritual that was neither awkward nor pretentious.

"Corton," Anne said admiringly.

"It's my worst vice. I love good wine."

"That doesn't sound like a vice," Anne said, watching him fill their glasses to the bottom of the curve.

"To you," he said, raising his glass. He looked into Anne's eyes, and his gaze held steady. Anne scowled, ready to protest. But what the hell? She clinked her glass to his, and tasted the best wine she'd had in months.

"Growing up," he said, "I thought there were two kinds of wine. Cooking sherry and altar wine. Then, about twenty years ago, I took a trip to France. I felt like I'd been hibernating or something. The food, the wine. The cathedrals."

"I love France," Anne said. Sipping the Corton, she watched Thomas Devlin slice mushrooms, and she remembered her last trip to France. Two Junes ago. Karen had been nearly three. They had taken an ancient *mas* in Provence, with lavender growing wild in the field and bougainvillea cascading from the stone terrace.

"It's a place to be in love."

"Yes," Anne said, thinking that the last time she had been there, she had been—wildly so. Don't think about it, she told herself, forcing her thoughts back to the present. She concentrated on her wine.

The silence between them felt comfortable as Anne leaned against the counter watching Thomas cook. He opened a can of beef broth and poured it into a heavy copper pot. He chopped a shallot, some carrots, one rib of celery, and added them to the broth. Reaching for a head of garlic, he glanced at Anne.

"I love garlic," she said.

"Good," he said. "If you didn't, I'd be sunk."

With the flat of his knife, he smashed a garlic clove. He threw it into the pot along with a pinch of salt, a few crackles of pepper, a big handful of barley, some chopped parsley, a sprig of fresh thyme, and the mushrooms. He added a big splash of Noailly Prat vermouth.

Now he reached for a shallow aluminum pan. He lined it with foil and placed the rest of the garlic inside. Some salt, pepper. He drizzled olive oil over the whole head of garlic, sealed it in tinfoil, and stuck it in the oven.

He worked with true grace. His mutilated hands were so huge and ugly, you would expect them to be merely powerful. But to the contrary, they moved with soft precision. Staring at Thomas's hands, Anne remembered holding them a week ago. Confused, she looked away.

"What's wrong?" he asked.

"About an hour ago I was thinking of you."

"That's nice," he said, and half his mouth smiled.

"It really affected me, the thing you told me at Ruby's that last time."

"About Sarah?" he asked. He stopped working, turned his back to the counter, and folded his arms.

"Your wife, yes. I've thought about what it must have been like for you, and in a way that comforted me. I'm sorry to say that—"

Anne's face twisted with confusion. She didn't know how to put these awkward feelings into words, but she knew she had to try.

"Don't be sorry! I can understand why—" Thomas moved toward her, but stopped when she stepped back.

Sweat stood out on Anne's forehead.

"It affected me, but I'm not sure I can handle it," Anne said. "It's too much. It's not like we can be casual friends, you know? We know everything about each other." Then, almost as an after-thought: "Everything that matters."

"And what is that?"

"I think of it as a monster," she said, as if she hadn't heard. "Something terrible that came along, the worst thing in the world . . ."

"And ate us alive," he said.

She shook her head, violently banishing the image.

"All of us. You and me and Karen and Sarah."

"Stop it!" she cried. "I have to go."

Thomas watched her fumble for her coat; he made no move to stop her. Standing by the kitchen door, she couldn't look at him.

"Not being friends won't make it go away," he said quietly.

"I just . . . it's better to be alone," she said.

"I used to think that."

Anne started to button her coat. Thomas walked across the room and put his hands on her shoulders.

"Monster. There was no monster," Anne said, picturing the sunny summer day, the open window, the bird. "It was just an accident."

"That's the monster," Thomas said. "That such a thing could happen."

He reached for her hand and they walked into the living room. Who was leading whom, she wasn't exactly sure, but it didn't matter anyway. Thomas sat at one end of the sofa and pulled her gently down to sit beside him.

"It's too much to take, isn't it?" Anne said.

"It gets easier."

"You know, that scares me. Isn't that strange? The way I feel, that's all I have left of her."

"You have her drawing."

"Yes," Anne said, a yawn escaping. Suddenly she felt calm and exhausted.

"Maybe you'd like to take off your coat and stay awhile," Thomas said, and when Anne glanced up at him she saw warm light and humor in his eyes.

"I'm tired," she said.

He reached across her for a yellow chenille throw pillow and placed it on his lap. He patted it.

"Put my head on your lap and take a nap?" Anne asked skeptically, but she found herself doing it. It didn't feel strange at all.

When she awakened, one side of her face was dotted with little imprints from the pillow tufts. She felt Thomas playing with her hair.

"Some guest," she said, still groggy.

"You're a good napper." He laughed.

"I'm afraid to ask. How long?"

"An hour and ten minutes."

"Not that you're counting," Anne said, pushing herself up on one arm. "God, I can't believe I did that. Do you think the soup cooked away?"

"It's probably just about done."

Anne's scalp tingled and her stomach growled. She closed her eyes, trying to remember her dreams. None came back. Perhaps she had slept too well for dreams to have penetrated the veil between unconscious and awake. The ticking of twelve clocks dominated the darkness. After a moment she brushed the hair out of her eyes.

"How do you feel?" he asked.

"Only starving," she said, pushing herself off the sofa.

They walked into the kitchen, which seemed very bright after the living room. Anne blinked, getting used to it, while Thomas checked the soup.

"Thank you," she said.

"Anytime you need a pillow," he said, patting his thigh. "My leg's not too asleep."

"That's not what I meant."

"Don't thank me, Anne. Just let me."

"Let you?"

"Help."

Thomas stirred the soup, wrapped a loaf of Italian bread in foil, and put it in the oven. Standing behind him, Anne stared at his back. The worn chambray shirt could conceal his skin, but not the muscles. He carried tension in his shoulders and spine, yet Anne sensed sweet relaxation coming from deep within him. Before she knew what was happening, she kissed his back.

It was a kiss so light, her lips barely grazed his shirt. She doubted that he felt it. The shirt was huge; it billowed out from where he had tucked it into the waistband of his jeans. Perhaps she noticed his spine stiffen just perceptibly; other than that, he gave no sign. He glanced over his shoulder so she could see only the good side of his face, smiling.

"Can you get the bowls?" he asked. "In that cupboard, by the sink?"

"Oh, is it ready?" she asked, feeling her cheeks redden.

"Timed perfectly," he said.

"Two bowls," she said. "No problem."

Chapter 8

The month of March, the season of mud, had come to the island. Plodding from her mud-encrusted E250 van to the front door, Gabrielle felt the earth trying to suck the rubber boots right off her feet. She curled her toes, holding the boots on, and barely made it inside intact.

The telephone was ringing. Her arms were full of grocery bags, her boots were covered in fresh slop, and the phone was all the way across the kitchen. She tried to kick off her boots—and her boots, which moments earlier had seemed eager to be slurped off her feet, suddenly clung to them tenaciously.

"Damn," she said, grabbing for the sponge mop as she hurried for the phone, tracking mud as she went.

"Hello?" she said.

"Hi, Gabrielle," came Matt's voice.

"Well, hello!" She hadn't heard from him in two or three weeks, and it made her happy to hear his voice.

Matt asked about Steve and Maggie, how Gabrielle's business was going, how the big house was coming along: all the niceties that disguised the real purpose of his call: to hear about Anne. Gabrielle didn't mind. It felt so pleasant to be talking to a man who really seemed to care, whether he actually did or not. She appreciated him for going through the motions.

For weeks now she'd been trying to get Steve to have a father-daughter talk with Maggie. She had a vague, unfocused fear that something was wrong with her, that she was depressed or heart-broken or something. Her friends hardly ever called anymore, and Maggie never went out.

"I miss you guys," Matt said.

"We miss you, too."

"I really messed up, didn't I?"

"Well . . ." Gabrielle didn't want to pass judgment. No one really knows what goes on in another couple's marriage. Gabrielle's loyalties, naturally, were with Anne. But she loved Matt, too. She had considered him to be a younger brother, and by leaving Anne, he had, in a way, left all of them.

"Does she talk about me?" he asked.

"Matt, you know I can't tell you. Just as I don't tell her the things you say to me." It was a white lie. Of course Gabrielle had always told Anne every single thing, confidential or not, that Matt ever said. She had no scruples or regrets about doing so, either. It was all part of the sisterly double standard.

"I'm trying to make some decisions," Matt said. "I'm considering a move to Paris."

"Oh my God," Gabrielle said, totally shocked.

"When Anne first left the city, I thought it was a big mistake," he said. "But now I'm not so sure. There's a lot of bad stuff for me here. Memories."

"Matt, you're nowhere near Gramercy Park now, are you? You're living closer to your office, right?"

"Well, East Eighty-third. But I have a client to lunch, and I remember going to the restaurant with Anne."

"Go to a different restaurant."

Matt continued, as if Gabrielle hadn't spoken. "I'll walk in Central Park at lunchtime, and I'm pulled to the zoo. Karen loved the zoo. She loved the polar bears, the seals. I'll watch the polar bears, and I'll feel her hand in mine. She's standing there, holding my hand."

Gabrielle had heard about cases of people who had lost limbs in terrible accidents. For months, sometimes years later, the people would swear they could feel the missing arm or leg. They'd feel an itch, or a pain, or just the normal heaviness of their old hand or foot. Doctors called the imaginary body part a "phantom" arm or foot or whatever. The idea of Matt feeling a phantom Karen squeezed Gabrielle's heart so hard, she wanted to jump into the phone and give him a hug.

"You're suffering in New York, Anne's suffering out here," Gabrielle said. "Why don't you get together and talk about it? Face the worst together?"

"I don't know," he said. "She won't let me in, I guess, and I feel too guilty to push. She's like a robot when I call."

THAT night Steve brought home pizzas and movies for dinner. Maggie was being her newly quiet self, and she asked permission to eat in her room. She said she had a math test the next day and needed to study. Steve had no objection. He praised her for her diligence, said she was making him proud. He was in a good mood: it was the first winter he'd had work in years, he was making fine progress on the house, and he liked coming home with treats.

But Gabrielle felt a dark cloud hanging over her head. Ever since Matt's call, she'd felt undone. She believed that a family's love was the most precious thing in life. One false move, too much taking each other for granted: you could lose it all in an instant.

"No," Gabrielle said to Maggie. "Let's have dinner together. I want to hear about your day."

"There's plenty to tell," Maggie said sullenly. "There's plenty to tell. Let's tell nasty mud stories. John Hildebrand got his Fiesta stuck in his driveway, up to the doors, and Bob Sullivan had to pull him out with his tractor."

"Way to go, John," Steve said, chuckling. He had his mouth full of pizza, and he took a big swallow of beer. Maggie shot him a look full of disgust. Sometimes it seemed to Gabrielle that Maggie hated him. She wondered whether Steve noticed his daughter's contempt, whether it made him feel bad.

"I don't have any mud stories," Maggie said.

"Wait. I have another," Gabrielle said, watching her daughter.

Maggie leaned on the butcher-block counter, tracing patterns in the wood. Her cheeks were pale, her hair not as lustrous as usual. Could it be drugs? An eating disorder? Gabrielle wondered, willing Maggie to look up so she could see her eyes.

"This one's really nasty," Gabrielle said. "Walking across our very own yard, I nearly lost my boots. I'm not kidding you. You know that gross slurping sound March mud makes?"

"Yeah," Maggie said, the corner of her mouth twitching in a smile. She glanced up, and her mother saw that her eyes were clear, her pupils normal.

Gabrielle felt her heart lighten.

"Like you're drinking a milkshake with a straw, and the glass is empty, but you keep going anyway? Well, our mud was trying to bring the boots right off my feet."

"That is nasty," Maggie agreed. "But please? My math test?"

"Okay," Gabrielle said, giving in. "But this is positively the absolute last time. From now on we eat at the table. As a family. And we come prepared with stories about our days."

Gabrielle and Steve sat at the table, watching the six o'clock news on TV. When had she stopped making everyone eat together? Gabrielle couldn't remember. Her catering business relied on the desire of people to entertain, to come together at a table laden with delicious food.

Slowly, over the last year, she had gotten slack at home. Steve wanted to eat in front of the TV, Maggie wanted to bolt her food and talk to her friends on the phone, and Gabrielle was just as happy sitting alone, reading recipes as she ate her dinner.

Talking to Matt today had really opened her eyes. She slid her arm across the table, took Steve's hand. He looked up with surprise.

"What?" he asked.

"We take things for granted," she said. "Each other. Our kid."

"We do not," he said. He kissed the back of her hand and released it, reaching for another slice of pizza. He resumed watching the news.

"Yes, we do," Gabrielle said. But Steve gave no indication that he had heard her. He didn't even glance her way. Leaning back in his chair, the front legs off the ground, he took another beer out of the refrigerator. His big belly hung over the waistband of his pants, and he burped.

Gabrielle waited for him to say "excuse me," but he didn't. Noisily, she stacked their plates. She felt nothing but anger at the world, and to Gabrielle the world and her home were the same thing. She had a husband who couldn't be bothered to use his manners, who didn't care enough to stay in shape for her. She had a daughter who'd rather stay in her room than be forced to spend fifteen minutes with her parents. Cleaning off the table, Gabrielle purposely blocked his view of the TV.

"Didn't anyone ever tell you you make a better door than a window?" he asked, giving her a good-natured push.

"This family had better shape up," Gabrielle said.

"Honey, what is wrong with you today?"

"Nothing. Unless you count being totally taken for granted by the people you slave for."

"I don't take you for granted. As a matter of fact"—Steve glanced around, to make sure Maggie wasn't in the room—"I've got a surprise for later. For you and me."

"What?"

"A horny movie."

Gabrielle nodded. She put the dishes in the sink. There had been a time when she'd tried to understand and even enjoy Steve's taste in X-rated movies. She'd told herself the material was erotic. She'd watch the scenes and try to feel excited. But the women's breasts were obviously as fake as their orgasms. The nipples uniformly erect, the breasts had the immutability of holy mounds. The men would come all over the plastic breasts and faces of every woman in the picture, like poor little puppies marking their territory.

Gabrielle wanted to like the movies, but they were too blatant or something. They didn't hold enough back; they never had enough of a story to work her up. She'd take a hit of Anaïs Nin or Nancy Friday over porn movies any day. Plus, she didn't love being naked beside such exemplars of male fantasy beauty.

Standing at the sink, she felt Steve come up behind her.

"You don't seem too thrilled," he said.

"I'm just having a bad day," Gabrielle said. "It's mud season."

"Maybe the movie will cheer you up. Or what comes after the movie." He slipped his arms around her from behind.

Gabrielle smiled ruefully. She couldn't help herself; she loved the man. Maybe he was fat, and maybe he was crude. Maybe he didn't pay quite enough attention to Maggie. Maybe Matt wouldn't rent movies with titles like *Thunder Honies* or *Wicked Delight;* maybe Anne had never had to share her bed with a beer belly the size of a basketball. Maybe what Matt and Anne had had was better, or at least more refined, but where was it now?

"What's the title?" Gabrielle asked.

"The movie? *Horny Figure Skaters,*" Steve whispered in her ear.

She laughed. What the hell? she thought. If it gives him pleasure, why not? She always ended up satisfied in the long run. The movies were definitely not her favorite part of their love life, but she had a firm belief that you don't mess with someone else's sex.

You don't judge, you try to understand. You don't have to feel the same way, but you have to respect their desires. You don't take people for granted.

"Come on," she said, drying her hands.

"You're great," Steve said.

"Just keep thinking that," Gabrielle said.

Dɪᴅ her parents think she couldn't hear their stupid movie? So what if they had the volume turned down? Maggie sat at her desk, trying to study. She tried to ignore the little squeaks and grunts, the shapeless music, coming from the next room. It embarrassed her, that her parents would watch such a thing. Joanie Mays worked at Island Video. She had a big mouth, and she loved announcing to the world who was renting from the plain-brown-wrapper bin.

Once Maggie and Kurt (back when there was a Maggie and Kurt) had skipped school and watched the video her parents had hidden under their bed. Kurt had loved it. After they watched it once, he wanted to watch it again.

To tell the truth, after the first two minutes or so, Maggie had closed her eyes. The girls looked so wasted. They seemed pathetic, pretending to enjoy what was obviously torture. The worst part, the sick part, was that they had sort of reminded Maggie of herself. How many times had she gone along with Kurt, doing whatever he wanted, just to keep him as her boyfriend?

Well, no more Miss Island Slut. Maggie hardly even missed him. She had seen Kurt's true colors in the back of Fritz's truck. If he really loved her, he would never have asked her to sleep with Fritz for money. It was the worst thing she could ever imagine happening. It was degrading and wrong, and it proved that Kurt didn't love her.

She couldn't get the movie music out of her head. With its throbbing backbeat, it reminded Maggie of the noise kids make when they're playing choo-choo. She wished her mother could read her thoughts and make her father turn off the sound. She didn't like thinking of her mother watching the movie. Her father, she might expect it of. But not her mother.

Maggie wished her father would demand more of her. He didn't care whether Maggie got A's or F's. He'd never once objected to her seeing Kurt, even though Kurt was every father's nightmare. He told Maggie he loved her "unconditionally," but Maggie wished for conditions. Rules and standards weren't so bad. They forced you to be your best.

She tried to imagine Karen all grown up, dating a boy like Kurt. It wouldn't happen in a million years! Uncle Matt would kill the scuz first. The first time he smelled beer on Karen's breath: zap. Grounded for life.

It's weird, thinking back, how Maggie now realized that she used to wish her father would tell her she couldn't see Kurt. She'd wish her father thought better of her. That he'd push her to make the honor roll. That he'd expect her to go to college. That he'd ground her for seeing Kurt instead of nice island boys like Josh Hunter or Ned Devlin.

Maggie hadn't touched her pizza. She didn't feel like eating, and knowing her parents were watching zombie sex girls made her even less hungry. Concentrating on a math problem, she tried to block it out.

I'm not like them

I'm not like them

I'm not like them

Maggie stared at the telephone on her desk. Sometimes she felt so lonely she thought she'd go nuts. The island was too small; it wasn't as if she would suddenly meet someone new, someone who didn't know every detail of her past, someone she would actually want as a friend.

The telephone was tempting her. Call Kurt, call Vanessa. Get back in touch. They're your friends, aren't they? Haven't they called about a hundred times to apologize? Didn't Kurt leave a red rose in your locker just yesterday? What makes you think you're better than them? The only person she actually felt like calling was Anne, and that was really ridiculous. Her aunt.

Still, thinking of Anne made it possible for Maggie to resist calling Kurt or Vanessa. Anne was awesome. She had lived in New York and traveled everywhere. She had style and mystery; you could imagine her as a spy. She was fighting her way through hell, and Maggie was with her every step of the way.

Anne had raven-wing hair and sex-goddess eyes. You'd never catch Anne watching dirty movies with a lazy blob. Uncle Matt had hurt her, and Anne hadn't stuck around to give him the chance to do it again. She had too much self-respect for that. Maggie could imagine Anne wearing an evening gown on the Riviera, posing in *Vogue,* dancing with a prince. Anne made anything possible.

What she was doing on the island was a puzzle to Maggie. Why would someone like Anne come back to this big stupid mudpie in the middle of the sea? Anne, who could live anywhere in the world, and we're talking *anywhere*—Rome, Paris, London, Rio de Janeiro—had come to the island. She was living in a tiny, bare apartment. She could make her collages anyplace. So why was she here?

In her deepest heart, her most treasured fantasy, Maggie believed that Anne had come back to the island because of her. Because of Maggie. Anne had lost Karen, and she had come to claim Karen's spiritual sister.

Okay, not claim. Anne would never take Maggie away from her family.

But something close to "claim." Anne and Maggie had a special bond, a love for each other that reminded Maggie of the ideal mother and daughter.

Sitting at her desk, Maggie turned her gaze from the telephone to her math homework. She wanted to make Anne proud. She had promised herself that Anne would never regret rescuing her and not telling her parents. She would make the honor roll. She wouldn't give in to loneliness and call Kurt.

She would not call Kurt. Anne wouldn't want her to. Maggie would gather the energy that loneliness made her feel and channel it into studying. Night after night she would do her homework, and at the end of the semester she would have a great report card to show for it.

Brown. Vassar. Harvard. Wheaton.

She could do it. Maggie could work hard this year and be accepted at a great college. She'd make Anne and her mother proud, and she'd show her father that she was worth more than he thought.

Suddenly she jumped. She had forgotten about the movie; in fact, she couldn't hear the soundtrack anymore. No celluloid bimbos panting and begging for what they did not want. Instead, what Maggie heard was quite human. The sounds of her parents' voices. She heard her mother moan, and she heard her father say her mother's name.

"Gabrielle . . ."

Maggie heard lust in the tone. Passion and desire. And if she didn't know better, she would swear that she heard the respect you get from love as well.

Chapter 9

One late Saturday afternoon, just before sunset, Thomas Devlin stood at Anne Davis's door. He had his caseful of clock tools; she had a broken ship's clock that had once belonged to her grandfather. He was eager to fix the clock, but even more, he couldn't wait to see Anne.

He had brought her a bouquet of spring flowers: daffodils, iris, and pussy willows. Waiting for her to answer the door, he shuffled his feet nervously. He shifted the case and flowers from one hand to the other and told himself to breathe steadily. His collar felt too tight around his neck.

Just then, as he heard her coming to the door, the fire alarm sounded outside. The air horn was located at the intersection of Transit and Benefit streets; its signal rang through perfectly. Thomas heard the message as the signal repeated. The emergency was here in town, down by the old docks.

All his nervousness disappeared, replaced by an adrenaline rush. Anne opened the door, and he handed her his tool case and the flowers.

"That's the fire signal sounding," he explained. "I'll be back when I can."

She nodded, obviously taken by surprise. It took only a split second for Thomas to register a catalog of information about Anne: her fragrance, the straight dark hair brushing her shoulder, an ivory silk shirt framing pearl-white skin. He wanted to kiss her.

"Be safe," she said.

"I will," he said, racing off.

"Come back," she called. "When it's over."

He waved, to let her know he'd heard.

Transit Street was full of people standing in animated groups, speculating about whatever might be happening down at the docks. The police cruiser sped by, splashing eerie blue light on the stone, shingles, and plate glass of nearby buildings. The people turned to watch it pass; bunches of them had begun to head for the docks.

Thomas Devlin ran down the hill. Sirens sounded in the distance, and a police car sped across India Street. Thomas didn't yet know what was wrong. He wondered whether he'd find a fire, an automobile accident, or a drowning. The air horn had told him where, not what. He ran through the steady parade of islanders, on their way to see what was happening.

Passing the busy ferry docks, he turned onto the deserted road that led to the old marine park. The place was full of abandoned and condemned warehouses, chandleries, and shipyards. Now he heard the electric static of amplified radio transmissions and idling diesel engines. Here it was: fire.

Smoke gusted through the air. The big red pumper hurtled down the road, Mike Hannigan driving. Thomas grabbed a chrome handle, caught his foot in another grab handle bolted to the side, and hoisted himself aboard.

"It's the Dauntless Chandlery, Dev," Marty Cole shouted over the big engine and the fire's hurricane wind.

"Deserted, far as we know," Leroy Adamson said, passing him a spare coat. Thomas Devlin scanned the scene as he slipped into his Scott equipment, pulling an air tank over the black rubber coat, making sure the breathing mask was clear.

The old chandlery was blazing. One brick wall had collapsed, and the multistoried interior pulsed with flames. Snakes of black wire dangled from the ceilings, old pipes glowed red-hot. Embers blinked along black sticks of charcoal: structural timbers and the forgotten spars of ships.

Mike parked the truck close enough for the crew to feel the fire's full force. Marty Cole scrambled out of his seat and jumped on the large chrome howitzer mounted on the pumper's rear deck. Throwing the handle, he fired a torrent of water at the fire. Guys already on the scene were smashing windows with poleaxes, and smoke poured from every broken window and through the roof; the structure had become a chimney.

A crowd of people milled around, at once exhilarated and reverent, and Dick Wade was shouting at them to stay back. Thomas Devlin peeled off a few hundred feet of two-and-a-half-inch hose. He ran it past Hugh Lawson and Bobby Caserta, already working a water cannon. They were all part of the same team, but they didn't greet Thomas or acknowledge him in any way. They were intent on fighting the enemy.

Thomas pulled down his face mask and leaned into the thick hose, the water pressure pushing back at him with the force of a linebacker as he aimed the brass nozzle at the chandlery's broken windows. Flames snapped along the old timbers like popcorn. Orange geysers of fire spewed from the roof, sounding like speeding traffic on I-95.

Guys backlit by flames attacked the windows with long-poled axes and bludgeons. They smashed panes with the zeal of high-school vandals, and the tinkling glass was as delicate and incongruous as wind chimes. Generators and pumpers sucking water roared through the night.

In Boston, Thomas Devlin had been at hundreds of fires as bad as or worse than this one, but still the scene gripped him. Fire was untamable, as fierce as weather, with the destructive power of a tornado or a Force-10 gale. He could tell by watching the other firefighters that they were in awe of this fire. To them, this fire deserved more respect than the average house fire, like the one at Anne's.

But this fire was no more lethal than Anne's or any other fire. The fire that had killed Sarah had one tenth the power of this one.

Engines 2 and 4 screamed down the access road, and Thomas Devlin heard Dick Wade call his name.

"Tommy! Leave the nozzle and get over here."

Thomas grabbed Josh Hunter, a friend of Ned's who was running by with a pike pole. He was a young kid, and the guys generally treated him as a gofer, sending him back to the trucks for tools.

"Josh, deliver that pike, then get back here and take the hose," Thomas said, and he caught Josh's dazzling expression of gratitude.

"Thanks, Mr. Devlin."

Dick Wade stood by his red Ford Bronco, barking orders into a mike whose cord ran through the open window.

"Tommy, I want you in the high bucket," Dick said to Thomas Devlin. He nodded at Engine no. 4, the cherry picker. "Go on up, and tell me what's what."

"Okay, Chief," Thomas said to the only man alive who could get away with calling him "Tommy."

It was unspoken between them, but Thomas Devlin and Dick Wade knew that they operated at a different level from the other volunteers. They'd been trained as Boston professionals. Out here, there was a tendency toward fire-groupie mentality; to some of these guys, disaster was their hobby. They worked hard, and there were heroes among them. But they hadn't had enough experience to really assess a blaze and know how to handle it.

You'd have to stick bamboo shoots under Thomas Devlin's

fingernails to get him to admit this, but he knew a lot of these guys were in it for the thrill of the police band. They'd sit around their kitchens after dinner, drinking Bud and listening to the scanner, waiting for a fire or a crash to make them instant heroes.

So Thomas Devlin clipped the walkie-talkie on his belt and climbed into the aerial. He gave thumbs-up to Bobby Sullivan at the helm, and the gears began to crank, hoisting the bucket to a vantage point high over the fire.

Surveying the fire ground from the high bucket, Thomas Devlin found the scene surreal. Reflections of the fire burned red and gold in the harbor and in puddles of water spilled from the hoses. Islanders clustered in small groups behind the police line, with more streaming down the access road from town.

The aerial lifted Thomas Devlin higher, the sturdy metal extensions unfolding. He gazed through black smoke and flames at the chandlery, a two-hundred-year-old hive of lofts, timbers, warrens, and machinery. He realized that he was witnessing the death of a key part of island history, and he felt his throat tighten up.

"Tommy, what do you see?" Dick's voice crackled over the walkie-talkie.

"It's three quarters done," Thomas replied.

"Do we need to ventilate? How's the roof look?"

"The roof's caved in."

"Okay, then. Let her have it."

"Roger," Thomas Devlin said. He braced his back against the bucket's rim and threw the nozzle's handle. The hose sprang to life, jetting water into the fire and pinning Thomas against the back of the bucket. Phantoms of smoke and steam escaped into the night.

Thomas Devlin was fighting the fire. He believed he had been born to do it. Police officers fought bad guys, soldiers fought enemies, and he fought fires. He had seen fires kill, had lost Sarah and nearly been killed himself in one. Certain things in life were black and white to Thomas Devlin. One of them was that fire was evil. Fire was a sneaky, deceptive devil hiding in the walls.

He felt alert, on edge, but not scared. Standing at Anne's door, waiting with his tools and the flowers, he had felt something close to panic. But not now. His feelings for the woman made him more nervous than staring into the soul of his enemy.

He was putting the fire down. He was in command. His eyes stung from the smoke, but he wouldn't look away from the flames. Not for a second. Anne's apartment was a quarter mile away. He knew the fire was contained, or would be very soon. The likelihood of it spreading to town, to Anne's building, was practically nil. Thomas Devlin knew that.

But deep down, as he aimed the water jet into the burning chandlery, he had the sense of protecting Anne. He would never admit it to anyone, especially not to Anne, but somehow he knew that he was fighting this fire to keep her safe.

He had made protecting people his life's work. All the burning houses he had entered, people he had rescued, the names he had once known blurred together in his mind. Well, one name stood out from the others, all by itself, as clear as morning.

Anne.

ANNE Davis walked east, toward the fire. Darkness had fallen, and there was a hellish orange horizon, like sunset, in the sky where the sun always rose. As she moved closer she saw the flames. Blue strobe lights bounced off the buildings and fire trucks. She looked around for Thomas.

She recognized many of the rescue workers who had come to her house. They raced around, carrying axes and long-handled saws, oblivious to the crowd. Anne blended in with a group of other townspeople, transfixed by the spectacle.

The old chandlery was burning. It had been abandoned since Anne was a child, when she and her friends used to play inside.

They had explored the old machine shop, the dusty sail loft, the vast storage shed. Graffiti covered the brick walls. Virginities had been lost here, and smoking skills acquired.

Faces in the crowd were solemn; there was an air of mourning about the scene. Anyone who had spent their childhood on the island must, like Anne, be feeling profound and sad disbelief.

"Anne Fitzgibbon, is that you?"

Anne turned to her left and recognized Polly Slater, a girl she'd grown up with. Although she hadn't seen Polly in fifteen years, maybe more, she instantly hugged her.

"Isn't it terrible?" Anne asked, turning back to the fire.

"It's unbelievable. I never thought I'd see this spot without the chandlery."

"Do you know how it started?"

"My husband overheard Chief Wade saying something about arson. I mean, what else could it be?"

"I don't know." Anne watched black smoke spiral into the sky, illuminated by the orange flames and blue police lights, and she wished she could paint it.

"Remember playing here?"

"I was just thinking about that. Remember swinging on those huge grappling hooks? Jumping off the lofts and swinging clear across the building?"

"God, we're lucky we didn't impale ourselves."

"I hope it wasn't kids here tonight," Anne said, frowning. She thought of Maggie.

"The kids don't hang out here anymore," Polly said. "They're not as forgiving of water rats as we were."

"Somebody could have fixed this place up," Anne said, thinking of the huge windows overlooking the harbor, the graceful brick archways, the big boathouse doors. It had been such a stately building, the workplace of generations of islanders. Anne's paternal grandfather had built boats here. And now it was burned beyond recognition.

"No one had the money," Polly said. "Listen, I'd better go find Mike. We're in the book, if you're out here for a while."

"Thanks," Anne said, watching her go. It's interesting, she thought: Polly was the first old friend she'd seen in months who hadn't mentioned Karen. It felt good just to blend in. To be one of a whole crowd of people at the scene of an emergency. A community emergency.

She resumed scanning the crowd for Thomas. Firefighters were everywhere, in their sooty yellow helmets and black coats, wielding hoses or axes, talking into radios. From a distance, it was hard to tell them apart. She looked through the men standing near the trucks. Her gaze traveled up the long, metal lift, and then she saw him.

Even from fifty feet below, he looked enormous. His body filled the small basket, and his broad back was silhouetted against flames leaping into the sky. The hose he aimed at the fire seemed alive. He was standing still, within the bucket's confines, but even from this distance you could see that he was full of action.

She blinked, the smoke stinging her eyes. She was staring at the man who had walked into a burning house to pull her out. The intensity in his posture was riveting; Anne couldn't look away. She felt awed by the fire, by its destruction, by the sudden realization of what a close call she had had. She felt awed by the man who had saved her.

She stood there a few minutes more. The fire was dying before her eyes. The flames were retreating; the character of the smoke had changed. It didn't seem as acrid, as menacing as when she had first arrived. She didn't know how long it would be before the fire was totally out; she didn't know when Thomas would be finished for the night.

It didn't matter.

She turned away and headed toward town. He had said he would come back when it was over. She was going home to wait.

.   .   .

IT was nearly midnight when he knocked on her door. She opened it almost instantly; she'd been sitting in the living room, having a cognac.

He stood in the hallway, soot covering his face and hands. He must have left his helmet and coat on the truck; he was shivering, and the hems of his pants and the sleeves of his sweater were soaking wet. His eyes were red and swollen; there was dried blood on the back of one hand.

"I'm sorry it's so late," he said. "I saw your light from the street."

"It's not that late," she said. "Come in."

"No, that's okay. But I said I'd come back, and I just wanted to let you know the fire's under control. It was the old Dauntless Chandlery."

"I know," Anne said. "I was there. I saw you."

"You did?" he asked, obviously surprised.

Anne stood in the doorway, hugging herself. Cold air swept up the stairs, filling the hallway. She reached out, to tug his sleeve. "Come on," she said. "I was waiting for you. I'd be disappointed if you didn't."

He shrugged and smiled shyly, ducking his head to enter the room. Anne closed the door behind him. When she turned around, she saw him passing a hand across his face. The smell of smoke was overpowering.

"I'm a mess," he said. "There wasn't a place to clean up down there."

"You can use my bathroom," Anne said. "I don't exactly have a shower, but there's a little handheld thing." She mimed spraying her head using the old-fashioned attachment.

Laughing, he showed her his blackened hands.

"I'll run you a bath," Anne said, patting his forearm and giving him a big smile. "It's the least I can do after you saved my life and made me soup."

He smiled. "You really don't have to, but okay. That'd be great.

I'm too wound up to go right home. It was quite a fire. There's just a shell left standing."

"Are you hungry?"

"No, Dick's wife brought sandwiches. But I wouldn't mind a glass of that." He pointed at the bottle.

"Coming right up," she said. She poured him a cognac, then disappeared into the bathroom.

She had a wonderful clawfoot bathtub, deep and long, coated with shiny white enamel. The building had endless hot water. She turned on the taps, and billows of steam filled the room. While the water ran she rummaged through the linen closet for the plushest towels. She found two dark green ones that matched the bath mat and washcloth; refolding them, she placed them on the towel bars.

Hesitating for one moment, she reached into the closet for a deep blue glass bottle. It held unscented bath oil, and she tipped it over the tub, pouring in a generous amount. Just before turning off the taps, she lit a single white candle. She didn't ask herself what she was doing, or what she wanted to happen. All she knew was that it felt good to be drawing a bath for Thomas Devlin. It felt good to be taking care of someone. To be taking care of him. Turning off the bright overhead light, she closed the door behind her.

"It's ready," she said.

He was standing in the foyer, right where she had left him. His glass was empty.

"I'm going to track soot and ashes all through your apartment," he said.

"I think I can handle it." Anne refilled his glass and led him to the bathroom. The hallway was narrow, and she felt very conscious of his proximity. Their arms were practically touching. She felt the hair on the back of her neck stand on end as she stood against the wall to let him pass.

"Thank you," he said, his hand on the door handle. "I'll make it fast."

"Don't make it fast," she said. "Have a wonderful bath."

He closed the door very gently behind him, leaving her alone in the darkened hall. She stood still, hardly breathing. She hadn't felt like this in a very long time.

She heard him ease off his boots, undo his belt buckle. Brass clinked against tile as his pants slid to the floor. Anne couldn't move. She stood frozen, listening to him step into the bathtub. She heard the warm water sloshing around, and she imagined how good it must feel to his body. Then she walked quietly into the living room.

Trying to concentrate on something, anything, Anne could think only of Thomas Devlin in the next room. She wandered into the kitchen and stared at a tarnished silver bowl. A feeling of deep longing pulsed inside her, so strong she could hardly stand it. She wanted to hold the man.

She moved nervously from the sink to the counter. She had never felt this way before, and she didn't know how to think of herself. Before, with Matt, she had been young and carefree, and everything had happened easily. Now her choices in life seemed to mean more. They carried more weight.

Her choices no longer came out of nowhere. They didn't sweep her along. When she was younger, everyone had loved her spontaneity, the way she could change course at the drop of a hat. She'd be walking the beach in January, and the next thing you knew she'd strip naked and dive into the icy sea. Before Matt, she had loved generously and often unwisely, and she had known or caused her share of broken hearts.

Even after her marriage and the birth of her child, she had still loved to play hard. She'd hated schedules, planning ahead, settling down. Matt's job was perfect, because it had meant lots of trips, changes of scene, new experiences. If there was one thing Anne had minded about Karen starting school, it was the inevitable loss of freedom.

Anne had once been passionate and wild. She had thought that part of her had died. All the color and joy had gone from her life, and she was too dulled to miss or mourn it. But now, standing in her kitchen, she felt it coming back. Not the wildness, but the passion. In total command, knowing exactly what she was doing, she walked back down the darkened hall. She stood at the bathroom door.

"Thomas?" she said.

"Yes?" came his voice, after a second, through the door.

Her hand trembled on the knob. She hesitated, then entered the room, closing the door behind her.

The room was swathed in candlelight. Particles of steam seemed to hold its warmth in the air. The bathtub faced away from the door; Thomas watched Anne over his shoulder. Their eyes met, and he didn't look away.

Anne knelt by the tub. She dipped her left hand in the water, as if testing the temperature. Then she trailed her fingers up his arm. His scars. The fire hadn't burned only his hands, the left side of his face. His back, shoulders, arms, legs: his entire body was a map of the fire. She couldn't look away. Tenderly, her fingers continued up his arm, across his back. All of a sudden, she didn't see the burns anymore. She only saw the man.

She kissed his right shoulder.

Thomas turned his head, brushing her cheek with his lips. His arms came around her now; she felt the warm bathwater through her shirt, soaking her skin. He held her so tight, as hard as she had dreamed. Her head buried in his shoulder, she wanted never to let go.

She shuddered, not because she felt cold. The warm wetness made her feel naked. He held her face between his hands, looked her deep in the eye. There wasn't a trace of shyness or awkwardness between them. Anne tried to read the expression in his blue, miraculously blue eyes. It was knowledge: knowledge of Anne, the true and hidden Anne. She had understood for some time, since that night at Ruby's, that she had met a kindred soul.

Still gazing into her eyes, he moved his hand to her mouth, grazing her lips. He pulled her closer, their lips almost touching. Every pause was electric, dizzyingly sweet. The kiss was slow and gentle, discovering each other's faces, mouths, for the first time. Anne felt Thomas's hand on the back of her neck.

Her shirt's wet fabric clung to her body. Slowly she reached down, to untuck it from her jeans. Thomas stopped kissing her, watching. She eased it over her head. Her full breasts were flushed in the candlelight, her nipples pink and hard. She watched Thomas's face. She had nursed a child. She had stretch marks.

"You're beautiful," he said.

She felt tall, full of pride and passion.

"So are you," she said, leaning to kiss him again. His hand brushed the outside of her right breast, then cupped it lightly.

"You're braver than I am," he said after a moment.

"Braver?" she whispered, thinking of earlier. She had seen him fighting the fire and thought no one could be braver.

"For this," he said. "I've wanted this . . . well, for a long time."

For the first time Anne felt shy. Since when? she wanted to ask. What was happening between them felt so important, deep and somehow ancient, that suddenly she wanted to know its history. But she didn't ask. Instead, she reached behind her for a towel. Heat from the radiator had risen, warming it thoroughly.

He pulled the stopper from the drain. They smiled: a moment of truth. He stood in the tub, the water pouring off his body. Anne shook out the towel, wrapped it around him. She stood on her toes, asking for another kiss.

"Down the hall," she said. "On the left."

Her bedroom was many degrees colder than the bathroom had been. Shivering, Anne stared at the bed. It was a joke: a single bed exactly like the one she'd had as a child. She didn't even know if Thomas Devlin would fit in it. When had she last changed the sheets? Over the weekend sometime. Not so long ago.

Standing in the dark, she took off her jeans and panties. She folded them, placed them on the straight-backed chair. Once again she had the image, as she had not since the day she'd signed the lease, of her apartment as a monk's cell. Feeling decidedly unmonkish, she pulled down the covers and climbed into the bed.

After a minute Anne heard the bathroom door open. A shaft of dim light fell into the hallway, then disappeared as Thomas blew out the candle. He made his way quietly to her room. Light from the street came through the tall bedroom window. Lying still, Anne called to him.

He sat on the edge of her bed. Anne stroked his arm; he was still warm from the bath.

"The bed's tiny," she said.

"It's okay," he said, sliding under the covers.

They faced each other, exchanging a long, openmouthed kiss. Then almost instinctively, to make room for him, Anne turned to face the wall. She felt his erection, hot against her bottom. His arms encircled her, and she half turned her head to meet his kiss.

They fit perfectly. His body closed around hers from behind, and suddenly the bed didn't seem so small after all. His left hand held both her breasts, kneading the erect nipples with exquisite friction. Reaching down, she guided his penis between her legs. They lay there for a few minutes, rocking in quiet rhythm, and then he entered her from behind.

Their bodies joined together; it felt to Anne so right and eternal. As if they were one, as if they had been together all through the ages. He held her so tight, her back pressing against his hard, flat belly.

"I love you," he whispered fiercely, and it was the truest thing she had ever heard.

"I love you," she whispered back, her voice rising with passion.

He touched her in ways she had forgotten or never known. She met his thrusts, reaching back to stroke his hips, his balls, turning her head to be kissed again and again. She came easily once. Then, quivering with pent-up emotion and desire, she waited for him. The rhythm of his strokes, his power inside her increased, and together they slid off the cliff into one avalanching orgasm.

They slept, or at least Anne did.

When she awakened, the bedside clock said four A.M., and Thomas was kissing the back of her neck. They made love again, hungry at first, like the night before. Then languorous, slow and lazy, as if they knew it was going to last. That neither one of them was about to disappear.

"I'd better go," Thomas Devlin said some time later. The streetlights were still on, but the black night had begun to soften. Anne had spent this hour awake many times since coming to this apartment, and she could read the sky. Dawn would bring clouds, rain clouds. She snuggled into Thomas.

"Not yet," she said, rolling over to press her body flat against the front of his. She gave him a long good-morning kiss.

"The first ferry will be loading in an hour or so," he said, kissing her forehead, cheeks, the tip of her nose. Her lips. "I want to leave before the town's awake. I don't want anyone talking about you."

"What about you?" she asked, touched by his protectiveness.

"You know it's different. It would do wonders for me, people knowing I'd been with you. My stock'd go right up."

"I don't want you to go," she said.

He kissed her, looked her in the eye, kissed her again.

"I'll be back," he said.

Anne nodded. She'd take it as a promise. Lying under the covers, savoring his heat and the smell he'd left on her pillow, she watched him dress. He had laid his clothes across the bathroom radiator, and they were something close to dry. He put them on, resurrecting smoke from the fire.

"I should have washed those for you," she said, not accounting for the fact that she didn't have a washing machine or dryer.

"We had better things to do," he said. He stood by the bed,

watching her for a moment. Then he kissed her once more, and he left. Anne listened to the door close. She heard his tread on the stairs. After half a minute she heard a truck start up. It fired right away. It drove up Transit Street, heading out of town.

After a while she couldn't hear the engine. Closing her eyes, Anne let herself drift back to sleep.

Chapter 10

With every passing day, Anne came to believe more and more in the existence of happiness. Not contentment. Not the state she had once known, where you sat back and thanked your stars, or forgot to thank them, for all that was good in the world. Contentment was gone for good. But happiness, soaring moments of bliss, opposed, as always, by the old sadness, was possible.

After that first night with Thomas in her little bed, they had spent other nights together. Once again at her house, but usually at his. His bed was big, and his house was isolated. Owls hunted over the potato fields. Sometimes she surprised deer, licking salt from the pines that lined his road. He had a garage in which to hide her car. After a few nights she stopped hiding it.

They walked the country roads after dark, holding hands. Thomas told her all about Ned. The pride he felt for his only son was evident and adorable. Anne loved hearing about Ned. She'd sit beside Thomas on the sofa, looking through old photo albums, and she had the feeling she would like the boy very much.

In Ned's baby pictures he was big and quizzical, and he seemed to love being tickled. There was a wonderful shot of Thomas kissing Ned's stomach, Ned doubled over in hilarious baby laughter. There were shots of Sarah, alternately delighted and solemn, as she regarded her baby. Anne knew there were similar photos of herself, boggled by the wonder of her own child, when Karen was that age.

You could tell, from Ned's picture, the moment Sarah had gone from his life. All expression left his face. At six, he became a blank slate. No smiles, no tears, no more laughter. He stared at the camera, his Christmas stocking hanging from the mantel behind him, and didn't flinch. Anne passed her fingers over that picture. She stared at it for a long time, and for those minutes she felt her new happiness balanced out by the old, familiar sorrow.

"He'll be home for spring vacation," Thomas said, his arms around Anne's shoulders.

"I can't wait to meet him," she said. "Do you think he'll mind?"

"Mind what?"

"You seeing someone."

"No, I think he'll like it."

"Have you ever before? Seen someone?"

"Not like this," Thomas said, kissing her cheek, the side of her mouth. "I've had dinners out. Movies. A weekend in Vermont one time. But nothing like this."

Anne nodded, the happiness coming back. She knew what he meant. It didn't matter that she'd been married all those years. She had never felt love like this.

"When did you start to feel it?" she asked.

"That's easy," he said. "The minute I saw you."

She laughed nervously. She didn't believe him or even want to believe him. What she felt for Thomas Devlin had evolved over months of getting to know him, of realizing that he was the only person she knew who had faced the horror. She didn't believe in anything as romantic as love at first sight anymore.

"No, really," she pressed. "When?"

"Anne, I told you. From the very beginning."

"It's not possible," she said, feeling her shoulders tighten, re-sisting the concept. "You didn't know me then. All you saw was some deranged woman in a nightgown in the snow."

"Yes, that's what I saw. And I *did* know you. The look in your eyes told me everything I had to know. I'd felt that intensity before, but I'd never seen it in another person. I fell in love with you right there."

"Hard to believe," Anne said, even though she did. She leaned against him, letting him hold her tighter.

"And you weren't deranged."

"A little," Anne said. "Maybe just slightly."

"Maybe you should invest in a lockbox, to keep the picture safe. I don't want you running back into any more burning buildings."

"It's in my bag," Anne said. "I keep it with me."

"You have it here now?"

"Yes," Anne said, afraid that he would think her paranoid. She had shown him Karen's drawing the day after they had first made love, when he had returned to fix the clock. She had explained all the elements in the picture, encouraged him to smell the crayon wax. He had appreciated it with her, listening to her tell about Karen, then sitting beside her in silence while time ticked by.

"I told you I was deranged," Anne said now, embarrassed.

"I think it's wonderful," he said. "It's not everyone who gets to carry paradise around with them."

Anne kissed him hard on the lips. He'd just reminded her why she loved him so much.

PEOPLE were talking. Gabrielle heard it first from Steve, who had heard from Emma Harwood. Emma delivered the morning paper. One morning last week, just before sunrise, she had leaned out the window of her late husband Arthur's Chevy 4×4 to pop Thomas Devlin's paper into the blue plastic tube bolted to his mailbox, and guess what she saw? The rosy fingers of dawn reflecting off the windshield of Anne's VW.

The nerve of Emma, telling tales on Gabrielle's sister to Steve, was a matter of ethics that Gabrielle would save for later. The more pressing issue was Anne.

Thomas Devlin was a decent enough, if mysterious, man. He kept to himself. You'd see him at the Firemen's Picnic on the Fourth of July, the Cross-Island Fair in August, the occasional roast-beef supper at Grange Hall. He cut a romantic figure, living such a lonely island life, and being so tall and scarred.

Gabrielle had once entertained notions of fixing him up with Monique Deveraux, her best friend from eighth grade. Monique had never married; she'd spent nine years hating men after being dumped by Winthrop Alcott, a rich summer kid from Baltimore who had dated her twelve summers straight, then run off with a girl from Bryn Mawr he'd known only four weeks.

Anyway, Gabrielle had thrown a cocktail party—her first and only, not counting the ones she got paid to do. She'd bought a pony keg, a case of blanc-de-blanc, and a half gallon of rum; she and Maggie had spent one hot summer day making pâté brisé and filling it with tasty aphrodisiacs like salmon roe, wild mushrooms, and smoked mussels. Gabrielle had felt giddy with the power of a born matchmaker.

The idea was a bust. Totally. Monique came on too blue-eye-shadow and décolletage, and Thomas couldn't stop blushing or think of anything more interesting to discuss than the record-breaking heat wave. Which had broken a full two weeks earlier.

Standing at her kitchen stove, slicing yellow onions into a skil-let, Gabrielle sighed. Thomas Devlin and Anne would never work. It warmed her heart to think of Anne sharing someone's bed. That would be lovely, if that's all there was to it.

But Anne was vulnerable. She might not be completely in command of her faculties. She might be ignoring one crucial fact: that she and Thomas Devlin were about the least likely pair on

God's green earth to last longer than it would take to break each other's hearts.

Anne needed excitement, travel, the best of things. She needed a man who could run an empire, a man others looked up to. She needed a lot of attention. From the time Anne was old enough to date, Gabrielle had watched her dismiss the island boys. They hadn't posed enough of a challenge. She wanted to keep a man guessing, and be adored for it. Island boys wanted meat-and-potatoes wives.

Thomas Devlin was too reserved, too withdrawn, to be Anne's sort of man. Anne needed a Fortune-500 CEO, a movie producer, something like that. Not Thomas Devlin—the local fire-fighting clockmaker. Gabrielle could understand the initial attraction, but she knew it wouldn't last. She only hoped no one would get hurt.

KURT wouldn't give up. It kind of thrilled Maggie, to see just how far he would go. Roses in her locker, notes passed in the hall, telephone calls every day, no matter how vehemently she refused to talk to him.

Still, she would not relent.

She had gotten an A on her history test, a B+ on her last math quiz, an A with an additional *Excellent and frightening!* on her English homework, a short story she'd written about a girl hitchhiking to Boston who gets picked up by a serial killer.

Vanessa called her stuck-up, and Eugene made pig noises when she walked past. It gave Maggie a kind of satisfaction. Let them waste their lives in the sewer, see where they wind up. Probably married to each other, fat and wasted, with a bunch of kids going to Island Consolidated.

What a life.

But one morning Maggie's resolve was tested. Waiting for the bus, she realized that she had forgotten her French homework. She could just see it: on the sideboard in the dining room, where her mother had made her put it so they could have a heart-warming family dinner at the table where she'd been studying.

"Shit," she said, checking her watch. She had about three minutes before the bus would arrive. She glanced around at her fellow schoolmates. Dennis Lawson, third grade. Dori Adamson, sixth grade. And let us not forget Skip Adamson, dweeb man of the sophomore class.

"Don't let the bus leave without me," she said to Skip in her most menacing tone.

"You know it won't wait," he said, visibly stunned that she would even speak to him.

"The ball's in your court," she said, leaving him reeling.

Running home, she smelled the damp island earth, the first mark of true spring. The crocuses, the first robin, the departure of the seals were false signs. You knew it was spring when, and only when, the air began to smell like dirt. Wet dirt. Let's be honest: you knew it was spring when the air began to smell like shit. The aroma of cow manure would drift downwind from Darlings' Farm, and you'd know summer was right around the corner.

Maggie raced into the house, grabbed her homework, and ran outside again. Her knapsack banging against her rib cage, she sprinted down the road. She heard the bus. At first she thought she'd made it. She thought the bus was just pulling in, but no: it was leaving without her.

"You die!" she hollered, cursing Skip Adamson.

Dejected, she was ready to meet her fate. She would walk home and ask her mother for a ride, and she would suffer the lecture on how her mother had never missed the school bus once in her entire twelve years at Island Consolidated. Then Kurt pulled up.

"Hey," he said, leaning over to open the passenger door.

"Hey," she said.

"Did you forget how to use the telephone or something?" he asked.

"I've been busy."

"Yeah, I notice you missed the bus. Want a ride?"

"No."

"Okay," Kurt said, not driving away.

"Thanks anyway."

"Okay," he said again.

She peered across the roof of his car, as if she were waiting for a much better, more exclusive bus. Feeling his eyes on her, she felt herself grow flushed.

"Thanks anyway," she repeated.

"Maggie."

She tried not to, but she had to look at him. "What?"

"I'm sorry. I'm so sorry for what I did to you."

"Yeah, well." She resumed scanning the horizon for the phantom dream bus. She'd gotten herself into such a state, she half believed it would drive up any minute now. Tinted windows, a glass roof, hostesses dispensing chocolate milk and blueberry muffins. God, the air smelled like spring.

"Please. Let me drive you to school."

She shot him a look.

"You don't want to be with me—I understand. I do. But how're you going to get to school?"

Reluctantly, Maggie opened the door. She climbed in. What was her alternative? Get her mother to drive?

Once in the car, she felt herself relax. Kurt had Led Zeppelin in the tape player, hardly audible. He fast-forwarded to "Stairway to Heaven," her favorite.

"Thanks," she said.

"Hey," he said, patting his pocket. "You feel like smoking a joint?"

For one bee-sting second she felt tempted. Nothing would feel better than getting stoned with Kurt, listening to Led Zeppelin, ditching school to spend the day driving around.

"No thanks," she said, smiling. Removing herself from the

danger zone. His frown told the whole story: he didn't want Maggie bettering herself. He wanted to keep her zonked.

Kurt gave Maggie a long, evil stare, loaded with disgust. "You're different," he said. "I don't even know you."

"You hurt me," Maggie said. "I hated that you wanted me to sleep with Fritz."

"How many times can I tell you I'm sorry?"

"I've only heard you say it once."

"That's because you won't answer my calls. I feel like such an asshole, asking your mother if you're there. She must be eating this right up."

Maggie didn't say anything. She had to admit he was right.

"You want to take after your aunt, right? Mrs. Above-it-all."

"If that's how you see her," Maggie said. She still felt a tug for Kurt: his ripped jeans, his glossy blond hair, the sexy sneer in his voice.

"She's fucking the freak," Kurt said.

"What?"

"Burns. You remember Burns? The guy who pulled her out after she lit the house on fire?"

"No way," Maggie said, frowning. They pulled into the school parking lot. Kids were still straggling off the bus, so she knew she had a minute.

"It's true. She's high-and-mighty one minute, and next thing she's down and dirty. Think of that while you're on your head trip," Kurt said. Hurt, he looked out his window, away from Maggie.

Maggie couldn't help herself. Some of the old feelings trickled back, and she touched his knee. Her finger poked through the hole in his jeans, rubbing his skin.

"It's not a head trip," she said. "I want to pull my grades up. This has nothing to do with you. Or my aunt."

"Yeah, well. I miss you, that's all."

"I miss you, too." There. She'd said it. Maggie glanced at the school and saw Vanessa standing by the door. She was watching Maggie and Kurt with a really sad look on her face.

"Please, give me another chance," Kurt whispered. "Let me prove how much I love you."

He had never said he loved her before. Maggie felt the color rise in her cheeks. All her plans, her resolutions to be a better person, her vow to stop seeing her old friends suddenly seemed ridiculous. Kurt stroked the side of her face with the back of his hand. Now he was leaning closer, kissing her ear, nibbling her neck.

"Let me prove it," he whispered.

"Okay," Maggie said.

Kurt shifted into first and peeled out right in front of Mr. Jephson, the boys' gym teacher. By the time they hit Orion Road, he'd lit the joint and handed it to Maggie. She let it burn for a few seconds, and then she took a hit. It was good pot, she realized as her head went cold. They were heading toward the lighthouse. She leaned against Kurt and trembled with the pleasure of being told he loved her.

Chapter 11

It had become a tradition that one Saturday every spring
Gabrielle and Maggie Vincent would take a shopping trip to the
mainland. They'd drive to Boston or Providence or one of the
malls, have lunch, and shop. Sometimes they didn't buy much.
New clothes weren't really the point. Going off-island was the
important thing: being together, seeing the new styles, getting
away from their neighbors.

This year Anne joined them.

She'd been happy to be invited along, but she'd hesitated before
accepting. She wasn't sure she should intrude on their mother-
daughter day. But Gabrielle had insisted, and Maggie had followed
up with a second phone call, for good measure, and finally Anne
said yes.

The ride over was typical for the early boat on an off-season
Saturday: hardly any cars, even fewer trucks, people sleeping in
their vehicles. Anne went into the cabin for coffee while Gabrielle
and Maggie dozed. Was it her imagination, or did conversation
stop dead when she approached the snack bar?

"Black coffee, please," she said to the girl behind the counter. Probably one of Maggie's classmates, she was about sixteen. Handing Anne the steaming Styrofoam cup, she looked fearful and apprehensive, as if she were serving a witch.

"Thank you," Anne said pleasantly. "Hi, Arnie. Hi, Mike," she said to two men standing together. Mike was a lifelong islander; Arnie had married one of Steve's cousins. The two men nodded at Anne, friendly enough.

"How're you doing, Anne? Been a long time since you made it through an island winter," Mike said.

"It wasn't too bad," Anne said.

"Sorry about your house," Mike said, and Arnie joined in, nodding solemnly. But from their discomfort, the way they shuffled their feet and looked quickly away, Anne had the feeling what they were really sorry about was Karen.

"Thank you," she said. "Thanks a lot."

Taking a seat, she turned to look out the window and distinctly heard one of them say "Dev." Anne sipped her coffee, not particularly bothered. As a matter of fact, it kind of pleased her, people knowing about her and Thomas. It was better than before, when she'd pass by and imagine she heard people whispering about Karen.

When she returned to the car, Gabrielle and Maggie were awake, discussing the shopping options.

"Boston, please? Please, Mom?"

"It's so far," Gabrielle said. "I was thinking the Warwick Mall."

"Anne, you're the deciding vote," Maggie said. Sitting in back, she leaned forward, her head between the two front seats.

"No thanks," Anne said. "I'm just along for the ride. Whatever you two want to do."

"Chicken," Gabrielle said. "Go for it."

"Honestly?" Anne said. "I'd rather go to Boston."

"Me and my big mouth," Gabrielle said cheerfully.

The ride up I-95 was fun. They tuned in to a radio station that

Maggie loved and couldn't get on the island, Q-105 or something, and listened to the morning-show hosts tear each other up.

It did Anne's heart good to see Maggie enjoying herself. She had really noticed a difference in her niece since the truck incident. Most of the time she seemed brighter, more alive. When they drove past the Wakefield exit, where Anne had found her at the Quality Inn, Maggie reached alongside Anne's seat and gave her hand a secret squeeze.

"Enough of this new-wave grunge rock," Gabrielle said after an hour on the road. "I want to hear love songs."

"You're not changing the station," Maggie said, gripping Gabrielle's seat back with great drama. "Tell me you're just kidding."

Gabrielle hit the seek-mode button, and selected a station playing Michael Bolton.

"There now," Gabrielle said.

Anne gave Maggie a sympathetic look.

"Love," Gabrielle said.

Anne looked out the window, trying to remember the last time she'd been to Boston. Karen had been a baby; Anne remembered carrying her down Newbury Street in a Snugli.

"I'm trying to set a mood," Gabrielle said. When Anne didn't reply, Gabrielle tapped her thigh. "I'm trying to set a mood. A romantic mood," she said.

"Really?" Anne said. "Too bad Steve's not here."

"Mom!" Maggie said sharply, as if she knew what Gabrielle was up to.

"What?"

"Don't be a jerk!"

Anne waited for Gabrielle to reprimand Maggie, for talking to her like that, but Gabrielle's attention was on Anne.

"I'm all ears," Gabrielle said, and suddenly Anne knew what she was after. Confessions about Thomas.

"Oh," Anne said. "I'm seeing someone."

"I'm glad you finally got around to telling me," Gabrielle said. "Too bad half the island beat you to it."

The words were lighthearted, but Anne heard hurt in the tone. She didn't really want to talk about Thomas; what went on between them felt so sweet and private, she couldn't imagine discussing him with her sister; with anyone. She didn't mind people knowing. Hiding their relationship seemed pointless, but she didn't want to explain it either. Still, she didn't want Gabrielle to feel bad.

"When did it start?" Gabrielle asked.

"I'm not sure, exactly," Anne said. How did you define "start"? Was it that night at the coffee shop? The first time they'd made love? Or, as Thomas said, when they'd first seen each other at the fire?

"First of all, I have nothing against Thomas Devlin," Gabrielle said.

"Good."

"But I'm worried about you."

"Gabrielle . . ." Anne said, the warning ringing in her voice.

"Mom!" Maggie barked.

"Just hear me out," Gabrielle said. "You listen, too, Maggie. Sometimes we're vulnerable to other people. To men. I'm lucky —I've been married to the same man forever, and he's a known commodity."

"You call that lucky?" Maggie asked in a stage whisper that made Anne smile in spite of herself.

"That's enough, Maggie! Anyway, Anne, Thomas is a good man. He raised a very nice boy all by himself, so he must be decent, and I've never heard otherwise. But look what you've been through! All you've lost this year."

"That's why I'm with Thomas," Anne said, feeling steady and secure and missing him.

"What about Matt? You are still married to him."

"Yes, but so what?"

"Don't you have feelings for him?"

Feelings? Anne couldn't begin to explain to Gabrielle the complicated swirl of emotions she felt for Matt. She had loved him with all her heart. She had borne his child. Together they had stood at the grave while that child was lowered into the ground.

"He left you, yes," Gabrielle said. "We all know that. But isn't it time to forgive and forget? Can't you give him another chance?"

Anne couldn't help it: rage boiled up from deep inside, and she lashed out, slamming the dashboard with the heel of her hand.

"Gabrielle, I lost my baby," Anne said, tears spilling out of her eyes. "I don't give a shit about Matt's feelings."

"But—" Gabrielle said.

"No. I don't want to talk about it anymore." But she took a deep breath and forced the words out. "Matt and I have been apart since . . . since Karen fell. It's been hell for him, I don't doubt that. But we've gone our separate ways, so we've been in separate hells. There's no going back now. Don't you see how impossible it would be?"

Maggie reached forward to clutch Anne's shoulder. When Anne reached for Maggie's hand, she found that it was wet. As if Maggie had been wiping away tears. Now she looked at Gabrielle and saw her crying.

"I'm so sorry," Gabrielle said, sniffling. "I can't imagine how it's been for you."

"Look," Anne said, composing herself. "I love you both. We all lost her, not just me."

"Isn't that the truth?" Gabrielle wept. "That little monkey. As pretty and smart as her mother. Sometimes I just can't believe it. I can't get it through my head. Here we are, the girls on a shopping trip, and she should be with us."

"I'm going to get her a present," Maggie whispered. When Anne turned, she saw Maggie staring at the back of her mother's head, tears streaming down her face. Anne had meant to tell Maggie to save her money, to say that Karen would want her to spend it on something for herself. But the sight of Maggie's face made her hold her tongue.

"Oh, honey," Gabrielle said, glancing over at Anne. She snuffled, rubbing her nose with the back of her hand. Anne reached into the glove compartment and pulled out tissues. She passed them around.

"Thank you," Gabrielle said. "Listen. If Thomas Devlin makes you happy, you have my blessing. Just . . ."

Anne waited, sensing that Gabrielle was getting up her nerve to deliver her older-sisterly last word.

"Just don't move too fast. And don't count Matt out yet. No matter what you say now, when Steve and I walked you down the aisle, we knew we were giving you to the right man. We knew it was going to be forever."

"You don't just give someone to a man," Maggie said, so scoffingly that Anne knew that the moment of grief had abated.

"Never mind," Gabrielle said. "You weren't there. You didn't see the look in Matt's eye when he took your aunt's hand. And I happen to believe that the look is still there."

Anne wondered what Gabrielle meant by that, but she didn't ask. She had to admit to herself that she didn't really want to know.

Browsing through a toy store in Back Bay, Maggie felt depressed. She had thought toy shopping would cheer her up, but she couldn't stop thinking of Kurt. She hated herself for getting high. For breaking her promise to herself. After having sex with him at the lighthouse, she hadn't heard any more words about love. It was back to the same old thing.

She almost wondered whether he had reeled her back in just to prove he could catch her. That she wasn't as good as she thought. It didn't matter. Vanessa and Kurt and Eugene were her friends, and that was that. After skipping school with Kurt, it seemed stupid to keep avoiding them. So everything was pretty much back to normal.

It wasn't as if her parents had even noticed her trying to change. She could get pregnant and become a crack addict or run for president or become a famous movie star: would it all be the same to her father? He'd walk Maggie down the aisle and just as happily give her away to Kurt as to anyone else. So who cared?

Suddenly Maggie saw the perfect toy. God, it was too cute to resist: a tiny white baby seal with coal-black eyes and a pink nose. It reminded her of the one she had once wanted to buy on the island, but it was nicer. The fur felt real.

Maggie had the awful thought that maybe it was made of real baby-seal fur. Back Bay was full of fancy fur stores and ladies wearing minks and sables, and she wouldn't put it past some store owner to stock the shelves with baby-seal toys made of fur from real baby seals who'd been clubbed to death on ice floes by poachers.

"Excuse me?" Maggie asked the salesclerk. "Is this, um, made of real seal fur?"

The salesclerk, who was twenty-two or so, gave Maggie a completely grossed-out you-are-garbage-look and said as snootily as possible, "Taking seal fur is against the law. A percentage of the proceeds from every single toy we kill goes to Save the Seals Foundation."

"Um, you said 'kill,' " Maggie said.

"Excuse me?"

"I think you meant to say 'sell,' but you said 'kill.' "

The salesclerk just shook her blond hair in bored disbelief and asked Maggie if she wanted the toy.

"Yes, please," Maggie said. "Wrapped."

She enjoyed watching the clerk, dressed to perfection in her Laura Ashley flowered dress, her pink Sam & Libbys, and gold charm bracelet, perform the menial task.

"Thank you," Maggie said, handing over her $24.50, smiling brilliantly, wishing she had worn full dress today: all her earrings, her nose ring, her Harley-Davidson belt buckle, and anything leather. Girls like the clerk gave her cramps.

She stuck the package in her knapsack. She was glad she'd bought the toy for Karen, but she wished she hadn't announced the idea to her mother and Anne. It called attention to herself in a way she hated. It reminded her of what a waif would do: embrace the tragic, waste away to nothing, and go around making people say poor-whatever-the-waif's name is.

That's not why Maggie had gotten Karen a present. She'd done it because buying the toy made Karen feel not so dead. Just the way that looking at Karen's drawing made Anne feel close to her. Maggie didn't really know what she was going to do with the seal toy. Keep it for a while. Maybe unwrap it and put it on her bed. Maybe leave it at Karen's grave the next time they visited it. Maybe throw it off the ferry.

She did know one thing. Somehow she was going to get her hands on the picture Anne called *Paradise* and have it framed. Maybe when she did, she'd get up the nerve to explain the white boxes.

Maggie had spent the morning shopping with her mother and Anne. They'd gone into every boutique on Newbury Street, trying on clothes they would never buy. Maggie had completely fallen in love with Betsey Johnson, but the price tags were a little out of her reach.

They'd had lunch at a pizza place that her mother kept calling a trattoria, just to remind Maggie and Anne that she'd once gone to Italy. Maggie could see right through the woman. She loved her, but sometimes she wondered whether she should point little pretensions like that out. She didn't want her mother to look like a fool to Anne.

Now Maggie walked up and down the streets of Back Bay, waiting until she met her mother and Anne at the parking lot, in time to make the boat. Maggie saw a lot of cool-looking kids. She wondered how many of them went to college in Boston. Wasn't Boston supposed to be College Town, USA?

A very cute guy was sitting alone on the curb, reading a book. Jean jacket, straggly brown hair, a soul patch and semigoatee. Maggie glanced over his shoulders. Poetry in some foreign language. Irritated, he looked up at her. "May I help you?" he asked.

"Can I bum a cigarette?" she asked, noticing that he was smoking.

He shook a Camel out of his pack, and she took it.

"Do you have a light?" she asked.

He handed her his own lit cigarette, and she touched it to the tip of hers, and she couldn't help thinking how weirdly intimate the whole thing was, like having sex with a total stranger.

"You go to school around here?" he asked.

"Not exactly," Maggie said, incredibly flattered that he would mistake her for a Boston kid.

"You look familiar. Did I meet you at a party at Emerson?"

"I don't think so," Maggie said, blushing like crazy. Emerson College! God, he thought she was a Boston college kid!

"Hmmm. I could swear." He went back to reading his book.

Maggie wanted to keep things going, but she didn't know how. She couldn't exactly make small talk about poetry or foreign languages. The Beantown Trolley rattled past, groaning under the weight of about a hundred fat tourists taking videos. When they showed the movies to their relatives, everyone would think the cute guy was Maggie's boyfriend.

"Well, see ya," she said.

"Yeah," he said, not looking up.

He'd already forgotten about her. He'd probably figured out that she was a dumb loser. Not college material.

NED Devlin had never felt so ready for spring vacation. His roommate's parents dropped him off at the mainland ferry terminal, and he boarded the late-afternoon boat feeling exultant, as if he were a conquering explorer returning home after a long, successful crusade.

He'd been accepted by Dartmouth.

The envelope, beautifully thick, had arrived in his mailbox last week. All the other colleges had said yes, too, but Dartmouth was the one that mattered. They'd offer him a partial scholarship and a work-study program, a starting spot on the freshman hockey team, and Ned was on top of the world. He was Hannibal crossing the Alps.

Standing on the ferry's top deck, he breathed the sea air. He'd told his father over the phone, but he couldn't wait to see him in person. His father always acted so proud of everything Ned did. Ned knew his father would want to celebrate about Dartmouth as much as he did.

As the ferry steamed into deeper water Ned started recognizing lobster buoys, and he knew he was getting closer to home. There were Marty Cole's buoys, painted neon pink and yellow, Mr. Hunter's, painted red and white. Once he started seeing island lobster buoys, he always relaxed. He felt the pressures of school blow away. This part of the ferry ride made him feel exhilarated, comfortable, slightly loose, the way two beers made him feel.

He'd been alone on the top deck, but now he heard voices. Women's voices. He felt too shy to turn. The air was cool. On dry land, the temperature had shot up to sixty-two or so, but out here, with the wind blowing, he needed his warm jacket. He could feel that his nose and the rims of his ears were red. When the voices receded, he glanced over.

Maggie Vincent and her mother and another woman stood across the deck. They were laughing, talking animatedly, not looking his way. He tried to hear, but the wind stole their words.

Maggie didn't look as tough as usual. When they were little, she and Ned had played together at Park and Rec. Ned had had a big crush on her. She was the second girl he had asked to dance; she would have been the first, but he'd had to get over his nervousness, practicing on Vanessa Adamson. In the last few years Maggie had been hanging out with idiots. Bored island kids who broke into summer houses to smoke too much pot, kids Ned didn't like.

Watching her now, Ned wondered what she was like away from her mother. She was joking around, making her mother and the other woman laugh about something. He could see they all liked each other a lot. But he wondered whether she was different with her school friends.

She glanced over, looked back at her mother, then glanced back at Ned. He had the feeling she was trying to place him. It had been over three years since they'd said two words to each other, and he knew he'd changed a lot in that time. He'd grown about a foot, started shaving, kept his hair shorter for hockey. But then it was obvious she recognized him. She waved and spoke to the others.

He waved back. Everyone was staring at him. For a second he thought they would cross the deck to talk to him. But Maggie pulled them into a huddle. They stayed where they were.

She'd probably told them what a jerk he was.

On the ferry home, a few hours earlier, Gabrielle had watched carefully for Anne's reaction when Maggie pointed out Ned Devlin.

"He's tall, like his father," Anne had said noncommittally. But suddenly she stopped talking and watched Ned—surreptitiously, Gabrielle would grant—for the rest of the trip.

Anne's mind had been going, that was for sure. Gabrielle had seen the little thinking frown on her face, the one that always gave her away. Gabrielle had learned to recognize it long ago. Whenever Anne had a problem to solve, whenever she wanted something badly, whenever she was just plain trying to figure someone out, she would get an intense look in her eyes and a barely visible frown on her lips.

If Gabrielle had to translate Anne's frown on the ferry, she would have to say Anne was wondering how it would feel to have Ned Devlin as a stepson.

"Oh, stop it!" Gabrielle said to herself. She was alone in the kitchen, cleaning up after dinner.

"Stop what?" Maggie called from the dining room, where she was doing her homework.

"I'm just talking to myself," Gabrielle called back.

"Keep it together, Mom."

"I will, sweetheart."

Gabrielle put the coffee cups and dessert plates in the dishwasher, wiped the counters dry, and went into the dining room. They had added this room on two years earlier, and Steve had done a beautiful job. A red oak floor, a bay window for Gabrielle's plants, and a chair rail. Gabrielle had chosen two different wallpapers: a colonial floral above the rail and a muted stripe below. All in shades of Williamsburg green and gold.

Maggie was leaning over her homework, making marks in a workbook.

"What's that?" Gabrielle asked.

"My SAT practice book."

"Oh." Gabrielle knew she shouldn't interrupt. Maggie doing schoolwork was a sight for sore eyes. You never knew how long the trend would last. Still, she had to talk to someone or she'd go crazy.

"What did you think of Anne today?" she asked.

"She's great."

"I mean about the Thomas Devlin thing."

"Like you said, whatever makes her happy."

"It won't make her happy. She just thinks it will."

"Mom, do you mind? The test's next weekend."

"I know, I know. I'll leave you alone in a minute. Did you notice how quiet she got after you pointed out Ned?"

"No."

"Well, she did. I have a bad feeling about this. She's not ready to be getting serious about anyone."

"Just leave her alone, okay, Mom?"

"I care, that's all."

"Where's Dad? I'm sure he'd like to help with this," Maggie said with a snort.

"He went back to the big house. With daylight savings, he says they'll be done in two weeks."

"What a hero."

"Maggie, I wish you'd show your father the respect . . ."

Maggie put down her pencil and arched her back. She tapped her fingers, as if she had something else to say.

"What?" Gabrielle asked.

"Do you think I'm smart?"

"Yes. I do. It's nice to see you concentrating on your school-work."

"Smart enough to go to college?"

"College is an enormous commitment, Maggie. It's four years of hard work, and a lot of money. If you prove you can get your grades up and keep them up, then I'd say you've earned the right to go to college."

"I'm trying," Maggie said, in a scared voice that reminded Gabrielle that in many ways, Maggie was still a little girl. Gabrielle gave her a warm hug.

"I know you are. I can see that. I'm very proud of you, and I'm even prouder that you've stopped seeing that troublemaker Kurt. He's a very bad influence."

"Mmmm," Maggie said, looking down.

Gabrielle didn't know what Maggie was thinking, but she could see that something was bothering her. Maybe she was afraid of disappointing Gabrielle by not getting good grades, by not getting into college.

"You know, not everyone has to go to college," Gabrielle said. "Many successful people go far with just a high-school diploma. I didn't go to college, you know."

"I know," Maggie said, still looking down.

"And I have a business that makes me happy and puts food on our table when things are slow for your father."

"Like nine months out of the year," Maggie said.

"Stop that." Gabrielle stood, her hands on her hips, regarding her puzzling daughter. As a child, Maggie had adored Steve. He took her everywhere, treated her the way other island fathers treated their sons. He taught her the right way to drive a nail, shingle a house, pour a foundation. To this day, he worshiped her. Gabrielle just didn't understand how Maggie could fail to realize that.

"Thanks for today," Maggie said. "Boston was fun."

"Wasn't it wonderful to get off the island? All those terrific shops, and that sweet little trattoria. I barely had room for dinner tonight. My quattro stagione was out of this world."

Maggie gave her a long, thoughtful gaze, and Gabrielle thought for a minute that she was going to say something. Instead, she closed her workbook and stood. She kissed Gabrielle on the cheek.

"I'll be in my room," Maggie said. "Thanks again for Boston."

"You're welcome, honey," Gabrielle said. She returned to the kitchen, but it was too tidy to pretend it needed any more cleaning. Standing on her toes, she reached for her current favorite cookbook, *The Mediterranean Table*. Summer was coming, and her business would start getting busy again. She'd look for recipe ideas and make some notes, to pass the time. Besides, who knew? Maybe Matt would call.

Chapter 12

Way back when, Matt Davis would rush home from a business trip, hardly able to stand it. The ride from Kennedy to Gramercy Park, those slow forty minutes, when he could practically feel Anne, were the worst part. The time would tick by as the car sped through Queens, with Manhattan right in sight, so near and yet so far. He had minded every second he was apart from Anne. For ten years, without abatement, he had pined for her when they were apart.

Later, after he'd fallen in love with Tisa, it had been the same way. On trips when he couldn't take her along, he would go nuts waiting to see her again. That first blush of erotic love was a powerful thing.

But now the first blush was over. He and Tisa had fallen into a routine not unlike that of long-married couples. They had gotten together about a year ago, been living together since September. She took his shirts to the laundry, his suits to the dry cleaner; from his trips, he now brought her duty-free scarves instead of jewelry. He had expected the love rush to thicken, to slow down a bit. He had not expected it to dry up. For him, at least, it had disappeared.

Now that Matt had a little objectivity, now that he could weigh the two relationships, he could see that he'd made the mistake of his life.

There wouldn't be ten years worth of pining for Tisa when he couldn't be with her.

He was with her now, in a cab stuck in Park Avenue traffic. They were late to some black-tie charity thing being thrown at the Waldorf by an old classmate of hers, and she was angry and hurt because he had taken so long getting ready. Because he hadn't wanted to go in the first place.

"Will you try to have a good time?" she asked, and there was more hurt in her voice than anger.

"Yes, of course."

"It's just that Trisha's never met you, and I want her to see how wonderful you are."

Matt slid his hand across the seat, to take hers. She was radiant tonight in a white Chanel party dress and black velvet cape. She was wearing the diamond-and-emerald necklace he had bought her last May at Fred in Paris, the pearl earrings he had given her on her birthday in Rome last July, and a cheap silk carré from one of last year's stock he'd picked up just before his flight home this morning. It was two A.M. French time; he knew he should feel jet-lagged, but he was too wired.

Anne had a boyfriend.

He had found out just hours earlier when he'd called Gabrielle from the Concorde. Some local guy Anne hardly knew. The two elements of Gabrielle's description of him that Matt had registered were "clockmaker" and "burn scars." The only way Matt could imagine Anne with a man like that was if she felt sorry for him. With her heart, and after what she'd been through with Karen, she'd be a soft touch for anyone with a sob story.

"Trisha's great," Tisa was saying, "and you'll love her husband. Shippen Maynard? He's practically the head of ITX."

"I know who Shipp Maynard is," Matt said, picturing the pretentious blowhard. With his Hong Kong suits, his custom-built shoes, his manicures and wavy silver hair. The ex-marine had a keg head and barrel chest, he was known for telling tales about the women in his life. He was not, as Anne had once said, a nice man.

"God, all you scions of industry know each other," Tisa said, her pretty laugh tinkling, telling him that she was over being mad. "I know, you all belong to the same club."

Matt laughed because, in this case, it was true. The Racquet and Tennis Club, just a few blocks south of where they were now. The cab crept through in traffic, a roiling sea of yellow cabs, all honking their horns and nudging each other. Sharks in a feeding frenzy.

"Remind me how you know Trisha?" he asked, to get his mind off Anne and the man.

"We were models together at the same agency."

"That's right. I was thinking you knew her from school."

"No. She's actually a few years older than me. Don't tell her— she'd kill me. But she's thirty-one."

"Horrors," Matt said.

"We had this booking together, it was a riot. On the beach in Miami, and I'm talking pre-chic Miami, when there were Cubans just everywhere and no cute hotels. We were doing swimsuits for *Vogue,* and that's when I got picked for *Sports Illustrated* and at first she didn't, but then she did because it turns out . . ."

Matt stopped hearing her voice. He suddenly remembered something that had happened on this exact block, five years earlier, in another yellow cab stuck in traffic heading uptown instead of down.

Anne was pregnant with Karen. She was four months along,

and she had an ultrasound scheduled that afternoon. Matt had come home at lunch so he could go to the doctor with her.

Entering their apartment, he had found Anne sitting on the floor with her glass, a pitcher of water, and a Xeroxed list of instructions. Anne was an obstetrician's dream. She followed her directions to the letter.

Catching sight of her, Matt felt his heart flip. She was *his* dream, pregnant with their child. Rounder than she had ever been or would be again, she had reminded Matt of a Raphael Madonna. All softness and goodness and maternal love, and somehow so sexy that all he wanted to do was take her to bed.

"You have to drink all that?" Matt had asked in disbelief, watching her down glass after glass of what seemed to be gallons of water.

"I need a full bladder," Anne had replied. "It'll push up the uterus so Dr. Ventura can get a good reading on the baby. I think we'll find out the sex today."

It was one of their few disagreements during the pregnancy. Matt had wanted to wait until the delivery room, for the great traditional moment when the doctor would hold up their baby saying "It's a . . . !" Anne had argued that the baby was growing in her body, and she wanted to know everything that was happening the first possible moment. In the end, Anne would win out. And Matt wouldn't mind at all.

When she had finished drinking all her water, they went down to the street. They walked around the corner, along East Twenty-first Street, and Matt hailed a cab. Anne was in a great mood. She looked beautiful, very happy, and she was telling Matt about ideas she had for the baby's nursery.

Anne, who even when not pregnant, was known for having to make frequent bathroom stops during any long trip, who on childhood car rides had been called "pea bladder" by Gabrielle, now seemed completely unaffected by all the water she had drunk.

"Are you okay?" Matt kept asking as the cab sped north on Park Avenue.

"I'm fine," she reassured him. She was fine through the Thirties, fine through the tunnel, fine as the cab snaked past Grand Central, around the Pan Am Building.

"You're still okay?" Matt asked when the cab emerged on the other side.

"I'll be glad to get there," Anne said, and for the first time her smile showed strain.

"On the double," Matt said to the cabdriver.

Traffic was moving, and they were nailing all the lights. Clear sailing, no stops all through the Fifties. They had to go only six more blocks to Sixty-sixth Street.

"I'm not going to make it," Anne said, her eyes watering, as if the level of fluid in her body had risen into her head.

"Think of the desert," Matt said. "Dry sand. The Gobi Desert. Morocco. Las Vegas."

They hit some traffic, and they got a red light at Sixty-first Street. Anne clutched the seat, her eyes closed.

"Can you walk it?" he asked. She shook her head without opening her eyes, furrows in her forehead.

When the car started creeping along, Anne looked at Matt as if she needed him to throw her a lifeline.

"Tell him to pull over," she said.

"You're going to be fine," he said. "It's just a few more blocks."

"I can't." She had her hand on the door handle, ready to jump out of the car.

"Try, honey."

"Okay. But listen: if we hit one more red light between here and the office, he has to pull over."

"Deal," Matt said, and he had no doubt that Anne was prepared to stand on the side of Park Avenue, pull down her pants, and urinate. He had never loved her more.

They made it. Anne ran into the office, past a legion of pregnant women, calling over her shoulder to the receptionist that she
needed to use the bathroom.

"Pee to the count of ten and then hold it!" the receptionist
yelled after her.

That was the day they learned they were going to have a girl.

Now in a cab with Tisa, traffic was beginning to move. Matt
stared at Dr. Ventura's building, remembering that day. Anne's
spirit, her incredible valor as a human water balloon. She had
savored every minute of her pregnancy and motherhood, even the
most ignominious.

He wondered whether Anne had registered the fact that Dr.
Ventura had sent flowers last August. To commemorate the death
of a child she had brought into the world.

Matt sighed.

"God, we're going to be late," Tisa said. She took a compact
from her purse and checked her makeup.

"I'm sorry I was so slow," Matt said.

"I'm so proud to be with you," Tisa said, her eyes wide and
hesitant, like a fawn's. Perhaps she had picked up on his mood. He
squeezed her hand.

Tisa gave him a restrained peck on the mouth, as if her lips had
shock absorbers. She had lived in New York long enough to know
that you don't kiss in taxicabs, that the wrong pothole could
knock out two sets of perfect teeth. It's funny, Matt thought. He
and Anne had made out in cabs all the time.

"How do I look?" Tisa asked worriedly as the cab swung
around the island, pulling up at the Waldorf.

"Stunning," Matt said, taking in her beauty. Her long blond
hair, her widely spaced almond eyes, her full mouth, her lovely,
graceful neck.

"Tonight will be fantastic," she said, grazing his cheek with her
own.

Matt paid the driver, and they climbed out of the car as another couple at the head of the taxi line jumped in. Matt tipped the doorman. His arm lightly around Tisa's waist, he followed her into the hotel lobby.

Tisa held their invitation in white-gloved hands. Standing side by side, they read the placard announcing that the Literacy for Homeless benefit was being held in the Starlight Ballroom. They piled into an elevator with fifteen people Matt vaguely recognized, and they disembarked on the eighteenth floor.

Matt took Tisa's cape to the coat check and put the ticket in his pocket. She stood in the foyer, as beautiful as a woman could be.

"Excuse me, darling," he said to her. "I need to make a quick call. In the excitement of coming home, I seem to have forgotten something important. A client."

"Matt! I'm not walking in there without you."

"How about powdering your nose? I'll be done in a minute."

Shaking her head, she gave him a long, fearful look. Then, realizing that people might be watching, she composed herself and strode off, with the poise of the runway model that she was, into the ladies' room. Matt headed for the bank of phones.

He dialed the island number Gabrielle had given him. Anne had rented an apartment in town, right at the head of Transit Street. Matt could actually picture her building. It was across from Ruby's, up the street from Atwood's, their favorite island restaurant.

The phone rang and rang. He checked his watch: eight-thirty. He counted twenty rings, and then he saw Tisa coming toward him.

"Tell him I'll call back tomorrow," he said into the ringing phone for Tisa's benefit. "Thank you."

"All done?" she asked as he replaced the receiver.

"I told you it would be quick," Matt said. Then, lightly touching the small of her back, he escorted Tisa into the Starlight Ballroom at the Waldorf-Astoria.

.   .   .

T HOMAS and Ned Devlin spent Ned's first two nights on the island together, just the two of them: steaks on the grill, along with hours of conversation and plans for Ned's future the first night, a night in town for pizza, beer, and pool the second.

Ned beat Thomas two straight games, and then they returned to their table to polish off the Last Call Saloon's Famous Anchovy and Extra Extra Garlic Pizza. Extra Large.

"I send you to the best prep school money can buy, and they teach you to hustle pool," Thomas Devlin said.

"Yeah, they call me 'Hialeah.' "

"Seriously?"

"Yeah."

"Do you take their money?"

"I'll put it this way. I haven't had to buy my own lunch off campus all year."

"Well, well," Thomas said admiringly. Ned never ceased to surprise him. Sometimes he seemed so absurdly young and innocent, you'd never suspect him of turning into a first-rate pool player. Thomas knew pool; he'd practically grown up in a Dorchester pool hall. It's where he had first met firefighters, and he associated the game with respect for the men. It was good to know his son could play as well.

"You're a little rusty," Ned said, drinking his beer. Narragansett, on draft. Bobby, the bartender, knew that Ned was underage, but whenever Ned came in with his father, Bobby would give him two glasses on the house.

"I don't play much anymore."

"You should. You're the best."

Thomas Devlin shrugged. "Too many other things to do."

"I know what you mean," Ned said wisely, in such a man-to-man tone that Thomas had to smile.

"It's nearly time to start the vegetable garden," Thomas said. "I started some tomatoes from seed, down in the basement, and I've got a big order coming on a boat next week. Lots of spicy stuff this year. Jalapeños, cherry peppers, broccoli rabe, a new purple basil."

"Pumpkins?"

"Of course."

"Gardening'll keep you busy," Ned said.

"It sure will," Thomas agreed, signaling Bobby for two more beers.

"I was wondering. . . ." Ned said.

"Anything you want to know about pool or vegetables, I'm your man," Thomas said.

"Actually," Ned said, "I was wondering whose toothbrush that is. The blue one, all wrapped in a washcloth in the back of the medicine cabinet."

"Oh, boy," Thomas said.

The day of Ned's arrival, Thomas had straightened up the house, hiding all evidence of Anne. It wasn't that he intended to keep her a secret; he just wanted to break it to Ned slowly. After Ned had been home for a few days, four or five, Thomas had planned to mention casually that he had a good friend named Anne, and how would Ned feel about having her over for dinner?

"Is she nice?" Ned asked.

"Very."

"She's the one you were thinking about when we toured the colleges?"

"How could you tell?" Thomas asked, stunned.

"Dad, I'm not blind. There's nothing but hormones gone rampant at Deerfield—I know the signs."

"I was planning to tell you, Ned."

"Yeah, I know. I've felt bad for you. You've been so nervous. So, what's she like?"

"Her name is Anne Davis. She's very beautiful, and kind. She's been through as much as we have." He paused. "I love her."

Ned nodded, playing with the salt-and-pepper shakers, taking in the news. Maybe Thomas should have held back that last part; maybe it was too much for Ned to handle. He scrutinized his son for a reaction.

"No one could ever take your mother's place, you know that," Thomas said. "I wouldn't want anyone to."

"Mmmm."

"Anne's very different from your mother."

"Like how?"

"Well, she's small, for one thing," he said, thinking of Sarah. Sarah had been nearly six feet tall, a magnificent athlete. She had skied in the Olympics, and Thomas could see her now, schussing the chute at Mad River Glen. Then, later, taking it easier (although not much) with Ned in a pack on her back.

"And Anne's pretty quiet," Thomas said.

"Mom wasn't quiet," Ned said, chuckling.

"You can say that again," Thomas said, wishing Ned would laugh a little harder. Ned's laugh was a direct echo of Sarah's. Sarah had loved to sing and talk and laugh, often all at the same time. It was a lot like living with a perpetual pep talk: exhaustingly lovable.

"It's been nice," Thomas said, "having a friend."

"I'm glad."

"How about you?" Thomas asked, thinking maybe Ned wanted to steer them off the topic. "Do you have any special girl?"

"No."

"Ah. Well, you will. I have no doubt about that."

"When do I get to meet her?" Ned asked after a moment.

"How about dinner tomorrow night?"

Ned seemed to consider this. Thomas couldn't quite read his face. There was a definite frown. His brows were knit, his mouth slightly downturned. But Thomas would have to call the expression thoughtful, pensive, rather than angry.

"We should make black-bean burritos," Ned said. "With that green salsa."

"I'm not sure we can get cilantro at such short notice. We usually have to give the market a head start on special stuff like that."

"Can you grow cilantro?"

"Sure," Thomas Devlin said, flushing with love and gratitude for his incredible son. "I'll add it to the list for next week."

"We should do fire nachos," Ned said. "With double jalapeños. Does she like hot food?"

"I think so," Thomas Devlin replied, although actually he was unsure.

"She'd better," Ned said. "The true test."

ANNE arrived at the appointed hour, ready for dinner. Parking her car, she took her time. She watched the house for signs of someone curiously peeking out, and she thought she saw a shadow fall across the kitchen window.

It had been a very long time since she had dressed so carefully for an evening. She had tried on and decided against black suede pants, a denim skirt, her oldest jeans and a sweatshirt, and a Putamayo black-and-white print dress. Instead, she wore newish black Gap jeans, a chambray shirt, and a tweed jacket. She recognized that she had chosen clothes that would be nonthreatening, but relatively attractive, to a teenage boy.

Gathering up the things she had brought the Devlins to go with dinner, she took a deep breath and headed up the sidewalk.

Thomas opened the door before she could knock.

Anne sensed the awkwardness of the moment. She wanted to embrace him, as she always did when arriving, but she held back. She didn't want to step on Ned's toes. Thomas stood on the doorstep, towering over her. She came up to about his waist. Their eyes, too busy darting around for Ned, hardly met. Thomas leaned down for a ridiculous nose-bumping kiss, and finally they laughed.

They'd caught each other in the act of overthinking the game. "Hi," he said.

"Hi," she said, handing him the bag.

"What have we here?" he asked, peering inside. But the moment of discovery was short-circuited as Ned entered the room.

Even if Maggie hadn't pointed him out on the ferry the other day, Anne would have recognized him instantly. From looking through the photo albums, she saw his resemblance to both his parents. His eyes and mouth were the same shape, and had the same far-off Irish sadness, as Thomas's. But when he smiled, as he did now, his face took on the look of Sarah.

"Ned," Thomas said, clapping his son on the back. "I'd like you to meet Anne Davis,"

"It's a pleasure to meet you," Anne said, shaking his hand.

He didn't say anything right away. He was too busy blushing and figuring out his handshake. It started off bone crushing, faded out, and came back just right.

"I saw you on the ferry," Ned said, a bundle of high color and twitches. Anne could tell he was shy, that it took great effort to look her in the eye, as he'd been taught.

"I saw you, too. Maggie Vincent's my niece."

"Oh." If anything, his color increased.

"Maggie and Ned were beach pals," Thomas said. "Back before he went to school off-island."

"Yeah," Ned said, frowning.

"She's something, that Maggie," Anne said, trying to feel her way along. Everyone felt so awkward, each person trying to make sure every other person felt comfortable.

"Is she a junior?" Ned asked.

"Yes. A year behind you," Anne said, letting him know that she knew about him. That she and his father had discussed him.

"College next year," Thomas said, smiting Ned's upper arm.

"Yeah."

"Congratulations on Dartmouth," Anne said. "I hear all the colleges want you."

This prompted a new round of blushes. Ned tried to frown, but he couldn't help smiling.

"Thanks," he said.

"Hell, what kind of hosts are we?" Thomas asked. "Anne, can we take your jacket? Would you care for a beer? A glass of wine?"

Anne slipped off her jacket, feeling Thomas touch her shoulder blades as he took it. She shivered, and smiled.

"Whatever you guys are having," she said.

"Beer," Thomas and Ned said at once.

"Great," she said, grinning.

They went into the kitchen, and Anne stood aside while the men prepared dinner. Ned seemed very mysterious as he popped a cookie sheet into the oven, shielding its contents from Anne's sight. The aroma of simmering black beans filled the room, and she watched Thomas assemble burritos. Sipping from a bottle of Dos Equis, she enjoyed the musky flavor of Mexico while being waited on by the two Devlin men.

After a few minutes a timer rang.

Ned pulled the cookie sheet out of the oven. He transferred nachos, sticky with melted cheese, to a serving plate, and set out a bowl of chilled salsa. He glanced at Anne, and she caught a devilish little smile.

"That smells delicious," she said.

"Please, help yourself," Ned said, passing her the plate.

Anne ate one nacho in two eager bites. Fire from the jalapeños shot down her throat and up her nose, but she loved the flavor. She took a sip of beer.

"Do you like it?" Ned asked.

"Oh, yes," Anne said, reaching for the bag she had carried in from the car. "I hope you won't be offended, but they're just a little mild for me. Would you mind if I added a few of these?"

Ned pulled the jar out of the bag: General Estada's Four Alarm Mouth-Burners, aka Chili Peppers, Eat Them If You Dare. Ned glanced up, puzzled, then caught the smile on Anne's face.

"You like hot food," he said.

"Love it."

He nodded, smiling.

When Thomas had warned her that dinner would be spicy, she had told him one of the three things she missed about New York City was the availability of super-hot food. New England did many things right, but south-of-the-border wasn't one of them.

Ned opened the jar and lifted a Mouth-Burner into the air. He dangled it over his open mouth, made sure Anne was watching, and popped it in. He shuddered, as if he'd just done a shot of tequila. Then, an obvious challenge, he handed the jar to Anne.

She looked him square in the eye, took a long drink of beer. She reached into the jar.

The pepper juice stung her fingertips. On contact with one cracked cuticle, it made her feel like shouting out loud.

"Go for it," Ned said.

Anne nodded. She shook the extra juice off a Mouth-Burner, licked it once, and swallowed it down.

"Wow," Thomas said.

Anne couldn't see through the flames. She daintily sipped her Dos Equis, wiped her mouth with the back of her hand. She wondered whether she had just killed all the nerve endings in her lips, but she smiled anyway.

So did Ned. So did Thomas. The night was underway.

For dinner, Thomas brought out lanterns Ned had made over the years. Most were shaped vaguely like coffee cans. Several were ceramic, swirls of clay forming van Goghlike patterns, with space for candlelight, coated with glossy black, blue, and silver glaze. Others were made of metal, with punched-out perforations through which the candle flames shone.

Ned made sure Anne had enough salsa, sour cream, and Mouth-Burners. He brought new beer when bottles were emptied. Anne asked him about Dartmouth, and he told her all about its English department, the hockey team, winter carnival, the medical school.

"Do you want to be a doctor?" she asked.

"I think so," he said.

"Really?" Thomas asked, and from the surprise in his tone, Anne could tell that this was the first time he'd heard it.

Anne waited, eating the delicious dinner they had made. She listened while Ned told about reading William Carlos Williams in English, thinking he'd like to be a doctor *and* a poet.

"Ned's a real poet," Thomas said to Anne.

"I know," she said, wondering whether she should say that Thomas had shown her Ned's poems, that they were some of the most beautiful words she had ever read.

"Anyway," Ned said, scowling again.

"Enough about you?" Thomas asked.

"Yeah."

"This is a great dinner," Anne said. "I haven't had food this good since I came back to the island."

"Where'd you live before?" Ned asked.

"New York," Anne replied. Thomas had told her that he'd said almost nothing to Ned, that he'd wanted Ned to find things out for himself.

"This must be a pretty big change," Ned said.

"Well, I grew up on the island."

"Still, New York is awesome." He smiled at his father.

"Ned and I saw *Tommy* in New York last Christmas," Thomas said. "Our first time there together in a long, long time."

"The time before was with Mom," Ned said.

"Right," Thomas said.

"We had lunch at Rockefeller Center," Ned said. "At that

restaurant right on the ice. It was Christmas then, too. The tree—"

"Did you skate?" Anne asked.

"Yeah. Mom and I."

"That must have been nice," she said, thinking that this was the winter she had been planning to take Karen ice-skating at Rockefeller Center. She, Matt, and Karen—three years old—had had lunch at the same tourist restaurant that Ned remembered, and it had been one of the high points of Karen's life. She had never stopped talking about it. The memory made Anne feel very close to Ned.

"So," Ned said, "how did you meet?"

"Meet?" Anne asked, still thinking of Karen.

"You and Dad."

"Well, we—" Thomas began.

"He saved me," Anne said. "My family's house was on fire. He pulled me out."

"He saved you from a fire," Ned said, staring at Anne. His words were a statement, with hard edges, and they made her uncomfortable. Just then he blushed and looked away, and she realized what must be going through his mind.

"Ned, I'm a fireman," Thomas said, his voice deep and steady.

"I know."

"What's the problem?"

"Nothing."

Ned shuffled a few plates together and carried them into the kitchen.

"I'm sorry," Anne said.

"Don't be. It's the truth. He has to know." Thomas covered her hand with his.

They sat at the table, watching the lanterns flicker, listening to Ned in the kitchen banging the plates louder than necessary.

"Maybe you should have told him before," Anne said.

"I honestly didn't think about the parallel," Thomas said

blankly. "It's what I've done for a living. I try to pull people out of burning buildings."

"I know," Anne said, giving his hand a squeeze.

They heard Ned leave the kitchen, walk down the hall. The water ran in the bathroom; they heard music coming from his room.

When he returned, he seemed as awkward, as uncomfortable, as when Anne had first arrived. He shuffled his feet and didn't want to meet her eyes.

"Dad, can I borrow the truck?" he asked.

"Sure, Ned."

"Thanks." He turned to Anne. "It was nice meeting you," he said.

"You, too. And thank you for dinner."

"You're welcome," he said, his expression sad and distant.

Anne waited until she heard the truck start before she said anything to Thomas. The engine caught and revved. Ned drove down the road.

"I'm sorry for telling him you saved me," Anne said.

"I did," he said, holding her tight.

"He's thinking of his mother."

"I know."

Anne felt Thomas's arms loosen around her. He walked to the window, to watch the taillights disappear down the road.

"I'm sorry," Anne said again, feeling empty.

"We can't change the past," Thomas said, staring into the distance, and Anne heard the emptiness echo in his voice as well.

N ED sped cross-island with no destination planned. In his mind, he replayed the last goal he'd made against Exeter. He saw it from the ice, he saw it from the stands, he saw it on national television with himself as commentator. His lips still sizzled from the Mouth-Burners, and he licked them, thinking of dinner.

Of his father and Anne.

Kids at school had stepmothers. That's the first thing he'd thought, the minute his father had admitted he had a girlfriend. Ned had steeled himself, prepared to meet anyone.

Mark's stepmother had turned Mark's bedroom into an office. Stephano's stepmother had brought her twelve-year-old son into the family and let him play with Stephano's Matchboxes, Tonka trucks, and remote-control speedboats. Jane's stepmother had enticed Jane's father to move to London, away from Jane in boarding school in Connecticut.

So, prepared to meet a typical stepmother type, Ned had been amazed by Anne.

Anne had seemed sweet, funny, easy to talk to. She liked hot food, and she'd made a good joke of it. She obviously liked Ned's father, and Ned had to admit, he thought she liked him, too.

So, why was he shaking? His entire body, every nerve under his skin. His teeth were chattering. Driving his father's truck, he tossed his head, to throw the coldness.

Why did his father have to meet Anne at a fire? He had had years of nightmares about flames, and he squinted, dispelling them now. He turned on the radio. The stations you could get out here were squat. He fiddled with the dial, trying to find something decent.

Why was his father able to save Anne, and not his mother? Just one of those things, Ned told himself.

He found WBRU, the Brown University FM station. An old Talking Heads song, a favorite of his parents, blared out of the speakers. He drove toward town, blocking his father, his mother, and Anne from his mind. He was on vacation. It was Tuesday night, and he didn't have to get up early the next day.

Chapter 13

On Friday night, while Anne was waiting for Thomas and Ned to pick her up for a movie, the telephone rang.

"Hello?"

"Hi, Anne," Matt said.

"Hi," she said, trying to sound steady.

"We haven't talked in a long time."

She didn't speak, waiting for him to continue. The sound of his voice was familiar, alien, infuriating, and endearing, all at once.

"Don't you think we should talk, Anne?"

"Do you have something to tell me?" Suddenly she felt positive that he was going to say he wanted a divorce.

"Lots of things. How are you?"

"I'm fine."

"I've left you alone, because you've made it clear that's what you wanted. But it's gone on long enough. We have a lot to talk about."

"You're right. I've been meaning to call you about the apartment. We should do something about it. Sell it, or rent it out. Unless you want to live there."

"How can you say that? We love that place. It's where we were a family."

"Were," Anne said, emphasizing the word. She had a piercing vision of the apartment, with all of them in it, and she pressed the heel of her hand into her forehead.

"Do you want it this way?" Matt said. "Living apart?"

"If you had asked me that one year ago, I would have said it was impossible. I would have said that I couldn't imagine life without you."

"I made a terrible mistake," Matt said. "And I've continued to make it by not asking you to forgive me, to take me back. Right after Karen died, I wasn't thinking at all. That's when I should have begged you to let me help you put things back together. Put *us* back together, Anne."

"But you didn't, Matt. I've been doing it alone, but I am doing it."

"Doing what?"

"Deciding to live."

"You don't just decide a thing like that," Matt said. "You might decide where you want to live, or who you want to be with. But you don't just decide *to* live."

"Oh, yes you do," Anne said. "That's what happened when I came out to the island. I saved my own life."

"Anne, please."

"You think it's bullshit?" she asked, her voice rising. "I wanted to be with Karen so badly. I wanted to follow her."

"Why didn't you come to me?" he asked.

In spite of the agony in his voice, Anne heard herself laugh. "Why didn't you come to me? Didn't you feel it yourself?"

"It was the most horrible time of my life," Matt said.

"Well, you had Tisa to help you through."

"If you're saying that Tisa makes up for losing Karen—"

"No!" Anne screamed. "I'm not saying that at all. Nothing, no other person could make up for her."

Matt's hard breathing came through the wire. Anne held the receiver in her lap for a moment, because she couldn't bear to listen. She already regretted her outburst.

"I'm sorry," he was saying when she put the phone to her ear.

"I'm sorry, too."

"You're getting some help through it?"

"My family's been great. And friends."

"One friend in particular, I hear."

"Yes," she said slowly, wondering who had told him. Gabrielle? Not that it mattered.

"Don't get involved, Anne. Please come back to me. Please? I want us to start over. I want us to fall in love again, resurrect what we had. Weren't we great?"

"I thought so," Anne said furiously.

"I want us to have another baby."

"No," Anne said, and she felt fingers of ice up and down her back. The night was shattered. "I have to go."

"Please . . ."

"Good-bye," she said, and she hung up the phone.

Fifteen minutes later, when she heard the knock on the door, she felt glad that Thomas and Ned were a little late. She had had a chance to compose herself. She'd caught her breath, washed her face, put on some fresh mascara. She'd swallowed down half a cognac while gazing at Karen's drawing. Now her hands were steady, her facial expressions under control.

But when she opened the door and saw Thomas standing there alone, she wanted to dissolve.

"What is it?" he asked when he saw her face.

"Ned didn't come?"

"He wanted to go out with Josh Hunter and some of his old friends. You know, it's Friday night," Thomas said with alert worry in his eyes. "Are you upset he didn't come?"

Anne shrugged, even as she shook her head.

"Tell me," he said.

"I don't know why people have kids," she said coldly, walking away from him. She stood by the front window, shivering as if she felt a great chill. She stared at the ferry docking, thinking of what Matt had said about another baby.

"Yes, you do."

She gave him a hard, punishing look, for daring to question what she did or did not mean. She felt very close to a dangerous edge, and she could see he knew it.

"Okay. Explain to me," he said.

She didn't feel like explaining anything. But she forced herself to try to be civil. She was in a rage at Matt and the imaginary baby, not at Thomas.

"Before Karen . . . well, when she was a baby, I'd go crazy worrying about things that could happen to her. I'd worry that someone would snatch her away from me, and I'd never see her again."

"Anne—"

"Those cartons of milk? With pictures of missing children on them? I'd have nightmares of them. I always bought plastic bottles of milk so I wouldn't have to see. Once Matt brought home a carton with the picture of a little girl, nine years old, missing since the spring before, and I threw it away. I couldn't even open it, have it in my house."

"Everything good in life comes with risks."

"It's not worth it," Anne said. Still looking out the window, she felt him hold her shoulders from behind.

"Would you trade the time you had with her?" Thomas asked. "To never have known her at all?"

"Yes," Anne whispered. "I wish I'd never had her."

"Anne," he said, rocking against her body.

Tears splashed out of her eyes, onto his hands folded across her upper chest.

"I know you don't wish that," he said.

"I do. I don't know how people do it. Before you have them, you have no idea. And then, you love them so much. You just want to protect them, and you know you'd die for them."

"Yes, you would."

"When something happens . . . when they die . . . it's like having a part of your body ripped right out. It's like you're being eaten alive. And it never ends. It just goes on, until you finally do die."

"You're going to heal," Thomas said. "I've seen it happening, with my own two eyes. Yes, you have days like this. You probably will forever. But I've seen you happy."

Even as she shook her head she knew it was true. But when these raw feelings of missing Karen came upon her, it felt as if they'd never go away.

"Come on," Thomas said softly, guiding her away from the window. "Show me *Paradise*."

Anne went to her bag and removed the cardboard folder she had made to hold the drawing. Together she and Thomas sat on the sofa, staring at the picture. It amazed Anne that even now, the drawing could bring Karen back as nothing else could. Holding it in her hands, she could almost believe that Karen was playing in another room, under this very roof. She felt herself becoming calmer, moving away from the edge.

"If there hadn't been a Karen," Thomas said in a gentle voice, sliding his arm around Anne, "you wouldn't have *Paradise*."

"Those white boxes," Anne said, almost hypnotized by the picture's power. "I've tried and tried to think of what they could be. How could I now know?" She looked into Thomas's eyes, as if somehow he had the answer.

"Maybe they're rocks," he said. "Or maybe they're just interesting shapes."

"Sandcastles," Anne said, thinking of her latest collage in the *Heaven* series.

"What happened tonight?" Thomas asked. "To get you feeling so terrible? Is it because Ned didn't come? Did that hurt your feelings?"

"No," she said. "I can understand. I make him uncomfortable."

"He just has to get used to the idea of me with someone. I've been alone for so long, he probably feels a little rivalry with you."

Anne gave him a sweet, sad smile. She had quite a different idea, but she decided to hold it back.

"He'll come around," Thomas said, almost mantralike, as if he was trying to convince himself. "So, if it wasn't Ned, what made you so upset?"

"Matt called," Anne said. "He says he wants to get back together with me."

"Who wouldn't?" Thomas asked, holding her closer.

Anne tilted her face up to kiss him. Holding his cheeks between her hands, she tried to put all thoughts of Matt out of her mind.

"We're going to be late for the movie," Thomas said after a moment.

"No movie," Anne said. "Make love to me, Thomas," she said.

AFTER about an hour of driving around the island, trying to decide whether they should go shoot pool at the Saloon or head for a party at Pirates' Cave, Ned and Josh still couldn't make up their minds. Bobby wouldn't serve them beer without one of their fathers there, so strike one against the Saloon. There would be a keg at the cave, but lately the cops had been busting parties and booking everyone who was underage.

In other words, everyone.

"The island sucks," Josh said. "There's nowhere to go."

"I know. I couldn't wait to get out here for vacation, and now I can't wait to go back to school."

"Thanks, man."

"Hey, not you. I'm just agreeing with you—there's nothing to do out here."

Josh was driving his family's rusty old Ford Taurus, the front bumper held on by wire. Ned listened to the engine, to a sticky valve, and wondered why Josh hadn't fixed it. Josh was a really good mechanic. When they were kids, Josh had always wanted his bike to be perfect. He was constantly giving it tune-ups. He'd even made a special stand so he could work on it in the garage. So now it didn't make sense that he'd let the family car fall apart. People who stayed too long on the island went mushy, lost their motivation.

"Anyway, next year it'll be a whole different ball game," Ned said. "You'll come to Dartmouth on weekends, I'll visit you at URI."

"I'll come to Dartmouth," Josh said. "But I'm not going to URI."

"What?"

"My dad's making me a partner. He's signing half the boat over to me."

"You're going to lobster?" Ned asked, stunned.

"Yeah. Listen, he pulls in good money. I never realized *how* good until he started telling me about the partnership."

"College isn't about money," Ned said. "I thought you wanted to get off the island."

"It'll just be for a few years."

"Right," Ned said. Jesus, he couldn't believe it. He and Josh were going to go out into the world, break off the island, find their dreams. Instead, Josh was finding quicksand. He was driving a rust bucket on land, and soon he'd be driving one at sea.

It's so bizarre, Ned thought. Certain people, like his father, came to the island looking for hope. They had lost their faith, or their heart's desire, and they came out here in search of whatever it was. He thought of Anne, then pushed her from his mind.

But for some people, the island was a trap. It sucked the souls out of people, drained them of the very hope the others had come here to seek. Ned couldn't look at Josh. He was afraid he'd see nothing but a shadow.

"Here's Pirates' Cave. What do you say?" Josh asked.

"Fine," Ned said.

They parked in the sandy lot with ten or so cars. Following the bonfire's reflections, they crossed the beach. The cave was an island oddity, carved into the face of a tall, craggy cliff. Formed of red clay and reinforced, so the story went, by granite hauled across from the mainland by pirates, it burrowed twenty feet into the hill.

Waves crashed, spraying Ned's face with foam. He licked salt from his lips, as the beat of Nirvana pounded from the speakers of someone's 4x4. Parked at the mouth of the cave, the Jeep guarded a keg wedged into the sand behind its left rear tire. Ned drew himself a beer.

Josh seemed glad to see his friends. He headed right between the Jeep and the fire into the cave, into the midst of kids Ned hadn't seen for a long time. Suddenly Ned felt out of place, and angry. He wished he hadn't come to the island at all.

He stood by the Jeep, staring into space. The bonfire threw dancing shadows on the water, skidding across the wave tops, turning the spray into fireworks.

"Ned Devlin," someone said, and Ned turned around.

It was Maggie Vincent, pouring herself a beer.

"Hi," he said.

"What are you doing out here?"

"I came with Josh," Ned said defensively. Was it that obvious that he didn't fit in?

"I meant on the island. Don't you go to boarding school or something?"

"Oh. Yeah—I'm on vacation."

"That's lucky." Maggie sipped some beer, licking off a foam mustache. She was as pretty as ever, if you didn't count all her

pierced earrings: hoops, studs, daggers, dice. Now that Ned had
met her aunt, he could really see a resemblance. Great big eyes, a
pretty mouth with a hidden smile.

"You're a junior now?" Ned asked.

"Yep. One more year after this, and I'm out of here."

"Where do you want to go?"

"College," she said with a funny defiance, as if she expected to
be challenged.

"I meant which college?"

"I haven't decided. I take my SATs tomorrow." She giggled. "I
suppose the grades I get will help me make up my mind. How
about you? Do you know where you're going yet?"

Ned was about to answer when Kurt stepped out of the cave.
He glared at Ned, and Ned glared back. Evil stares at twenty paces,
Ned thought. What a jerk.

Maggie just about leaped away from Ned. But when she
reached Kurt, he turned his back. She followed him into the cave.

God, Ned hated guys like Kurt, who turned their girlfriends
into puppies. Assholes who probably didn't even care for the girl.
He knew some at Deerfield. They'd go to a dance somewhere like
Miss Porter's, and meet a girl. They'd turn on the charm, act all
sweet and sensitive, and exchange addresses with the girl. They'd
write back and forth a few times. They'd get together at a dance,
or a football game, or meet in New York or Boston on vacation.
They'd sleep with her.

With guys like that, sex always changed things. Suddenly it
would be the girl doing all the letter writing. You'd see about a
hundred messages from her at the bell desk. She'd send care pack-
ages. She'd try to befriend the guy's friends, hoping for information to help her understand what was going on.

God, it was really pathetic.

Ned wandered into the cave, looking for Josh. The smell of pot
was strong in the air. People had flashlights and candles, but you
couldn't really see too much. Ned kept bumping into people and

getting dirty looks. He must have said "Excuse me" a hundred times, and he felt like a clumsy jerk who didn't have one friend among these kids he'd grown up with.

His throat closed up, from the smoke and a lonely feeling deep inside. No one, not even Josh, was talking to Ned. He'd expected his vacation to be fantastic. As a kid, he'd always been too shy, not popular, bigger than anyone else. Kids had called him "gawk." But coming home this time, he'd felt so proud of his acceptance to Dartmouth, he had thought that somehow things would change. That all of a sudden people would start to see him for who he really was.

He'd been feeling down ever since dinner with his father and Anne. He felt disappointed in himself for not being able to accept her. She'd seemed really nice; his father obviously loved her. His father had an almost embarrassing sparkle on the entire time he was around her. That was hard for Ned to take. His father's demeanor, and the stuff about the fire.

Moving through the cave, Ned suddenly caught sight of Maggie and Kurt. They were arguing. Kurt was stone-faced, giving Maggie a sneer of disdain while she clutched his arm, obviously trying to convince him of something. When Kurt shook her off, Maggie headed for the mouth of the cave. Ned followed.

The sea air hit him in the face, and it felt great. Breathing deeply, he watched Maggie head straight for the keg.

"You shouldn't be drinking any more of that if you have SATs tomorrow," Ned said.

"What the hell?" Maggie said, tension making her voice thin. "I probably shouldn't even bother taking them."

"Is that what Kurt says?"

Maggie filled her glass, as if she hadn't heard him.

"As a matter of fact, it doesn't bother him one way or the other," Maggie said. She held the big plastic cup with both hands, not drinking from it.

Don't you wish it did? Ned wanted to ask. *Don't you wish he'd want you to do well?* Ned had come to the island as an outsider, in second grade. His father had sent him away to Deerfield, to remove him from the tempting island mind-set: don't bother trying, because you'll never get away anyway.

"What time is the test?" Ned asked.

"Nine."

Ned checked his watch: midnight.

"If you go home now, you'll still get a pretty good night's sleep."

"I don't have a car, and Kurt wants to stay."

Ned wished that he had driven his father's truck, but his father had wanted to take Anne to the movies. For ten seconds he considered asking Josh if her could borrow the Taurus to drive Maggie home, but with his luck the heap would fall apart before they reached the main road.

"I'll walk you home," Ned said.

"It's about three miles to my house," Maggie said.

"Three miles? That's nothing. It'll make you good and tired, and you'll fall straight to sleep."

Maggie took one long look at the mouth of the cave, as if she was trying to make up her mind. Flashlight beams and candle flames flickered eerily. Porno for Pyros had replaced Nirvana, and kids were dancing.

Maggie poured her full beer into the sand. Then, wordlessly, she and Ned headed down the beach, to the hard sand by the water's edge. Making their way, they listened to the waves breaking. They'd walk a mile or so on the beach, then scramble up a dune and head cross-island by road. Maggie would be home within the hour.

Chapter 14

Relearning life, Anne discovered, was not without its setbacks. Ned's resistance and Matt's insistence had hit her hard, and she found herself holed up at her worktable, spending hours every day trying to capture *Heaven*.

Her callused fingers ached from the scissors' pressure. Her eyes stung from the close work. She was blocking out real life, inhabiting a twilight world of fantasy and collage. She'd cut the tiny bits of paper, move them around like parts of a puzzle. Presently they would form one aspect of Anne's vision of heaven, and she would fix them to the paper with glue.

The cherubs, womb, sandcastle, Karen's profile, the ferry decorated for Christmas, a box of crayons.

She left her new message machine on all the time. She and Thomas had gone too far too fast. Anne wasn't ready for the closeness he had come to expect. Her last conversation with Matt had proved it: you don't just walk out of marriage into someone else's arms without a lot of thought.

Just look at Thomas and Ned: Ned's reaction showed that the

ties of family counted a whole lot more than a winter's worth of
sweet feelings between two strangers. Anne found herself making
a collage of Thomas's cottage in the snow, but she set it aside.
That picture didn't fit with the rest of her series.

"Please, pick up the phone," Thomas's voice would come off
the answering machine. "You're there, I know it. Please talk to
me."

Then, later, he spoke more harshly. "Why are you doing this?
Do you feel guilty because we were too happy?"

Warily, hearing his message, she answered the phone, stopping
the broadcast.

"I'm working," she said. "That's all. I'm concentrating on my
work."

"You're acting so cold," he said. "As if you've gone underground."

That sounded right, Anne thought: underground. She'd shut
herself up with her stamps and scissors and her quest for heaven,
and she wasn't letting in much earthly air or light.

"I'm sorry," she said. "But I have to do this for now."

"You're not a coward, Anne," he said sadly. "But you're acting
like one. You let a seventeen-year-old boy get under your skin and
break us apart."

"It's not Ned," Anne said, wondering at his use of the word
"us." Because in spite of her ties to Matt, something vivid and
true had been happening with Thomas. It might not be family,
but they had made an "us."

"Just do me a favor," Thomas said. "Don't keep leaving me to
your machine. Talk to me once in a while."

"I will," Anne said, hating and not understanding how guilty
she felt.

AND with the island's high season approaching, Anne got a
callback from one of the jobs she'd applied for back in March.
She'd be secretary for one of the whale-watching operations, just

down the street from her apartment. The owners were island newcomers, and they didn't care anything about Anne as long as she could use a word processor, handle the phones, and keep track of reservations.

Making collage was dream work, and Anne knew she needed to wake up. Pure survival instincts made her accept the job. She needed to get out of her apartment, out of her own head. Her collages were heavens of the past; the apartment had started feeling airless and murky, a trap.

WHALES ARE WAITING! proclaimed the banner over the door to her new office. The background was white sailcloth stitched with royal-blue letters, and a chubby turquoise whale with a smile like the Pillsbury doughboy, spouting a geyser of gold dust. Subtle.

She used her key to let herself in. First, she played back the messages on the answering machine. Memorial Day weekend was just about a month away, and reservations were pouring in from everywhere. Washington, DC; Hartford, CT; Winnetka, IL; Tucson, AZ; Kansas City, MO; Reno, NE; Iowa City, IA.

Out of her lonely life, into the mainstream.

Everyone wanted to see the whales, to feel the awesome surge you'd get from seeing a great humpback whale breach the ocean's surface. The company was called WhaleRush, Ltd., and the owners made no bones about the fact that they were playing on sex.

"Whales love each other," Sam Crichton, the owner, told Anne. Sam and his wife, Lori, were oceanographers trained at Woods Hole and Scipps, and they'd found a way to parlay their expertise and love of whales into cash. "Whales have courtships, marriages, heartbreaks. They sing to each other. When they're happy, they zoom into the air at sixty miles an hour just to tell the world they're in love. We hang aquaphones over the side, and we pick up these songs, so beautiful and heartsick you'd swear it was Roy Orbison himself. People eat it right up."

They sure did. Anne took down reservation after reservation, from people who wanted to see the whales. Then she got the following message:

"Are you avoiding me? Meet me for lunch at Ruby's at twelve-thirty, and I'll forgive you."

Gabrielle.

Anne rolled her eyes. She considered calling her sister to tell her that she would be too busy to have lunch today. She didn't feel like seeing anyone. Thomas's phone call was sticking with her, making her face some hard facts.

She typed out letters of confirmation to the people who had called. A travel agent called to ask whether WhaleRush gave volume discounts, and Anne told her it was company policy to do so only after fifty paid-in-full bookings. Robin Drexel, the woman who owned the stationery shop next door, stopped by to see if Anne could convince the Crichtons to consider ordering from her instead of the wholesale stationers they used in Boston.

At twelve-thirty she taped a "Back at One" sign to the door and headed down to Ruby's.

Gabrielle occupied a booth halfway down the room, on the right. Her arm shot up upon sight of Anne.

"How's work?" she asked as Anne slid into her seat.

"I like it."

"The chowder's great here. So is the clam hash."

"I'll have clam chowder," Anne said to the waitress.

"Chowder. And a BLT," Gabrielle said. Then she focused on Anne. "Will you please tell me what's going on? Why haven't I seen you for I-don't-know-how-long?"

"New job, spring, I don't know."

"You're mad at me."

A silence fell over the table as the waitress delivered Gabrielle's chowder.

"Yes, I am," Anne said when the waitress was gone. "What makes you think it's okay to tell Matt I'm seeing someone?"

"Because he cares." Gabrielle stared at Anne with amazing intensity, ignoring her soup.

"What does that have to do with anything? Don't I have a right to privacy?"

"You are still his wife."

"God, I sometimes forget how puritanical this place is. Yes, I still have the marriage license, but no, Gabrielle: we are not still married. Not in any way that counts."

"Tell me you don't love him."

Anne shook her head hard, to show how stupid she thought her sister was acting.

"Tell me."

"You don't just stop loving someone," Anne said slowly, with deliberation. "But that doesn't mean the marriage is solid. I do love Matt. I always will. But I don't ever want to think of him as my husband again. Got that?"

"You don't mean that."

"And I don't want you telling him about me," Anne said.

"Anne, he's been my brother-in-law for more than ten years. He and I have a relationship, too."

"Then tell him about yourself. About Maggie, Steve. But don't discuss me and Thomas with him."

With Gabrielle's chowder untouched, the waitress brought the rest of their lunch. Anne dug right into hers.

"Well," Gabrielle said, rebuffed. She stared at her soup, as if she were too devastated to eat it. Anne refused to take pity on her.

"What does Steve say about the house?" Anne asked.

"It's almost ready."

"Just in time for summer."

"Are you sure you don't want to move back there?" Gabrielle asked, beginning to eat.

"Positive."

"You own two perfectly lovely places, and you choose to rent a tiny little apartment. I'm not criticizing," Gabrielle added, at Anne's look.

"I can't live in the past," Anne said. "I don't want constant reminders."

"Hearing you say that," Gabrielle said slowly, "makes me wonder."

"About what?"

"About whether that's the reason you don't want to try again with Matt. Because he's too much of a reminder."

"That's ridiculous."

Gabrielle hummed thoughtfully, as if she held all the secrets of the universe in her older-sister soul.

"I have a proposition to make," she said. "It has to do with the house."

"What?"

"That bed-and-breakfast idea I had," Gabrielle said, withdrawing several sheets of paper from her bag. "I really think I could make it work. I'd run it and pay myself a salary, but otherwise we'd split the profits fifty-fifty. I've called around, and people are getting a hundred dollars and more a night in high season."

"It's fine with me," Anne said. "But what about your catering business?"

"I'd just operate from over there. You know I love that kitchen."

"What would you call it? You can't exactly stick with the 'Big House.' "

"Why not? We could have a cute little jail theme. Handcuffs and manacles by the bed, striped pajamas." Gabrielle chuckled. "No, I was thinking of 'Fitzgibbons'."

"I like that," Anne said, nodding. "Sort of a tribute to Mother and Dad."

"Yes, that's what I've been thinking. Although they'd probably turn in their graves. They were so proud to own the bakery, to be 'prosperous Americans.' Prosperous! Anyway, at least they didn't have Irish dirt under their fingernails anymore. I don't think they'd take to the idea of opening the family homestead to paying strangers."

"Let's hope they never find out," Anne said.

"I thought I'd run a few ads before Memorial Day. In a few Sunday papers. You know those country-inn listings?"

"Won't that be expensive?"

"Honey, we'll make it up the first weekend."

"Sounds exciting."

"Well, if you get tired of the whale business, I'm sure we could create a position for you."

"Actually, I'll shill for Fitzgibbons'," Anne said. "I'll convince all the tourists to leave their hotels for the best guest house on the island, with breakfasts by the Seduction Table."

"Great," Gabrielle said, jotting it down. "I'll stick that in the ads." She looked up. "Are you still mad at me?"

"No."

"Why don't you and Thomas come to dinner some night soon? Next weekend?"

"I'll ask him. Thank you." That left her an out, Anne thought sadly. She could always say he wouldn't be able to make it, that he'd made other plans.

"You're welcome, my sweet," Gabrielle said, with the relieved air of a woman whose olive branch had just been accepted.

ANNE was coming for dinner and Thomas was in the garden, passing time. The earth was ready for planting. Each spadeful of dirt was dark and rich, free of big stones. Earthworms and wood bugs squiggled for cover while robins perched nearby, waiting for Thomas Devlin to go inside. He uncovered two carrots, a potato, and a trove of leeks left from last year. Not many things brought him more joy than gardening, but this year he readied his vegetable patch with a heavy heart.

Anne was pulling away from him. Her feelings for him were different, and he felt the shift as surely as he felt the change in seasons.

Since she had taken the new job, he'd heard nothing but forced cheer in her voice. She'd talk about the office, the customers, the Crichtons, with great enthusiasm. Nothing could please him more than knowing Anne had found satisfying work. But she was treating him like a stranger: reporting the facts of her day with the upbeat blankness of a weather forecaster.

No matter what she said, he dated the growing distance between them to Ned's visit. Certainly Ned's reaction to the circumstances of Thomas and Anne's first meeting was disturbing, but also understandable. Thomas had no doubt that Ned would get over it. More upsetting to him was feeling Anne withdraw from him.

In the months since he had known her, Thomas Devlin had found pure happiness. That Anne could love him had seemed to him a miracle. With half the skin on his body burned off, he knew how repulsive he looked. He had never expected to be touched by a woman again. He could not say that he had given up hope of it; since the fire that deformed him, he had simply ceased to consider the possibility.

But that night at Anne's apartment, when she had entered the bathroom and looked upon him without flinching, when she had touched his naked body, her soothing strokes so full of love and acceptance, Thomas Devlin had felt redeemed.

That he was the person she chose to tell about Karen had made him want to sweep her into his arms, into his home, and make her his wife. That's what he wanted more than anything: to marry her. From that cold winter's night, when he had pulled her from the fire, until now, his feelings for her had been building and growing.

When Thomas Devlin thought of Anne Davis, he knew that he had found his heart's desire.

Now, working his garden, he listened to the clocks in his workshop chime six o'clock. She would be arriving soon. He had
caught some flounder that morning, which he planned to serve
for dinner. But for some reason, as the dinner hour drew closer, he
felt less and less hungry.

He placed his tools inside the shed. Tomorrow he'd tune up the
lawn mower; he'd cut the grass over the weekend. It had gotten
shaggy in just the last few days. Daisies were blooming like crazy
this year.

On his way into the house, he picked a bunch. Sticking them in
a mason jar on the kitchen counter, he thought of how casual they
looked. Nothing special like roses or gladioli or tulips. They didn't
convey much of anything. They were too simple an offering to
indicate a fraction of the heart-pounding trepidation he was feeling right now.

Hearing Anne's car in the driveway, he had to force himself to
not head outside to greet her. For the first time since they'd gotten
together, he was holding himself back. He had so much to give
her, and he knew she wanted to push it away. He felt scared. She
knocked on the door, and reluctantly he went to answer it.

"Hi," she said, not quite meeting his eyes.

"Hi."

They stood in the living room, not saying anything. Thomas
stared at her, willing her to face him, to look into his eyes and see
all the love he had for her. But her gaze was focused downward.

"We'd better talk, huh?" he asked.

She nodded, and when she sat in the wingback chair, instead of
choosing the sofa or heading for the kitchen, Thomas's heart sank
further. It meant that she didn't want to be touched—either sitting side by side or crushed together in the cozy kitchen.

"I've been moving too fast," Anne said, finally able to look in
his direction.

"You have?"

"Yes. You swept me off my feet."

"I didn't try—" he said, frowning.

"I know. That's not what I'm saying. You were—are—wonderful. You came into my life, and I felt the world change. Just like that. You brought me hope, and light, and the most amazing love."

"I still feel it."

Anne glanced away, her eyes full of pain. "This is so hard," she said.

"It doesn't have to be."

"The thing is, by being with you I was ignoring a whole lot else. I'm still married, for one thing. My sister said that to me today, and I practically told her to go to hell. But the fact is, it's true."

"Do you want to go back to him?" Thomas asked, the hardest eight words he had ever spoken.

"No."

"Then, what?"

"This office job I have is incredible. It's so simple—little tasks I could have done in my sleep a year ago. Not like collage—there my dreams just carry me along. But the job takes all my concentration. It's like I was in a terrible accident, and I'm just learning how to walk again."

"I'd say that's pretty accurate."

"Seeing your son so upset really shook me up," Anne said. "It made me think that I'm not ready for this."

"'This'?"

"Us. It's too much for me right now, Thomas. I feel responsible for Ned. For how he feels about me, and for how that will come between you and him."

"He's just a kid. He'll adapt if we're patient and give him time."

"Ned's not the problem between us. I am," Anne said slowly, as if she was assessing how much she should say. "But Ned *is* having a hard time."

"It's just a silly rivalry."

Anne gave him a long, hot look. She was in the grip of some strange passion, but it wasn't love and it wasn't lust. The expression in her eyes was intense and dangerous, and it spooked Thomas Devlin as much as it excited him. But presently it passed, and she was again calm.

"I disagree with you," she said.

"Tell me your theory."

"He wishes the fire had killed me, not his mother."

Her words thudded in his brain as he tried to make sense of what she was saying.

"That's crazy," he said. "He knows it's not possible, a trade, whatever you want to call it, like that. The fires were years apart."

"Still, it's how he feels."

"What you're saying doesn't make logical sense."

"I didn't say there was anything logical about it. It's something he feels in his gut. I know, Thomas. Because every time I see a four-year-old . . . I would trade the life of that child to have Karen back." She paused.

"Anne—"

"I think that's how Ned feels about me, and I'd say it must be very hard for him, knowing that you don't feel the same."

"I don't," Thomas said.

"I know."

Thomas shrugged, tried to smile. His mouth felt set and grim, and his stomach was nervous.

"What are you telling me?" he asked.

"We have to stop seeing each other."

"Anne, don't say that. We can take it slow, if that's what you need. If you don't want to stay overnight with me, I'll accept that."

"I do want to, but I can't," she said in a measured tone, her obvious need for control his only clue that she was finding this as difficult as it was for him.

"And we can't take it slow," she said. "You must know that."

"Why can't we?"

"Because we know we're rockets."

That made him smile; he saw her try to smile back.

"This is wrong," he said. "You do know it's wrong."

"I'm sorry," she said, rising. "I'm not going to stay for dinner. It would be too . . ."

"Painful," Thomas said, and immediately he agreed with her: they couldn't take it slow. They couldn't go back to polite friendship. He couldn't sit across a table from her and make idle conversation knowing that she would be walking out his door that night and all the nights to come.

"Yes, painful," she said. As they stood together by the door the moment seemed to demand a physical gesture. A kiss? A handshake? A smack on his own head for being so stupid in somehow making her want to go?

"I hope you come back," he said. He heard his voice hiding so much. It sounded cordial, inviting. Nothing like what he felt inside: the north wind, a bullet whistling through the night, a ship sinking just yards from its home port.

"Thank you," she said. Standing on her toes, she brushed his neck with her lips. But before he could hold her close, give her a last kiss, she was gone.

Thomas Devlin stood in the doorway, watching the woman he loved back her car into the street. She didn't even glance his way, to see him waving good-bye. When he walked into the kitchen, because even though he wasn't hungry it was dinnertime and his kitchen seemed the place to be, he saw the daisies. Simple flowers he had picked for her. Flowers that conveyed very little, certainly not a broken heart.

Chapter 15

There were negative actions and positive actions, and while the first kind brought confusion, the second kind brought power. When Maggie had turned away from Kurt because of what he'd done in Fritz's truck, she had felt confused. She doubted that she deserved better than he. Yes, his proposition had been despicable, but deep inside she had still cared for him, had still needed to have him for her boyfriend. Loathsome and despicable, but her boyfriend nonetheless.

This, her second and final time leaving him, was an example of positive action. For once, she was acting for her own good, not just reacting out of hurt. Maggie felt power blooming inside her. She had taken her SATs and left the test feeling damned decent. Her grades for the quarter following her breakup with Kurt were A's and B's, landing her on the honor roll. Things were becoming clear.

Walking home with Ned Devlin that Friday night, Maggie had realized there was more in the world to talk about than pot, keg parties, tattoos and body piercing, and what everyone might be doing that night. She and Ned had talked about What Things Meant. Characters in books and movies. If they had to be a fruit or vegetable, what kind would it be? (Ned would be an apple, Maggie would be beets. The redness of their choices had seemed to be significant, and they had talked about that.)

That night Maggie had felt more sure that she wanted an education. College. Maybe a master's degree. She had liked spending time with someone smart who took her seriously. She wasn't in love with him or anything, but she wanted to write Ned a letter, to let him know how the SATs had gone.

Her homework finished, she curled up on the love seat with some of the personalized stationery Anne and Matt had given her for Christmas two years ago, that she had once thought to be dorky but now considered classy.

"Hey, Princess," her father said, heading straight for the TV.

She didn't say anything, but watched him tune in to the Red Sox game. He had his trusty Bud and a bag of pretzels. It seemed that her parents had traded places: her father had finished his work at the big house, and now her mother was there every night, turning it into a country inn. A commercial came on. Watching her father switch channels, just being himself, Maggie didn't feel as pissed off as usual. She was a woman on the way up.

Dear Ned [she wrote],
Thank you for walking me home that night. The SATs went really well, mainly because I didn't have a hangover, so thank you for that, too. I did forget to bring an extra pencil (wasn't that the last thing you said before you headed off into the night?). In fact, I forgot to bring *any* pencils. I had to borrow one from the girl next to me, and by the time the test was over, I had it worn down to the wood. I just hope the computer can read my little rubbings. (Unless they're wrong, in which case, what the hell?)
How does it feel to be graduating? I know you said gradu-

ation was in early June, so you only have about a month. Will you be sad leaving Deerfield? It sounds like a really pretty place. Sometimes the Ye Olde New England stuff can make you feel carsick, but it sounds like Deerfield knew to let well enough alone. At least, that's how you made it sound that night.

Let's see . . . Deerfield, Dartmouth. Both places begin with a "D." That must mean something!

I wish I were graduating. I can't believe I have another entire year on this island. I know you love coming out here for vacations, but I think it's going to drive me crazy. Literally. I'll wind up in a loony bin, and with my luck it'll be right here, on the island. *Help!*

Anyway, good luck with your finals. Did I tell you that I made honors last quarter? I know, big deal. Good luck with graduation, also, and have fun. I guess I'll see you when you get out here in June. Until then—

Maggie Vincent

P.S. Thanks again for walking me home. I've been think-ing, and I was wrong about Vanessa. She'd only think she's a pomegranate. Actually, she's lettuce.

Maggie addressed the envelope with the post office box Ned had given her that night. She took a stamp from the rolltop desk that had come off the Grace Line ship her father's father had captained. Licking the stamp, she glanced at her father. She had heard a hundred romantic tales of her grandfather, Captain Twigg Vin-cent, all from the lips of her mother. She wondered why she had never heard any from her father.

"Did you like your father?" she heard herself asking.

"Sure, I did. Everyone likes their father."

Dream on, Maggie thought, but instead of feeling sarcastic, she felt sad.

"What was he like?" she asked.

"Very stern. Never saw him without a coat and tie. Not once that I can remember. He loved my mother."

"And you, right? He loved you, too."

Her father slugged some beer, newly absorbed with the baseball game.

"Two outs, Princess," he said, intent on the screen. "Bottom of the third. Let me root for my team, okay?"

Maggie had left the room before her father had even noticed that she hadn't answered.

NED Devlin kept having dreams of children on trapezes. Flying high above the ground, laughing and soaring, knowing for sure that they would be caught if they fell. In the dreams he'd see his face, Josh's, Mike's, and Maggie's. But when he woke up, sometimes with a smile on his face, he'd be thinking of Karen.

Maggie had talked about her a lot on their long walk home.

He had never known Karen Davis. It was possible that he had met her; the island was small, the summer season short, and during her lifetime he had worked at the carousel, the Ben & Jerry's shop, and the ferry snack bar. He'd seen a thousand little kids. He wondered about it now, the likelihood that their paths had crossed.

Final exams were upon him. It was strange, taking the last tests of his high-school career. Accustomed to studying hard, to trying his best, he balked this time. He had already been accepted to Dartmouth. What could happen? If he got straight F's, if he blew every essay question, would Dartmouth renege on their word?

The truth was, he didn't want to find out. He studied his ass off for finals as if they were the sole factors to determine his future. Even Mike, his roommate extraordinaire, the man who during all four years had never once gone to bed before finishing every single assignment, even if it took until three A.M., had slacked off for senior finals.

Not Ned. He didn't want to curse his dream. One afternoon he took time out to address invitations for his graduation. To the Wades; to distant relatives; to Maggie (what the hell—she'd never want to come); and to his father.

He had considered including a note along with his father's invitation, asking to please invite Anne. But in the end, Ned did not. He didn't want Anne there.

As nice as she seemed, as much as his father obviously liked her, he didn't want her to come to his high-school graduation. That was a place for his mother. His mom would have been so proud of him. She would have stood in the crowd, the light of her love for Ned shining in her eyes. God, he knew that was true.

He wanted his father to be happy. Ned, who had never been attached enough to a woman to rely on her, had imagined how hard it was for his father. His father had loved his mother so much. He had lived with her, made her pregnant with Ned, been present with her in the delivery room when Ned was born. Ned had heard the marriage vows, and when it came to his parents, he believed the promises: to love, honor, and cherish.

His mother wasn't going to put in a surprise appearance at his graduation. Ned knew that. He didn't believe in the supernatural. When he sent his father the invitation, he knew that he should write: *Please ask Anne to join us.*

He couldn't do it.

Anne had made an impression on him. She had looked at him as if she could read his mind. She had told him, without speaking out loud, that she loved his father. That she was ready to love him, too.

"Shit," Ned said out loud. He'd gotten himself so churned up thinking about everything, he couldn't concentrate on his physics final.

Balmy May air rustled the papers on his desk, tempting him outside. You could hear voices drifting over from the playing fields. Grabbing his lacrosse stick, Ned loped down the dorm stairs. He didn't see another soul; his dorm was deserted, as if a plague of spring fever had wiped everyone out.

The school grounds were all trimmed and blooming, in shape for graduation. Running along the brick walk, Ned passed two junior girls with their boyfriends. They were sprawled on the grass, sort of entwined with each other. Ned wondered how it was that guys even younger than he could seem so relaxed with girls.

That got him to thinking about Maggie Vincent, and he quickened his pace right up to a sprint. Walking her across the island that night had been really fun. At first he'd felt nervous, afraid that she'd think he was too much of a nerd. But she was so nice. Really sweet and funny, a little shy about telling him her ideas at first; very playful, getting right into the game of determining the vegetable counterparts to people they knew.

At one point, when they'd scrambled up the bluff, she had stumbled. Wanting to steady her, Ned had held her hips, and electricity had flashed all through his body. It knocked his knees out from under him, and he actually wobbled. He'd been afraid, for just one second, that he was the one who needed help. But then he planted his feet and knew he'd be okay.

The shock came back, again and again, when he remembered the feeling of her soft hips beneath his hands. It radiated almost stronger in memory, until he thought it would drive him crazy. Even now, running at top speed, he had to clench his fists a few times to convince himself that he wasn't touching her.

Maybe she actually would come to his graduation. Stranger things had happened. He smiled, imagining the look on Mike's face if she showed up. The smart thing for Ned to do, if he really wanted Maggie to come, was to tell his father it would be okay to invite Anne. But Ned had just wasted an hour of study time deciding he didn't want that, and he wasn't one to compromise his principles just for the sake of romance.

Romance, what a joke! Maggie had probably forgotten all

about him by now anyway. Ned ran along, past clusters of kids he'd spent the last four years with, and not one of them realized that his hands and the part of his brain that dared to call it romance were on fire.

Fᴛᴢɢɪʙʙᴏɴs' was really shaping up. Starting a bed-and-breakfast wasn't much more complicated than setting up your own home. Except for two rooms' worth of stuff upstairs, they had lost very little to the fire. Gabrielle's first order of business had been to wash, and wash again, every piece of fabric in the house. She went through a gallon of bleach. Steve and his crew had given the rooms fresh coats of whitewash, and they smelled brand-new.

The house had been in the family for forty years, and it was already furnished in the comfortable New England summer style that was very much in vogue. Her guests didn't have to know that the house's character had evolved from the fact that her family had had no money.

The stuff she had once considered dowdy was now being written up in all the house magazines. People actually paid extra for sun-faded chintz love seats, for well-washed white chenille bedspreads, for paper-thin white curtains with ball fringe, for comfy white wicker.

The dining room had corner cupboards with painted pale pink interiors, like the inside of conch shells. Stacked on the shelves were countless pieces of Blue Willow china. At the time her mother bought it, it was all the family could afford. But now Gabrielle saw pieces of Blue Willow at antique stores for twelve dollars a plate.

She bought new sheets for all the beds, gave them a good washing in fabric softener, and hung them in the sun to dry. The entire time she was working in the house, she had big pots of fruit simmering on the stove: wild island strawberries, wineberries, and blackberries for the preserves she would serve at breakfast.

The window boxes were given a fresh coat of sea-blue paint,

then filled with red geraniums, white petunias, and cascades of English ivy.

As Memorial Day drew near, when the first guests would arrive, Gabrielle asked Maggie to stop by after school every day. Naturally Maggie had put up a fuss, but in the long run she did as she was asked. She'd have the bus drop her off at Salt Whistle Road instead of her usual bus stop, eat her snack, and get to work.

Today Gabrielle had plans to resurrect the herb garden that she and Anne had started as young girls. Overgrown and choked with weeds for many years, it now showed signs of promise. Gabrielle had been hacking away at it all week. Just yesterday she had uncovered the flagstones her father had laid so his daughters wouldn't have to get their feet muddy weeding it.

Anne was coming out to see the house, and to help with the herb garden. The whale business was in full swing, and she worked both days on the weekend. Her only time off was Monday afternoon and all day Tuesday, when she would hole up with her collages, but Gabrielle had staked a claim on her time after lunch on Tuesday. Crouched by the circular stone wall that marked the garden, planting a ring of lemon-drop marigolds because they supposedly discouraged slugs, Gabrielle heard Anne arrive.

She must be touring the house, Gabrielle thought, when Anne didn't appear right away. It was Anne's first time seeing the house since Steve had finished his work, and Gabrielle thought it was best that Anne did it alone.

"I'd pay to stay here," Anne said, coming out the back door in cutoff jeans and a yellow T-shirt.

"Didn't he do a great job?" Gabrielle asked, relieved by Anne's reaction.

"You wouldn't even know there'd been a fire. I was really expecting to see some changes, but he kept everything exactly the way it was."

"Steve doesn't mess with family history," Gabrielle said.

"God, look at this old place," Anne said, turning her attention to the garden. "The last time we got our hands dirty here, we were probably younger than Maggie."

"I should have consulted you on the plants, but here's what I got: rosemary, mint, oregano, woolly thyme, sage, dill for the middle because it grows tall, basil, and parsley."

"And look at the flowers! We never had flowers here before," Anne said.

"I thought the borders could use some color. I was thinking silvery leaves—"

"Artemisia," Anne said, nodding her approval, fingering the plant.

"And white, deep blue, and yellow flowers. So, rockcress, lobelia, and marigolds. They're supposed to torment various bugs and other varmints, I forget exactly which plant does what. Your friend Thomas told me."

"Thomas?" Anne said, her gaze rising.

"Yes, I saw him at the garden center. Apparently, he's quite a gardener. He helped me pick all this out. I must say, he didn't seem too enthusiastic when I personally invited him to come to dinner with you."

"We're taking a break from each other," Anne said.

"He didn't look very happy," Gabrielle said. "That must be why."

Anne was working the soil with a trowel, not even bothering to slip on the bright orange, green-thumbed garden gloves Gabrielle had found in the basement. Gabrielle herself wore white ones with a dainty blue flower print, but right now her attention was on Anne.

"Do you wish I'd just shut up and blow away?" Gabrielle asked.

"No, but you do seem determined to monitor my love life," Anne said. "First you want me back with Matt, now you tell me Thomas looks unhappy. I'm not ready for any of it," she said.

Gabrielle had drawn a diagram of where she thought each plant should go, but Anne was just plunking herbs into holes she had dug.

"Thomas told me you don't plant basil too near the wall, because it likes sun," Gabrielle said, feeling slighted by Anne.

Without speaking, Anne dug up the plant and stuck it right beside a blue-gray flagstone.

"In case you'd like to know," Gabrielle said huffily, "I have a map for this garden."

"I didn't know. I'm sorry."

"That's the purpose of communication," Gabrielle said. "You talk, I listen. I talk, you listen. That's the way things get done. You should try it sometime."

Handing Anne the diagram to study, Gabrielle dug a hole with all the dignity she could muster. Just see if she'd let Anne know how hurt she felt by Anne's propensity to keep every damned thing to herself. Gabrielle took the old metal watering can, sprinkled a little water in the hole. Then a little plant food. Finally she patted the rosemary plant into the soil.

Now Anne was reaching for the watering can. Gabrielle refused even to glance over. Let Anne follow the garden map or not—Gabrielle wasn't going to police her. She heard some water trickle out. Then, just as Gabrielle was reaching for the flat of artemisia, she felt something hit her back.

She turned, in time to see Anne forming a second mudpie and lob it into Gabrielle's lap.

"You brat!" Gabrielle said. "Stop that!"

Without changing expression, Anne scooped up another handful of mud. Bemused, she stared at her older sister, taking her time as she patted the mud into a fat ball.

"Don't you dare, Anne. I'm warning you—"

Anne tossed it. Gabrielle caught it on her left breast. Hardly thinking, she grabbed the hose. She let Anne have it full force. Squealing, Anne ran behind a hedge, ducking for cover. But

Gabrielle kept charging, pulling the hose through a break in the privet and catching Anne from behind.

Laughing hysterically, Anne lowered her right shoulder and ran straight at Gabrielle. The tackle didn't hurt as much as Gabrielle had feared it would; it was as if she and Anne were dancing, and Anne had suddenly decided to dip her, and good. Anne's arms were around her, and they were both cracking up too hard to speak as Anne lowered her to the ground.

The grass was soaking wet from all the water Gabrielle had sprayed, and the sisters fought to keep each other from getting up and running away.

"What is going on here?" came the irate sound of Maggie's voice.

"She started it," Gabrielle said.

"I did not," Anne said, giving Gabrielle's dripping hair a serious pull. "She deserved it for being nosy."

"You can't have it both ways," Gabrielle said. "Either you didn't start it, or I didn't deserve it. That's like a double negative."

"You two are mental," Maggie said solemnly.

"She called us mental," Anne said to Gabrielle.

"I heard her."

Grabbing the still-live hose, Anne stuck her thumb over the nozzle to increase the pressure, and gave Maggie a severe dousing.

At first, Maggie just stood there, stunned, while Anne lay on the wet grass spraying her with water with the intensity of a warrior. Then, very calmly, she walked to the spigot on the side of the house and turned off the water.

"She's good," Anne said, to Gabrielle, raising an eyebrow.

"She learned from the best."

Maggie walked over in her baggy plaid shorts and red T-shirt, sopping wet from head to toe, and sat cross-legged beside her mother and Anne.

"Maybe this would be a good time to ask if I can go to a friend's graduation," she said.

"Like whose?" Gabrielle asked, raising herself up on one elbow. Something cajoling in Maggie's tone had Gabrielle's maternal antenna twitching full power.

"Ned Devlin's."

"I didn't realize you were such good friends," Anne said.

"Neither did I," Gabrielle said.

"Well, we sort of are. We bumped into each other while he was home for vacation, and we started talking, and I don't really know, but he sent me an invitation to his graduation from Deerfield."

"Oh, honey, I don't know," Gabrielle said. "That's awfully far away."

"Please?"

"Let me think about it," Gabrielle said.

"Okay," Maggie said, surprisingly ready to let the matter drop without exacting an immediate promise. Every day Gabrielle saw more signs of her daughter growing up; she felt proud, yet nostalgic for the past, when Maggie was just a little girl.

"Did you tell Anne?" Maggie asked shyly.

"Tell her . . . ?" Gabrielle asked, then realized that Maggie was talking about the garden. For a moment Gabrielle wished Maggie hadn't said anything. It had been so much fun, laughing with Anne this last fifteen minutes, as if they hadn't had a care in the world beyond throwing mudpies. But Gabrielle wouldn't disappoint Maggie by changing the subject.

"Go ahead," Gabrielle said. "You tell her."

"We want the garden to be in memory of Karen," Maggie said in a rush, as if she feared being rebuffed.

Anne just sat there, in obvious shock. Her mouth was slightly open as she looked from Maggie to Gabrielle.

"It's because we loved her so much," Gabrielle said. "And we want her on the island. A place where we can visit her."

"Her grave's in Pennsylvania," Anne said dumbly.

In the aftermath of Karen's fall, Anne's grief had been such that she had allowed Matt to bury Karen in his family's plot. They hadn't planned for, or even considered, the possibility of her death. At the time Matt's decision had seemed best. On a long hillside, the cemetery overlooked apple orchards and a gentle river. Karen was buried among her grandparents and great-grand-parents from Matt's family. The grave site was lovely, but so very distant.

"I know she's far away," Gabrielle said. "That's why Maggie thought of the garden."

"Oh, it was your idea?" Anne asked, reaching for Maggie's hand.

"Yes."

"I wish we'd brought her to the island," Anne said.

"We have her in our hearts," Maggie said. "I know that sounds stupid, but it's true. I think of her every day."

"This will be her place," Anne said, her gaze drifting to the garden-in-progress.

"We won't tell anyone who stays here. Strangers, I mean," Maggie said. "We'll keep it in the family."

"Did you see the herbs and flowers I picked out?" Gabrielle asked. She headed over to the garden, and Maggie followed.

When Gabrielle looked over her shoulder, to ask Anne whether she'd had the chance to study the map she had made, she saw Anne sitting where they had left her. Anne was staring at the sky. She wasn't smiling, and she wasn't crying. Her expression was somewhere in between, and there was a very far-off look in her eyes. If Gabrielle had to guess, she would say that Anne was somewhere in western Pennsylvania. Near the top of a long slope, listening to the current of a lazy river, with the scent of apple blossoms heavy in the air.

Chapter 16

The word came that Ned was to be the valedictorian of his class. Every day the mailbox was full of parcels postmarked Hanover, NH. They contained information for Thomas Devlin about events at Dartmouth, which, as the parent of an incoming freshman, he might enjoy: football games starting in September, a three-day parents' weekend in October, the hockey and basketball seasons, Winter Carnival in February, and much, much more.

He knew that he should be bursting with pride for his son, but he wasn't. He couldn't ever remember being so disappointed in Ned. The disappointment was like a pellet lodged in his throat, and he couldn't get rid of it. He carried it around with him all the time.

He made more trips into town than necessary, just hoping to catch sight of Anne. Sometimes she'd be standing at the counter in her office, explaining the boat ride to a pair of tourists. Or she'd be talking on the phone, her pencil scribbling down the details of a reservation. Often he wouldn't see her at all.

Once, as he downshifted his truck, he ground the gears so badly it sounded like a car being mangled at the junkyard. Anne looked up, and their eyes met. Thomas felt himself blush. He tried to smile, but by the time he got his mouth working, he had already passed her window and was halfway down the block.

That night he was huddled over his workbench, adjusting the counterweights on Ginny Cole's wall clock, a handmade beauty her brother had brought her back from Switzerland. Work helped Thomas forget the knot in his throat. It made the time fly, so at eleven, when the phone rang, he was startled to see the hour. He dove for the receiver, hoping to hear Anne's voice. He heard Ned's.

"Sorry to be calling you so late, Dad," Ned said. "But it's about my graduation. There were a few things I was wondering."

"Like what?"

"Did you get the letter from school? About me being named valedictorian?"

"Yes. Congratulations." Thomas tried to put a little warmth in his voice, but he couldn't quite succeed.

Ned laughed nervously, sensing that something was up. "I thought you'd call me when you found out, that's all. It's pretty cool, huh?"

"It's amazing. I'm proud of you, Ned."

Ned seemed to be waiting for Thomas to say more. When he didn't, Ned cleared his throat nervously.

"The other thing is, you know Maggie Vincent? Anne's niece?" Ned asked.

"Yes."

"She and I have kind of been writing letters back and forth since my vacation, and I was sort of wondering if you'd mind driving her up for vacation."

Thomas Devlin felt so riled, he had to count to ten before speaking. Here was Ned, asking him to drive to graduation with a girl Ned hadn't said two words to over the years, mentioning

Anne's name only as a matter of reference. Not once, in any call or letter, had Ned told Thomas to please feel free to invite Anne.

"What do her parents say?" Thomas asked.

"Well, I talked to her a little while ago, and they said it's okay with them if she can get a ride."

"What about all your stuff? Won't you need the extra room for carting home your things?"

"We'll stick it in the back of the truck. I'll have it all packed in boxes so it won't fly around."

"What if it rains?" Thomas asked, running short on objections. He felt reluctant and cranky, and he knew he was being unreasonable. They could always use a tarp and tie-downs.

"We can cover everything with a tarp," Ned said, his father's son. "There's plenty of room for three people in the cab. Especially Maggie. She's small."

Like her aunt, Thomas thought, hearing an unfamiliar, brand-new tone of yearning in Ned's voice.

"I guess so, then," Thomas said.

"Thanks, Dad. This'll be really fun. You won't regret it."

"I'm sure I won't."

"It's just a couple of weeks away. I can't wait."

"Me neither," Thomas said.

Silence filled the line.

"What's wrong, Dad?" Ned asked. "You sound funny."

"It's just late," Thomas said.

After they had hung up, Thomas stretched out on the cot in his workshop and thought about the truth of those last words.

Love doesn't come along every day, at least not for him. Well into his middle age, he felt love so strong he could imagine dying of it. Lying there, he closed his eyes and folded his hands on his chest. He felt racked with pain and disappointment, and he wondered whether it was possible for his emotions to do serious damage to his heart.

He didn't begrudge Ned his girl. If Ned wanted Maggie, Thomas was all for it. He only wished that Ned could grow up a little, that Ned could wish the same, in return, for his father.

ON the Saturday of Memorial Day weekend, the entire island was invited to the grand opening of Fitzgibbons'. The day was brilliant, so clear you could practically see the houses on Cape Amelia, all the way across the sound. Anne drove down Salt Whistle Road in a parade of cars. Bed-and-breakfasts were springing up everywhere, but all the islanders knew they'd get good food at any grand opening thrown by Gabrielle.

Anne wore a white linen sundress and wide-brimmed straw hat; she walked barefoot across the front lawn. People milled around, holding cups of punch and tasting the food. A checkered cloth covered a long table laden with shellfish stew, clam pie, island spring rolls, peppercorn-cheese straws, crudités from Gabrielle's garden, and a slew of homemade muffins, chocolate cake, and oatmeal cookies.

Anne recognized old friends and some of the emergency workers who had last come to this house the night it was on fire. She encountered none of the hostility she had felt all winter. Perhaps she had redeemed herself, in the islanders' eyes, by staying through the worst weather. Everyone seemed friendly, as if the festivities had put the island in a good mood.

Weekend guests, Gabrielle's first, had forgone the beach, bicycling, whale watching, in favor of the party. Anne picked them out of the crowd: one couple had been into the office yesterday, to sign up for the afternoon trip. Gabrielle was talking to them now. Leaning against the porch rail, regaling them with some dramatically told story, she was in her glory.

Anne moved through the crowd, hoping to come across Thomas. The firefighters kept to their own, clustered with their wives and, in some cases, parents. Thomas wasn't among them. Even though she knew it was for the best, Anne couldn't believe that weeks had passed since she had seen him. Some nights she would awaken in a sweat, terrified at whatever impulse had made her drive him away. Then she'd lie awake, unable to fall back to sleep, wondering whether she had forever lost her knack for love.

Sometimes she dreamed of seeing him on a crowded street, calling his name and waving wildly. Only, the louder she called, the faster he seemed to walk away. Many nights, especially after those dreams, Anne would stare at the telephone, thinking of things she could say if she called him. But she didn't.

This party would be the perfect place to bump into each other. Anne was sure he knew about it: Gabrielle had tacked up signs all over the island, placed an ad in last week's paper, and sent out flyers. She imagined their meeting, awkward at first, but then comfortable. It was a coward's fantasy, one that required no direct action on her part, and she knew it.

Maggie circulated with a pitcher full of punch. "Would you care for some delicious, refreshing punch?" she asked Anne.

"Sure," Anne said, holding out her empty cup. Maggie had trimmed and brushed her hair. She wore a pink-flowered sleeveless dress, the straps crisscrossing in back. Anne couldn't ever remember her looking so demure.

"You look pretty."

"Is it too suburban? Do I look like I could walk into a country club without getting kicked out?"

"No, and yes. In that order."

"Good. 'Cause I'm wearing it to Ned's graduation. Mom broke down and said I could go. His father's driving me."

"Thomas?" Anne said. Just saying his name made her heart flip over. As if she could somehow have conjured him up, she glanced around the crowd again.

"Yeah, Mr. Devlin. Mom says you're not going out with him anymore."

Anne heard the question in Maggie's voice, but she didn't want to talk about it. Before other people knew about her and Thomas, they had discovered amazing love, deep and true. But Thomas had a son, and Anne had a not-quite-ex-husband, and she was still too damaged to withstand the upset and confusion that their love for each other seemed to cause everyone.

"Have you seen him today?" Anne asked.

"No, but I'm sure he'll stop by. This is *the* place to be on the island."

"It does seem to be."

"Well, I'd better keep passing out punch," Maggie said. "I'm on the time clock, paying off this dress Mom bought for me."

"Go to it," Anne said. She wandered through the crowd, heading in the direction of the herb garden. She hadn't visited it since she, Maggie, and Gabrielle had consecrated it in Karen's memory. Maybe by the time she was done, Thomas would have arrived.

But twenty minutes later, when Anne returned to the heart of the party, there was still no sign of him. By the end of the afternoon, when the last islanders were pulling away from Fitzgibbons', leaving the house to the family and their paying guests, Anne knew that she had to face the fact that Thomas Devlin was not coming.

MAGGIE had looked at a map, but she didn't have any real sense of how long a drive it was to Deerfield. She and Mr. Devlin had caught the first ferry. He had excused himself as soon as the boat pulled away, probably to go inside for coffee so he wouldn't have to talk to her for the entire trip. Maggie knew the feeling. Relieved, she bunched the blue blazer she had borrowed from her mother into a ball, wedged it against the truck window, and dozed off.

She'd managed to fake sleep all along I-95, but now they were on the Mass Pike, and she had the feeling she was being rude. Honestly stretching, she pretended to yawn.

"Good morning," he said.

"Good morning," she said, feeling shy. Now he would feel like he had to make conversation with her. He would ask her about her plans for the future, what she thought about the decision to enlarge Island Consolidated School, what her favorite subjects were. She took a deep breath and waited.

But he didn't say a word. He just drove along, his elbow leaning on the door rest. He didn't whistle or hum, and he didn't ask whether she would mind if he turned on the radio. He seemed extremely comfortable with silence.

Maggie took a quick glance at him. He wasn't a bad-looking man, if you didn't look at his face. Even taller than Ned, he had great big shoulders and arms so muscular they looked like they might pop his sleeves. He wore a blue suit and black loafers that were extremely huge. Maggie wondered where big people like Mr. Devlin did their shopping. Life on the island was probably pretty inconvenient for him when it came to stuff like needing new shoes or pants or anything else for that matter in a hurry.

She snuck a peek at his hands. They were speckled with white and reddish-purple craters, like a gory mad scientist's vision of the lunar surface. Just picturing those hands on Anne made Maggie shudder. It was hard for her to imagine Anne going to Mr. Devlin from a man as handsome as Uncle Matt.

But Maggie knew that Anne cared for him very much. She had recognized that expression in Anne's eyes, at the grand opening when she'd asked Maggie if Mr. Devlin had arrived yet. It was a look of love, and boy do I know looks of love, Maggie thought.

How many times had Maggie stood at her bedroom dresser, listening to a crying song on the radio and thought of Kurt while staring at her own reflection in the mirror? Not recently, not since that night at Pirates' Cave, but she hadn't forgotten. She knew the gaze: faraway, sad, full of longing for what you wanted more than anything in the world.

Ned had been a jerk about Anne, and he knew it. Maggie's parents would die when they got their phone bill, but many the late night lately had found Maggie and Ned on the telephone,

telling each other everything. One of the things Ned talked about
was how bad he felt for not wanting Anne around. He couldn't
help the way he felt, but that didn't mean he had to like it. Seeing
Anne, especially with his father, made him feel too bad about his
mother.

"Get over it," Maggie urged him. "Your father deserves a life."

"I know," Ned said, but even so, he couldn't soften toward
Anne.

"Does she know how I feel about her?" Ned asked, and Maggie
knew he hoped the answer was no.

"Anne's pretty sharp about stuff like that," she had to tell him.

"Do you think they broke up because of me?"

"You have delusions of grandeur," Maggie had said, although
secretly she thought it was a possibility.

Now, riding along beside Ned's father, she thought back on
their telephone conversations with sheer amazement. In all their
time together, Kurt had never told her one one-hundredth of the
things Ned had. Maggie had kept so much locked inside, because
Kurt never wanted to talk. She'd found herself pouring everything
out to Ned: about Fritz, about what Kurt had wanted her to do,
about Karen.

Sometimes she spent half the call with tears running down her
face. Ned couldn't see her, but he could hear it in her voice, and
she never even felt embarrassed. All this with a guy she'd never
slept with, or even kissed.

Sometimes he told her he wished he could give her a hug, and
she'd smile because he sounded so cute and innocent. One thing
he hadn't admitted was the status of his virginity, but Maggie was
fairly certain that it was intact.

"I know Ned is glad you could make it today," Mr. Devlin said,
and for a split second Maggie had the horrible notion that he'd
been reading her mind.

"So am I," Maggie said.

The conversation went dead again as the truck passed through some of the most gorgeous countryside Maggie had ever seen. She had been reading college catalogs in the school library, and there were a few really interesting colleges in the Berkshires. She had happened to notice that Dartmouth wasn't all that much farther north. One thing she hadn't been able to tell Ned yet was how much credit she gave him for helping her get a new start: take her SATs, stop hanging out with druggies, and believe in herself. She'd tell him someday.

Glancing at Ned's dad, she noticed his eyes. He had no eyebrows or eyelashes, and there was something about the lids that made Maggie think that he'd had a lot of plastic surgery around there. For a second, with his funny-lidded eyes, he reminded her of Fishy, her childhood goldfish. Alone and sad and swimming in circles. There was something lost about Mr. Devlin. He didn't exactly have Anne's look of love; it was something worse. It was a look of lost love.

"We missed you at the grand opening," Maggie said.

"I'm sorry I couldn't make it. Everyone said it was terrific."

"Anne was looking for you," Maggie said.

When he didn't reply, she was afraid she'd said the wrong thing. That she was meddling, just like her mother. But then Mr. Devlin looked over at her.

"She was?" he asked.

"Yes. She asked me if I had seen you."

"Oh."

"Yeah."

"Um, how is she?" Mr. Devlin asked, a thoughtful frown on his poor scarred lips.

"Holding herself together," Maggie said. "She's been through a lot."

"I know."

"Yes, I have the feeling you do," Maggie said kindly.

Silence blanketed the cab. Outside, the sun had risen above the tree line, making every pine needle sparkle with dew. It would be a beautiful day for graduation. Maggie had never been to a prep school, and she felt more excited with every passing mile. For once, she felt perfectly dressed. She had even borrowed her mother's pearl stud earrings. She had left her usual array at home, all except for her lucky pair of dangling dice. Only two earrings in each ear: very restrained.

"Thank you," Mr. Devlin said a few miles down the road.

It's nothing, Maggie had been about to say, but she stopped herself. She nodded at him. They both knew what he meant. In a very real way, she had just given him a gift, and thanks were not the least bit out of line.

STANDING at the podium, addressing the crowd under the hot midday sun, Ned was roasting in his cap and gown. Sweat trickled into his ears, down the back of his legs, into his shoes. Everyone else was feeling the heat, too. Half his classmates were giving him goony looks, rolling their eyes and pointing at their watches. Ned knew that they could take it. All his concern was reserved for one person, the girl sitting between his father and Mike Mallory's mother, the slightly sunburned beautiful girl to whom Ned had directed his entire valedictory address: Maggie Vincent.

Just before taking the stage, Ned had had the paralyzing thought: what if I bore her? After all, most of his speech was about his class, about their four years at Deerfield and what would happen next. But there she was, seeming to hang on every word he said, giving him a constant smile of encouragement.

A lot of his friends in the graduate section kept leaning over, looking down their rows to catch a better sight of her. Ned knew it was crazy, but he felt almost prouder to have Maggie at his graduation than to have been chosen valedictorian.

Looking into the audience as he spoke, his eyes met his father's. He had been afraid of this moment. His father had been so reserved in their conversations lately; Ned knew he had let him down. But as if nothing had ever happened between them, his father was beaming.

"Get over it," Maggie had told Ned one midnight call recently. "Your father deserves a life."

Ned had expected to look at the seat beside his father's, the place where his mother should have been, and feel strong sorrow that she was missing his high-school graduation. That she would miss his college graduation, and his medical-school graduation, if such a day should ever come. Ned had been afraid that he would look at the seat beside his father and see his mother's ghost shimmering with dreams of what might have been.

That's why he hadn't wanted Anne to come; he hadn't wanted her in his mother's place.

But the strange thing was, when Ned looked into the audience, all he really saw was Maggie. One night they had talked from midnight until the sky turned milky blue with dawn. They had talked about the island, Deerfield, their parents, their worst nightmares (Ned's was one where his hockey coach's wife had blood dripping out of her teeth, like venom from a snake's fangs, and she was trying to bite him), countries that had had at least two names in their lifetimes, dictators, the difference between Indian and African elephants, anything that would keep them from hanging up.

He couldn't wait until his father got that phone bill.

Now he was coming to the end of his speech, the part where he would read his favorite poem by Wordsworth, the one that would always remind him of Deerfield. He imagined Wordsworth's part of England to be very similar to Deerfield: rolling hills, river valleys, bitter winters, verdant springtimes. When he had read the poem to Maggie over the phone, by the end he was as choked up as he felt now.

His last four years had been as happy as possible for a boy living many miles away from his father and a lifetime away from his mother. Deerfield was the reason. And so, Ned turned his attention from Maggie Vincent and his father to the friends and teachers he would miss so much. Giving them all a big smile, he took a deep breath and launched into "Lines Composed a Few Miles Above Tintern Abbey."

"Five years have passed; five summers, with the length/of five long winters! . . ."

Ned Devlin's Deerfield years had come to an end.

Chapter 17

Whether Maggie Vincent realized it or not, she had given Thomas Devlin heartsease. Just hearing that Anne had asked about him, that she still thought of him, however occasionally, went far toward soothing his mind. It gave him a mission. Anne might say Ned wasn't the problem, but Thomas knew that deep down he was at least part of it.

The mission would officially begin by giving Ned a talking-to. This required prying him loose from Maggie. Now that the island school was out, before summer jobs began, the two of them had become surgically attached. Long days at the beach, on the tennis court, or just hanging around the yard.

When Ned was little, Thomas had hung a tire swing from a high branch in one of the oaks, and now Ned and Maggie swung on it for hour after lazy hour, all wrapped up in each other.

Thomas had to vie with Ned for the use of his own truck; he had gotten used to the sight of Ned driving down the road, his arm around Maggie's shoulders, Maggie's hair blowing out the truck's open window. Ned would beep and wave as he passed his father, working in the garden.

One afternoon, in the midst of restaking the tomato plants that had doubled their height in the last heat wave, Thomas saw Ned and Maggie pull into the driveway.

"Hey, Dad," Ned called, heading into the house with Maggie.

"Just the man I wanted to see," Thomas called back.

The kids ambled over, all sunburned and tousled, lightly holding hands.

"Maggie, I bet you know how to make great lemonade," Thomas said. "This old farmer could sure use a glass."

"Just point me to the lemons and sugar," she said.

She already knew the way to the kitchen. Ned started after her, his toes practically catching her heels, and Thomas had to smile at the sight of his son in thrall to love and, probably by now, sex.

"Hang on, son," Thomas said. He adjusted his old Red Sox hat, to shield his eyes from the summery glare.

"What's up?"

"Let's grab some shade," Thomas said, leading Ned to the picnic table he had placed among the scrub oaks so many years ago. Every year his skin got more sensitive to the sun, no matter how much sunblock he used. He blinked the stars out of his eyes, taking off his dark glasses. When having a serious talk with someone, especially your child, Thomas Devlin was a firm believer in letting them see your eyes.

"I've been letting you get away with being a bully," Thomas began.

"Me, a bully?" Ned asked, incredulous.

"Yes. When it comes to Anne."

"Oh, Dad," Ned said, impatiently, as if this were old news. He glanced at the kitchen door, agonizing as the seconds away from Maggie ticked by.

"Maybe you and I should have had this talk a while ago. On

your spring break. The minute it became clear that you have a problem with her."

"I don't have a problem with her," Ned said, spoken like a sullen child.

"She thinks you do."

"What difference does it make?" Ned asked. "You should do what you want."

"And not care about how you feel?"

"It's just . . . shit." Ned stopped, as if he couldn't get the words from his brain to his lips.

"The parallels to your mother," Thomas supplied.

Ned shrugged. An acorn fell onto the old pine table with a knock. For a few moments both men were absorbed watching a squirrel at work a few branches above their heads. Thomas felt his breath coming easier than it had in two months, and not for the first time he wondered why people make it so hard to talk to the people they love. They imagine the worst, they set up obstacles to prevent the truth from coming out. But in the end, when they finally muddle through, they find relief.

"It was hard to take," Ned said finally. "The part about you saving her from a fire."

"When I couldn't save your mother."

"Yeah, that part."

"Anne understood before I did," Thomas said. "She told me that you sort of had to hate her for surviving when your mother could not."

Ned didn't answer, but his expression told Thomas that Anne had been right.

"You're going to have to work that part of it out," Thomas said slowly. "I'll help as much as I can. You always have Dr. Struan to talk to." The psychologist that had helped both Thomas and Ned in the years since the fire. "But I love Anne. I don't know if she'll have me, but I want to be with her."

Ned nodded, looking his father dead in the eye for the first time since they'd sat down. He seemed about to speak, but then he caught sight of Maggie, hovering by the kitchen door with a full glass pitcher of lemonade, obviously not wanting to interrupt. She was a good girl with fine sense, Thomas thought.

"Is that it?" Ned asked.

"I'd like a last word from you."

"Dad, in families there's no such thing as a last word," Ned said.

However, for the last word on this subject at this moment, Ned's grin and the way his arm shot into the air, waving Maggie over, told Thomas the whole story: love would reign. It was as much of a blessing as he could hope for.

The three of them sat under the tree, sipping from glasses of lemonade made with just the right measure of mouth-pucker and sweetness.

"How's your aunt?" Ned asked Maggie.

Surprised, Maggie's eyes flickered from Ned to Thomas. "She's fine," Maggie said, smiling.

"Keeping busy, is she?" Thomas asked.

"Working, mainly."

"That's good," Thomas said as he watched Maggie's smile turn impishly sly.

"She only gets a day and a half off a week," Maggie said. "And next Monday afternoon, she wants to take me whale watching. She thought she should experience firsthand what she's pushing on helpless tourists."

"That sounds very smart."

"Anyway, the thought of being cooped up on a glass-bottomed boat, or whatever it is, twenty-five miles out with a bunch of cameras—it's not my thing."

"Sounds like a ball," Ned said wryly, proving to Thomas exactly how besotted he was. Thomas happened to know that Ned loved whale watching.

"Anyway, if I bail on her, there'll be an extra spot available. I mean, if you know anyone who might like to go."

"I'll keep that in mind," Thomas said, smiling at this young woman, his son's girlfriend, who obviously had a brilliant future as a matchmaker.

MOST Mondays Anne left the office at noon. She would head home and get straight to work at her table. This morning she had decided her next collage would be a stained-glass window. She would copy one of Notre Dame's magnificent rose windows from a postcard she had tucked away, and she would add the collage to her series. That would stop her from puttering, as she'd been doing lately, with the picture she had started of Thomas's snow-covered house. It didn't fit the series, but she kept going back to it.

Today, however, she was going whale watching with Maggie. She joined the parade of twenty-three passengers on their way to the town dock. In spite of herself, she felt excited.

Like most jaded islanders, she knew marine animals were everywhere. The jetties and ledges were thick with harbor seals all winter; porpoises played in shallow island waters; you could see whales on nearly every ferry crossing, if you were patient and kept your eyes peeled.

This expedition promised something even better. The boat would head twenty-eight miles out from the island, to Hurricane Banks. Marked by a few shoals, this was the spot where the continental shelf dropped into deep water. The currents were powerful, and they constantly circulated tons of plankton, attracting the whales.

Leaning against a piling, Anne looked around for Maggie. They had ten minutes to board the vessel, and there was no sign of her, and she was beginning to wonder. But aside from the obvious pleasures of Maggie's company, Anne would miss something else if Maggie didn't show up: Maggie was bringing lunch.

"I have a message from your niece."

At the sound of Thomas's voice, Anne whirled around. She hadn't seen him for so long, she just stood there, taking everything in. He stood back, beyond arm's length, looking nervous and uncomfortable, his shoulders hunched.

"From Maggie?" Anne asked finally.

"Yes. She won't be able to make it today."

"Oh."

"It's my son's fault. He becomes severely disabled when she's more than six inches away."

"My sister tells me Maggie has the same problem."

"Ah," Thomas said. A gentle smile tugged at his mouth, but his eyes darted nervously around. "Maggie thought maybe I'd like to take her place."

Anne could see by his posture, his discomfort, that he expected her to object. She didn't like being pushed into things, but she couldn't deny how good it felt to see him.

"I do have this extra ticket," Anne said. "This morning I had to turn away at least ten people who'd hoped to get aboard, and I hate to see the seat go to waste. Want to come whale watching?"

Thomas nodded, grinning. "I can't think of anything I'd rather do," he said.

Onboard the vessel, the deckhands pulled up the gangway right behind them. Bill Hannigan, the captain, waved to them. The young deckhands, who went to Anne for their paychecks every Thursday, gave them a warm welcome.

Moses Court, third mate and year-round volunteer firefighter, pointed out the best spot on the starboard rail.

"We have a good forty-five-minute ride out to the Bank," he said, "but when I give you the high sign, stand right there and look twenty degrees off the bow. They're playing like crazy out there."

"Are there always whales?" Thomas asked.

"Not like today."

"How do you know they're out today?"

Moses winked, tapping his forehead with his index finger. "We're psychic," he said.

"Radio contact," Anne explained when Moses walked away. "All the different captains call each other to let everyone know where the action is. The season is short, and they're all after the same thing."

"Enough money to make it through the winter," Thomas said.

"Right. There's enough business to go around, so there's no need to be cutthroat. I hear them all day, on the radio in my office."

Anne and Thomas strolled around the boat. They shouldered around Cape Amelia, and the captain set a course for open water. Standing in the bow, Anne felt the chill of fresh air at sea. Thomas was so close, their arms were nearly touching. She shivered, from the breeze or his proximity. It came upon her so strongly, she had to step away.

"Maggie sent along the lunch she said she'd bring. Are you hungry?" Thomas asked.

"Starved."

They settled onto a long, blue bench on the top deck. Here the hot summer sun counteracted the stiff sea breeze, making Anne feel sensual. She watched Thomas unwrap the lunch Maggie had sent. There was curried chicken salad with slivered almonds and red grapes on sweet brown bread, chilled watercress soup in a silver flask, and fresh orange juice mixed with sparkling water.

They ate the delicious food, ignoring the seagulls perched on the rail, crying for a handout. It wasn't until Anne tasted the dessert, chocolate cognac truffles, that she figured out the picnic's romanticism. Maggie had obviously raided the Seduction Table.

Instead of mentioning it, she just smiled at Thomas. He returned the smile, rolling his eyes in rapture.

Full and content, Anne leaned back, taking the sun on her face. This felt good, being with Thomas right now. They were miles out to sea, together among strangers, far from his son and her sister and the gathering torrent of letters from Matt. Anne reached for Thomas's hand, and she held it. He squeezed back.

While people around them talked excitedly about the action they would see at the feeding grounds, Anne and Thomas quietly watched two minke whales approach the port side, take air, and disappear beneath the water's surface. No one else noticed.

With the twin diesels throbbing two decks below and the rhythmic waves bearing them farther away from the island, Anne let herself relax. Don't take it anywhere, she told herself. She didn't think about how this had happened, she didn't analyze Maggie's actions; she simply enjoyed this moment in time.

Presently, Moses waved down from the bridge, directing them to the starboard bow. Anne led the way, touched to be accepted as an islander insider by the ship's crew. She and Thomas leaned against the rail. Waves broke over a barely protruding rock, and at first Anne thought it was a whale. Then she saw the real thing.

Whales everywhere. She cried out, before she could stop herself. This was more magnificent than anything she had imagined, better than the brochures she handed out every day, better than the sales pitch she had been giving.

People crowded along the starboard side, squashing Anne into Thomas. His arm went around her, and she leaned into his body.

Whales were feeding: coming to the surface, breathing the air, then sounding with a graceful arch of the back. As they dove, their great tails would rise straight above the surface, like a two-pronged Neptune's spear. And the whales were breaching: zooming with torpedo force out of the water, seeming to hang in the air, then smashing back into the sea.

Anne offered Thomas the binoculars, but he nodded that she should use them first. She focused on one old whale, floating on his back, sunbathing. He, like most of the others, was a hump-back. They had long white flippers and knobbly spines, relatively elegant sloping snouts, and the biggest one Anne saw looked about seventy feet long.

The captain circled the feeding grounds along with several other companies' boats. It might have felt hokey or commercial or exploitive, but to Anne it felt spectacular. She lowered the binoculars. She wanted a large field of vision, to take in the whole scene. Cameras clicked and whirred, and the passengers exclaimed every time one of the whales came to the surface.

At some point during the show, Thomas's arms came around her. They encircled her from behind, and Anne felt his mouth against her ear. He whispered something.

She couldn't hear his words above the noise of the crowd and the big diesels, but she felt his warm breath. She half turned, just enough to brush his cheek with her lips. She wanted to ask him to repeat what he had said, but finally she did not. Turning back to the whales, she believed she already knew. Only, she wasn't quite ready to hear.

O N a hot June afternoon, with the sun high in the sky, in the tall grass between his yard and the potato fields, Ned Devlin lost his virginity. He saw shooting stars. For the first time in his life he made love to a girl. Or, rather, Maggie made love to him.

Lying in their bathing suits on a blanket, Ned exulted in the sun beating down on his body. His outer thigh touched Maggie's, sticky with sweat, Ned felt the happiest he had ever been in his life. Without opening his eyes, he reached over for Maggie's hand. Where the bottom of her bathing suit should have been, he felt bare skin.

He raised his head to look.

Bare skin. Head to toe. She was on her stomach, her arms folded under her head. She was looking at him with that very Maggie smile that told you she had a secret. He could see the plump white curve of her breast peeking out above the blanket, her bottom a round, firm mound with tan lines.

Ned had never seen full-body tan lines before.

"Hi," she whispered.

"Hi," he whispered back, paralyzed practically all over, but not quite. He hardened instantly, and he felt her watching.

"I'm glad I decided not to go on the whale boat," she said.

"So am I. Um, what happened to your bathing suit?"

"It fell off while your eyes were closed."

"Wow."

Playfully, she tugged his waistband.

"Maybe if you close your eyes again," she said, "yours will fall off, too."

But first, Maggie inched over, to kiss him on the lips. Their eyes open, they watched each other. Ned felt her soft mouth covering his, her tongue teasing him. Then she stopped.

"Now close your eyes," she said.

Blood pounding in his ears, Ned obeyed. He felt her fingers, cool against his skin, untying the drawstring. Then, easing his suit down his legs, her fingers trailed along his buttocks. Involuntarily, Ned moaned, arching his back.

Before he could open his eyes, he felt hot, moist velvet caressing his penis. A magic fabric, it enveloped him totally with softness and friction and wet heat. Only, it wasn't cloth of any kind. It was Maggie's mouth. She slid her lips up and down, taking every inch of him, stopping now and then to encircle the tip with her tongue, all the while fingering his balls with a featherlight touch.

Ned hadn't believed that such arousal could be possible. Opening his eyes, he saw Maggie. Their bodies were naked together, and she was kissing and sucking his penis. He was actually seeing this, feeling this, happen to him. Maggie, with her plump creamy white breasts and bottom, was crouched over Ned with an expression of joy on her face.

By the time she crawled up the blanket, to press her body full-length against his, rockets were going off in his head.

"Maggie," he whispered, kissing her lips, her eyelids. Very shyly, he cupped her breasts in his hands.

"Kiss them," she whispered.

"I—" Ned began. He couldn't believe he was doing this. He had never seen a live woman naked, he had never dared to feel a girl's breasts. Here was the woman he had fantasized over for months now offering her breasts to him.

She gave him a warm, steady gaze, to let him know it was okay. Then, hardly able to breathe, Ned lowered his lips to her left nipple. It was a pink diamond, so erect he couldn't believe it. He kissed it. He kissed her right nipple. A tentative lick, and then he let himself suck it.

"Mmm," Maggie said, squirming in his arms.

Did that mean he was doing it right? Ned wondered. Almost instinctively, he touched his own nipple, to see how it felt. The pressure made him feel even sexier than before.

"Make love to me," Maggie whispered.

Ned raised himself up on one elbow. He pushed a lock of hair out of Maggie's feverish eyes. Suddenly she looked worried, even frantic. For some reason, knowing that he needed to reassure her, Ned relaxed a little. He kissed her eyebrows. Gazing deep into her eyes, he felt himself drawing the tension out of her.

"I love you," he said in a clear voice.

The worry lines left her eyes.

"You do?"

"I'll never say anything to you I don't mean," Ned said.

"Let's promise we'll never lie about love," Maggie whispered. A tiny tear trickled out of the corner of her eye, and tenderly Ned licked it away. Who could hurt a girl like this?

"I promise," he said.

"Make love to me," she said again.

Then, as if Ned had done the act many times, as if the act was programmed into him, he gently raised his body above Maggie. She reached for his penis, guiding it between her legs.

This was the most amazing thing Ned had ever known. Surrounded by her slippery wetness, he let himself glide in and out. He lowered his body against hers.

She cried out, and at first he was afraid he was crushing her. But when he looked at her face, he saw the pleasure. They moved together, embracing, their eyes locked. Electricity tingled in his penis, charging through his body. He felt it flooding into Maggie, as her little pussy expanded and contracted with each of his thrusts.

He'd been in control, but suddenly he felt himself losing it. Each time he pushed down, he felt her silky breasts against his chest, teasing and nuzzling, the image of her diamond nipples scalding his brain. His eyes closed, his teeth clenched, Ned let go and let gallons of white-hot come explode from his body.

Collapsing on top of Maggie, he somehow had the presence of mind to keep from squishing her. Gasping for breath, seeing stars, he held himself one inch aloft on his elbows.

"I love you," he said. "I love you."

Maggie rubbed his back, holding him close. She seemed to be massaging him into an enchanted dreamworld; drugged by their sweat and musk, he was about to fall asleep when he heard her whisper.

"Please?" she asked in an impossibly small voice. "Could you do me?"

"Oh, sure, I'm sorry," Ned asked, totally flustered. His hands moved nervously, unsure of how to use them.

Girls didn't come the same way as boys, he knew. He'd read about that spot on their bodies, the clitoris, and he even knew, from looking through *Penthouse,* approximately where to find it. But what did you do with it? Boys had seven inches of nerve endings to work with, and girls had a distinct epicenter.

He didn't have to worry. Without any inhibitions, Maggie guided his fingers to her pussy. She let him hold the back of her hand while she showed him the exact spot and the right rhythm with her own middle finger. After a moment he eased her hand away. He felt, rather than saw. There it was, just as prominent as a tiny penis. He rubbed, as she had done, and when his finger dried and the friction seemed too great, he licked his own finger.

They lay in the tall grass, naked and sweating, with Ned bringing Maggie along until she relaxed her back and screamed, startling a flock of starlings. The birds took off in formation, like a great black cape being shaken over the field. Enfolding Maggie in his arms, Ned was overcome with emotion.

After many minutes had passed, he whispered his confession: "That was my first time."

And she whispered hers: "It was mine, too. No boy has ever cared enough to do that for me."

"I do," Ned whispered, and he kissed her lips to seal the promise.

In a limousine on the way to JFK Airport, Matt Davis glanced through the travel section of Sunday's *New York Times*. He was on his way to Monaco, a quick twenty-four-hour trip, to meet with an exiled Hungarian countess, best known for her scandalous love life and a surprisingly successful series of exercise videos. Now she wanted to launch her own perfume.

The travel section featured Monaco in the "What's Doing" column, and Matt's secretary had thoughtfully tucked the paper under his arm as he had left the office. Scanning the article, he saw that it rounded up the usual suspects: the casino, the Grand Prix, the Vieux Port, the aquarium, Jules Millet's three-star restaurant. Since Matt had been to Monte Carlo more times than he wished to remember, he flipped past the column.

Maybe it was time to think about summer vacation. This would be his first year without Anne or Karen, without going to the island. Well, there was always Maine. He could take a cottage at Port Clyde, where he had summered as a child. Or something even more remote, like Swan's Island or Bass Harbor. But when he came to the country-inn section, his eyes were drawn to the listings on Anne's island.

He read each one: Atwood's Inn, the Surf Hotel, Harwood's B&B, and Fitzgibbons'. His mouth dropped open as he read:

FITZGIBBONS': Sea views, ocean breezes, warm family atmosphere, best island breakfasts. Contact Gabrielle Vincent.

With his eyes glued to the paper, he reached for the cellular phone and dialed the familiar digits, the same old number that had always rung at the big house.

A young woman, whose voice Matt did not recognize, answered on the fifth ring.

"I'd like to make a reservation," he said. "For this weekend."

"You're in luck," the girl said. "We have just one room left. It has single beds."

Karen's room, Matt thought. The room that had been Anne's as a child. "That would be fine," he said.

"For how many people?"

"Just one. For Friday and Saturday nights."

"Your name, please?"

"Ventura," he said, using the first and most ironic alias that came to mind: Anne's obstetrician. When Anne found out what he had done, she would warm to the fact that he'd booked the room under Dr. Ventura's name.

"Great, Mr. Ventura," the girl said spiritedly. "See you in two nights."

"I can't wait," Matt said.

Chapter 18

Ever since seeing the whales with Thomas, Anne had spent most of her time thinking about him. She could list the reasons to be apart, and each of them was valid. Neither she nor Thomas liked rocking the boat, they cared deeply for the people in their lives, they didn't want anyone to be hurt. When they had met, Anne had been in free fall, and she didn't believe she should be with another person until she found herself on solid ground. But then she'd remember how it felt to hold him, and all the rest would turn to mush.

The truth was a blue star, blazing brighter than any other in any constellation: Anne Davis and Thomas Devlin were meant to be together. Fire and sorrow had brought them to each other, and love had developed from there.

It was Friday, four days since they had returned to shore after whale watching. Sitting in her office, Anne couldn't wait for a momentary lull in the action so she could call Thomas.

Two couples from Providence were standing at the counter, telling Anne about the whales they had seen. Their eyes wide, gesturing with extravagance, they were all talking at once. One couple looked about sixty, twenty or so years older than the other two, and Anne guessed that they were the younger woman's parents.

Grinning at their pleasure, she listened to the descriptions and remembered what she and Thomas had seen.

"Excuse me," she said just as they were leaving. "I know it's none of my business, but are you related?"

"Why, yes," the older man said. "This is our daughter and her husband."

"You look like your mother," Anne said, smiling at the younger woman.

When they had waved good-bye, now discussing where they should have dinner that night, Anne thought of how lucky they were. On vacation together, obviously enjoying each other's company, a family making their way through life all together. You saw it all the time, without realizing how extraordinary it was: men and women who stayed married to each other, children who watched their parents grow old, parents whose children outlived them, sisters who stayed close through thick and thin.

Very slowly, feeling lucky to have Gabrielle, Anne called Thomas.

"Hello," came the familiar deep Boston accent.

"Hi," she said. "Are you busy?"

"Not one bit," he said, and she heard metal hitting metal, as if he had dropped something in his workshop.

"I had such a great time on Monday. I've been thinking about you ever since."

"You didn't mind me taking Maggie's place?"

"The opposite, in fact. It was wonderful. I was wondering . . . would you like to come over tonight?"

"Oh, we're doing fire drills at six," he said, disappointment heavy in his voice. "Ned's just joined the squad, and we made plans to grab some supper with the other guys."

"How about afterward?" Anne asked.

"Afterward would be fine," Thomas said.

In trying to run an inn and a catering business at the same time, perhaps Gabrielle had bitten off more than she had imagined. But *not,* she said to Steve and Maggie, more than she could chew. They were huddled in the laundry room at Fitzgibbons', having a family conference, the washer's spin cycle keeping their words from earshot of the employees.

"Learning to delegate is the most important part of running a successful business," she said.

"You're here all the time, babe," Steve complained. "Maggie's always working here or out with her boyfriend. We have no home life anymore."

"Steve, you know the season is short. We're banking double what we did last June, and that's all there is to it. What I need from you is support, not criticism. You make me feel guilty if you act all neglected."

"Do you know his name?" Maggie asked sullenly.

"Huh?" Steve asked, a whipped expression in his washed blue eyes.

"I have a new boyfriend," Maggie said. "I was just curious about whether you've noticed or not."

"You're young," Steve said. "You don't need to settle down with one guy. Have a ball—life's too short."

"That's what I thought," Maggie said. "You haven't noticed."

"The preppie. I've noticed."

Maggie turned her back, heading out the door.

"Here—take these," Gabrielle said, hoisting a plastic basket laden with wet sheets. She heaved it over to Maggie. "Get one of the other girls to help you hang them on the line."

Wordlessly, Maggie took the basket and left.

Gabrielle had a thousand things to do. She had to run into town, pick up brochures and ad proofs from the printer. Tonight the Wickershams were having fifty for cocktails, and Gabrielle was doing lobster strudels, sugar snap peas filled with mint cream, and oyster fritters with coriander-pepper sauce. But first, she had to set Steve straight on Maggie.

"Maggie wants you to notice the boys she goes out with," Gabrielle said.

"I've noticed. Dev's son. She went to his graduation. Why does she have to get nasty about it?"

"Because she's trying very hard, Steve. You know how hard it is to grow up out here. And it's *ten* times worse for her than it was for us. Ned's a smart kid. He's not into drugs, he really likes Maggie. She wants you to see the difference between him and that rotten Kurt."

"Well, I just think Ned's a little stuck-up. That's all."

"He's shy," Gabrielle said, but she could see by Steve's scowl that he wasn't buying it. Exasperated, she started pulling towels out of the washer.

"So, what's the job you want me to do?" he asked huffily.

"Make a sign. All the guests tell me they drive past, looking for us. I thought something discreet, blue and white, with just 'Fitzgibbons',' for the end of the driveway."

"It's great, pushing forty-five, with your wife making all the money," Steve said to the ceiling. "And your daughter dating rich kids, looking down on you."

"Put your damned ego aside!" Gabrielle said. "You show her no encouragement at all. You treat her the same when she flunks as when she shines."

"I love her no matter what."

"That's not what I mean, and you know it. She needs praise for the good choices she makes. She spent last year in very rocky water. Kurt was bad news, and he was taking Maggie right down with him."

"Maggie's a good girl. You worry too much," Steve said, beginning to page through a discarded tool catalog, as if he'd already forgotten the job he had agreed to do.

"Listen, if you don't want to make the sign—" Gabrielle said, her temper rising.

"I'll make it, I'll make it. What the hell? No one's building anything anymore—it's not like I'm rolling in work."

Gabrielle listened to him slam the door. She shook her fist at the air behind him, swearing out loud. She knew Steve was insecure about not finishing high school, never moving off the island, unable to provide for his family the way he wanted. During their leanest times, she had resented him for those things and more.

But Steve was her husband, and she loved him. She also loved her daughter. She wanted to set an example for Maggie, to show her that women could succeed as well as or better than men. Above all, they were a family. In time, Steve would realize that Fitzgibbons' was a family business, his as much as anyone's, and maybe he and Gabrielle could start to work together. Instead of resenting each other.

M AGGIE's mother had appointed her chief chambermaid. For that she got paid seventy-five cents more an hour than anyone else, and she got first priority on the schedule. Also, she got to hand out the assignments. In other words, she got to boss the other chambermaids, including Vanessa, around.

Usually she stayed out of Vanessa's way, but today she felt like talking. Most of the other girls were in different grades at Consolidated or summer kids who lived most of the year off-island—girls she didn't know very well. So for help in hanging the sheets out to dry, Maggie called Vanessa.

Early-morning fog had lifted, and the day was turning hot and muggy. In her official uniform (white shorts and navy-blue polo shirt), Maggie carried the laundry basket out back and began pinning a pillowcase to the line.

"It's so humid. These'll never dry," Vanessa said, coming slowly across the grass.

"Eventually they will."

"Why doesn't your mother just use a dryer, like everyone else? This is so much more work."

"Like that's important," Maggie said. "She wants the bed to have that fresh-air smell."

"God, you have changed," Vanessa said with potent disgust, shaking the wrinkles out of a sheet. "What Mommy says, Maggie agrees with. Didn't used to be that way. I suppose these preppie suits were your idea, too."

"Not quite," Maggie said. She had fought her mother tooth and nail to be allowed to wear cutoffs and a halter, but her mother had definite standards you couldn't argue her out of. Maggie should have known, after years of watching her mother iron the little black dresses and starched white aprons she made her waitresses wear.

"I can't believe you gave up Kurt for Ned Devlin. He's not even cute."

"That's your opinion," said Maggie, who found Ned a) adorable, b) sexy, c) super smart, and d) in love with her. Kurt had possessed only the first two qualities, and Maggie had found they definitely weren't enough.

"You just never seemed like the type who would turn your back on your friends."

"I still want to be friends," Maggie said.

"It hasn't seemed it."

"Well, I do. It's just, why is everyone out here so afraid of someone changing? What's so bad about wanting to do better in life?"

"Better than who?"

"Better than no one!" Maggie said. "I'm not talking about competition. I mean, doing the best you can. I feel as if people like me better when I'm stoned and stupid. Even my father."

"Your father?" Vanessa asked, her mood improving. Parent bashing had always been one of their favorite pastimes.

"Yeah, you know. He's still the same."

"Hitting the Bud while your mother does the work?"

"Pretty much," Maggie said, feeling a tickle of guilt for saying so. "He doesn't like Ned either. I don't think he wants me going out with someone who might do better in life than him. See what I mean? Everyone out here has the same complex."

"So, what's Ned doing for the summer?"

"Learning to be a fireman. He just started, and already he got to go to a sort-of fire. Some stupid renters lit a fire in the fireplace without opening the damper, and it smoked them out."

"I'm just glad you're not turning your back on everyone else," Vanessa said, returning to what she considered the important stuff. "We miss partying with you."

"Yeah," Maggie said noncommittally. Before Ned arrived for the summer, she had missed partying with them, too. The temptation of beer and pot and old friends was strong, and she didn't yet know if she had the willpower to keep it under control. To resist getting swept over her head.

"Well, it's Friday," Vanessa said, "and Eugene and Kurt are picking me up after work. We'll probably head over to the cave to party, if you want to come."

"Thanks anyway," Maggie said.

"Tomorrow, then. Or whenever. Ned should give you one night off to hang out with your old friends."

"I'll see," Maggie said, even though the answer was, and would be, no.

JET-LAGGED to within an inch of his life, Matt Davis ran from JFK's Air France terminal to the waiting helicopter. He'd been planning to fly to La Guardia, where he would catch a shuttle to Boston and make that day's last scheduled flight to the island. He had been traveling for forty-eight hours, back and forth through the time zones so fast his head was spinning.

His meeting with Countess Nazarena Splagda had been surreal, in her compound full of exotic animals and waited on by her staff composed entirely of midgets—not dwarves, as she had haughtily informed him. The meeting had been attended by her body-guards, lawyers, business manager, literary agent, sons, ex-husband, and current lover, the wife of a prominent Texas heart surgeon.

A full day's worth of that, and then a slew of transatlantic lies to Tisa, telling her that negotiations were stalled, that he would be home on Monday. Three days late. Then the plane from Nice to New York.

Buckling himself into the helicopter's front seat, Matt settled back. He could go straight to sleep. But the flight to La Guardia was just ten minutes long.

"Is this for hire?" he asked the pilot.

"The aircraft?" the mustachioed pilot asked sternly, with a tankload of military behind the voice.

"Yeah, the aircraft."

"Let me call control," the pilot said.

Matt heard the roters slapping overhead. His eyelids fluttered, and he felt himself drifting off.

"It ain't cheap," the pilot said, quoting Matt the price.

"Fine," Matt said, not even opening his eyes. "Take me to the New Shoreham airport."

It didn't happen often—maybe three or four times a summer. But when the Island Volunteer Fire Department got together for burgers and beer after a drill, you could bet the farm that things would get rowdy. Wives and girlfriends were excluded. Although most of the women considered themselves lucky, some of the men complained that their wives gave them a hard time, that they resented being left out.

Thomas Devlin would trade the whole thing to spend the evening alone with Anne. Ever since she'd called him, earlier in the day, his heart had been pounding with the thought of "afterward." He couldn't wait to see her. But they were breaking Ned into the department, and Thomas wanted to introduce his son to the camaraderie of firefighters.

With Ned helping Marty Cole at the grill, Thomas stood in the sandpit out behind the firehouse, pitching horseshoes with Dick Wade. The sun was down, but there was still enough light to see. Every so often one of them would hit the stake, and the resultant clang would get the other men cheering and hollering.

Dick was tall and portly, getting old fast. The evening was warm and muggy, and Thomas could hear him wheezing. The emphysema that had made him leave the Boston force early had gotten much worse this last year. Thomas loved him like a father. No one told Dick what to do, but Thomas could see the exertion was getting the better of him.

"Come on," Thomas said. "Let's stand aside and let some of the others take their turn."

"All right," Dick said, winded. "You young turks ought to learn some patience," he said to Mike and Hugh, but Thomas caught the grateful look in his eyes. They headed for a pair of webbed folding chairs.

"That son of yours will make a good fireman," Dick said.

"He will," Thomas said. He knew it was brave of Ned to try. At the chimney fire yesterday, Thomas had watched Ned stare wide-eyed, with fear and respect, at the oily black smoke billowing out the front door. Fire was Ned's demon. Thomas had been surprised, and secretly pleased, when Ned had asked if he could volunteer.

"Nothing makes a man out of a boy faster than fire," Dick said.

"If that's true, it happened to Ned long ago."

"I'm sorry, Dev. You're thinking of Sarah."

"She's been on our minds a lot this summer. Ned didn't take too kindly to my seeing Anne Davis."

"To hell with that, son. Life is too short to let our children rule it. If Richard Junior and Beth had their way, Mamie and I would still be living in Roxbury, and their old rooms would be little shrines, full of all their baby things. Blooey to that, I say."

"Ned's coming around. I just have to convince the lady she shouldn't be so worried about it."

"A pretty one, that Mrs. Davis," Dick said. "She's put a sparkle in your eyes, that's for sure. Mamie and I are going to want to meet her before the wedding."

Thomas laughed, and clapped Dick's knee. "You're getting ahead of yourself."

"No, I don't think I am," Dick said, his squint giving him that sly-fox look. "I've known you a long time now, and you don't go about things in a casual way. If she's the one, you're going to marry her. And she's the one."

"How can you tell?" Thomas asked, feeling absurdly happy.

"Just look at you!" Dick said, the Irish of his childhood seeping into his thick Boston accent. "Blushing like a boy at the mere mention of a wedding. You'll be needing a best man. And if Neddy's got a problem with it, you know who you can count on."

"I've always been able to, haven't I?" Thomas asked, smiling with affection for the old man.

WAITING for Thomas, Anne sat on her living-room sofa, a blank piece of stationery on her lap. The night was beautifully hot. A gentle breeze came through the open window, raising goose bumps on her arms. It's not the breeze, she told herself: it's anticipation. Soon Thomas would arrive, and they would be together. She would feel his fingers in her hair, his kiss on her lips, and they would make love until he had to leave. But there was something she had to do first.

Anne sighed. She forced herself to concentrate on the letter she had to write. She had avoided this for too long, but if she was going to give herself over to loving Thomas Devlin, she had to take care of unfinished business.

First, she pulled Karen's drawing out of its folder. She stared at it long and sternly, asking herself if she was sure. Mommy, Daddy, Gramercy Park, vacations together on the island: was she ready to give that up?

You didn't choose what happened before, she told herself. But you have to choose now. You have to decide. And so, she began to write.

Dear Matt,

I have dreaded the day that I would write this letter. For several months I have had moments when I thought I was ready to write it, but then doubts would surface, preventing me. I promised myself that as long as I had questions, as long as I felt ambivalent, I would wait. But now I am ready; I no longer have those doubts. I want a divorce.

It's hard to believe that we have been married eleven years this month. So much of that time I was happier than I had ever believed possible. You showed me the world. Every trip we ever took is etched in my memory. My birthday in Venice, when you took me to a Vivaldi concert in that pink jewel-box theater; Ireland, where we found my grandfather's grave in that little churchyard north of Galway; all those enchanted trips to Provence, in search of the most beautiful flowers.

And, of course, our daughter. The day she was born I loved you more than ever before. I truly believe I couldn't have gone through those twenty hours of labor without your strength and love and sense of humor (although I distinctly remember wanting to kill you at the time—how many times did you have to tell that piece-of-string joke?).

Anne put down her pen, smiling at the memory. She didn't want to write the next part. There were things she needed to say about Karen, to make this difficult letter complete, and she couldn't quite bring herself to write them. Thomas would be arriving soon. She had hoped to have this done by then.

Just finish the letter, she commanded herself. Reading over the words she had already written, she searched her mind for what would come next. Downstairs, the front door closed, and she heard footsteps on the stairs. So be it, she thought, laying the letter facedown on the coffee table. She went to the door to answer his knock.

But the man standing in her hallway was not Thomas.

"Hello, Anne," said Matt.

His eyes looked bloodshot, as if he had not slept in some time. But they were bright, and they couldn't hide the pleasure he felt in seeing her. He looked as handsome as ever. Tall and lean, with boyishly tousled brown hair, a straight nose, and a charmingly crooked smile. His rumpled dark suit hung elegantly on his athletic body, and although he affected his usual air of "who cares?" confidence, Anne could see his hands shaking.

"Will you invite me in?" he asked, the tone in his voice a possible indication that he feared perhaps she would not.

Wordlessly Anne stood aside, and her husband walked past her, into her apartment.

Chapter 19

Matt made a quick study of Anne's apartment. Tall white walls with hardly any pictures on them, a few pieces of shabby furniture, the windows overlooking the harbor the room's best feature. Aside from her typically messy worktable, there wasn't a trace of Anne's personality present. She didn't plan to stay here forever. He turned to her, grinning.

"How have you been?" he asked. "God, it's good to see you!"

"Why are you here?" she asked, sounding shell-shocked. She looked lovely: her jet hair longer than he had seen it in years, not a trace of makeup on her porcelain skin, black palazzo pants and a black mesh tunic clinging to her beautiful curves. She looked sexy as hell, and all Matt wanted to do was kiss her.

"It's been more than six months since I've seen you," he said, just drinking her in. "Do you know, for the last eleven years, until now, I don't think we've gone more than a few days without each other. Eleven years this month."

"Yes, I was just thinking that," she said, turning away from him.

Her voice was flat, unwelcoming, as if she were afraid of feeling something for him.

"May I sit down?" he asked.

"You should have called," she said, whirling around, fire in her gray eyes. "You know my number."

"This morning I was in Nice," Matt said. "Yesterday at this time I was returning to my hotel from a meeting with a perfectly vile countess who wants her name on a perfume guaranteed to 'stimulate the male sex glands.' Her words. She doesn't give a hoot whether it smells like orchids or roses or musk or horse manure as long as it makes men horny."

Anne passed a hand across her eyes, standing stiffly across the room from him. Frowning. Shit, Matt thought. Usually his tales of fame-crazed would-be perfume hawkers cracked her up. But he had miscalculated. The jet lag had totally thrown his timing off.

"I'm sorry," he said. "I thought you'd think it was funny."

As if he had sprung a slow leak, he felt the adrenaline start to whistle out of him. For days, he had thought of nothing but seeing Anne. In his fantasy, his old ways had worked: he had half expected to settle into the sweet banter he had prized with Anne, that had totally eluded him and Tisa. He felt dizzy.

"What are you doing here?" she asked again.

"I came to see you," he said, subdued now. "To try to work things out."

"Matt—"

"Please, listen. Just for a minute." He took a deep breath and swallowed. He felt his resolve coming back. "I made a mistake. I really messed up. Losing you is the worst thing that could happen, and I did it myself. I miss you so much, Anne."

"Matt—"

"On my way to the plane I started thinking about summer, how this would be my first summer without coming to the island with you. Then I happened to be glancing through the travel section, and I saw an ad for the big house. Gabrielle's turned it into a hotel?"

Anne nodded, her expression still hard.

"So, I made a reservation."

"At the big house?" Anne asked with disbelief.

" 'Fitzgibbons',' as I believe it's called in the ad."

"Gabrielle knows about this?"

"I doubt it. Some girl, not Maggie, answered. And I made the reservation under a different name." Matt hesitated. He wanted to tell Anne that he'd booked himself in under Dr. Ventura's name, but he restrained himself. He sensed that he would not win favor, groveling for brownie points. Better that she find out on her own.

"That's sneaky."

"I know. But maybe it gives you some idea of how desperate I am to get you back. And I will, Anne. You can't talk me out of it."

His heart overflowing, Matt moved closer to his wife. Her hair smelled freshly washed; he detected no traces of the perfume she had always worn, the one he had had created especially for her on her thirtieth birthday. He had given it no name, for no one would ever find it at any store. It was Anne's alone.

He gazed down at her, willing her to look up. If she did, if her expression had softened even slightly, he would caress her cheek, tenderly kiss her lips. He would make her his own again. He wondered whether she could hear his heart, pounding like crazy in his chest.

Not even thinking, he sank to his knees, took her hand. So tiny, filled with such delicate bones. The feel of her hand brought back such memories, tears came to his eyes. She didn't pull away, but she wouldn't smile at him.

"Please, Anne," he said. "I love you. Please forgive me."

He felt her stiffness. Pain flashed across her eyes as she looked away, then back. She stared down at him, as if memorizing his face. Perhaps she was remembering his proposal: on his knees, at twilight, at a beach not five miles away from this very spot. If it weren't so late, he would invite her to dinner at Atwood's, the restaurant where they had dined later that night, the first place she had appeared in public wearing his ring.

She wasn't wearing it now. For the first time since entering the room, he noticed. No diamond, no wedding band. But he held his tongue. His life was on the line, the decision hers. She stood tall, her gaze flickering from his eyes to his mouth to the air above his head.

"There's something I have to show you," she said, gently withdrawing her hand. She walked to the sofa, leaving him alone on his knees, as if he was saying some frantic prayer. Which he was.

"Please," she said. "Come sit down."

Slowly, he raised himself off the floor and walked to the sofa. She seemed to want him to sit beside her, and for some reason he felt afraid. Objects swam in his vision. He couldn't focus, and his throat felt dry. On the table in front of him were two sheets of paper. One appeared to be a child's drawing, and the other was blank. She handed him the blank paper. When he turned it over, he saw her handwriting.

How many times had he seen that handwriting? No one in the world could know it better than he. All the notes she had left on the refrigerator, the shopping lists, the checks she had signed, the notes she had tucked into his luggage. He had never, not once in all the ten years they had lived together, gone away from home without finding one of Anne's notes nestled in his underwear. Notes so full of her wit and love. So full of Anne herself.

His throat choked up, he forced himself to read.

When he came to the word "divorce," he heard himself say "oh!" He looked at Anne, but she was facing away from him. When he had finished reading, he lowered the paper to his lap.

"I should have had the courage to say it out loud," she said in a measured tone.

HOME FIRES

Matt's head was buzzing. He heard her speak, but he couldn't make sense of her words. Mechanically, as if he was in a trance, he reached for the other paper on the table before him.

"What's this?" he asked dumbly, staring at the picture. The images blurred, but he tried to focus.

"Karen drew that," Anne said.

Of course. He had never seen it before, but he should have known. How many pictures had she drawn him of herself, Matt, and Anne? She had been so proud when she would visit his office with Anne and see her own drawings taped to his walls.

He stared at each element of the picture. The family, the park, the beach, the birds she had loved so much, two strange concrete blocks.

"It's a picture of her life," Matt said.

"All the things she loved," Anne said, her voice breaking. "She called it *Paradise*."

"Poor little girl," Matt said. "Poor little girl."

"She did it that day," Anne said, sitting closer to Matt, taking one side of Karen's picture in her hand. She stared with frowning intensity, her chin trembling. A tear from Matt's eye plopped onto the manila paper, and Anne immediately dabbed it dry with her finger. As if afraid he might do serious damage to the picture, Anne eased it away from him.

"Please," he said. "Let me look. Why didn't you show it to me before?"

"I don't know," Anne said. "You were both gone. The picture was all I had."

Matt slid his arm around Anne's shoulders, and she cried into his chest, her tears soaking through his shirt to his skin. He closed his eyes, smelling her hair. He wanted to freeze the moment forever. He wanted never to leave this spot. He wanted to grow old and die with Anne in his arms, Karen's drawing resting between them on their knees.

After a few minutes her sobs subsided. She wiped her cheeks and drew away from him. She looked at him with clear gray eyes. He knew immediately what she was going to say.

"I do," she said. "I want a divorce."

"We have so much," he said.

"We did," she said. "But it's gone now."

"It would hurt Karen," he said.

"Matt—" Anne raised her hands to her ears, then dropped them.

"No one else can understand what we've gone through," Matt said. "We lost our only child, Anne. That binds us together forever. Whether we like it or not, that's our fate."

"Yes," Anne said. "It is. And if we had come together last August, right after she died, if we had stared at her picture like we've done tonight, and tried to survive together, maybe . . ."

"There's still a chance. There is. In this entire world you couldn't find someone who loves you like I do. Someone who knows what you've been through."

"There is," Anne said softly. "And I have found him."

Matt's blood went cold. The man Gabrielle had told him about.

"Have you slept with him?" Matt asked, feeling fearful. But the words came out sounding harsh, like an attack.

"Don't be a fool," Anne said, tearing herself off the couch. She tucked Karen's picture away in a folder and carried it to a table across the room.

"Have you?"

"Try to keep your dignity," Anne said. "This, coming from you? Have you forgotten what started this whole thing?"

How could he forget? Matt reddened, picturing himself and Tisa in bed together, Anne standing in the door.

"That's over," Matt said, knowing it was. He hadn't exactly broken up with Tisa yet, but he hadn't cared for her in a long time.

"I don't care," Anne said. "I hope you're happy. I truly do.

Writing the word 'divorce,' I felt like my heart would break. But it's the right thing. I know that. I love someone, Matt."

"That will pass," Matt said impatiently. "Trust me."

"No," Anne said, shaking her head. "It won't. And I'd like you to leave now."

Matt stood his ground, trying to stare her down. But it was he who looked away first. He wished he had brought in his suitcase and briefcase instead of leaving them in the hall. If he had to walk out, he wanted to do it with a flourish.

"I'll be at the big house," he said. "Until Sunday night. I want to see you again."

Anne shook her head. "No," she said.

She unlatched the door and held it open, not looking at him. Footsteps sounded in the stairwell, and they both glanced over the handrail. Here came one of the biggest men Matt had ever seen. A good ten years older than Matt, with a massive frame and gnarled hands.

"Leave," Anne said under her breath.

Matt ignored her. He stood beside her, watching the man mount the stairs. When he reached Anne's landing, an expression of puzzlement clouded his grotesque eyes.

"You must be Thomas Devlin," Matt said in his best boardroom voice. He reached out a hand. "Matthew Davis," he said.

The giant looked at Anne, as if to ask her permission. Then he shook Matt's hand. Not a bad handshake, Matt had to admit.

"Mr. Davis," the man said steadily.

"Matt, leave," Anne said.

"She's a married woman," Matt said pleasantly, grabbing his suitcase and briefcase. "Keep that in mind."

Bounding down the stairs, as if he weren't jet-lagged beyond exhaustion and cracking in half with grief, Matt expected to hear Anne or the man call after him. When they didn't, he glanced up, over his shoulder. And saw the door close softly behind them.

.   .   .

IF Anne Davis were his wife, if another man showed up and tried to take her away, Thomas Devlin would throw him against a wall. He would take his punch. He would hunt him down and make him hurt. He would not shake his hand and offer a sarcastic warning in a friendly tone of voice.

Holding Anne tight, he felt her entire body quivering.

"Shh," he whispered into her ear. "Shhh. It's okay. You'll be fine."

"I asked him for a divorce," Anne said.

"That must have been hard," Thomas Devlin said, his heart soaring.

"Very," she said, in a high, thin voice.

"I love you," he said.

"And I love you," she said, "but I can't tonight. I couldn't wait to see you, but I can't be with you now."

"I understand," Thomas said. He felt disappointed, and a little hurt, but not rejected.

She pushed herself away, her eyes blank.

"Tomorrow?" she asked, worry lines in her forehead. "I need to be alone right now. I didn't expect to see him, and I'm upset."

"You must be confused," he said.

At that she smiled, and she gazed up at him with enormous eyes. She caressed his cheek with her hand, and he held it there.

"Oh, no," she said. "I'm not confused. I'm not confused at all."

"Tomorrow, then," Thomas said.

"I'll make us a picnic," Anne said. "After work?"

"I'll pick you up then," Thomas said, giving her one more long kiss before yielding to her wish and leaving her alone.

THE next morning, when Gabrielle walked into the dining room with a pot of fresh-brewed house-blend coffee and a basket full of blueberry muffins straight from the oven, she couldn't believe her eyes.

There, sitting at his usual place at the table, was Matt.

"Hello, stranger," he said, grinning. He wore tennis whites, and he was reading the morning paper.

"What in the world are you doing here?" she asked, momentarily stunned. She put the scalding coffee pot right down on the pine table and hurried over to give him a crushing hug.

"I missed you," he said.

"My ass," she snorted. "You miss Anne."

"That is so," he said, bowing with his classic, courtly charm.

"You need to call her right away. She'll kill me when she finds out about this."

"I saw her last night. She knows you had nothing to do with it. She called me sneaky."

"What happened?"

"Her boyfriend showed up. After she asked me for a divorce."

"Oh, Matt. I'm sorry," Gabrielle said, trying to gauge his tone. He might have been telling her about a movie he had seen, a book he had read. He spoke with his usual pleasant flair, with no signs of distress.

Matt held up a crossing-guard "stop" hand, that crinkled smile on his face. "I'll wear her down," he said. "I don't take no for an answer."

"We're talking about Anne," Gabrielle said dubiously, thinking of her sister's amazing powers of refusal.

"And we're talking about me. I know a thing or two about determination."

God, the man did a good job of masking his feelings, Gabrielle thought. He had frown lines a mile deep in his forehead, and he looked as if he hadn't had a decent rest since last August. But he was damned if he'd let anyone know.

Outside, car doors slammed. The girls were arriving for work. Gabrielle steeled herself for the moment when Maggie would come looking for her. She didn't have to wait long.

The dining-room door swung open, and Gabrielle heard Maggie gasp.

"Hey there, Maggs," Matt said, opening his arms. "Give your uncle Matt a hug."

Maggie just stared at him.

"You don't belong here," she said.

"Maggie! Remember your manners," Gabrielle admonished, embarrassed and not knowing what to do.

"I'm here to set things right," Matt said evenly. Was it Gabrielle's imagination, or was that coldness glazing over his eyes?

"Anne told me what you did," Maggie said darkly.

"She did? I'm surprised."

Gabrielle just listened with amazement to this exchange that excluded her totally.

"Yeah, she did. So don't expect me to be thrilled to see you. You hurt her."

"That's between me and Anne," Matt said, with definite iciness.

Although Gabrielle had no idea of what he and Maggie were talking about, she felt her opinion of him beginning to shift. Very slowly but definitely, she found herself regarding him with distaste. She wished that he had found somewhere else to stay.

"What do you want us to do first today?" Maggie asked, turning her back on Matt, facing Gabrielle.

"Let's go into the kitchen," Gabrielle said, nudging her daughter's shoulder.

"I'm looking for a tennis partner, Gaby," Matt said. "Can I convince you to play hooky?"

"I'm sorry," she said, turning on a little glacier of her own. "We have lots of work to do."

Together, Gabrielle and Maggie left Matt alone at the dining-room table. Gabrielle glanced back at him once. He sat still, gazing out the window. He looked lost and a little crazed, sitting in his old spot at the table. As if the house were still the family's own and he was just waiting for Anne and Karen to come walking through the door. Gabrielle felt a tug of pity. She nearly went to him with a comforting hug. But there had been something cruel in his coldness, and she didn't want to explore further.

Chapter 20

Matt's presence in the house threw everything off-kilter and put Maggie in a terrible mood. All the guests had left the ˜inn, for the beach or wherever, and Maggie was standing at the dining-room table, trying to polish up the spot where her mother had put the coffeepot. No hot plate, no nothing: when stove-hot wet glass meets bare wood, you get ugly rings that don't come out.

Her mother had obviously been curious about the exchange between Maggie and Matt, but Maggie had to hand it to her: her mom had been cool, asking no direct questions, probably figuring that if Anne wanted her to know, Anne would tell her herself.

Maggie had heard her mother's van pull out about ten minutes ago, so she made her way to the phone. Anne answered on the first ring, as if she'd been sitting on it.

"Prepare yourself," Maggie said. "Matt's here."

"I know. I saw him."

"You're not taking him back, are you?" Maggie asked. God, what if she was? Just three hours ago Maggie had stood at this very table, defending Anne and cutting Matt down to size. She would feel extremely stupid.

"No," Anne said, and Maggie blinked with relief.

"I'm sorry I missed whale watching last Monday," Maggie said.

"You are?" Anne asked, a big smile entering her voice. "Will it hurt your feelings if I tell you I'm not?"

"He's nice, isn't he?" Maggie asked.

"Yes, very. You gave us a push, and we needed it. Thank you."

"Anytime," Maggie said, grinning with shy pride.

"How's Ned?"

"Oh, he's great. We should double-date sometime. He wants to."

"He does?" Anne asked, and Maggie could hear that she'd gotten Anne's hopes way up.

"Well, he wants to want to. That's a step in the right direction, you know?"

"Yes, it is. All in good time," Anne said.

Just then Maggie caught a whiff of sweet, acrid smoke. Pot? She sniffed again. Yes, definitely.

"I'd better go," she said to Anne.

"Okay. Thanks again for what you did for me and Thomas. And, Maggie?"

"Yeah?"

"You've come a long way. I want you to know that I've noticed. You're a different Maggie than the girl I found at the Quality Inn. Keep it up, okay?"

"Okay," Maggie said.

In some ways, Anne was right. Maggie was entirely changed. She had different goals—shit, she *had* goals. That in itself was new. She didn't need to desecrate herself just to prove something to her friends. No more holes in her body, no more tattoos, no more waking up every morning with cottonmouth and a pounding headache.

On the other hand, the old Maggie was still in there. The smell of pot was luring her, just the way a flute calls a snake. But smoking it was just an evil habit, a way to avoid feeling bad. What did she have to feel bad about? Nothing. It was a gorgeous summer day, and after work she and Ned were going to sail with Josh out to Sandymount Island.

Outside, behind the hedge by Karen's herb garden, she found Vanessa sharing a joint with Céline, a summer girl from Montreal.

Céline had bored, languorous eyes and a pouty mouth, with very blond hair teased up and long bangs combed in a slant across her face. Maggie wondered whether she spent hours in front of the mirror practicing that sex-crazed look.

At the sight of Maggie, Vanessa took a hit and passed the joint.

"Don't do that here," Maggie said.

"Shut up and take it." Vanessa giggled.

"Vanessa—"

"You *are* getting stoned, and you are coming out with us tonight. So don't even think you're not."

Maggie felt really strange, watching her friend smoke grass in Karen's herb garden. It seemed disrespectful to Karen's spirit. Maggie knew this didn't make sense, but she didn't want to set Karen a bad example. She put her hands on Vanessa's shoulders and began gently pushing her into the backyard.

"Are we playing choo-choo?" Vanessa asked. "Come on aboard, Céline."

Now Maggie felt Céline's hands on her waist, and the three girls wove toward the kitchen door. By the time they got there, all three were laughing, and Vanessa had finished the joint.

"That's better," Vanessa said. "Making beds and cleaning toilets with a buzz is the only way to go."

Céline said something in French; not comprehending, Maggie laughed along, relieved. She had withstood the temptation, and she'd gotten them out of the herb garden. Best of all, in just a few hours she and Ned would be sailing the open water.

Maggie couldn't wait.

A T the vegetable stand during her lunch hour, shopping for tonight's picnic, Anne bumped into Gabrielle. They'd been standing under the same daffodil-yellow-and-white-striped tent, oblivious to each other. Choosing tomatoes, Anne was lost in the white noise of bumblebees cruising the plums and cars whizzing by on Billow Road. Suddenly someone standing right next to her reached out to fondle a tomato, and Anne recognized Gabrielle's hand.

The sisters jumped at once.

Startled, Anne slapped her own chest.

"God, you gave me a start," Gabrielle said.

"What are you doing here?" Anne asked. "You have your own vegetable garden."

"My tomatoes aren't coming in yet. They've been slightly neglected in favor of the inn this year."

"I understand you have a prize guest staying with you."

"I swear, on my own husband, that I didn't know Matt was coming. Vanessa Adamson took the reservation, and he booked it under a phony name."

"Well, it's over," Anne said, lowering her voice as a sunburned couple sauntered by. "I told him I want a divorce."

"You know," Gabrielle began, making sure the couple was out of earshot, "that I totally disapproved of that?"

"Don't start," Anne said sharply.

"Just listen, you. I've changed my mind. I think. Something went on between him and Maggie this morning, about something he did to you . . . ?" The question in Gabrielle's voice went unanswered, and she continued. "Anyway, I saw a cold side of him that I didn't like. I just want you to know."

"He's sad," Anne said. "He screwed up, that's for sure. But now he knows he has to give up."

"He must have done something awful to hurt you," Gabrielle said, gently probing.

"Mmmm," Anne said, examining a tomato.

"Why won't anyone tell me what he did?" Gabrielle asked, suddenly wound up like a top. Her fists clenched, she was pure nervous tension. Her wide mouth froze in a grimace, and Anne could tell Gabrielle had attracted the attention of other shoppers.

"What happened was humiliating," Anne said under her breath.

"Here I am, trying to be supportive of you, and you're still shutting me out. You and Maggie are closer to each other than you are to me. Don't think that doesn't sting."

"Gabrielle," Anne said, shocked by her sister's display of raw pain.

"I know. I know all about it. That rapist, that lunatic in the truck, he was probably a serial killer. And does she call me? She does not. Instead of her own mother, my daughter calls you for help."

"Maggie told you about that? Good," Anne said.

"She did not tell me," Gabrielle said, plump tears squeezing out the corners of her eyes, falling onto the tomatoes. "I overheard her, months ago, when she thought I was asleep, talking on the phone to Ned. I was standing in the hallway, listening to her tell this boy the most horrendous, terrifying story I have ever heard. I was afraid to make a sound. If she heard me, she would stop talking, and I would never know what had happened. All I could think was, she might have been killed!"

"I didn't know what to do," Anne said slowly. "She was in trouble, that was obvious. And she was afraid to have you find out."

"Am I so mean? Am I such an ogre?" Gabrielle asked in a voice between a whisper and a wail.

"No, the opposite," Anne said, reaching for her hand. "We never want to disappoint you."

"Disappoint me!" Gabrielle said. "I feel so shut out right now. . . . You've confided in Maggie some dreadful thing about Matt, Maggie's all concerned about making sure your love life with Thomas runs smoothly. I'm out of it entirely."

"No, you're not. I'm sorry if I've treated you that way," Anne said, knowing that she had.

"I have to leave now," Gabrielle said, her lower lip quivering. She scrubbed tears out of her eyes.

"Gabrielle," Anne called, wanting to make peace. "I'm fixing a romantic picnic for tonight. Can you help me out? I need an idea."

But Gabrielle just waved the air behind her, stumbled into her van. That's when Anne realized just how hurt her sister felt. Never in her life could she remember her sister turning down the chance to help plan a meal.

G ABRIELLE drove twice around the island, then took a walk on the deserted end of Salt Whistle Beach. She felt bleached with frustration and agony. Everyone thought she was a brick. Solid Gabrielle, the nurturing sister, mother, and wife. Take her for granted, appreciate her, it didn't matter: she'd keep giving, no matter what.

It had been that way since she was a little girl. She had been a teenager when her parents had died; she had taken on the responsibilities of raising Anne without once looking back. She had sacrificed her senior prom, because she didn't have a sitter. She had missed out on college, travel, all the things she had wanted for Anne.

Maybe that explained it: Anne and Maggie. They had both been raised by Gabrielle, and that gave them a sisterly bond. Well, Gabrielle had had enough of that. They weren't sisters.

A westerly breeze blew square off the water, drying her tears.

The sun had gone behind some pillowy clouds, lighting them orange and purple from behind. Gabrielle had a dinner party to cater that night, a clambake for eighteen. She had barely started preparations, but she didn't feel inclined to leave the beach.

Standing at the low-tide line, her bare toes burrowing in the wet sand, she felt the cool waves lick her ankles. When had she last come to the beach without a bunch of people to feed? She was always making beach picnics, hot-dog roasts, champagne suppers.

She'd been feeding strangers for years. And now, as if making a nest for her own family were not enough, she had opened her family home to travelers. What fueled this compulsion to feed every hungry mouth from the ferry dock to Salt Pond? And now she was luring them from off-island with mouthwatering ads in Sunday papers everywhere.

For now, nothing fueled Gabrielle. She took a deep breath, forced herself to walk back to her van. In less than two hours she was supposed to have a pit dug, the fire going, and seaweed steaming. Forget it—she'd do the short-form clambake tonight. On top of the stove, in big iron kettles. To hell with the customers, if they didn't like it.

When she returned to Fitzgibbons', Gabrielle found Brian Pearse, a young lawyer from Boston, waiting for her on the front porch. She had chatted with him and his wife last night. They had seemed pleasant, perhaps a little shy, asking her about beaches on the island. It didn't take long for Gabrielle to figure that they were after Haley's, the nude sunbathing beach. She gave them directions to find it, including the only place they could park their car and not get towed.

"Hello," she called. "Did you find the path to the beach all right?"

He assured her that he had. He seemed hesitant, as if there was something he wasn't quite sure he should mention.

"Is there something wrong?" Gabrielle asked, frowning.

"I hate to even say anything, but we're missing a bottle from our room. My wife remembers packing it, a little bottle of Grand Marnier. Maybe one of the girls accidentally moved it while cleaning. . . ."

"I'll check into it," Gabrielle said, thin-lipped.

Marching into the laundry room, she found Maggie, Vanessa, and Céline folding sheets. She did a piercing survey of their eyes, the dilation of their pupils, and thought maybe she detected something funny about Vanessa's. She closed the door behind her.

"I've had a complaint," she said. "From one of the guests. A bottle is missing from his room."

Both Vanessa and Céline were wide-eyed, innocent as lambs. Only Gabrielle's very own Maggie showed signs of guilt. A deep blush crept up her neck, straight to the roots of her hair, and her gaze darted everywhere except Gabrielle's face.

"I'd like to speak with you in private, Maggie," Gabrielle said with what she considered admirable restraint.

Matt stood in the kitchen, helping himself to a glass of milk from the refrigerator. Gabrielle felt like snapping at him: *You're just like any other guest, keep out of my kitchen.* Full of seething, unfocused anger, she walked straight past, ignoring his greeting.

"Creep," Maggie said under her breath.

"Save it," Gabrielle said.

She led Maggie out back, to the potting shed. The place hadn't been used in years. Full of old flower flats, dusty potting soil, cobwebs, and garden tools, Gabrielle had planned to make it next year's project: a honeymoon cottage, separate from the main house. But right now she saw only the dust and filth, and she felt mocked.

"How could you?" she asked, turning on Maggie.

"I didn't take it!"

"Then look me straight in the eye and tell me who did. Was it Vanessa? Céline?"

Maggie gave a sullen shrug, and Gabrielle slapped her face. Maggie looked up, her mouth an O. Gabrielle had never, not

once in her entire life, slapped her daughter. She felt shocked by
what she had done, but she didn't regret it.

"Shall we march right inside?" Gabrielle asked. "So you can
point out the culprit to me?"

When Maggie didn't answer, Gabrielle exhaled. "No, I didn't
think so. Do you have any idea of how hard I work? Do you know
how unlikely it is for an inn like this to really succeed? It takes
word of mouth, Maggie, and if guests head home and tell their
friends that the chambermaids are thieves, do you think people
will want to come? Do you? Answer me!"

"I didn't take it," Maggie whispered.

"Guess what? I don't care whether you did or not. You
wouldn't tell me the truth if your life depended on it. I don't even
know what to believe anymore."

"I would tell you. I swear, Mom. I didn't—"

But Gabrielle was in a blind rage, too far gone to listen. Her
fury was a ball of yarn, a tangle made from Maggie and Anne's
secrets, Matt sneaking into her guest book, the theft of the Pearses'
Grand Marnier, and a serious disappointment in herself. Here she
was, more concerned with betrayal than the fact that she suspected
her sixteen-year-old of stealing liquor.

"You're grounded," Gabrielle said as calmly as she could.

Still touching her red cheek, her eyes full of tears, Maggie stared
at her mother. You could practically read Maggie's thoughts, in
beseeching little bubbles above her head. But she seemed to decide
that speaking wasn't worth the trouble. She left the potting shed
without once looking back.

Ned Devlin and Josh Hunter had just spent the afternoon climbing ladders at the fire station. With Marty Cole supervising them,
they took turns climbing the super-tall sky ladder on the back of
Engine no. 3. At first Ned went slowly, one rung at a time. Lift
the left foot, carefully bring the right foot beside it. Left foot

again, let the right foot catch up. Both hands gripping the ladder. Don't look down.

Marty and Josh taunted him from below, good-natured teasing that made him realize that they'd been in his position once. The way they were poking fun at his fears, he knew that they had once felt the same ones.

But Ned's third time up the ladder, he caught the hang of it. He whipped up and down, a squirrel in a maple tree. Looking down was no problem, and he started to enjoy the view: you could see all around the island, blue water everywhere, as if you were in a plane coming in for a landing.

Marty wanted to clock them, to see who was faster. Ned was game, but Josh said he'd gotten fouled playing basketball the night before, and he still had a stiff ankle. "Yeah, sure," Marty said. Anyway, it was just as well: Maggie would be getting off work soon. Ned's father needed the pickup to take Anne out, so Ned had to rely on Josh for a ride.

"I can't believe you're scoring on Maggie Vincent," Josh said, heading cross-island to Maggie's family inn.

"Not exactly 'scoring,' " Ned said, scowling. He didn't want people thinking that was how he saw Maggie.

"Listen, buddy," Josh said. "She may have a lot going for her, but one thing you have to realize: with Maggie you always score."

"Knock it off," Ned said. He flipped on the radio, but nothing much besides static was coming in. He turned on the scanner instead.

"Sorry, man," Josh said, sounding sincere.

"Yeah," Ned said, still pissed off. He knew he shouldn't care about what Maggie had done before they started going out, but imagining Kurt or anyone else touching her the way he did . . . it nearly drove him out of his mind.

Sometimes, kissing her, caressing her silky skin with his hands, Ned's mind would fill with images as sharp as if he were watching them on a movie screen. Once, picturing Maggie kissing Kurt, he bit his own tongue so hard he drew blood and swore out loud.

Pulling up in front of the inn, Josh let the Taurus idle. Spitting dark exhaust, the car shuddered in the street; both boys leaned forward, looking for a sign that Maggie was done with work.

"There's Vanessa," Josh said. "Looks like maybe she's waiting for her ride. We could ask her about Maggie."

"Maybe I should just go in," Ned said doubtfully. He knew this inn was Mrs. Vincent's pride and joy, and he didn't know how she'd feel about him, all scruffy and ready to go sailing, making a grand entrance. Maybe the back way—but here came Vanessa.

"Hi Josh, hi Ned," she said.

"Is Maggie finished with work?" Ned asked.

"Not quite," Vanessa said, dimpling prettily. She'd been much nicer to Ned now that he was going out with Maggie. When he'd come on-island last April, she wouldn't give him the time of day. None of the kids would. But being with Maggie seemed to open every door.

"Do you know how much longer she'll be?" Josh asked, checking his watch. Ned knew he was thinking of the tide. They had to be on the water within thirty minutes, before the tide started rushing back in. Josh kept his boat, a JY-15, down by Panther Hole, where the flood washed through like Niagara Falls. You couldn't get anywhere on an incoming tide: it was like sailing on a treadmill.

"You giving her the night off?" Vanessa asked Ned sweetly.

"What do you mean?"

"Oh, we just want to steal her away for a few hours. You can join us later. But we're all mad at Maggie, forgetting all her old friends just because she has you now."

"That's what she wants?" Ned asked, amazed.

"She'd think it was really big of you," Vanessa said. "Sometimes you have to let go a little, in order to hold on. And Maggie doesn't like possessiveness."

Ned knew he had a tendency to hold too tight, and it scared him. He certainly didn't want to scare Maggie away.

At the firemen's picnic the other night, he had overheard some of the guys saying their wives were feeling hurt and pissed off because they'd been left at home. Everyone had an opinion on the subject, and the war stories were flying. About stag parties; excursion to the Playground, a strip club in New Bedford; how all the best women accepted a man's need to have the occasional night out with the boys.

"No guy wants a clingy wife," Marty Cole had said.

Listening to Marty and the others, Ned had faded into the background. He could relate more to the women, sad for being abandoned even for one night, than he could to the guys. Right now Vanessa was striking a nerve. He wanted to be with Maggie every free moment. He tried to act super nonchalant, as if what Vanessa was saying was no big deal. As if he didn't care a bit about Maggie going out without him.

"So, you say there's something happening later?" Josh asked.

"There's always something happening later," Vanessa said, but she was still watching Ned for his reaction. He had the feeling she was daring him to make a wrong move. Ned knew that Maggie had misgivings about her old friends, but he also knew she felt guilty for abandoning them. It was a genuine conflict, and Ned didn't make it easier for her. Anytime she brought up Vanessa, Eugene, or especially Kurt, he would feel his muscles stiffen as if he were contemplating a high dive.

"Go sailing," Vanessa urged. "Have a great time, then come back and meet us. We'll probably head for the cave. You'll find us."

"Who's that?" Josh asked, gesturing at a cute blond girl observing the car from the front porch.

"Céline Dutremble," Vanessa said. "She's eminently available. I'll introduce you to her tonight."

"Summer kid?" Josh asked, practically salivating.

Vanessa nodded. She held a backpack, and from it she slipped a bottle. "Want a hit?" she asked. "Go ahead. It'll keep you warm on the water. And get you in the mood for later."

"Where's Maggie now?" Ned asked, peering toward the house. Josh uncorked the curvy brown bottle and took a sip. He passed it over to Ned, but Ned shook his head.

"Getting chewed out by Leona Helmsley," Vanessa said. "Her mother is really taking this hotel idea a little too seriously. But don't worry. I'll tell her you'll hook up with us later. Okay?"

"Sounds cool," Josh said. He threw Ned a radiant smile. "Whaddya say, buddy? We'll catch the tide, be back in time for the party?"

Still staring at the house, Ned nodded.

"Yeah," he said. "Okay."

"HE wanted to go sailing," Vanessa said. "He waited, but there was something about the tide. Don't worry—he's meeting us later."

"Why didn't you call me?" Maggie asked, glowering at Vanessa. She couldn't believe Ned would just go sailing without her. They'd made plans. Now she was grounded, and she couldn't even tell him.

"Chill out," Vanessa said, giggling. Maggie could see she was tipsy.

"And thanks for letting me take the blame," Maggie said. "What are you doing, stealing from the rooms?"

"What about it, Miss High-and-Mighty? You're really letting that dork-ass rule your life. You never minded stealing before, as long as it was for you."

"Oh, Vanessa," Maggie said, depression settling in. Now she didn't know what to think. Ned hadn't even waited for her, and here was Vanessa making fun of him.

"You'll see him later. He's coming to the cave."

"He said so?"

"Yeah."

"I'm grounded," Maggie said.

"So what? It's summer, and you have a boyfriend. Break the rules," Vanessa said, throwing her arms around Maggie. Maggie held on, because Vanessa was her oldest friend and because at that moment she didn't have anyone else. She felt lost and deserted, and a sob was lodged in her throat.

A rattletrap VW beetle stuttered down the street, making both girls look up. Burnished gold, lacy with rust, it was a typical island surfmobile. Maggie stared to see who was driving, and recognized Kurt.

"Come on," Vanessa urged. "Come with us. You'll see Ned in a couple of hours."

"No," Maggie said, watching Kurt. "Not with him."

"He's just one of us. We were a team, weren't we? God, how would we have gotten through the last few years without each other? Come out with us, for old times, and you can be in Kurt's face with Ned later."

"I'm grounded," Maggie said, but even as she spoke she saw her uncle Matt coming in her direction. He raised his finger to catch her eye. Shooting him a defiant glare, Maggie turned back to Vanessa. "Okay," she said. "Let's go."

Chapter 21

The big question was, who would sit where? Half the backseat, behind the driver, was taken up by a big cooler full of beer. Kurt was driving, Eugene was in the front passenger seat. Maggie wanted to sit in back, on Vanessa's lap or vice versa. But before she could speak, Eugene had leaped out of the car, into the back, pulling Vanessa on top of him. Maggie had no choice but to sit in front. Next to Kurt.

"How's everything?" Kurt asked with a sidelong glance at the exact moment that Eugene slid into the cooler and came up with four fresh Molsons.

"Fine," Maggie said, her stomach all worried about what Ned was doing and what he was thinking. She accepted the opened beer and took a long drink.

Kurt's progress down Salt Whistle Road was halting. He would accelerate, get the clutch and the brake mixed up, pull the car off the center line with just enough time to miss oncoming cars. To Maggie, it was obvious he had been drinking all day. Her eyes on the road, she reached behind her head for the seat belt. But there was none. This was not a new car. No seat belts, no headrests, only an AM radio.

"Where did you get the car?" she asked.

"Bought it," Kurt said. Burping, he gave her a sinister sidelong glance.

For how much? Maggie wanted to ask. *Fifty bucks?*

"Hear you have someone new," Kurt said.

Maggie realized that this was a mistake. She breathed deeply, listening to the suck, suck, sucking sounds coming from the backseat. Kurt was drunk and feeling mean, and Vanessa and Eugene were making out.

"Don't hog it," Eugene said, and Vanessa giggled. She handed the half-empty bottle of Grand Marnier into the front seat. Kurt drank from it, and Maggie didn't even bother looking at Vanessa.

They were speeding down the Cross-Island Highway. The road twisted and turned, and when Kurt hit the brakes, you'd hear the tires putter, trying to grab. Maggie felt afraid.

"Where've you been, baby?" Kurt asked, reaching for her bare knee. Maggie let him tickle it. She kept her eyes on the road, as if her own vigilance could keep him from driving into a ditch.

"I said, where've you been? Hand me a brew, will you?"

Maggie didn't flinch.

Half turning, one hand on the wheel, Kurt reached into the backseat and jostled the lid off the aluminum cooler. It rattled to the floor, causing Eugene to laugh.

"You want a beer, you just ask," Eugene said, handing Kurt a bottle and replacing the cooler's cover.

The car bounded down the highway, the pavement still buckled with frost heaves and the constant effects of shifting sand. The salt marshes were on their right, miles of reeds and creeks, tidal flats and shorebirds. Crossing the bridge at Old Whisper Creek, the golden light of early evening collected in the marsh grass. But Maggie was too edgy to notice.

"So, I hear you're fucking the preppie," Kurt said, raising the glass bottle to his lips.

Maggie was about to say, *Let me out of here,* when Kurt swerved into the oncoming lane. The car ricocheted off a stone wall. Kurt braked, and Maggie was flung full force into the dashboard. The car careened madly, spinning in impossibly perfect circles, like an ice dancer. Screams filled Maggie's ears, and she realized they were her own.

Later they would determine that a mere four seconds passed from the moment of impact. Maggie's head throbbed. Suddenly she realized that Kurt's hands weren't on the wheel. As the car twirled Maggie grabbed frantically for the wheel. Like a wildcat, it fought her grip.

Vanessa and Eugene squealed.

Four seconds.

The guardrail, a flimsy corrugation, in place forever, came at them. They smashed into it and stopped dead. The sparkling creek beyond. Orange sun streaming through clouds. Maggie's arms flew up, across her face. Glass cracking, bang, her head. The screams: Vanessa, Eugene, Maggie, a gray heron.

Liftoff, into oblivion.

Flying through the rushes, their soft tops sweeping the car like brushes at the drive-through car wash.

Blood in the eyes, a baby at home in her mother's womb.

The pulse, the tidal pull of the moon in its crescent phase and the heart pumping blood through the uterus, the placenta, the embryo. The slap of waves, of your mother's blood.

Sleep.

In the end, Anne had settled on smoked bluefish with buttered brown bread and capers, fresh tomatoes, mozzarella, and basil, and Ruby's chocolate-chip cookies. What her picnic lacked in seductive flair, it would make up for in heartwarming spirit. The air felt balmy, and Anne dressed for the sunset in a flowing coral dress, a black cotton sweater tied around her shoulders, and silver hoop earrings.

She packed everything into a paper grocery bag, wishing she had one of the six or so wicker picnic baskets from the big house. She knew that it should feel strange, fixing a beach picnic for Thomas with Matt on the island. But it did not. If anything, she took perverse pleasure in it, and that worried her. But Matt had made his bed with someone else for so long, and he hadn't asked her permission.

Thomas would be here at any minute to pick her up. On a whim, Anne lifted the receiver and dialed the big house.

"Fitzgibbons'," came the voice of a subdued Gabrielle.

"Hi, it's me," Anne said.

"I am so mad at you," Gabrielle said, her voice instantly high-pitched. "Have you seen Maggie?"

"No. Why?"

"Because I grounded her, and she's nowhere to be found. Somehow she's got the idea that I'm the one who punishes her, but she can always go running to you."

"No!" Anne exclaimed. "That's not true!"

"Well, when she shows up on your doorstep later, will you please ask her to call me?'

"If she does, I will," Anne said, alarmed by the high note in Gabrielle's tone.

"Meanwhile Matt is sitting at the table here, moping, and I just want to kill him," Gabrielle said, her voice shaking. Anne couldn't remember hearing her so upset.

"I love you," Anne said. But her sister had already hung up.

Before she left that evening, Anne left a note on her apartment door:

Maggie—
CALL YOUR MOTHER!

A.

.　　.　　.

W<small>AKING</small> slowly, Maggie explored her mouth with her tongue and came upon something hard. The car door had caved in, trapping her right arm, but she worked her left hand free and cupped it under her lower lip. Along with a mouthful of blood, she spat out a tooth.

She heard whimpering in the backseat. Sleep threatened to drag her away, but she forced herself awake to try to determine where they had landed. Still in the car seat, she was on her back, like an astronaut ready for takeoff, looking straight up through a broken windshield at the sky. Bands of purple and gold streaked across clouds. She could hear the sound of gurgling fluid. The blood rushing in her ears.

"Maggie," came the weak voice.

She blinked, trying to focus. Blood dripped from cuts in her head into her eyes. Squirming, she felt a jagged pain slash down her back, and the world went black.

When she awakened again, the sunset was still there. Still bright, and so close.

"Maggie," she heard again, above the gurgling.

Very painfully, she half turned her face. There was Vanessa, up to her chin in brown water. Sitting on Eugene's lap, she was trying to hold Eugene's face above the surface. That was the rushing sound, Maggie realized: the car had flown into the creek, and water was seeping in through the car doors.

Kurt was slumped over the wheel, passed out. Brown sludge and red blood coated the windshield inside and out. But out the side window, Maggie could see they had plunged off the road into the shallow marsh. Somehow the car's back end was sinking faster than the front. She heard little squeaks of panic coming from Vanessa, and she tried to think, to keep from passing out.

"The water," Vanessa said. "We're going to drown."

Without speaking, saving her strength, Maggie reached her left arm across her body and tried to open the door. It wouldn't budge. Stove-in at a forty-five-degree angle, the door metal speared her right side. Her right elbow was pinned into her body, totally useless. When she took a deep breath, pain stabbed her chest; she must have broken some ribs.

"Kurt," she said. "Kurt."

He wouldn't respond. With her left hand, with all the energy she could muster, Maggie tapped his knee, his thigh. Nothing.

"We're going to die!" Vanessa cried, a diluted wail.

"Whassa matter," Eugene said.

It hurt Maggie too much to turn fully around. Painfully, she moved her left arm between the two front seats, reaching back to Vanessa. Weeping, gulping air, Vanessa grasped Maggie's hand.

"Whadappened?" Eugene asked, and then Maggie heard him spitting out water. Salt water was flowing steadily into the old Volkswagen through the engine in back, the rust holes, the doors.

"Keep holding my hand," Vanessa pleaded.

"I will!" Maggie said, even though it hurt unbelievably to hold herself in that position. Every time she moved her spine, silver dots flashed through the blood in her eyes.

Eugene thrashed, spewing like a geyser to keep his throat clear.

Vanessa tugged his chin, stretching it to keep his mouth clear of the rising tide. "Please," she cried. "Don't go under."

"Can you move?" Maggie asked, her senses beginning to clear.

"No, I'm pinned between the cooler and the car door. Maggie, I'm hurt," Vanessa said.

"We'll be fine," Maggie said resolutely, squeezing Vanessa's hand. Her shoulder muscles were aching with massive lactic acid and hot knives were stabbing her spine, but she would not let go.

Why wouldn't Kurt wake up? Now that Maggie's adrenaline was kicking in, she called his name again and again. She heard Vanessa shouting it. The rescue squad should be on the way. Someone must have seen them go over. Someone had already dialed 911, and Ned was on his way now. They would be here any moment, pulling Maggie and her friends to safety.

Was the sunset quite as bright as it had been? Suddenly the

thought that darkness was falling filled Maggie with dread, and she must have moaned.

"What?" Vanessa screamed. "What?"

"It's okay," Maggie said. "I'm sorry."

"Eugene, try, try," Vanessa was pleading. "Hold yourself up! Try! Maggie, help!"

Maggie struggled to free herself from the car. How bad could it be? The windshield, and most of the front, was sticking straight out of the water. The car felt stationary. Yet water was pouring in from behind, and the car felt like it was sliding backward, downward, its nose in the air. Sinking.

"Maggie!" Vanessa said, water clogging her throat. She spit it out.

Maggie noticed the lid of the metal cooler. It had flown into the front seat from behind, come to rest on the dashboard. Wedged between the windshield and the steering wheel, it stayed in place, a sharp-edged piece of aluminum.

Her eyes blinked, her consciousness flickered. There was the evening star, the crescent moon swinging in the western sky. A brilliant sunset blazed. From the backseat, Maggie heard her friend sucking sludge.

"Maggie," Vanessa gurgled, her voice desperate. She yanked her hand away, and Maggie heard it slapping at the seats, the window. The sound of rushing water filled Maggie's ears. "Maggie . . ."

Maggie tried to turn, to see Vanessa, but her body wouldn't obey. The level of water had risen, and Maggie could no longer hear Vanessa's voice. Blinking the salt and blood away, she saw that darkness was falling.

Something bobbed into her lap. Maggie flinched, terrified. Something horrible from the marsh had swum into the car. She tried to clasp, but could not reach, Vanessa's hand.

"Vanessa?" Maggie asked, shaking. Vanessa wasn't answering.

Overhead, the moon bobbed and weaved, as if the car in which Maggie sat was tilting precariously. The water level was rising. It had been at her ankles, then her knees, and now it was at her waist.

"Vanessa!" Maggie called, but again, no answer.

Maggie's consciousness flickered again. Blackness, then the waning colors of sunset again.

"Vanessa!"

The thing danced in the tide. It thumped Maggie's chest, reminding her that it hadn't gone away. They had plunged into a marsh, a saltwater creek. Could it be a blue crab? A bass? Hardly daring to look, Maggie opened her eyes.

It was round, and heavy. Bloody strands trailed from one end, like the tentacles of a jellyfish, and minnows nibbled at them. With her left hand, Maggie Vincent held the thing steady. She took a deep breath, turning it over.

It was Kurt's head. It stared at her with sightless eyes. Like a wax model, with pale cheeks, blue lips, hair streaming in the current. Small fish darted at his eyeballs, into his ears and nostrils. Veins and arteries dangled from the neck, and blood flowed into the water.

The lid of his metal cooler had decapitated him on impact. Maggie heard her scream rise through the dusk, piercing the island air. She held Kurt's head in her good hand, trying not to think of her two oldest friends drowned in the backseat, and the fact that the tide was rising to claim her.

Screaming with horror, Maggie watched a torrent of sandpipers skitter across the windshield of Kurt's car. Their tiny white bellies grazed the broken glass, then disappeared. She was going to die here.

DRIVING cross-island from town, Thomas knew he had never felt happier in his life. The evening would be perfect: another half hour of silvery-purple sunset, and then a night of stars. Such clear weather in June was unusual. When Anne had suggested a beach picnic, Thomas had known there was only one spot: the secluded cove at Tim's Lookout.

They drove along in his truck, holding hands across the bench seat. Every so often Thomas couldn't help shooting her a helpless look of love, and she'd throw one right back. They spent most of the trip with big grins on their faces, thrilled just to be together.

Rounding the bend at Old Whisper Creek, Thomas noticed wide black skid marks on the road.

Braking, he followed them with his eyes. Just off the side of the low bridge, he saw the nose of an old wreck clearing the surface of the tidal marsh.

"I don't remember seeing that before," he said, gazing at the car's rusty hood tilting skyward.

"Me neither," Anne said.

Thomas gave her an apologetic glance. It was probably nothing, but he had to check. Striding to the edge of the pavement, he heard Anne give a low wolf whistle. He blushed, in spite of himself. He was a middle-aged guy in jeans and a sweater. She could be having cocktails on any terrace in Newport or Edgartown if she wanted to. Why in the world would she want to be with him?

But when he got close to the guardrail, his heart quickened, and not because of Anne.

"What is it?" Anne called, getting out of the car.

"This just happened," Thomas said, noting for the first time the cracked guardrail, broken reeds, and fresh tire tracks in the mud.

He heard Anne gasp, and he turned to see her face. A mask of horror, she was staring at the car.

"Maggie!" Anne screamed.

There, her face barely visible through the car's window, was Maggie Vincent. The tide zipped fast through here, creating the noise of a loud whirlpool. But if you listened hard, you could hear Maggie crying, pounding on the car door.

Before he knew what was happening, Anne was pulling off her sandals, plunging into the water. He watched her fight the current swirling from the marsh to the sea, swim straight for the automobile. Her dusky pink dress tugged her down, but she reached out a hand for the girl trapped inside.

"Don't touch it!" Thomas bellowed.

Anne stopped, treading water, a frantic look on her face. Kicking off his shoes, Thomas dove into the water. Holding his breath, he swam beneath the becalmed Volkswagen, the current rushing past him.

The automobile's rear end floated freely in a wildly flowing torrent. What prevented the entire car from sinking, from filling with seawater instantly, was the fact that its front axle rested precariously on the tangled root system of an old tree. The illegal dumping practices of some local landowner had just saved Maggie's life. If it weren't for the twisted roots of some forgotten oak, she would have already drowned.

Thomas surfaced, sputtering.

Anne treaded water, meeting his eyes. She glanced from him to her niece and back again.

"It's a seesaw," he said. "The car could go under any minute."

Maggie was panicking, rocking the car back and forth with her efforts to open the mangled door.

"Maggie!" Anne called in a ringing but perfectly calm voice. "Don't move. I'm here with you. I won't let anything happen."

Out of panic, Maggie rattled the door for another moment. But then Anne's serenity touched her, and she met Anne's eyes. She gulped the rising water, her head tilted back. And she nodded.

"What can we do?" Treading water steadily, Anne asked Thomas these words in a perfectly easy voice, her eyes on Maggie.

"We need help."

"Go get it," Anne said, with no change of tone.

Thomas struck out for shore. He scrambled up the bank and ran for his truck. Clicking on the CB, he called in a code. For not even one second did his eyes leave Anne in the swift current or Maggie pinned inside the car. Peggy Lawson was dispatcher.

"Send an ambulance," Thomas commanded, giving his location. "Divers. The hydraulic tow, and the Hurst. On the double, Peggy."

"Roger, Dev," she said.

MAGGIE was swimming with Anne. They were separated by a bloodstained window, but they were together. If only Maggie could wrench herself free of the metal holding her prisoner. She could wiggle into the creek, and Anne would take care of her. Anne would carry Maggie to her mother, and everything would be okay.

Something veiled Maggie's eyes. Ripping off a shred of seaweed, she nearly lost her breath. The sun was going down. Soon it would be as dark as a blindfold. Wadding the seaweed into a ball, she swallowed a muddy mouthful of salt water. Kurt's head kept coming back. She pushed it out of the way, hysteria bubbling into her throat. Could Anne see?

Maggie felt the water rising on her body. It was up to her chest. The car lurched, tilted forward. She screamed, frantic. But then, as if the car had found the fulcrum's sweet spot, it held steady. Maggie huffed every breath, straining out water. It helped to know that Anne was right outside, but she couldn't stand to open her eyes. She was terrified of seeing Kurt's head.

THE call came just as Ned and Josh were tacking in from a totally frustrating sail. The tide had been stronger than usual, and in spite of Josh's genius reading of the tide charts, they hadn't made it past the breakwater.

"What's that?" Ned asked at the sound of Josh's beeper.

"Emergency," Josh said.

Whizzing into the dock, they occupied themselves with hoisting the centerboard, lowering the sails, walking the boat over to the ramp, and loading it onto the dolly. Only when they had reached Josh's Taurus did they hear the scanner, broadcasting to volunteers everywhere:

"Submerged vehicle," the woman's voice crackled. "Passengers trapped inside. That's Old Whisper Creek where she meets the Great Salt Breachway."

"On our way, Peggy," Josh blurted into the microphone.

Thinking of Maggie, wanting to go straight to her, Ned nearly protested. Then he gave his own stupid hormones a good talking-to. You signed on to the force, he told himself. Someone needs your help. Think about what's important in life.

Someone needs your help.

Chapter 22

Reports of a sunken car spread like wildfire among islanders, and so did the rumor that four island teenagers had died in the wreck. Gabrielle heard it while presiding over the Rocheleaus' clambake.

Standing outside at the buffet table, making sure everyone got a lobster and enough clams, or grilled sirloin steaks for the two guests who did not care for shellfish, Gabrielle was dressed in a sand-colored linen dress with a big silver necklace. Even though she was still riled at Anne and, especially, Maggie, she gave all the guests her best smile. You never knew who might be a potential client.

"Excuse me, Mrs. Vincent?" said Paula Draper, a pretty girl one year ahead of Maggie at Consolidated, one of Gabrielle's most reliable waitresses.

"Yes?" Gabrielle said, filling a cup of extra melted butter for one of the guests.

"Would it be okay if I used the telephone inside?" she asked. "Someone just said there was a bad crash out on Cross-Island, and a bunch of kids died. I just want to call my boyfriend, make sure he's okay."

Gabrielle frowned. Usually she would say absolutely not, no using clients' telephones for personal calls. But she nodded. Something inside her chest was doing cartwheels. Watching for Paula to return, she spilled a ladleful of butter on the white tablecloth.

Paula emerged from the house smiling. She started toward the tables where guests were seated, but Gabrielle waved her over.

"Well?" Gabrielle asked. "What did you hear?"

"Oh, Jay's fine. But it's true, supposedly. Some car went into the water with kids inside."

Gabrielle walked away from her station without thinking to ask Paula to cover for her. She walked toward the house, and then she started to run. Through the front door, trying to remember where she had seen a telephone. Kitchen wall. Her hands shaking, she called home. The answering machine picked up.

Maggie might have gone to Anne's, she told herself. But Anne's number rang and rang.

She dialed the number at the big house.

"Hello, uh, Fitzgibbons'," came Steve's voice.

"Steve, is Maggie there?"

"Not that I know of. I'm just sitting here, shooting the shit with Matt. He kinda needs a shoulder, you know?"

"There's been an accident. All I know is it happened somewhere on Cross-Island, and kids are hurt."

A long silence while Gabrielle's panic seeped through to Steve.

"I'm sure everything is fine," Steve said slowly. "I'll drive out to check, but what are the odds—"

"It's Maggie," Gabrielle said, her voice spiraling down a wind tunnel.

Patting her pockets for keys to the van, she headed out the door and intercepted Paula.

"You're in charge," Gabrielle said. "Do everything right, and you'll get an extra fifteen percent."

"Okay," Paula said, flashing Gabrielle a concerned look as Gabrielle ran toward the driveway.

Gabrielle drove the van around the circular drive. Cars were parked thickly here; she had to maneuver carefully to avoid swiping them. She edged past the thick briar hedge onto the road that would take her to the Cross-Island Highway.

The sun's last light was fading, and all the cars had their headlights on. At first, Gabrielle didn't make the connection, but then she realized it was too dark to see. Trembling, she fumbled for the switch; as the beams illuminated the twisty, sand-strewn road she found herself—not an especially religious woman—saying the Lord's Prayer out loud.

In the dark, Anne could no longer see Maggie. The wind had whipped up, and small waves were splashing against the windshield, which protruded seven inches above the water's surface. Anne had wriggled out of her dress, to keep herself afloat. She gulped water as a larger wave broke over her head, temporarily turning her around.

She talked out loud to Maggie, doubting the girl could hear her. Needing to reassure herself that Maggie was still alive, every so often Anne would dare to tap on the window. After a moment, as if it took enormous effort or she had dozed off, Maggie would always tap back.

Sea creatures grazed Anne's legs. Something sharp, like a fish's dorsal fin. Whispery eels, minnows, cunners. Seaweed wrapped itself around her legs, and she kicked it off. She refused to feel afraid. She was feeding all her strength to Maggie.

The rescue vehicles had arrived. On the road above her she heard booming engines, the sizzle of radio static. Glaring ice-blue strobe lights skittered across the creek's murky surface, bouncing off silver marsh grass on the far bank. Divers in wet suits with air tanks strapped to their backs swam around the car, assessing the delicate situation. She heard them talking when they surfaced, saying the car was hanging by a thread.

Thomas was among them.

Get out of the water, he had told Anne, but she would not.

I understand, he had said, you're terribly worried, but you're not helping. Something could happen to YOU.

I promised Maggie, she had replied. I'm staying.

Anne, blue-ribbon swimmer at Salt Whistle Beach in second, third, fourth grades. Junior lifesaver, senior lifesaver, Red Cross–certified to be a lifeguard.

Staying with Maggie.

How can a car be hanging by a thread when it's balanced on the entire root system of some giant tree? I can't help Karen, but I will not *will not* let you die.

Tap, tap. Hi, Maggie.

I wish I could see her. Can she see me in the blue light from the fire trucks, the police cars, the ambulance waiting to take her straight to the hospital, wrap her in blankets, bandage her wounds, put her to bed after a nice hot supper?

Thomas swam over with a life jacket, bright yellow, so Anne could float more easily without treading water. She'd also be easier to see from shore. You don't mind putting this on? he asked, helping her into it. A kiss.

Tap, tap. Hi, Anne.

Anne swallowed more water, overcome with the relief of hearing Maggie answer. How much longer would this take? How terrified Maggie must feel! The black night brings cold, fear, darkness, the dark's only consolation being the fact that it makes invisible that horror. Anne had seen the human head bobbing under Maggie's chin just before the sun went down.

"So, what do we have here?" Josh, the old hand, asked Marty Cole when they arrived at the scene.

Why was Marty staring at him like that? Ned wondered, looking behind him, to see if Marty was watching something over his shoulder. This scene was a thrill, all the big equipment and the guys ready for anything, the lights flashing like crazy.

"Ned, your girlfriend's in there," Marty said, his hand on Ned's forearm.

"In where?" Ned asked, stopping cold.

"There," Marty said, pointing.

All you could see in the black creek was a pane of glass, a windshield, maybe, reflecting the strobes and spotlights.

"Maggie's in the car? That went into the water?"

"Yeah. They think she's alive."

Ned ran to the edge of the bridge. Guys were swimming around, on and under the surface, scuba tanks on their backs.

"I want to go in," he said out loud.

Here came Chief Wade, limping over to see him. Ned knew he was supposed to be polite, that the chief would probably tell him to stand back and watch, they were doing everything they could. To hell with that! Ned started to push past him, but the chief grabbed his arm.

"Slow down there, Neddy," the chief huffed. "No sense getting yourself hyperventilated."

Did this damned old wheezebag have any idea of what was happening? Maggie Vincent, the girl Ned loved, was in that car, and there was no way Ned wasn't going to try to save her.

"Excuse me, Chief," Ned managed to say, knowing that if the old man tried to hold him back he was prepared to deck him good.

"You're built like your dad. Too big for the wet suits we got available. Get yourself a tank and a buddy, and be careful going in. Call out to your father, let him know you're coming."

Ned nodded with gratitude, ripping off his shirt as he ran to the dive truck.

.   .   .

G ABRIELLE arrived at the scene at the same time as Steve and Matt. Together they ran to the police line, where throngs of islanders and vacationing curiosity seekers jostled for a better view.

"Hey, watch it!" someone yelled as Gabrielle stepped on their toes. Shouldering her way to the front of the crowd, with Steve and Matt right behind her, Gabrielle could hardly breathe. She kept hearing the words "kids," "dead," "drinking," "drowned."

A bright yellow tape kept everyone back from the fire trucks, from the scene, and two young police officers were patiently explaining to a woman Gabrielle recognized from a recent party that yes, there were casualties and no, no one was allowed to get any closer.

At the sight of Gabrielle and Steve, Joe Nevers, a cop who occasionally worked construction with Steve, stopped talking. Without saying a word, he lifted the yellow tape to let them pass. Gabrielle ducked, and by the time she straightened up, she was weeping. She had known in her mother's heart, but Joe Nevers had just confirmed that Maggie was in the car.

Leaning into Steve, Gabrielle let herself be led forward, into the circle of Maggie's fate.

Y ES, there she was. Right in that flash of blue-white light. Maggie tried to keep Anne in her sight, but Anne was bobbing around in the dark water, sometimes hidden by the waves.

Inside the car, the water had risen just higher than Maggie's chin. The chilly water numbed her body, making it possible to perform the contortions necessary to breathe. The car was sliding backward, so to keep her mouth in the air pocket, Maggie had to lean forward, her breasts pressed tight against her thighs, her head tilted way back. Her nose just grazed the windshield.

Unconsciousness kept reaching for her. Her head would wobble, and she'd wake up sputtering dirty water. Stay awake, she told herself out loud. Stay awake. But talking meant moving her mouth too wide, and water would rush in. Blowing it out, she struggled to breathe.

Anne?

Anne was gone. Don't go, don't leave me, Maggie thought, panicking. Men with black hoods, scary frogmen, kept popping their masked faces out of the water. The sirens she had heard, the flashing lights, the emergency vehicles on the bridge above frightened her, instead of comforting her as she had thought they would. They were trying, of course they were trying, but time was ticking by.

The big equipment said terror to Maggie. Didn't you always see it on the news? All the fire trucks, the ambulances, the police and firemen, hundreds of people struggling to save a boy who had crashed through the ice, a girl who had fallen down the well?

Hundreds of heroes working all through the cold night to save the little boy, the little girl, Karen, Maggie. And the same people still there the next day, daybreak a time for hope, but what do you always see on the TV? The police chief shaking his head, the parents crying, the child being carried away in a little shroud on a stretcher.

Even when Maggie closed her eyes so she wouldn't have to see all the useless rescue activity, the blue lights pulsed through her eyelids. The sea's gentle rhythm pushing Kurt's head lightly against her chin: there, there. A tuft of his hair in her mouth.

Crying, she spat, and tried to push it away with a sweep of her left arm. Her sobs like a pump's intake, her own emotion choking her to death. Drowning her.

Tap, tap.

There was Anne! Maggie couldn't see her, but just outside the car, right on the other side of the window glass, was Maggie's aunt Anne.

Or was it Karen? Peering at the glass, Maggie saw, illuminated by the emergency lights, the bright face of a little girl.

"Karen?" Maggie asked.

Yes, it was! The Little Mermaid herself, returned to life with a squadron of helpers—dolphins, friendly blue fish, wise crabs, and brave lobsters—to save Maggie. In the months since Maggie had last seen Karen, in all that time apart, Karen had grown up.

Karen had turned into a beautiful young lady.

That very last day on the beach, when Maggie and Karen were building their last sandcastle, hadn't that been Karen's wish? Hadn't Karen squinted up at Maggie, shielding her pretty eyes from the sun, and said, "I can't wait to grow up. To be like you."

What a sweet dream, something to get lost in . . .

Where am I? Maggie wondered suddenly, tossing her head, choking on a mouthful of seawater. She felt puzzled and frantic. *Frantic!* To have her back hurt so fiercely, to be so freezing cold. To be up to her nose in salt water!

Tap, tap.

Right! Karen.

What a regal sandcastle they had built that hot, August day. The balconies decorated with pebbles, the walls adorned with misty green and blue-green sea glass. Karen shielding her eyes, peering up at Maggie. "I can't wait to grow up," Karen had said. "To be like you."

"How do you want to be?" Maggie had asked, drizzling wet sand on the castle for turrets.

"Pretty, with earrings."

"Earrings?" Maggie had asked.

"Like those," Karen had said, pointing. She had crawled close to Maggie, her sandy fingers touching the earrings that dangled from Maggie's earlobes. Back then, like now, Maggie had worn only one or two pairs.

Maggie had reached up to feel which ones Karen meant.

"Oh, the pair of dice," Maggie had said, smiling.

"When I grow up, I'll have earrings like those," Karen had said.

Maggie could see her wearing them now. In the sea on the

other side of the glass, the seaweed dancing around her, Karen was beautiful, back to life, keeping Maggie company, and wearing the dice earrings that meant she was all grown-up.

Tap, tap, Maggie.

Tap, tap, Karen.

Pair of dice.

Paradise.

"WE'RE going down with a hook and a towline, and we're going to pull the sucker out of there," Hugh Lawson said, water streaming off his face mask.

"It's our only bet," Mike Hannigan said. "The tide is shooting through the hole, and the car's slipping inches every few minutes. She could go down at any moment."

"Can't we open the doors?" Ned asked. His lungs ached with unbearable worry and from being unaccustomed to pulling air through a regulator. The divers were gathered on the creek's bank, right beside the bridge. Up on the road, Marty Cole was backing Big Bertha, the truck with the fiercest towing power, to the edge.

"Can't, son," Chief Wade said. "Outside water pressure is too great, and besides the doors are all bashed in. Crash impact does that."

"We attach the hook to the front axle," Hugh said, "and Marty winches her in nice and slow."

"I don't want any of you boys anywhere near the car when Marty starts pulling," Chief Wade said sternly. "If she goes down, I don't want any heroes pinned underneath. And get Mrs. Davis the hell out of there."

"Haven't been able to thus far," Hugh said wryly.

"She'll stay right next to me," Ned's father said, his eyes trained on the crayon-yellow life jacket bobbing alongside the car.

"Ready up there, Marty?" Chief Wade bellowed, precipitating a violent spell of coughing.

"Ready," Marty called back.

"I'm afraid of that front axle breaking," Ned's dad said, frowning. Bigger by half than any man there, as he stood, he looked like a sea monster rising from the creek.

"It's the only place we can get some grab," Hugh said.

"It's all rust."

"The car's a fucking rust bucket, and the axle is our only hope," Hugh said.

Ned started into the water after his dad, but Chief Wade grabbed his weight belt.

"Hold it right there," the chief said. "You've done your part. The hardest thing about being one of us is knowing when to sit back and watch. You can't do it all."

"My girlfriend's in there, Chief," Ned said. Surprised, and humiliated, he burst into tears.

"See what I mean, Neddy? You've done your part. Wait here with me." Ned crouched beside the chief, staring with blurry eyes at the sinking car. He felt grateful that the chief didn't reach over with a consoling hug or pat or anything. He'd spent so many holiday dinners with this guy, the chief felt like a grandfather, and Ned didn't want them to acknowledge his tears in any way.

"Anybody can save her, it's your dad," the chief said in a low, husky voice. "I've seen him at accidents, like the time a car ran over a bicycle, and everyone was fussing around with the Hurst tool. Your father just picks the car up with his bare hands so we can pull out the cyclist and get him some first aid."

"If he could have done that for Maggie," Ned said in a voice without hope, "he would have by now."

"Get her out of the water," Matt said through clenched teeth to the crowd at large. His eyes were on Anne, still treading water next to the car. He imagined the car sinking, creating a vortex, pulling Anne under.

"Please, God," Gabrielle was praying through tears streaming down her face. "Please let Maggie be alive. Let her be rescued."

Matt stood close to his sister-in-law, and all eyes were on Anne. She had become their lifeline to Maggie.

Dumb bastard, he thought dully. This is the kind of family you threw away.

You're going to go home to the smell of nail polish, the music of exercise videos, the flavors of mâche and arugula, the warmth of a Sterno stove. You stupid, fucking asshole, you gave up a woman who would freeze at the side of her drowning niece for one who hasn't spoken to her sister in five years. Asshole, he thought, shithead.

"Merciful God," Gabrielle wept, shuddering convulsively. Matt slid an arm around Gabrielle, and suddenly he felt Steve's arm, encircling her from the other side. Together the Vincents were praying out loud. He stopped swearing at himself and listened.

The words didn't come easy to him, and his effort was creaky. But silently, standing with his sister- and brother-in-law, Matt Davis remembered how to pray.

"Allow this couple's daughter to live," Matt prayed with tears veiling his eyes, "as you couldn't allow ours. Don't let them suffer as Anne has this last year. As I have. Bless Karen's soul, even as you keep Maggie safe on earth. Please, Lord, bless us all."

ANNE felt exhausted from the effort of making her arms and legs move constantly against the cold current, and from the knowledge that the end was near. No matter the outcome, good or bad, it would occur in the next minutes. Hugh Lawson and Thomas were swimming out, pulling the long towrope between them. Now they split up: Thomas came toward her while Hugh dove down to attach the hook to the beetle's front axle.

Pulling her back, farther and farther away from Maggie in the car, Thomas wrapped his arms around Anne.

"We have to give Marty enough space to pull her out," he explained when Anne tried to struggle against his embrace.

"Will this work?" Anne asked, her teeth chattering. Half turning, she looked through Thomas's face mask, hoping to see reassurance in his eyes.

"It has to," he said.

Now Hugh was sidestroking over, his air tank glinting in the eerie blue light. Hugh gave a thumbs-up, and the great hydraulic winch began to grind.

It strained and whined, like the spinning wheels of a car stuck on ice. Anne focused her eyes, for any sign that the car was budging.

Did Maggie realize that this was it, that the winch would either pull her free or not? Was Maggie aware? That during the next moments she would either be freed from the car or drown at the bottom of this creek?

All through the past year Anne had tortured herself with the same questions. Did Karen know? During the fall had she realized what was happening? Listening to the high-pitched whine of the winch gears, Anne stifled her sobs.

Cacophonous mechanical noise: metal punches in a factory, presses in a print shop, work trucks rumbling out of the city garage. Water magnified the ugly sound, filling Anne's ears. She stared at the car, its front end seeming to lift ever so slightly.

Then, peace. With no tension on the towline, the winch motor settled down to a gentle hum.

"The car?" A voice called from the bridge, and then another voice. "The car!"

Where the car had been, there was only flat, black water. The car had sunk without a trace.

"The axle broke," Thomas said. Taking a deep breath, struggling out of his air tanks, he started swimming. Anne followed behind, gasping for breath.

"Was it here?" Thomas yelled to people on the banks. "Is this the spot?"

"Right there! My baby!" Anne heard Gabrielle scream. "Maggie, Maggie!"

Thomas dove.

HOLDING his air tank in his arms, Thomas Devlin breathed steadily through the regulator. Awkwardly, he unhooked the light from his belt, shone it along the creek bottom. Eelgrass fluttering in the current, a school of mackerel, and there: the car.

The car had slid off the tree trunk, its four tires resting square on the silty, pebbled bottom. It wasn't going anywhere now, so Thomas had nothing to lose. His light caught Maggie, her cheeks full with her last breath of air, her left hand clawing at the windshield. And here was Ned, swimming fast toward the car.

There was not a sound in the world except for Thomas Devlin's heart beating in his own ears.

Get back, he gestured with his hand, urging Maggie away from the windshield. But of course she could not see him. All Maggie Vincent could see was his bright light, shining through Old Whisper Creek like a cruel full moon.

He took one last breath and then, because he needed to use both his hands, he dropped his light. Shrouded in black water, he planted his feet on the car's crushed hood like Ahab on the white whale. Using his air tank as a weapon, like a harpoon, he struck the windshield again and again. Now Ned was beside him, beating the glass with his fists. Each time the metal connected, Thomas heard a gentle *ping*.

On the fourth try, he felt the windshield give way. Ripping the glass out with their bare hands, he and Ned reached in for Maggie. Struggling, she clutched their wrists. They pulled, but she was stuck.

Fumbling, Ned took a breath from the regulator, then eased the rubber mouthpiece into Maggie's mouth. She fought, terrified at first, but then she began to breathe. Watching Ned cradling Maggie's head, feeding her air, made Thomas realize that Ned was saving the woman he loved, and he felt flooded with pride.

Pushing Maggie against her seat, feeling his way because he could see nothing, Thomas Devlin put his feet through the windshield and wedged them against the caved-in side door.

Suddenly, an army of white lights began swimming from his left. Pinpoints at first, like candles being carried in a distant procession. They drew closer, fanning out, surrounding the submerged car and bathing it in shimmering light.

With one monstrous heave, Thomas Devlin kicked out the dent in the crumpled door, freeing Maggie's trapped right arm. Wrapping her in his arms, as gently as possible, for it was obvious that she was badly hurt, Ned eased her out through the windshield.

The men surrounded Thomas, Ned, and Maggie. Hugh offered Thomas a breath from his regulator, and Thomas saw Ned pressing his own mouthpiece to Maggie's lips.

His heart full, his chest aching, this is how Thomas Xavier Devlin, former altar boy, namesake of the saints, father of Ned and lover of Anne, saw it:

They were angels and archangels, cherubim and seraphim, the men of the Island Volunteer Fire Department. And here they were, bearing Maggie Vincent, alive, straight to heaven, direct to paradise, safely home to her parents and Anne and all the people who loved her, miraculously back to the place where she belonged.

A cheer arose among the crowd, from the bridge over Old Whistle Creek back to the cars parked two deep along Cross-Island Highway. Policemen surrounded Gabrielle and Steve, who had to be helped down the bank because they couldn't see through their tears. The divers and Anne floated Maggie in to shore, Anne and Maggie's heads pressed so close together you almost thought they were one.

Shrieking with joy, Gabrielle waded straight into the creek, embracing Anne, lunging for Maggie, being carefully restrained by Chief Wade, who reminded her gently that they had to be very cautious, at least until they determined the extent of Maggie's injuries.

Steve and Gabrielle knelt in the shallow creek, on either side of their daughter, whispering in her ears as the EMTs strapped her securely to the stretcher, Gabrielle's hands fluttering, from Maggie's hair to her eyebrows to her throat. Bright lights from the bridge illuminated the three Vincents like actors in a play, like figures of the holy family in the floodlit crèche on the church lawn at Christmas.

Standing tall, watching her family, Anne seemed oblivious to the fact that she wore nothing but a black lace bra and panties. Water flowed off her beautiful body, so magical and feminine, like Venus in *The Birth of Venus,* only without the scallop shell, only more magnificent than any woman Botticelli had ever painted.

The Uffizi Gallery, in Florence. How long ago had it been? Their second year of marriage? Their third? They had stood before the famous painting, so large it occupied a whole wall. Throngs of tourists surrounded them, pressing forward, pressing them together.

They had gazed upon the famous painting, so famous that everyone in the world knew it, you wouldn't be surprised to see it on a Hallmark card, a children's cartoon show, the crass place mat at any seafood joint, they had gazed at it for many moments, trying to figure out its magic.

The crushing crowd pressing them together, so that feeling Anne's bottom press against him, Matt had grown aroused, had reached around her to cup one breast and kiss her neck, right there among a hundred tourists in the Uffizi Gallery, and staring straight at Venus, holding his wife, Matt had known he had the more beautiful woman.

And there she was now, knee-deep in the muddy creek, naked

except for her lace underwear, the bra one Matt recognized well, one he had brought her from Christian Dior last summer, an offering, a sleight of hand to keep her from realizing that he was having an affair behind her back.

Matt gazed not at Maggie Vincent, his niece who had so narrowly escaped the sweet spot of death, that perfect window of opportunity where life can end instantly. That moment when you might not even recognize how lucky you were to escape, how grateful you should feel.

Matt didn't gaze at Maggie, whose life had been saved by the same capricious forces that had let Karen die. He gazed with eternal love and deepening regret at Anne, his wife, who was being embraced, being swaddled in warm, dry blankets, by the man she loved. He narrowed his eyes, to focus on Anne and that man.

Anne, who couldn't take her eyes off of Maggie—as if she still couldn't believe they'd been able to save her, as if she were afraid the tide could rise and sweep Maggie away.

Matt watched Thomas Devlin hold his wife, caress her face, pat her hands with his own, as if trying to warm them, as if his weren't at least as cold as hers after spending all that time, over an hour, in the tidal creek. Now Anne looked away from Maggie, to Thomas Devlin. She reached up, held his face, and smiled into his eyes. She was speaking to him, but Matt couldn't, didn't want to, hear what she was saying.

Thomas Devlin encircled Anne with his arms. His love for her was plain. And the way Anne looked at Thomas Devlin left Matt with no doubt that her heart was overflowing. Matt stared, boring the image into his brain. He was so intent on committing the picture to memory, he almost didn't notice that Anne was looking in his direction.

Staring at him.

Alarmed, at first. She looked worried, as if she feared that Matt would interrupt the scene. Their eyes locked, and the longer she watched, the more her fear melted away. His mouth twitched in a half smile, and she smiled back. Good work, kid, he thought. You saved her.

Now, noticing that Anne was looking into the crowd, Thomas Devlin followed her gaze. No smiles here. Matt stared, expressionless, his eyes narrowing just perceptibly. Thomas Devlin didn't look away, and he didn't loosen his grip on Anne.

"Take care of her, you bastard," Matt said, not possibly loud enough for anyone to hear. But Thomas Devlin nodded. As if he knew exactly what Matt meant, as if he were prepared to lay down his life for her. Matt let himself nod back.

A flurry of activity. The cops clearing the road, bullhorns bleating that it was time to leave. They'd gotten Maggie strapped in safely. Sirens beeping, people running to their cars. Thomas Devlin kissing Anne, saying something. A quick glance at Matt. Easing himself away, then lifting one end of Maggie's stretcher. A kid who could only be Devlin's son lifting the other.

Overhead the *pop pop pop* of helicopter rotors. *Pop pop pop.* Coming in loud and fast.

"I'm sorry, sir, you'll have to move. We need to load the girl into *LifeStar,*" said the polite young police officer who had initially let Matt and the Vincents past the yellow lines.

"I'm her uncle," Matt said, holding Anne's gaze with his eyes.

"Still, sir. Please."

Matt nodded, saluting Anne. She tipped her head back, raising her hand.

"Okay, officer," he said. "Good job."

"Thank you, sir."

Even as the helicopter hovered overhead, Matt whispered to the woman who had been his wife, "I love you."

And then he left.

Chapter 23

Maggie stayed in the hospital for three weeks. She had four operations for a broken jaw, a fractured right lower leg and ankle, a fractured right wrist, and minor plastic surgery for the cuts on her face.

She had her jaw wired shut. Stainless-steel wire holding her jawbone in place. They fed her chalky milkshakes through a straw, and it was nearly impossible to talk.

She wore a long leg cast on her right leg, up to her thigh. Her leg had been so stiff in anticipation of the impact, her right foot instinctively pushing down the imaginary brake, that her foot and ankle had gotten mangled. Both bones in her lower leg, the tibia and fibula, had shattered. The surgeons had implanted stainless-steel screws for at least six weeks, probably eight.

In her right wrist she had a colles's fracture. Although Maggie couldn't remember, the doctors told her that when she saw the crash coming, she had probably thrust out her right hand to brace herself. As her palm smashed the dashboard her wrist became a train wreck: an "S" deformation up to her elbow.

Maggie wore a long arm cast, up to her shoulder.

She had a contused kidney, which sounded scary but which actually meant "bruised." But it meant having tons of uncomfortable tests and IV pylograms, where doctors shot dye into her body and by magic it bypassed all her other organs and went straight to her kidneys.

Her parents practically lived at the hospital. Well, not exactly, but they had rented a room with long-term rates at the Howard Johnson in Kenmore Square. Every day Maggie's mother would tear a sheet off the calendar on Maggie's wall, to show how fast the time was passing.

Her parents had gone home to the island for the funerals. At first they told Maggie they were taking care of business matters, but when Maggie scowled, turning her head away to glower at the wall, they admitted the truth.

"We thought it would upset you," her mother said. "That you won't be able to be there."

Maggie nodded, starting to cry. She had to keep her emotions under control, to keep from forcing her jaw open. You can't cry hard and keep it inside, Maggie was learning. But the thought of Vanessa, Kurt, and Eugene in their coffins, being buried in the ground on this beautiful sunny day, was too much for her to stand.

The memories came pouring in, and her chest started heaving so hard, she was rocking the bed. All she wanted to do was scream. Just scream! For the fact that she had listened to Vanessa drown, unable to do one thing to stop it. Her mother tried to hold her, to calm her down, but Maggie was out of control. She was weeping and thrashing, screaming inside, and she was going to explode.

Her mother ran for the nurse, and suddenly the nurse was rushing in with a syringe, and she stuck it into the spongy orange thing on the IV machine, and the cold drug ran straight into Maggie's veins and made her forget.

When her parents returned to the hospital that night, they

looked pale and tired, but they didn't tell Maggie anything about the funerals. And Maggie didn't ask.

Her mom had had to call and cancel all the reservations for June and early July at Fitzgibbons'. That part made Maggie really sad, and although she didn't speak—couldn't, really—she must have shown her mom with her eyes.

"Honey, being with you is more important. We only have one daughter. Daddy and I are staying right here until we take you home."

When she went home, the doctors told Maggie she would need a wheelchair for a while. Maggie didn't care; she wanted to get out of this place that smelled like ammonia. Ned wrote letters, and he called. Even though she couldn't really talk, she loved hearing his voice. He had taken some medical books out of the library so he could read about her injuries, and he would explain certain things to her that the doctors had left out.

Anne visited on her Tuesdays off, and for some reason, that was when Maggie would feel saddest. She would think about her friends, what had happened. She would remember being with Anne in that black water, and they both would start to cry. Quiet tears, though. Not an explosion, like before. Just both of them sad.

The odd part was, Anne never talked on her visits. Everyone else seemed to think that because Maggie couldn't speak, they should talk twice as much. Her parents, even Ned, proved they had amazing talents of small talk, of making conversation about things you had never thought possible. But Anne just sat there, reading or holding Maggie's hand, as if she had decided to save her words for a time when Maggie could come back with some of her own.

Maggie's parents spent every day at her bedside. Her father would occasionally get a scowl on his beardy face and have to excuse himself, but her mother was there all the time. Maggie's mother had the strongest look of love and concern in her eyes,

Maggie could feel it seeping straight into her bones, as if directed by hypodermic infusion.

Maggie had been too hurt to apologize to her mother right away. But after a while, when her painkillers began to wear off and the truth of her feelings poked through, she let her left hand stray across the woven white blanket to her mother's.

Sitting on the edge of the bed, Gabrielle had been dozing. Startled, she wakened at Maggie's touch.

"Hello," Gabrielle said.

Maggie gestured that she wanted a pen.

Although Maggie was right-handed, she did her best with her left hand.

I'm sorry, she wrote in squiggly scrawl, *for going in the car when I was grounded. If I hadn't, this might never have happened. They might still be alive.*

Her mother took a long time reading the note, and then she looked straight at Maggie.

"What happened to them is not your fault. Do you understand me? Yes, you used poor judgment by getting in that car. But you are *in no way* responsible for their deaths. I know you're sad, honey."

Maggie nodded.

"When Dr. Scheer takes the wires out, we're going to find someone for you to talk to. A good psychologist, to help you make sense of everything. Ned's father recommended some-one. . . ."

Maggie nodded, then closed her eyes. She was really awfully tired.

One day her parents arrived with Cheshire-cat grins on their faces. They looked ecstatic, and just seeing them made Maggie's eyes start smiling. Her father did a corny little wiggle across the floor, waving an envelope in the air, sitting on the edge of her bed.

What's that? Maggie asked, tossing her chin.

"Your SAT scores," her father said.

"Your father said we shouldn't open your mail," her mother said, "and I said that I absolutely agreed as a matter of principle, but in this case we didn't want to show you if the news was bad."

Did that mean she had done well? Maggie's eyes darted from her mother to her father. Her father had made a cage around her with his arms, and he was looking at her so seriously, as if he was honestly seeing her, that Maggie had to wonder whether this was the genuine Steven B. Vincent. He opened the envelope, placed the paper on her blanket, where she could clearly read the results: *650 Verbal, 600 Math.*

"Maggie, I am so proud of you," her father said. "I have to admit, I didn't expect this. You really showed me something."

Maggie gazed up at him quizzically.

"No father was ever happier to have a daughter, and in my eyes, I guess you could do no wrong. So, while maybe I've erred in turning a blind eye to some of your shenanigans, I've also failed to notice your successes."

Maggie couldn't believe he was actually saying this. She just stared at his eyes, wanting to hear more.

"Those other poor parents," he said, "they don't have a second chance to pay attention. That's what I think of. How lucky I am to have this chance. To tell you that you make me proud. I'm popping my buttons."

He patted his big belly, and even though her eyes were wet with tears, Maggie let out a giggle.

"Hey!" he said. "No comments about my blubber. Remember what you used to say when you were a little thing?"

Maggie nodded.

"You'd say, 'Daddy, you're just right with a little left over.' "

"She also used to call you 'El Plumpo,' " Gabrielle reminded them gently.

"She can call me whatever she wants," her father said, leaning down to kiss her cheek. Maggie worked her left hand out from under the blanket and slung it around his neck, to hold him close a minute longer. The accident had taught her a few things, too.

THOMAS Devlin convinced Anne to take a week off from work, and in those seven days they came to acknowledge what they had known all along. That they had fallen in love, they wanted to be together.

In his years of being alone, Thomas had sometimes glanced through the personal columns, amused by the sameness of the ads: *If you like long walks on the beach, drinking wine by the fire, listening to music, quiet drives through the country . . .*

Yet, in the week Anne had taken off, those were exactly the things they did. Nothing fancy, nothing extreme. They hardly even talked, as if the most important things could only be sensed.

They made love. One night when the almanac predicted a wild meteor shower in the northern sky, they drove out to Cape Amelia. That side of the island was mainly a nature sanctuary and some old abandoned potato fields, uninhabited except for osprey, foxes, deer, and one old coyote.

That coyote was the only one left on the island. Once there had been an entire pack, but through the hard winters their numbers had dwindled to two. And right after the last bad snowstorm, the town crew found the body of this guy's mate, frozen stiff in a snowbank just down the field. The night of the meteor shower, Thomas and Anne heard his howl. It was piercing and empty, somehow elegiac, and it made Anne move closer to Thomas in the truck.

"He won't last another winter," Thomas said.

"Poor old guy," Anne said, scanning the field for him.

"Let's not think about the coyote," Thomas said.

"No, nothing sad tonight. Shooting stars'll be just perfect."

"I hope it's clear enough," Thomas said, bending low over the steering wheel to look at the sky. The air was warm, and the atmosphere was slightly murky with haze.

"You know what?" Anne asked. "I don't care if we don't see even one."

Thomas slid his arm around Anne's shoulders, and the next thing he knew, he was caressing her breast. Then she was reaching down to stroke him, right through his jeans. Unbuckling his belt while he drove, undoing his zipper, slipping her small, cool hand in through the front of his boxers, and making him stiff.

They parked at the edge of the bluff, their headlights catching the silver crests of breaking waves. Thomas's breath seemed to be coming from somewhere in the vicinity of his collarbone as Anne reached up to kiss him.

"Shall we get out of the truck?" she asked so throatily that at first Thomas thought she was teasing him. But no, she was just as affected as he was. Ned had left an old beach blanket in the truck, and Anne shook it out, spread it on the dry, whiskery grass.

There wasn't much of a moon, but what there was illuminated Anne's breasts, the pale curve of her waist, the gleam of her dark hair. Thomas Devlin was lying on his back, having his shirt slowly unbuttoned by this woman he loved so much, and he thought he'd burst with the joy of it. He let out a yell so plaintive that the coyote answered in kind.

"Lovesick," he explained to Anne, pulling her down to him.

"Poor coyote. All alone."

"No, I was talking about myself," Thomas said, smiling as she kissed him, sliding her beautiful, full breasts against his chest.

"Good," she whispered in his ear. "That's what I like to hear."

"You'll be hearing it plenty," Thomas whispered back. And then turned his attention to the matter at hand.

ON a muggy July afternoon, with distant thunder rumbling toward the island, Gabrielle mixed a pitcher of lemonade in the kitchen. Low drumrolls sounded an ominous message. The air was moist and heavy, the sky colorless. But Gabrielle sang. To her the day was brilliant and fine, breezy, exquisite: Maggie was home.

Heading for the herb garden with a tray of lemonade and fresh gingersnaps, Gabrielle listened to the music of Maggie's voice. The wires had come out of her jaw two days ago, and she talked all the time, making up for three weeks of silence.

Her tone was low, sometimes sorrowful. She would talk about her injuries, or, with obvious wonder, about how amazing it had been to be rescued. But she never mentioned her friends, and she hadn't ever told Gabrielle and Steve about Kurt's head. That detail they had learned from Anne and Thomas.

When Gabrielle had heard it, she had wondered how Maggie could stay sane. It gave Gabrielle nightmares and kept her awake long into the night, the image of her daughter trapped in a sunken car with *that,* and she truly wondered how Maggie could have withstood it, how she could carry the memory with her through life.

Victims of certain horrors deal with things differently than other people, Dr. Struan said. She was the psychologist Thomas had recommended, and Gabrielle would be taking Maggie to Boston every Friday morning to see her. The tendency to block certain memories, Dr. Struan said, can be necessary in the early days, but with therapy and the support of family, the worst can be faced.

Now, walking toward the herb garden, Gabrielle faced the best: her beautiful daughter and godsend of a sister. Would Maggie have survived in that water, so seriously injured, in shock, and trapped with the horror of death, without Anne at her side? Gabrielle doubted it.

"Thirsty, girls?" Gabrielle asked, balancing the tray on the herb garden's uneven old stone wall.

"Wonderful," Anne said, reaching for a glass. She took one for Maggie also, and Gabrielle slid a plastic straw into the lemonade.

Maggie held the glass in her good left hand. She stared into it for a moment before taking a small sip. Gabrielle waited for a comment, a compliment or the opposite, one of the signature Maggie-isms.

But nothing. Maggie just gazed thoughtfully at the herb garden, her right arm in its cast resting on the baby-seal toy bought on that long-ago shopping trip.

"This is the best," Anne said. "All three of us back on the island, sitting in Karen's garden."

But without Karen, Gabrielle thought, her heart flipping as she smiled at Anne. Hadn't Anne come a long way? She seemed so happy with Thomas, so strong. Having nearly lost Maggie, Gabrielle had a different insight into what Anne had endured the last year.

"It's good to be home," Maggie said quietly. "Do you know what time it is?"

"Four o'clock," Anne said, checking her watch. "Why? Are you expecting a certain Ned Devlin?"

"Yes," Maggie said, smiling. The scars on her face were raw still, dramatic testimony to her ordeal. If anything, Gabrielle thought they gave her delicate features even more appeal and distinction, along the lines of a Cindy Crawford mole or a Lauren Hutton tooth gap.

"Are you going out?" Gabrielle asked.

"No. His dad has the truck. We're just going to hang around. Maybe he'll push me down to the beach."

"These roads are too rutty," Gabrielle said. "Potholes and frost heaves all over. That wheelchair will be bouncing every which way, and your muscles will ball right up."

"Mom . . ." Maggie said just as Anne said, "Gabrielle . . ."

"He did save her life," Anne said.

"Mmmm," Gabrielle said, savoring the deliciousness of a family scuffle.

The three women sipped their lemonade for a few minutes,

lazily enjoying the herb garden. Gabrielle listened to the thunder, wondering when the sky would open up and break the heat wave that had held the island captive for the last twenty-four hours. The rumbles were definitely louder, the storm closer, and Gabrielle was just about to ask her sister and daughter to bet on exactly when the first drops would fall, when Anne spoke.

"I miss Karen," she said.

All eyes were on her. Anne never discussed Karen, at least not with Gabrielle, and Gabrielle hardly dared to breathe.

"Don't you?" Anne asked, her eyes wide, searching from Gabrielle to Maggie.

"Yes, sweetheart," Gabrielle said.

"So much," Maggie whispered.

"She would be so happy, to know that you're okay, Maggie," Anne said, holding Maggie's good hand, stroking it with her thumb.

Gabrielle watched the gaze pass between them, her sister and daughter, and she felt nothing but joy. What more could she ask than a family who loved each other? What an idiot she had been to let the jealousy get to her before.

She didn't want to analyze too deeply the role she might have played that moment when Maggie decided to get into the car. You make a lot of mistakes as a mother, and most of them slip by. But what about the ones that don't?

"I bought this seal for Karen," Maggie said, handing it to Anne.

Anne accepted it, nodding. As if it didn't seem strange to her that Maggie would be buying a present for Karen months after her death. "She'd have loved it," Anne said, handing it back to Maggie.

Maggie frowned, trying to wiggle a finger down the cast on her right leg. Distracted, as if she wanted to scratch an itch, suddenly she focused on Anne.

"You know that picture?" she asked. "Karen's picture?"

"Paradise?" Anne asked.

"Yeah."

"Sure. Of course."

Gabrielle felt her spine start to stiffen. After so recently, like ten seconds earlier, vowing to renounce jealousy, here it came again. What picture, what paradise?

"What are you talking about?" Gabrielle asked, with exaggerated pleasantness.

"Karen drew a picture," Anne said, staring at the canvas bag by her feet.

"Her last drawing," Maggie said, now stroking Anne's hand. "The one Anne went into the fire after."

"You went in after a picture?" Gabrielle asked, incredulous. Anne had risked her life for a piece of paper?

"Show her," Maggie said.

"I'm surprised I haven't before," Anne said, withdrawing a manila folder from her bag. She carefully removed the drawing, examined it, and handed it to Gabrielle.

"It's beautiful," Gabrielle said, stunned.

"Karen told me it's a picture of paradise," Anne said. "It's of all the things she loved."

As Gabrielle examined the scene Karen had drawn tears filled her eyes. How many drawings of Maggie's had Gabrielle thrown away? What if one of them had been all she had left to remember her only child? Gabrielle recognized every person, every object in Karen's picture, and she tried to keep her shoulders from heaving.

"Anne," Maggie was saying. "There's something I have to tell you. About the picture."

"Is it the white boxes?" Anne asked tremulously, reaching across to point at the funny squares in the middle of the drawing. "It's the only part I don't understand."

"Yes," Maggie said. The tone of her voice, the way her eyes flickered from Anne to Gabrielle to the picture, was mournful, laden with regret.

Anne sensed it. She stopped like a doe frozen in headlights. "What?" she asked.

"See, I don't think Karen meant that the picture was of paradise," Maggie said, reaching for one of her ears. With difficulty, using one hand, she unhooked one of her earrings and closed it in her palm.

"What, then . . . ?" Anne asked.

"Last summer Karen told me she wanted to grow up. She wanted to be a big girl. Is this too awful for you to hear?"

"Of course she wanted to grow up," Anne said, her gaze locked on the drawing, but her voice eager for details. "Tell me."

"These earrings," Maggie said, handing one to Anne. "Karen said she wanted some like these. She wanted to be pretty, with earrings, earrings like mine. I think they sort of symbolized growing up to her."

Anne turned the earring over in her hand, and then Maggie unhooked the one in her other ear and passed it over.

"A pair of dice," Anne said. "Paradise." She stared at Karen's drawing, her mouth taut. She looked from the two spotted white squares on the page to the earrings in her hand. "Pair of dice."

"She just wanted to grow up," Maggie said fiercely, wiping her cheeks. "That would have been her paradise."

"Oh, God," Anne said.

"It's so sad," Maggie said, crying freely now. Gabrielle slid her arm around Maggie's shoulders, feeling them shudder with sobs. "It must kill you, Anne. I think of how you feel, and I want to go crazy. I was in the car, holding Vanessa's hand, and she just . . . went. I think of you and Karen, and I'm so sorry."

Anne couldn't speak, staring at the picture. But she reached over to comfort Maggie.

"I wish I could," Anne said, "I wish I could have it back, that last day." She sounded like a zombie. "If I can't have Karen, I wish I didn't know the secret. Earrings that she'll never wear!"

Anne wept hard for half a minute, then stopped as if she would never cry again. She stared blankly at the green spiky leaves of a rosemary plant in Karen's garden.

"I'm sorry," Maggie said, sniffling. "I know what you wanted to think. The feeling was true—she loved everything she put in her picture. I wasn't going to tell you. But then I thought, wouldn't you want to know the truth? No matter what?"

"Anything about Karen, I want to know," Anne said. "It's just a letdown. I wanted to think . . . never mind."

"Honey," Gabrielle said to Maggie, a grin starting in her throat, spreading to her mouth and ears. "Did Karen know that your earrings were called 'dice'? Did she ever say that word?"

"No," Maggie said, frowning. "I never thought of that."

"We never had dice at home," Anne said. "Matt and I didn't exactly spend a lot of time playing board games."

Her face crinkling with possibly the largest smile she had ever encountered, Gabrielle shook her head.

"Maggie, sweetheart," Gabrielle said. "I'm afraid you're wrong. About the earrings."

Maggie shook her head, but here came the sound of Ned. Still out of sight, he was whistling some tune Gabrielle couldn't recognize, coming down the path. At the sight of Maggie, he stopped in his tracks. He looked at her for a long moment, growing pinker by the second, then cleared his throat.

"Hi," he said.

"Hi," Maggie said.

"Hi, Anne. Hi, Mrs. Vincent," he said. "Big storm coming."

"Sure sounds that way," Gabrielle said, making up in friendliness for Anne, who was still rapt in Karen's picture: Anne's face a mask of confusion, as if Maggie's words had been an earthquake toppling Anne's world. Gabrielle couldn't wait to get Anne alone.

"Maybe we shouldn't head for the beach," Ned said to Maggie.

"Inside would be okay," Maggie said, her eyes darting to Anne. "My dad rented me some movies."

"Popcorn in the kitchen," Anne said to Ned. "Don't scrimp on the salt, and use real butter."

"Sounds good," Ned said.

Maggie stared at Anne, but Anne didn't look up. Her attention seemed riveted to the white patches in the midst of Karen's last drawing. Paradise. Again, Gabrielle's lips twitched in a smile. Maggie glanced at her quizzically, and Gabrielle nodded. Go off with Ned, she gestured. Anne will be okay.

When Ned had pushed Maggie, still frowning with concern over her shoulder at Anne, into the big house, Gabrielle cleared her throat.

"What?" Anne asked dully, as if significant hope had been lost.

"Upstairs," Gabrielle said. "Into the attic. I'll show you paradise."

WHY did it matter so much? Anne asked herself. This one drawing. There were twenty not unlike it in the second top right kitchen drawer in the apartment on Gramercy Park. All with similar depictions of Anne and Matt, the island, the park, the familiars of their life.

That afternoon had felt so ordinary, like all those other pictures in the drawer. Pages ripped from a calendar, sheets of drawing paper torn off a tablet. One would follow the other, day into night.

Into night.

Following Gabrielle up the attic stairs in the house where they had been raised, Anne had the impulse to stop short, pull Gabrielle into a hug, refuse to go farther. Gabrielle was just trying to make her feel better.

What did Gabrielle know about Karen's drawing? Perhaps it was Anne's worst attribute as a younger sister, keeping so much back from Gabrielle. So often Anne would feel sad, or desolate, or worse, and she would think of calling Gabrielle. But would she? *No.*

Gabrielle made it too easy. Gabrielle was always there.

No matter what Anne did, no matter how terrible, Gabrielle still loved her. Gabrielle wanted to make everything right, to *make* Anne's life "normal." Normal! And how could Anne accept that kind of love when she sometimes hated her own self, despised what she had allowed to happen to Karen?

"Here it is," Gabrielle was saying.

"Here what is?" Anne asked, looking everywhere but at Gabrielle. How long would Anne be able to keep herself together? It was obvious that Gabrielle was just trying to "cover up" for Maggie, to make up for Maggie's revelation about the dice earrings by pointing Anne in a different direction. And while Anne appreciated the gesture, she no longer had the graciousness simply to weather it politely.

Cobwebs draped from the rafters, and the smell of smoke was surprisingly strong. Where Steve had replaced floorboards and roofing, there was an alarmingly bright section of golden pine. But Gabrielle led Anne to the opposite end of the attic, the part that they had played in as children.

The first raindrops grazed the fanlight window. Then more, and then they were pelting the roof. The drops rattled the uninsulated eaves like machine-gun fire. The tension in Anne's chest built until she thought she would explode.

"Gabrielle," Anne said. "You don't have to do this."

"Do what?"

"Try to make me feel better. I don't know what you have in mind, but just let it be. I love Karen. Maggie was just telling the truth. It doesn't change the way I feel about the picture."

"Anne, sweetheart," Gabrielle said, holding Anne's hand and gazing into her eyes with a crinkled, bittersweet smile. "Sit down." With the heel of her hand, she gently pushed her sister down onto an ancient crate containing strips of fabric their mother had saved to weave into braided rugs.

"Gabrielle," Anne said, passing a hand across her eyes, as if she didn't think she could stand more of this.

"Anne?" Gabrielle said in a strong, steady voice. "Remember when you went back to New York last summer, to see Matt? And left Karen with us?"

"Of course!"

"Well, one morning when Maggie was off with her friends, Karen and I were alone together. We went to the beach, and then we came up to the house for lunch. She was a little excited, because you were coming back to the island that afternoon."

"I remember," Anne said, spinning her memories back one year.

"Somehow I got the idea to come up here, to the attic, and let her poke around our old toys and things. To calm her down."

"Didn't we love to play up here?" Anne asked. "It was one regret I had, living in an apartment—no attic for Karen to play in."

"We sure did," Gabrielle said, her smile widening. "So did Karen. I showed her these."

Anne watched as Gabrielle reached into an old armoire and withdrew two small dress boxes. While the cardboard had once been glossy and white, it had mottled with age. The corners had broken down, and gray dots of age and mildew speckled the boxes' surfaces. Anne hadn't seen these boxes in many years, but recognizing them from Karen's drawing; she felt her heart start to pound.

Gabrielle was watching for Anne's reaction. Seeing that Anne had made the connection, she kissed Anne's cheek.

Gently, so as to not further damage the frail box lids, Gabrielle removed them. Inside each box, wrapped in fragile tissue paper, was a white lace christening gown. One had been Gabrielle's, and the other had been Anne's. Years later, when the sisters had had daughters of their own, each had dressed her baby girl in a gown for her own baptism at the island church.

"You showed them to Karen?" Anne said, picturing the scene.

"I did," Gabrielle said. "I told her the happiest day of your life was the day she was born. That you held her in your arms and couldn't believe how lucky you were. Just the way I felt about Maggie. And how, at different times but in the same church, we dressed our little girls in these beautiful gowns, and we knew we had found paradise."

"Thank you," Anne said, holding Karen's dress, her cheeks damp. "For telling me. I needed to hear that."

"Thank you for bringing my daughter back to me," Gabrielle said, leaning over to kiss Anne's head, wrap her in a sisterly embrace. "I believe we would have lost her if it wasn't for you."

Anne's hand found Gabrielle's, and they stayed there, huddled together in the dark end of the attic, while rain pounded the roof. Her eyes closed, Anne was holding on to a strong sense of Karen. Karen had been here, in this very spot, barely a year ago. If she strained to hear, if she mixed in the sound of the rain, Anne could almost hear Karen's voice ringing in the eaves.

"Oh, excuse me. I didn't mean to interrupt," came Thomas's voice. "Maggie told me I might find Anne up here. Hi, Gabrielle."

"Hi, Thomas," Gabrielle said, giving Anne a final pat before letting go.

Anne blinked, bringing herself back from the sweet sensation of Karen. The feeling was gone now, taken by a gust of wind, the blink of an eye, the crack of a lightning bolt.

Holding out her hand, Anne let Thomas pull her up. Her arm

around his waist, she walked with him to the stairs. The feeling might be gone, she thought, but it wasn't lost. She could always get it back, because she knew where to look. Making collages of heaven had brought her closer to Karen, and she knew that Karen would understand why she had finally let herself include Thomas's house in the series.

Not everyone glimpses paradise during their lifetime. Only the lucky ones.

About the Author

Luanne Rice is also the author of *Blue Moon, Secrets of Paris, Stone Heart, Angels All Over Town,* and *Crazy In Love,* which was made into a TNT Network feature movie. She lives in Connecticut.